Summer Nights

by Erik Boman

Published December 2

This book uses some actual locations and family names, however all events are fictionalized and all persons appearing in this work are fictitious. Any resemblance to real people, living, dead or damned, is entirely coincidental.

Proofread by Pauline Nolet, Editors' Association of Canada

Cover image montage by Wandering Mind

www.wanderingmind.net

WANDERING MIND

Also by Erik Boman

The Detective Lena Franke series

Siren Song (Book #1)

Other books

Southbound
A dystopian thriller set in Sweden/UK

Short Cuts
Collected short stories

Short Cuts 2: Stories from the Brink of Dusk
Collected short stories

SUMMER NiGHTS

Chapter 1

Norra Ängby

Tuesday

21:10

The couple inside the house have only hours left to live.

Felix studies the building from his vantage point inside the forest. The property must be expensive; its unfenced lawn borders one of the suburb's many small woods, and houses with adjacent woodlands always rake in money when sold. Having the wilderness so close brings a sense of authenticity, or so some say.

How this supposed genuineness is defined is unclear. Maybe it's a sense of tranquillity or privacy. Whatever the case, the trees are good for hiding.

He rests his back against the enormous rock behind him. Too huge to be removed, the boulders lie scattered throughout the whole district. One can find them in the strangest of places: in meadows, on front lawns, in playgrounds and behind shops. Many hundreds of years ago, when the local Vikings worked on their weapons and vessels, the general belief had been that giants had hurled the great stones across the land, for fun or when arguing.

The image is tantalizing: massive blocks of stone sailing through the air and crashing down without warning. One moment calm and quietness, the next destruction and chaos. Not unlike the way he will bring ruin to the unsuspecting pair in the house. Except that in difference to the giants, he has a plan. His strike will have meaning.

And it will be as precise as a surgeon's blade.

He has spent over an hour examining the doors and windows through his binoculars. Nothing must go wrong. Once he moves in, he will be briefly exposed; Stockholm's summer nights are prolonged sunsets that meld into dawns, and the house has movement-triggered floodlights. But few will be awake later, in the small hours of Wednesday morning, and those not asleep will be staring at pages or screens.

Getting across the lawn unseen will be easy. Then remain the windows, but tips on the Internet have taught him how to cut through them quietly. He will be inside in less than thirty seconds. No one will spot him as long as he stays low. In the fading light, his second-hand army jacket and grey jeans are as effective as a camouflage overall. Anyone looking in his direction will see only a blur of muted natural hues. As soon as he's inside, he will use surprise, speed, and duct tape.

That idea, of course, has not come from browsing the Net, but from Timmy.

He shifts and turns his binoculars to the living room.

Seated at a table are a man and woman in their late twenties or early thirties. On the table are large plates and white boxes with steaming food: Thai takeaway from Ängbyplan, the nearest underground station. The woman smiles while the man laughs. They are young, unblemished, and successful. Half his age but twice as rich. Successful and energetic, while he fights to endure every day.

He would never have thought that such a glowing, homely façade could hide evil beyond understanding. The house is a polished skin around the blackest of fruits. No one has recognized the man inside for what he truly is. No one, except for Felix.

A rustle among the leaves behind him makes him tense, then relax. Timmy is here at last. His one true friend. Not always in view, but never far away.

"Where are you?" Felix asks. "I get nervous when I can't see you."

"I'm right here."

The shadows on Felix's left shift, and Timmy walks out from behind a large rock. His eyes are large and bright in the waning glow of the setting sun. A slow gust of wind ruffles his hair, and he sweeps it out of his eyes with a quick, clumsy brush that makes him look like a skittish squirrel. Just as he always does when he's excited.

At least this is what Felix thinks he remembers: his recollections of Timmy are elusive. Not even now, when they are face to face, can Felix recall what Timmy said or did yesterday, only that they have met and talked for hours. But they are friends. Comrades in a world that hides secrets and promises pain at every turn. And starting tonight, they will turn the tables and direct some of their suffering back at the culprits.

"Are you sure it's him?" Felix asks.

"Don't you recognize him?" Timmy's eyes turn to the dining couple behind the window. "He came at us with knives and questions, one sharper than the other. You must remember."

"I do," Felix says. "I just want to be sure he's the right man."

Tim nods. "We've looked him up. In fact, you should make both of them pay."

"That sounds dangerous."

"They're part of the same breed, Felix. They cut our minds open and let the light in."

"I know." Felix's heart speeds up every time Timmy touches on their shared past.

"And it was far too bright," Timmy continues. "We were burned, and we can't see properly anymore. That's why I'm here to point the way. Our tormentors have had their fun."

"So now it's our turn," Felix says, hoping for more confirmation.

Timmy nods. "That's right. They pulled us apart and stuffed us with their seeds."

"And we bring the harvest to their door," Felix finishes. "Isn't that so?"

Timmy does not answer. When Felix looks around, his friend is gone.

Felix goes back to studying the house. Timmy always chooses to appear and vanish at the strangest of times. Even now, at the brink of their first task, Timmy is unpredictable. They have planned and discussed the mission for many nights, however. Timmy will be close. Waiting on the fringe, ready to instruct and direct. Only Timmy knows how to extract the ideal revenge.

Felix knows better than to disagree with Timmy. On the few occasions when he has doubted his friend, Timmy got angry, and there is nothing as terrible as Tim's wrath. So Felix has promised both Timmy and himself to do as Timmy instructs.

He waits until the light in the bedroom goes out. After that, he lets another hour pass, sitting still until the neighbourhood sinks into the brief, hesitant lull of Swedish summer nights. Finally, he runs crouched across the backyard, sticking to the shadows wherever possible.

His moment has come.

Chapter 2

Lena's phone buzzes just as she sticks her spoon in the starter dish.

She curses herself for leaving it on, but then remembers she set the phone on silent before they sat down at the table. Silent as in absolutely quiet except for severe emergencies. Earlier that day, she was explicit in telling the exchange that nothing short of a confirmed apocalypse is disastrous enough to interrupt her. It is her night off, and as she normally does not do nights off, there better not be any mistakes. Or calls, for that matter.

And despite all the precautions and warnings, the damned phone is ringing.

She chases the scowl from her face when Gustav frowns at her over the table. He has planned this evening for weeks. Made the effort to book a restaurant even she knew was one of the hottest in Stockholm. Double-checked times, ironed his suit, and studied the menu in advance. His enthusiasm rubbed off on her so much she had dug out a dress that still fits her.

Although she tries not to move too quickly. She has not worn it for at least three years, and during the majority of those months, she has been dedicated to a murderous weightlifting regime that has rewarded her with a different physique, as well as countless glib comments. Even now, more than one guest is unable to glance at her bare shoulders. Some things change slowly.

But she wants this to work, so she must do her part and show some real commitment. Gustav deserves that and much more. Her preoccupation with work has erased some of her previous attempts at relationships, while others have been cut short by her aversion for socialising or leaving home other than on her bike.

That will not happen again. Gustav's eagerness to eat out and spend hours in cafés is exhausting, but his interests weren't a surprise. After all, he is a creative director at a production company whose irreverent name she often struggles to remember. And while she is unsure exactly what his job entails, it does not sound like a role for asocial loners.

She slips the phone out of her pocket and kills the buzzing.

They're seated in the middle of the room. Even though it's the middle of the working week, almost all of the thirty-odd tables are occupied. The restaurant is a bold crossover-kitchen venture housed in a refurbished downtown parking garage. Rough concrete walls, minimalistic halogen lighting, some kind of jazzy dubstep from concealed speakers. Its prices can make accidental visitors flinch and run for cover, so when Gustav demanded the dinner is on him, she didn't argue.

Her preference would have been a simple pub or pizza place, but that would not have gone down well with her date. That does not matter. Tonight, she will not come across as impossible. One of her colleagues once stated that Lena was as compromising as a wet tomcat, which is not true, but there is no reason to underpin rumours. There are enough of those flying around already.

Her phone buzzes again. She glances down at the screen. A one-line text message from Gren, her superintendent.

Call me.

She sighs and closes her eyes. Much to her own surprise, she was looking forward to eating out. An evening of intelligent conversation and soothing silence in the company of a man who does not judge her. Someone who is genuinely interested in her.

The plan is set in her mind: later, they will take a taxi back to his flat, rummage in the fridge for snacks, break open another bottle of wine. Then, the still-unfamiliar smell of his linen, the soft murmur of downtown traffic, and the closeness of his body.

Of course it was too much to ask.

"Anything wrong?" Gustav asks.

Lena can hear the almost undetectable bitterness in his tone. He already knows. Gustav is unlike her in many ways, so it's far from astonishing that he is perceptive. In contrast, she gets by on stubbornness and luck. Not that there seems to be any of the latter around tonight.

"I'll be right back," Lena says.

"What's the matter?" The hint of annoyance in his voice changes to open concern.

"Probably nothing," Lena says, knowing it's not true. "And whatever is going on, someone else can deal with it. I'm not working tonight."

Lena excuses herself through the corridor outside the wardrobe, slips past the three suits that man the entrance, and walks out on the street. The summer evening is warm and mild, which in Stockholm means that most sidewalks are filled with people walking aimlessly or milling around outdoor serving areas. Some stand still and gaze at the sunset with slightly stupefied expressions on their faces. Even in summer, warmth is a rare boon in this town.

She turns her face to the deep orange glow that fills the western sky. A few hours of decent daylight left. After that, a short spell of relative darkness, followed by an early, drawn-out dawn. Better than winter, but maddening in its own particular way.

Although not nearly as galling as the text message that burns in her pocket. It means she has to take off. Gustav will be disappointed, then offer her a ride and immediately arrange for another dinner, probably at an even better restaurant. He is an efficient machine while she is an overworked steam engine.

One block away, an underground train emerges from a tunnel onto a short strip of unsheltered railway. Showers of sparks fall away from its wheels as it shoots past. Just as the train vanishes into another tunnel, steel grinds against steel and gives off a sharp, piercing shriek. The pained wail echoes away into the fissures between her recent memories.

Six months ago, she went through two days and nights that threatened to pull her apart at her already patched-up seams. Hours filled with running through snow after a man bent on murder. Confusion, stress and violence. Moments of vertigo, sudden flashbacks, and impossible voices in bathrooms. The howl of the blizzard still plagues her dreams like a warning of what might happen if she drops her guard or looks the other way.

She takes out her phone and presses a speed-dial button.

"What?" her superintendent says by way of answering.

"How bad is it?" Lena asks him.

"Where are you?" Gren asks.

Lena's last hope of the call being a mistake dwindles away. Gren knows that she is off, but rather than apologizing for phoning her, he wants to know her whereabouts. Just as if she were on alert. The superintendent is a man of protocol and procedure. He would not call Lena on an evening like this unless he feels that he needs her particular views or help. Only when he is seriously troubled can he be distracted enough to forget his armour of formality. In Lena's experience, this is a bad sign.

"I'm in the city," Lena says. "Trying to have dinner."

She keeps the rest of what she wants to say to herself: *I'm also attempting to nudge Gustav and myself into serious-relationship territory, and this call isn't helping a single bit.*

"Can you make it to Norra Ängby in twenty minutes?" Gren asks.

Lena realises that Gren sounds out of breath. "Aren't you forgetting something?" she demands.

"You don't have a car?" he asks. "I can have a patrol pick you up in two minutes."

"That's not what I—" Lena breathes out slowly and resists the urge to hang up. That will only result in her having to call him back to apologize, which is the last thing on her mind.

"No," Lena says. "I don't have my car here, because I was planning to be reasonably drunk before heading home with someone who right now is wondering why I'm on my phone. Can you see the picture I'm painting here?"

"Cut it out, Franke."

Lena blinks and looks at the phone in her hand. This is unlike Gren. Not saying sorry for intruding is one thing; snapping at her is an entirely different matter. The superintendent is not just winded; something has thrown him, and in a rough way.

"I'm sorry," Lena says, forgetting that she meant not to be apologetic. She has to get back inside. Gustav is waiting, and the night is growing colder by the minute.

"I am the one who should apologize," Gren says, sounding a little more like his normal self. "It's just – there's a scene here that you need to see."

"There are at least three or four other detectives who can go there. I hate to say this, but tonight's the worst night you could've picked for calling me."

"You're correct." Gren pauses to catch his breath or maybe to get Lena's full attention.

"I have four other very competent detectives at my disposal," he says, "all of whom are on duty and able to get here in fifteen minutes flat. I'm also aware that you haven't had time off since who knows when and that you're on a date."

"How do you know about that?" Lena is so surprised she cannot keep the edge out of her voice.

"The whole office is aware."

"You have to be joking."

"For heaven's sake, we're not blind. But my point is that I'm not calling the other detectives. I am calling you."

"Why?" Lena asks.

She's not sure she wants Gren to answer her question. Reasons for the call have already lined up in her mind. Most likely, the scene in Norra Ängby is related to one of her old cases, and the superintendent thinks Lena can pick out leads that the other detectives might miss.

But for that to be the case, the scene must be seriously problematic. Cherry-picking detectives for assignments leads to people feeling overlooked or even distrusted, which in turn often results in office dramas. The last time it happened to her, she engaged in a one-sided shouting match that almost saw her suspended.

Still, this is the lesser of her fears. A more disturbing reason can be that Gren's case is linked to one of the two events that cling like a leech to both her psyche and her reputation. Twice in her past, her career has put her in situations so severe she has been forced to undergo mandatory follow-up therapy. First the botched raid against the paedophilia circle, then the madcap manhunt for John Andersson, which shut down several city blocks and a major airport.

But John is locked away and watched around the clock at a secure facility. And given what happened during the disastrous raid, Gren would rather try to bring in the Scotland Yard than call Lena to a similar scene. It has to be something else.

"To be honest," Gren says, "I asked the exchange to put me through to you without thinking twice."

"They would've told you that I'm off."

"I ordered them to put me through anyway."

"Why?"

Gren is silent for a moment.

"Because I don't think anyone else can deal with this," he says.

Chapter 3

Lena steps out of the taxi near a crossing in Norra Ängby some fifteen minutes later. It took her almost a minute to convince the sceptical driver that, despite the dress and the smell of wine on her breath, she is a police officer as well as in a hurry. After a half-sincere threat to commandeer the taxi, the sullen driver took her to the quiet suburb without a comment apart from a few glares in the rear-view mirror.

Using taxis to travel to crime scenes is unconventional, and in violation of at least a few regulations, but she had no choice. Gren is known for his calm and relatively good sense of judgment. If he thinks it's urgent, there is a good reason.

She looks around while the taxi drives away. The western half of the sky is cast in reddish gold as day dissolves into night. Behind her, a long slope leads down to what resembles the gates of a manor. Across the street are a small grocery store, an even smaller restaurant, and a dry-cleaner. The signs are tidy but lack the self-conscious minimalism of their inner-city brethren. In front of her is a typical slice of the suburb: box-like two-storey houses in variations of white, red, blue and green. She has passed through this district a few times, always sticking to the main routes to avoid getting confused by its layout or the repetitive architecture.

The scene is only a few blocks away from the crossing. Two police cars are parked under a pair of the huge maple trees that line the road on both sides. She can see the cordon tape is visible from where she stands. Among the thick hedges and trimmed apple trees, the strip of bright blue and crisp white is a glaring anomaly. It is almost as strange as being called in to examine a crime scene while wearing a dress.

She walks towards the police cars as fast as her dress allows. The neighbouring houses will be filled with people jousting for a good angle with their phones and posting updates on their social media channel of choice. With luck, she might be able to escape before someone manages to get a good shot of her face.

Despite their astronomical prices, the houses are small; she passes by each one in just over a dozen strides. Many of them have been extended in every direction and manner allowed by boundaries and permits. Some of the lawns are reduced to narrow green strips. By now, it's a familiar sight: the buy-and-sell mania of the past decade has wiped out acres of lawns and driveways, here and throughout the rest of suburban Stockholm.

Almost every window in sight is lit, as if in a collective effort to add to the frustrating lack of darkness. Most windows are oddly small, and with the extensions eating up much of the space between the houses, a soft gloom presides under the trees in the cramped backyards. Much of the greenery remains, though, and summer has unleashed every scent. The city's aromas of cement, water and smoke are dispelled by thick copses of pine and nearby old nature reserves. The air is so rich it's almost difficult to breathe.

She knows little about the area beyond what she learned from her phone during the taxi ride. Around two thousand houses, a massive grid of barbed hedges, and a pair of miniature plazas. Add to that a few schools, a lake surrounded by thick forest, and numerous patches of woodlands. Practically all the houses were hammered together in one great rush in the nineteen thirties by families eager to carve out a space larger than a small flat.

Today, the district is a dream for well-off couples who do not fear ongoing DIY when roof tiles blow away or boilers go bust. Expensive cars fill most parking lots, TVs the size of billboards flicker on walls behind linen curtains, and new children's bikes are locked together in tidy rows.

But she has also gleaned that the area is home to lots of memories from past centuries. Dozens of Viking grave mounds hide in the clusters of pines, and not far from where she's walking stands a rune stone. Many years ago, the ground was under water, and its presence lingers in the restless soil. Someone had commented online that nights are never quiet here; all houses are sinking, imperceptibly but irreversibly, which causes cracked foundations and splits in the wall.

She slows down when she nears the scene. Over twenty people linger next to the cordon tape. Most of them are teenagers, whispering and looking sideways at the house. All have their phones out. The constable on security is a slightly overweight man in his fifties with an acne-scarred face. His name is Gunnar, if she remembers correctly: she has met him before at some point.

Gunnar catches Lena's eye, nods at her, and goes back to keeping an eye on the onlookers while he listens to his radio. Behind one of the police cars is a discreet black van she hoped not to see: the coroners are on the scene. She expected that there would be casualties but had hoped she was wrong.

Lena nods back and looks the house over. Dark yellow façade, two storeys, both extended out back. A pair of windows face the street. The blinds are down, but the harsh glare of the coroner's lights filters through the gaps. Behind tall hedges behind the house are five adjacent properties. Lena sees no faces in the other houses' windows, but people must be there, out of sight but anxious to see what kind of catastrophe has taken place in their haven.

"Good to see you," Gunnar says when Lena reaches the scene. "I suppose Gren called you out of the blue," he adds with a look at her dress.

"You should be a detective." Lena ducks under the tape. "We're short on sharp eyes."

He smiles at Lena's jab; few things alleviate the horrors of vicious crime scenes better than a round of sharp banter. She wonders on which side of the fence Gunnar stands: among those who support her, or together with the larger crowd who thinks she should have been publicly reprimanded for interfering with the national task force six months ago.

"Patrolling the suburbs is excitement enough for me," Gunnar says. "Peace, quiet and petty thieves. Most of the time, I should say." His tone is friendly but sombre. He doesn't have to look at the house to underline the irony.

"Is Gren inside?" Lena asks.

Gunnar nods. "Together with four other officers. And the forensics, of course."

"Keep an eye on the audience. I wouldn't put it past them to sneak into the garden for a better photo for their next status update."

Lena walks a few steps up the driveway, then turns around and motions for Gunnar to come closer, out of earshot of the spectators. The constable is not a senior officer and therefore not part of the actual investigation, but he knows the area. Sometimes neighbourhood policemen can spot invaluable signals in the noise of unfamiliar places. A quick conversation won't hurt. Whatever unpleasantness waits for her in the house is not going anywhere.

"What do you think?" Lena asks Gunnar when he stands next to her. She keeps the question vague on purpose.

"Definitely murder." Gunnar tries to keep the emotions from his face, but he looks tired and worn.

"Beyond that?" Lena asks. The presence of the coroners has already told her as much.

"I can't really–" Gunnar stops as he notices Lena's expression. "A random madman," he continues. "You'll see what I mean. But that's not very helpful, is it?"

"No murders are random. Only accidents are."

"I see what you mean," Gunnar says. "In that case, I would guess revenge. Some kind of psychotic jealousy act. If she or he wanted this to be some kind of warning, I've no idea what to make of it." He takes a deep breath. "The poor bastards. They were young, you know."

"Were they children?" A cold wind washes over Lena, but Gunnar shakes his head before she has time to conjure any abhorrent visions.

"Late twenties," he says. "I've seen them once or twice, working in their garden or painting the house. I'm good with faces."

"You said 'she or he'," Lena notes. "Have you any reason to think the suspect is a woman?"

"I haven't got any reason not to." Gunnar looks uncomfortable. "Although even I know murderers usually aren't women."

"You're quite right. Who was the first one on the scene?"

"I was," Gunnar says. "My radio happened to be on and I live five minutes away. Before you ask, I almost always have it switched on."

"You weren't on duty?" Lena asks. "Then why did you come?"

"This is my turf. It's that simple."

Lena makes a mental note to touch base with Gunnar again. He appears more observant than the average uniform, and she gets his need to help when things go south in his own backyard. The same urgency grips her every time her radio beeps. Perhaps it hasn't let go since she joined the force. And unfortunately, her turf is the size of a city.

"The distress call was made by a neighbour," Gunnar continues. "He's in the ambulance right now. I gleaned from the radio call that the caller hadn't made much sense, but I understood that it concerned a probable double homicide."

"Please tell me there's an officer watching him?" Lena asks.

"Two, I think. The man is in tatters. He said they'd left one of their cars blocking his driveway. Apparently it wasn't the first time. So he'd gone over to knock on their door, found that it was open, and looked inside. Eventually he'd manage to call the police."

"He actually entered the bloody house?"

"There wasn't any need. One of the bodies is on the hall floor. I saw it myself." Gunnar pauses. "That's why I said it's a madman who did this."

A knock on a window from inside the house startles Lena. She looks up and sees Gren peering through the blinds. He frowns and waves at her. *Hurry up.*

"Brace yourself," Gunnar says.

Lena walks up the driveway and the short set of stairs. Her plan is to get in, help Gren in whatever way she can, and rush back to the city as fast as possible. Gustav is waiting at his flat. When she told him she had to duck out from the dinner, he was all understanding and helpfulness, putting on a show so perfect she almost bought it. But she could see through the pretence: he is disappointed and, even worse, worried.

The front door opens outward. It is partially closed, possibly to obscure the view from the neighbours. From inside the house come hushed voices and the soft rattle of tools. On the door handle is the signature black coating left behind by the crime scene technicians when they sweep for fingerprints. The radiance of the coroners' lights spills out onto the small concrete landing like a film of snow.

"Mind your step, Lena," Gren calls from inside. "And pull the door shut behind you."

Lena pulls the door open, squints in the glare of the brilliant spotlights, and looks down.

And understands why Gunnar thinks a madman has descended on his suburb.

Chapter 4

"Two victims were found at the scene," Lena says. "One man and one woman. The man's name was Emil Backman, twenty-eight years old, born in Gothenburg before he relocated here about ten years ago. The woman, Pia Oscarsson, was twenty-seven. She was born and raised in a suburb just north of the city."

She drinks from her water bottle and clears her throat. The air conditioning in the briefing room is poor at best. Tonight, when every seat is taken, what air the system manages to circulate is stale and hot. The light from the projector feels like an interrogation lamp. Which is no wonder, given that all twenty-seven woman and men in the room are watching her as much as they are listening to the brief.

Some expect her to go off the rails before the investigation has started in full force. Few bought her story about how the door in the bathroom was broken because of an accident; they know her temper and history too well and think she might crack at any moment. There are probably bets on whether she will see the case through. Or even manage the briefing.

Thankfully, she had left a black T-shirt and a pair of red track pants in the locker, or she would still be wearing a dress. That would have done little to underpin her image as a professional member of the police force. Now she looks like a stressed-out jogger instead, but she counted her blessings.

"They were married two years ago," Lena continues. "Neither had a criminal record or suspicious affiliates. Over the past six years, they bought two flats in areas close to central Stockholm before they purchased the house about four months ago. All books are in order. Large mortgage, but that's to be expected given the address."

"That's a fast property career," another detective notes. "What were they doing for a living?" He frowns at the screen on which the details of the case are projected.

He is short and a few years younger than Lena, perhaps in his early thirties, with a round face and sailor-style sideburns. His surname is Jacobson, and his accent suggests he is from southern Sweden, but that is about all she knows. He has been at the department only a few months. Going by the rumours, he is bright but careful, which fits his mole-in-the-daylight looks. But he is also one of the few in the room who is studying the screen rather than her body language.

"Both were doctors," Lena says. "The woman was a trauma specialist who moved between the city hospitals. Her husband was a general practitioner."

"So the woman was a high earner," Gren suggests.

"Her husband did pretty well for himself too," Lena says. "He did some consultancy for large businesses, advised them on private care options and such. Both made a fair amount of money. We've done a quick review of their bank accounts, but they look clean. No weird transactions or funny withdrawals."

"Could it be a rival corporation trying to intimidate the competition?" someone in the room wonders.

"His clients were in the cosmetics industry," Jacobson replies. "Lots of capital, but as far as I know, they're not known for scare tactics. And I really think this is beyond the animal welfare activists. But I suggest we keep all options open."

"I agree," Lena says.

Stranger forms of blackmail and attempts at coercion happen all the time. Some are so outlandish even the media shy away, often out of fear they would be accused of making the reports up.

"The crime site is clean," Lena continues. "No suspicious prints or footsteps have been found so far. The suspect entered through a basement window. He or she used a plastic adhesive sheet to punch a hole in the glass. No neighbour has seen anyone leave or enter. We'll do another round of interviews tomorrow morning."

"Let's go over the cause of death," Gren says softly from the back.

Lena skims the paper in her hand while people shift in their seats. It's the first time she shares the official report, but everyone in the room already knows. Details about cases often filter through the department and out beyond its walls within minutes. The speed is determined by the unusualness of the information, and gruesome facts always ramp up the whispering game. This case will have spread among the force and spilled onto the streets in record time.

"As most of you will have heard," Lena says, "the victims were stabbed repeatedly around their necks and the lower part of their torsos. Both died from near-immediate organ failures. This level of violence suggests that the killer is a man, so we're acting on that presumption. The injuries were severe, but I don't think this was a professional hit, and the coroners agree."

"How come?" someone asks.

"Because the scene is a right mess," Lena says. "The man was stabbed eighteen times and the woman three. And that's just a preliminary count. Some of the cuts are mere grazes while others are deep, but few struck arteries and other typical soft spots."

"Perhaps the victims put up a fight?" Gren wonders.

"The man did." Lena clicks a button, and a sketch of the floor plan appears on the screen. "He was found on his back just inside the door. I think he fell backwards when he tried to defend himself. There was a spilled glass of water near his body, so I'm guessing he'd been to the kitchen when he was attacked.

"His wife was still in bed," Lena continues. "No sign of struggle there. My theory is the attacker was hiding in the bedroom and waited for the right moment, which came when the husband left the room. The murderer first targeted the woman and then confronted the man."

She pauses.

"The next slide shows close-ups of both victims' faces."

Lena presses the button to display the photo, but she keeps her back turned to the screen. She has seen enough. No number of high-resolution images of thrashed skin and flesh can help her at this stage, at least not for the moment. The key to finding the perpetrator will be found in the circumstances. And there must be a key, or they are in trouble. Gunnar's idea of a casual killer still rings in the back of her head.

"Once both victims were dead," Lena continues, "their eyes were removed."

The room is silent. Everyone in the room is aware of this particular detail, but hearing it as part of a brief makes the deed tangible and real.

"How?" Jacobson wonders.

"They were gouged out with a blunt tool," Lena says. "Possibly a kitchen spoon. As you can tell, it wasn't a precise operation. The autopsy report will be ready tomorrow."

"Could it have happened by accident?" someone asks. "I mean, there are cuts all over their faces."

"Maybe one eye," Lena says, "but not four. This is deliberate, and it's our most important lead when we're looking for similar cases. Any kind of removal of body parts is of interest. Especially when it's likely that the motives are jealousy or extortion."

"How the hell do you blackmail somcone after poking their eyes out?" wonders an officer at the back of the room.

"It could be a cautioning," Jacobson suggests. "Terror tactics, perhaps by a mob. Heaven knows they do worse things."

Lena shakes her head while she sorts her papers. Some syndicates are inhuman when they try to rattle their rivals, but they always have objectives like money or intimidation. This wasn't public enough. And hit men are often either overly brutal or very precise. This murder spans both those scales.

"What's your hunch, Lena?" Gren asks.

Someone inside the darkness outside the glare of the projector mimics the sound of a gun being cocked and fired: *cha-click-boom*. Several officers stifle laughs.

Lena waits in silence while she brings her temper under control. Snide remarks during briefings is a time-honoured way of venting stress and worry, but the unwritten rule is to keep the sarcasm general, not personal. This was aimed directly at her. And she has heard similar remarks before. The joke suggests that her preferred approach would be to shoot someone. Once again, her history hangs over her like a cloud, colouring every word she says.

She picked up on the distaste that filled the room as soon as she crossed over the doorstep. Revulsion at this crime, resentment over the cruelty of people in general, and aggravation that the most spectacular investigation in a long time is run by a detective with a citywide reputation for rash moves and unhinged behaviour.

Many officers have track records brimming with collapsed cases and mishandled interrogations, but the norm was to ignore the past and look forward. Especially if the man or woman concerned was seen as a good cop. Not so in Lena's case. The label was etched in too hard. All she could do was keep it from sinking any deeper.

"Stop that immediately," Gren orders the unseen would-be comedian. "Lena, tell us what you think about the motive."

"Jealousy," Lena says. "That's my primary suspicion. My secondary is a warning of some kind."

The notion feels threadbare even as she says it. As assaults against couples go, infuriated ex-boyfriends are the usual suspects, but physical attacks on former loved ones with this level of brutality are rare. Sabotage, slander and violence, sure. Those types of crimes are more common, but often underpinned by signs of rage.

This is different. The word that springs to her mind is *biblical*, although while assaults on religious pretexts happen on a daily basis, they are seldom the reason for assassinations in Scandinavian suburbs.

So another cause, then. An unknown incentive buried beneath who knows how much dirt. And Gren has picked her to helm the hunt. If she didn't know her superintendent better, she would suspect that he either wants her to fail in public or that he has lost his mind.

But Gren is not petty or deranged. He believes in her. Consequently, she's stuck in the spotlight and surrounded by disgruntled officers waiting for her to crash and burn in a spectacular fashion.

It's shaping up to a tremendous weekend.

"Where did you find the eyes?" Jacobson asks.

"We haven't located them yet," Lena says.

"Jesus Christ," someone mutters. Hushed speculations and questions fly across the room. People scratch their necks, cross their arms, and peer at the screen.

"I don't have to repeat this," Gren says and raises his voice, "but please remember that discretion is paramount. This is the kind of story that'll have us under siege by the press in no time."

Lena shares Gren's desire for silence, yet his ambition is pointless. The press will start to pepper them with questions very soon. There are too many people involved already, too many nodes through which the information can flow. Leaks are inevitable.

The crime scene is pulling at her. She wants to go back and start searching for clues. A nagging feeling urges her to hurry, and it's not because she has picked up the scent of the cause behind the murders. This sense of urgency comes from the total lack of a clear reason. There will be a motive, but so far, it is inexplicable, and vagueness is every sane police's enemy.

Both bodies were transferred to an ambulance an hour after Lena arrived. A quick tour of the house provided her with a few critical facts: there weren't any blatantly obvious clues to the identity of the murderer, and there were no other victims, at least not found during her superficial search. She had been relieved by the lack of toys or pictures of children. As relieved as one could be on a scene of that kind.

A team of officers and forensics will go over the house next morning to document, label and bag anything that might help the investigation. They will do a much more thorough job than she possibly can, but she'll join them to go over the surroundings and try to replay the atrocity. Then she'll start knocking on doors.

If only she were able to leave this stuffy room. As she has done so many times over the past months, she wishes Agnes was here, but the junior officer is still missing. No obituary, no call, not a word in print or online. Stress is still the official reason for Agnes's absence. Her desk is used as temporary storage for various office supplies and folders, which is an odd symbol of respect. Usually, other officers with smaller workspaces pounce on bigger desks as soon as they are vacated.

Lena sometimes wishes someone had taken Agnes's seat. The unoccupied chair is a constant reminder of her absence, just like the water dispenser outside the briefing room. No one any longer unplugs it to spare Lena from its hideous gargle. Only Agnes had noticed Lena's discomfort around the machine.

"That's all." Lena slams the laptop shut. "Tomorrow, we'll do more door knocking, and the techs will do a secondary sweep of the house. I'll be available around the clock."

Her phone buzzes. She slips it halfway out of her pocket and glances at the display. It is Gustav. She has missed three calls, all by him.

The censored version of what has happened is prepared in her mind. There's no point in worrying him. He would want to make sure she does everything in her power to protect herself and keep out of harm's way, which is exactly opposite what policing is about.

But his concern is a price she has to pay, and she will hand over the money no matter what it takes. The time for aloneness is over. No more hiding in the woods.

Chapter 5

Felix watches the morning from his living room sofa. This early in the day, Norra Ängby is drowsy and quiet as it emerges from another brief respite from daylight. Only the birds are restless. Thousands upon thousands, they chirp ceaselessly as they zip around apple trees and birches. Each creature is facing the daily struggle to maintain territories, attract partners, fend off predators, and improve nests. A furious, never-ending battle.

His neighbours think the avian wildlife is a quaint feature of their suburb. No one but him sees the tragicomic similarity: just like the birds, they too are startled by the morning into immediate hysteria. Mortgages dangle over their heads like sabres suspended by fickle employers and the whims of global finance. And so they dart to their various ventures in cars and on trains, returning at nightfall after having fought off the threats one more day.

He used to be one of them. As far as his fellow suburbanites know, he still is. Those years spent pretending he was like his neighbours had taken a tremendous toll. Hoping to fit in, fretting over appearances, worrying over the opinions of his peers. And his struggle has been far more difficult than theirs; his childhood was not one of privilege and gentle honing for a life among peers.

He was born into captivity and brought up by torturous trials. For countless days, every hour was filled with punishments, medication, and bouts of fitful sleep. His escape was possible because of wit and speed. He clawed his way to freedom. After spending months in institutions while authorities tried and failed to establish his origins, he fought to adapt to a world he had not known existed, and he had managed.

Then came the years of battling to be accepted. Decode the rules of primary school, understand the thorny woods that is high school, and negotiate the slopes of adult everyday life. He stuck to accepted avenues: degrees, internships, ambition. Always mimicking those around him, nodding when others agreed, showing his teeth when his colleagues grinned.

But no longer.

His living room is an oasis from the birds' hustle and bustle. All the furniture is dismantled, thrown away, or stored in the basement. It keeps the room free from clutter and distractions. Only a single sofa remains, placed in the middle of the room and facing east so he can watch the dawn and its accompanying cacophony. The birds are a useful reminder. Even roads to salvation have bumps, cracks and pitfalls, each of which can nudge him in the wrong direction.

Fortunately, Timmy had arrived and showed him an easier way.

His friend had pointed out how trying to blend in is a wasted effort, doomed to fail at any given point. There are easier ways to find a lasting equilibrium. Why spend years climbing the mountain of life when the playing field can be levelled with the swipe of a knife? Revenge trumps pretence any day, Timmy claims.

Felix rises and goes to his kitchen. Another window, but with a similar view: stress and struggle lacquered with cutting-edge technology and three-course dinners. And hiding in the parade of smiles are the evil ones. One man split into countless replicas, each as vile as the other. There are so many he must stop. Hundreds of potential crimes that must be prevented.

There are many obstacles in his path: recurring nightmares, sudden pangs of regret and unwanted questions surfacing among his daily thoughts. His faith is anything but solid. It will take time before his conviction is as unwavering as Timmy wants it to be. Time he will have only if he is careful.

A soft hiss behind Felix is followed by a hint of frigid wind. Timmy has come to visit him again. Relieved, he turns around.

Timmy sits on the edge of the kitchen table, his knees pulled up to his chin. He looks between Felix and the windows while he taps his fingers on his legs.

"Why do you so often come here?" Felix wonders. "To the kitchen, I mean?"

"It's a place for contemplation." Timmy winks. "Which makes it easier for me to get in. You've no idea how many grand schemes have been drawn up in front of stoves."

Felix isn't sure what Timmy means by this, but he doesn't ask for an explanation. Timmy is here. That is enough.

Timmy steps down and pads up to the kitchen window. His steps are perfectly soundless, but also careful.

"You look troubled," Felix says.

"We have a small problem." Timmy nods at the window. "A woman-shaped one. She's a scalpel taken human form, slicing away what's meant to be healed over, out of sight, kept secret."

"Do you mean the chamber?" Felix wonders.

Timmy shakes his head. "That's irrelevant. Those rooms are empty. The beds stripped bare, our old desks covered with dust, all the nurses gone into permanent hiding. It doesn't matter if they go there, except for one thing."

"It can lead them to us," Felix guesses.

"Only if they're clever. And this woman stops at nothing. I should've known they'd call her in."

"You talk about her as if you know her."

Timmy smiles thinly. "She's something of a celebrity where I'm from. Actually, forget I said that. What has me all riled up is that she's dancing on my doorstep, but she refuses to come inside."

"Can't you make her go away?" Felix asks. "You've told me before how you've silenced others who might hunt us."

"Everyone hunts me." Timmy's smile is a band of white in the gloom. "I'm used to being the prey. It's you I'm worried about. We have much left to do."

"I can visit her tonight," Felix suggests. "I'll bring my knives. She can be made to stare, just like the others."

"Not this one. She's too dangerous. And there's another woman in the mix."

"Another police officer?"

Timmy shakes his head. "This is someone I've worked on for years, but the stubborn cretin refuses to do herself in. My biggest worry is that the two meet."

"What can I do?"

"Leave the policewoman to me," Timmy says. "She's running through the night, and she's picking up speed. Soon she'll stumble. When she does, I'll be there to catch her."

Chapter 6

Stockholm, Östermalm

Thursday

07:12

Lena wakes with a gasp and sits up in the bed.

For a few confused seconds, she's completely disoriented, but then she recognises Gustav's curtains. She has spent three nights in the bedroom, and some features are already familiar enough to be comforting. The crisp smell of his fabric softener. The bookshelves filled with style guides and business magazines. His stark white walls and designer coat hanger draped with his suit jacket and her T-shirt. The dim sunlight sliced into pale slivers by broad vertical blinds.

Gustav mumbles in his sleep and shifts closer to her. In the weak light, the blanket over his body is a mound of slopes and valleys in cotton the colour of wet sand. A foreign landscape that hides an increasingly valuable treasure. When she arrived at his flat after visiting the neighbours, he met her with a tight embrace, a glass of wine and, eventually, all of himself. No questions or meaningful looks.

Her phone rings. She understands what pulled her out of her deep sleep. She reaches for her trousers on the floor, digs the phone out of her pocket, and takes the call.

"Franke," she rasps and clears her throat.

"Oh, hello. This is Gunnar. I'm at the scene in Norra Ängby again. Or near it, I should say."

"You must have a good reason for calling this early," Lena says, suspecting that he has.

"I read through the case description when I got up this morning," Gunnar says. "I saw what's missing."

"The eyes," Lena says.

She pushes down the surge of unease. The wrongness of the victims' disfigured bodies is a nail in her consciousness. A murder this savage pushes the crime out of the realm of regular homicide and into a deeper, more unpredictable pit. But even the worst tangle of madness has patterns and frayed ends. Somewhere out there's a thread dangling free, waiting for her to pull it.

"Precisely," Gunnar says. "I suspected as much when I saw the body yesterday, but I wasn't sure because of all the blood. You see what I meant when I said it must be the work of a lunatic."

"We're considering a range of ideas," Lena says. "A deranged individual is one of them. But to be honest, it's not my number one theory."

"How many traces have you got?"

"Very few at this point," Lena says. A more accurate count is zero.

"Then I might be able to help."

"Have you found a lead?" Lena stands up and reaches for her clothes.

"In a way," Gunnar says. "I think I've found the missing eyes."

*

Lena steps out of her car thirty minutes later and slams the door shut, startling a robin in a nearby tree into panicked flight. She locks the door and cracks her neck. Four hours of uneasy sleep have left her more tired than before she went to bed. The coffee she picked up from a petrol station is both dreadful and apparently void of caffeine. It promises to be a long day.

She learned that Gustav had stayed up most of the entire night, reading and drinking coffee in his kitchen, sneaking back to fall asleep next to Lena only when it was six o'clock in the morning. He had wanted her to feel safe. After only ten or so dates, he is alert to her moods in a way no one else has been, or at least not many others. He is stylish even in his protectiveness.

Still, her brief downtime wasn't enough to bring the world into full focus. It didn't compensate for a long week, followed by an interrupted evening out and a murder case that's a good candidate for the grisliest investigation of the decade.

She drains the last of the coffee, tosses the takeaway cup onto the floor in her car, and looks around. The dawn is turning the houses' terracotta rooftops into molten rectangles. Today will be hot, but the cool of last night lingers in the air. Real warmth is several hours away. Two days ago, heavy rain fell over most parts of Stockholm, but the daytime heat has vaporized every trace of moisture.

At least the air is fresh enough to revive her a little. Sprawling and cut through by waterways, Stockholm is not cursed with the persistent smog of many other capitals, but breathing in this suburb feels different. Trees fill every available space and filter out most artificial scents until only a cool humidity remains. If she were here in her private time and were unaware of what had happened in the house a few minutes away, she would have enjoyed the view.

But Gunnar is waiting for her, and what she's about to examine will darken the day in ways no amount of sunlight can wash away.

Squeezed in between two houses is a path up along a heavily wooded hillside. According to Gunnar's directions, the right-hand path will take her straight to the location where he's waiting for her. Two patrol officers from the local department have joined him, and the individual who found the eyes – a young man out walking his dogs, according to Gunnar – is also there.

She has just entered the forest when Gustav calls.

"I'm sorry I took off so fast," Lena says.

"Don't worry. Did you go back to that place?"

"We've found a clue," Lena says. "And they're waiting for me, so I had to run."

"I get it. I'd hoped you would've stayed here a while longer. No one makes breakfast in bed like I do. There would've been eggs Benedict with coffee."

"You're making me hungry."

"Just according to plan, then. Any chance you might be free for lunch today?"

"I really hope so. I'll call you when I know for sure."

Lena doesn't add that the odds are microscopic; bad cases like these make lunch breaks a luxury that never seems to materialize.

"I know that you don't want me to ask too much about your work," Gustav says.

Lena closes her eyes and sighs.

"And I know that you can't tell me much anyway," he continues. "Which is fine, and I mean that. But I want you to look after yourself."

"Of course."

Lena almost speaks through her teeth. Gustav's concern is genuine, but his timing is wrong. She cannot afford distractions right now. At least he's not demanding answers or trying to hold her back like some of her previous partners did. He is only voicing his apprehension. She can't ask him not to do that. She needs to get used to meeting him halfway.

"There's nothing dangerous out here apart from a couple of hungry officers," Lena says.

"Did they really have to drag you out of bed?"

"They didn't," Lena says. "I rushed here because it's my job."

Gustav hears the growing edge in her voice. "I get it," he says. "I'm sorry. No more questions. Call me when you can. Please?"

"As soon as they let me go."

"I miss you."

"Don't give up on your breakfast ideas just yet," Lena says. "I'll come over tonight if I can. If that's all right?" she adds after a moment.

"I can't wait."

Lena says goodbye and pockets her phone. After a moment, she switches it off. Breaking the link feels like releasing mental ballast that weighed her down. No more disturbances until she has a firm grip on this new scene.

She follows the path and soon spots Gunnar. By his side are two patrol officers, a man and a woman, both radiating the kind of energy Lena lost somewhere by the roadside years ago. When they see Lena, they straighten up and adjust their belts. They wear their uniforms with the discreet awkwardness of recent graduates from the academy.

A short distance away stands a short, blond man in his late twenties. He's flanked by a pair of huge dogs that are looking at Lena. Black and brown, with wide mouths and long, sturdy legs. Rottweilers, she guesses. Dog breeds are not her forte, but it doesn't take an expert to see that the animals are nervous. Perhaps they can sense blood on the air.

Lena studies the two officers. Both are doing their best to look relaxed, but while they might be alert, they fidget with their gloves and eye the woods as if expecting a rabid beast to bear down on them at any moment. Given the recent events, their attitude is understandable.

Gunnar nods at Lena and squints in the low-angle sunlight. He looks as if he wants to shake her hand, but his veteran local-officer manners hold him back.

"Sorry to chase you up so early, Detective."

"I'm glad you did," Lena says. "Were you listening to the radio again?"

"I was on duty, actually. The call came through to our station first. I heard the details and realised what it might be about. To be honest, part of me wishes I hadn't."

"Is he the one who rang?" Lena points at the man with the dogs.

Gunnar nods. "Just after seven," he says. "It took me a while to understand what he was going on about. I told him to stay put and give me directions, and he didn't object."

"Where are they?" Lena asks.

"Over there."

Gunnar points away from the path. Some ten metres away is a knee-high rock with a flat top, partially hidden by a sheet of white plastic. Lena recognizes the material as part of a body bag. One of the officers must have brought it from the local police station.

"I inspected the – well, items when I got here," Gunnar says quietly. "I'm not a crime scene technician, but I would say that there's no doubt."

"I'll have a look in a moment," Lena says. "What can you tell me about him?" She nods at the two other officers and the man with the dogs.

"I know him a bit," Gunnar says. "His name's Ronny. He walks his dogs quite often up here."

"Have you run him through the system?"

Gunnar nods. "Nothing out of the ordinary. He's pretty rattled, and I can't blame the man."

"Does he know what he's found?" Lena asks.

"I'm afraid so," Gunnar says. "That's why he called the police. And his house is just down the street from the scene, so he knows something's happened there. He made the connection straight away."

"It doesn't take much to join those dots. Let's talk to him."

Lena walks over to Ronny and looks him over.

"I'm Detective Lena Franke," she says to Ronny. "When exactly did you make the discovery?"

"About ten past seven," he says. "I remember, because I spent ages trying to make the call."

"Why trying?" Lena asks. "Bad coverage in here?"

"My hands were shaking. It took me a while to dial the number."

Lena looks around the forest. The shadows are long, and the rock of particular interest is at least five or six steps away any path she can see.

"Where were you standing when you spotted them?" Lena asks.

"Right here. Although I was walking, of course."

"You must have good eyesight," Lena says. "I can barely make out the white plastic, and it was even darker an hour ago."

"I didn't see anything," Ronny says. "Freke found them."

"Your dog?" Lena guesses.

"It's him over there." He points at one of his pets. "He went for the rock as if it'd been a fried chicken. After I took a closer look, I called straight away."

"I appreciate it," Lena says.

"I haven't touched them." Ronny glances at the white plastic sheet. "Or let the dogs close."

"That's equally appreciated," Lena says. "Have you seen anything out of place in the area?"

"Other than what I found this morning?" Ronny asks. "Or the police tape two houses away? Can't say I have, really." He clears his throat and swallows, then starts at the distant sound of a car horn.

"Save the sarcasm," Lena says. "It's possible that you have valuable information, even without knowing it. Anything you've noticed can be important."

"Sorry," Ronny says. "Everything else is normal as far as I can tell. That's almost the worst, if you see what I mean?"

"Yes," Lena says. "I do see what you mean."

She turns to the female officer, who stands to rapt attention just behind Ronny. When she meets Lena's eyes, she tenses and shifts her feet, but her face is open. Perhaps Lena's reputation is less tarnished this far from the city headquarters. Or the woman might just be good at looking neutral.

"Anything to report?" Lena asks.

"We've searched the perimeter," she replies, "but we haven't found any other evidence. A few people have walked past, although all of them were kids. A few of them asked what we were doing here. We said there'd been a campfire."

"Why the hell are there children in here at this hour?" Lena asks.

"They were on their way to their primary school," the officer explains. "It's a few minutes that way." She points east along the path.

"Kids wandering around the forest on their own?" Lena wonders.

"It's pretty much the norm in Norra Ängby." The woman shrugs. "And these woods are in the middle of the suburb, so lots of people cut through them. All the small forests here are full of paths."

"Isn't that lovely," Lena says under her breath.

So there are plenty of ways to nip from one place to another without using roads or parkways. Tracking the movements of a suspect here would be a massive headache. If they ever manage to pin down a likely offender, that is.

"Search the area again," Lena says, "and get every constable available out on the streets. Check for anything out of place. Although try to look inconspicuous. What's the matter?" The officer is unable to keep a pained look from her face.

"Being low-key here might be difficult," she says to Lena. "Most who live in this place would be surprised to see an officer on patrol more often than once a month."

"Then they'll have to put up with a change of scenery," Lena says. "Gunnar, get on the radio and pull your people closer."

"Do you think the perpetrator is still in the area?" the male officer asks.

"There's always a risk. I'd have the dog patrol here if I could, but they can't make it until after lunch."

She called them as soon as she hung up on Gunnar, but the two German shepherds on duty were busy on the outskirts of Stockholm, several hours from Norra Ängby. It's her vintage brand of non-luck.

Shielding her eyes from the sun, she peers into the forest. The contrast between the morning sun and the hard shadows make for a confusing landscape. Someone could hide twenty metres away and be next to invisible.

"You can go home," she says to Ronny. "Leave your contact details with one of the officers. I'm likely to be in touch soon."

"Are you going back to town?" Gunnar wonders.

"Once I've had a proper look here," Lena says.

She walks into the forest and looks down at the sheet of white plastic. After a moment, she lifts a corner and crouches down for a closer look.

Four glistening, spherical pieces of bluish white rest on the moss-covered surface of the rock. They are definitely eyes, and given what happened last night, there's no need to check if they're human. The eyes are discoloured by red and purple blotches, and the pupils are round discs of faded brown and green. They match the descriptions of the victims.

Wrenched away from the bodies to which they belong, the eyes look anything but human. It's hard to imagine that they have helped someone navigate childhoods and grown-up lives. Even thinking of them as eyes feels wrong. That word is imbued with significance: eyes are windows to souls, silent conveyors of meaning. They are focal points of attention for both the minds behind them as well as those who look into them.

These have been reduced to dislodged chunks of broken and bloodied tissue. The links to the minds were broken. Their meaning was reduced to dust. The only thing that remains is decaying flesh and a hidden message. Because one thing is certain: the eyes were left here for a reason.

Lena takes out her phone and calls Gren.

"We've found the eyes," she tells him as soon as he answers.

"Where?" Gren asks. "Did you miss them when you swept the house last night?"

"They're in a forest, and so am I. Send a team of technicians here as soon as possible so they can bag the evidence and check for prints. They aren't likely to find any in here, but I want to make sure."

Lena gives Gren a rundown of how the eyes were discovered, followed by directions to the location. She tells him that three other officers will meet up with the technicians when they arrive.

As she speaks, she removes the plastic sheet completely and walks around the rock. The eyes are centred on the top of the rock. All of them have been positioned to stare sightlessly in the same direction.

"Who found them?" Gren asks.

"A dog walker. I'm fairly sure he isn't our man. We've checked him."

"Make sure he understands the repercussions of talking to journalists." Gren sighs. "We're already fielding calls about this case. Mostly from worried people in the neighbourhood, but the reporters are in the mix."

"He's pretty shaken," Lena says. "Which means he won't say a word or throw himself on the phone as soon as he can."

She stands up and tilts her head. Unless she's mistaken, the pupils point east, almost ninety degrees away from the house where the murders took place. She walks around the rock again and kneels down to follow their imagined line of sight. Only trees and bushes fill her view. The sun shoots spears of reddish golden light, forcing her to squint.

"Jacobson has looked up the records of the area," Gren says. "Give him a ring as soon as you can."

"Is he assigned to this case?" Lena asks.

"Yes," Gren confirms. "Play nice with him."

Lena isn't sure what to make of the news. Since Jacobson appeared at the department, he and she have exchanged only a few words. He is almost a complete stranger. The man has the characteristics of someone too brainy for his own good: he speaks his mind whenever he wants, and he's cautious in the extreme. Then again, he never gives her repulsed looks in a meeting or when passing her in the corridors. And rumours have it that he's dedicated, despite his slow, soft manners.

"I know you've never worked with him," Gren continues, "but he's very competent. He actually asked me to team him up with you. Don't worry, you're still running the investigation. I've texted you his direct number."

"What's his background?" Lena asks.

She rises again and takes a few steps past the rock. Perhaps the eyes are supposed to look at something beyond the woods. Maybe a particular house in Norra Ängby or an object even farther away.

In some notorious instances, murderers have left clues to help detectives track them down, usually as part of twisted games meant to end with a spectacular capture or showdown. Those cases are so rare they make jackpot-winning lottery tickets look as common as confetti, but the placement of the eyes is not accidental. They have been arranged with far too much care for that.

"I'll let you ask him those questions," Gren says. "By the way, the board is taking an interest in this investigation. They're keeping close tabs on it."

"On me, you mean?" Lena asks. After the debacle last winter, she would be surprised if the police command is not scrutinizing her every email.

"They know that the media will descend on the house like an avalanche," Gren says. "This investigation will draw lots of attention. But to be honest, it's possible that the board wants to assess your work as well."

"When they get in touch again," Lena says, "tell them to assign me every available technician we have on the force. I might have to search an entire forest."

Lena walks towards the sun while she talks to Gren. A trio of birches split the light into two horizontal pillars of glittering white. She moves slightly left so one of the trunks blocks out the sunshine.

When she no longer is blinded, she notices a speck of white on one of the trees.

"I'll do what I can," Gren says. "Call me in an hour and give me an update."

Lena doesn't reply. As she walks closer, the white patch turns out to be a Post-it note. It has been pinned to the middle tree. The paper is crisp and unblemished. In its middle is a single line of text.

Look deep and draw.

She turns around and looks back at the white plastic on the rock. The note faces the eyes perfectly.

"What the fuck is this?" Lena says.

"Please don't argue with me," Gren says, thinking Lena's expletive was aimed at him. "I'm the one who put you in charge of the case, remember? All I ask is that you keep me posted—"

"Hang on."

Lena lowers the phone and jogs back to Gunnar and the two local officers.

"Did it rain here the day before yesterday?" she asks Gunnar.

Gunnar thinks for a moment and nods. "We had a proper shower," he says. "It went on for hours."

Lena runs back to the note pinned to the tree. The neat handwriting is not smudged. She raises the phone to her ear again.

"Gren?" she asks. "Are you still there?"

"What's going on?" Gren asks. "Why are you cursing?"

"Get the technicians here right now. We have a hard lead."

"Really?" Gren sounds relieved. "That's what I was hoping to hear."

"That was the good news," Lena says. "You're not going to like the rest."

Lena's thoughts race while she fills Gren in on what she has found. As she speaks, she sums up what she knows to herself.

A woman and a man callously butchered for an unknown reason. Their eyes plucked away and left for anyone to discover. Four words that might help her find the killer or which perhaps have no meaning at all outside the deranged psyche of the murderer. At any rate, they can scratch the idea of corporate blackmail or espionage, and discard all motives related to jealousy or debt. This is different.

And, she knows, much worse.

Chapter 7

Lena leaves the café in central Vällingby and walks past a string of fashion retailers. The parking lot is less than a minute away, but she's doing her best to finish her breakfast before she gets back to her car.

A cup of coffee, a large bag of nuts and an enormous baguette sandwich with triple tuna filling. A decent load of proteins and enough calories to run a boat engine. It will at least see her through the morning. Her training regime makes her a serious gourmand by default, and stress always makes her cravings even worse.

The hour is the blessed window between breakfast chaos and lunchtime mayhem, and the broad pedestrian streets of Vällingby are almost empty. A group of children mill outside the local movie theatre. Behind her, a street sweeper works his way across a plaza outside the entrance to the underground trains. The sky is an almost undisturbed blue. No more rain in sight, at least for now.

The coffee in her hand is a Godsend. Three espressos with just enough milk to dull the bitterness are bringing her thoughts up to cruising speed. At the same time, she is frustratingly unfocussed. Even though Gustav is back in the city, working away on whatever project he is engrossed in for the moment, he is still present in her mind. It's as if her consciousness were a waiting room and he was standing outside the window, constantly looking at her.

45

This constant feeling is the reason behind the near-lethal amount of caffeine in her hand. If it doesn't enable her to home in on the important questions, nothing will.

Look deep and draw.

A sequence of random words, someone's stab at poetry, or an actual lead. By now, the technicians will be dusting down the paper and other surfaces around it. Given that the note is in a forest, the odds of finding any prints are against them. Unless the author of the note is an idiot, unusually clumsy, or truly wants to be caught.

In the meantime, Lena will work on the words or make sure that her temporary partner does his bit. Going by Gren's tone, Jacobson will end up as her permanent teammate if they get through this case without too many public confrontations. It won't hurt to remind him that she's running the investigation; his borderline arrogance betrays a bit of overconfidence.

She arrives at her car, puts the food on the roof, and calls Jacobson.

"This is Franke," Lena says. "I need you to research this bloody riddle we found. I suppose Gren has filled you in?"

"Hello to you too," Jacobson says. "Yes, Gren gave me a quick rundown. Actually, I was just about to call you. Are you on your way in?"

Lena presses her phone to her ear; Jacobson's voice is so quiet she struggles to hear him over the wind.

"I'm going back to the scene," Lena says. "The neighbours might have more to say now that we've found the note. Not that I'm planning on mentioning it, obviously, but it can prompt new questions."

"What will you ask them?"

"Not sure yet. I'll figure it out on my way there. But we need to make sure there's nothing too obvious we're missing about that text. It might be part of a poem or the lyrics to a song."

Lena sips from her coffee. Every mouthful is bliss. If she ever grows sensitive to caffeine, her career is as good as over.

"First of all," she continues, "I want to do some basic searches around the message on the note. Look up the words online and see what you find. We might get lucky."

"I've tried," Jacobson says. "There are thousands of hits, so instead I–"

"Search for the exact combination of words."

"I was about to tell you that I've done that too. And I have an interesting hit."

Lena swallows her coffee so fast it leaves a trace of hot fire down her throat. She curses through a coughing fit, drops the cup on the ground, and sucks in air.

"Are you sure?" she rasps.

"I'm positive," Jacobson says.

"What is it, some lyric from a song?" Lena is reflexively sceptical; it cannot be this easy. No investigation ever is.

"It's a blog. Not much text, but thousands of images. Empty factories, big tunnels, open manholes, things like that. They're quite well shot, I'd say. Looks professional to me."

"Is the blogger some kind of photographer?"

"It seems so, unless she or he gets the pictures from another source. There are no mentions of real names or any pictures of the author's face. Or anyone else's face, for that matter."

"What do you mean there's no real names?"

"All the posts are signed Cronus."

"All right, run a check on that."

"He was the father of Hades. In other words, a god. So I don't think we'll get much from that name. Oh, look at this."

"What?" Lena clenches the phone in her hand. Jacobson definitely has to learn to stop drip-feeding her information.

"I found the words I searched for on an actual photo. They're in the caption. That must be why the page came up when I searched for it."

"And?"

"The words look as if they're painted on a wall. The letters look pretty large, but it's hard to say for sure."

Lena leans against her car. Another hard lead. A trickle of adrenaline finds its way into her bloodstream.

"Send me the link to the page," Lena says. "I want to see this website before we bring the blogger in."

"The link is in your inbox. By the way, I just checked the owner of the domain. The address is in Sundbyberg."

"That's just north of here." Lena turns slowly and looks over the roof of her car at the woods beyond Vällingby Centrum.

"I've emailed you the street and the number. I checked the map, too. It's a flat near the river."

"Get in your car," Lena says. "Meet me two blocks away from that address. I'll decide on a rendezvous point when I've checked the area. You'll have the exact location in five minutes."

"I'm on my way."

"Call in two more cars when you're on the road," Lena continues. "But be discreet. If there's someone at home, we don't want to be seen."

Lena yanks the car door open and drops her breakfast on the passenger seat. If the blogger had lived on the other side of the planet or even in another city, the match could be a coincidence. But Sundbyberg is too close for the connection to be a dud. The blogger has answers.

And in a few minutes, Lena will have them too.

Chapter 8

While Lena drives, she checks the map on her phone and chooses a meeting point a few hundred metres from the blogger's home. The owner of the domain address and the actual blogger can be two different individuals, but it's likely they're at least superficially familiar with each other. Names in investigations often work like links in a chain. The challenge is to hook them together the right way.

Once she has sent the location for the rendezvous to Jacobson, she opens the link he emailed her. The blog is a poorly designed chaos of green text on a dark grey background. Reading the tiny paragraphs is impossible without stopping the car, so while she waits at a red light, she zooms in and skims a few posts.

As Jacobson said, there are hundreds of images. Most are in black and white or tinted green. The theme is obvious: the blog concerns urban exploration, an increasingly popular hobby that involves visiting or breaking into closed-off and derelict facilities. Abandoned hospitals and disused stretches of the railway network are favourite targets.

Some do it just to snoop around, others for documenting their experiences. The police deal with this type of daredevil semi-criminal on a regular basis. Some will break all kinds of laws just to gain access to a bricked-up sewer.

49

But Stockholm's huge subterranean landscape is also used by people more sinister than curious delinquents with cameras and maps, and sometimes the so-called explorers tip the police off about suspicious activities in this or that forsaken tunnel. Such information can lead to successful raids and arrests.

In a second email, Jacobson has sent a link directly to the page where he found the text. Jacobson will not be at the meeting point yet, so she pulls over and clicks the link. Within seconds, she finds the snippet of text she's looking for right at the bottom of the page, just below a shot of dark letters on what looks like a concrete wall.

Look deep and draw.

As Jacobson said, the texture of the letters suggests that they're painted directly on a concrete wall rather than printed on a sign. She blows up the image as much as the phone allows and looks closer. Each letter is curved in a peculiar, almost infantile way that makes her think of the ornate titles of children's books.

More images flash past as she scrolls up. Empty rooms brutally lit by hard camera flashes, rusted metal bed frames, a metal cabinet, and a pair of windowless steel doors. The heading at the top of the page reads *The Secret Lab.*

"What the hell is this?" Lena mutters to herself.

She shivers despite the warmth, as if a string of arctic chill has snuck into the air conditioning and found its way down her back. The sound of the traffic seems muted as she scrolls down. From far away comes the screech of a car braking hard, but the noise sounds to her like a faint, desperate scream.

After bookmarking the page, she brings up a map and enters the address Jacobson sent. A rental property on the outskirts of Sundbyberg. One tenant by the name of Jimmy Franzen. She has been to the suburb only a handful of times, so its layout is mostly unfamiliar, but there is a station that serves both underground trains as well as several buses and the commuter train. Which means a lot of traffic.

She runs the name and address through the system. No driving license, only a grainy photo that could have been from his military service, although he has no record of such service. He looks pale and gaunt, with a small nose and almond-shaped eyes that give him a vague but almost comical feline look. His hair is dyed an impossible black, but the roots are ginger. He stares into the lens with the kind of steely non-focus that suggests a wandering mind in a bad mood. The photo is five years old, so Jimmy would have been in his late teens when the picture was taken.

Her phone buzzes. A message from Gustav: *Hey. Free for lunch?*

Gustav will have to wait for her reply. If this Jimmy is at home and can contribute something useful, she has to move fast. Should he be out, or if they're forced to bring him in, they will have to move even faster. Whoever left the message on the tree is not done.

*

Sundbyberg is a tiny suburb wedged in between a river and a broad bundle of commuter train rails. Almost all the properties are blocks of flats between three and six storeys tall. Over the past ten years, an incessant construction frenzy has resulted in modern apartments sprouting up on nearly every available patch of land.

Near the station and close to the river are strings of offices and supermarkets housed in a few drab bastions left behind by the sixties. A few century-old houses huddle in the shadow of the recently erected blocks.

Jacobson waits for Lena exactly where she proposed that they should meet. To reach Jimmy's flat, they will walk up a short hill and continue across a parkway. Four police cars are parked just out of view. There's no chance that Jimmy has seen them come, even if he's hanging out of his window.

Eight officers stand next to Jacobson. All of them are armed and wear protective vests. They look between her and Jacobson as if unsure who will give orders, or maybe who they should listen to.

Lena parks behind the last police car and walks up to Jacobson.

"Why the crowd?" she asks him. "We're going to talk to him, not lay siege to his flat."

One of the officers snorts, but she can't see who it is. Jacobson looks characteristically disinterested as he glances at the parkway.

"If I hadn't said otherwise," he says, "there would be four times as many cars here right now and at least thirty more officers. I had to explain to Gren that I'd promised you to bring only a small team. This case has everyone on their toes. They're keen to get the man."

"You never promised me anything," Lena notes.

"True," Jacobson says. "But I agree with your plan."

Lena raises her eyebrows. To the best of her knowledge, she hasn't shared any details of a plan with Jacobson. At least not beyond trying to keep a low profile. Which, she realises, is what Jacobson is referring to. His comment also conveys to the other officers that it is Lena who's running this mission.

Perhaps she'll endure working with him for the time being, after all. If only she can understand why he comes across as so detached. His reserved manner is enough to drive a Samaritan person crazy. She'll find time to ask him about that, and make him snap out of it.

"Detective?" one of the officers says. "Why aren't we waiting for backup?"

"You are the backup," Lena says.

"No offence," the man continues in flat tone, "but the target is a suspected murderer, right? What happened to those poor people isn't a secret. This might be a trap. He could be waiting for us."

Lena swallows a frustrated moan and looks at the sky before she turns back to the officer. Anyone who thinks of another human being as a target is unlikely to stay calm and restrained.

"Listen up," she says. "Jimmy is very unlikely to be our man. He is entangled, maybe even guilty of something, but he's not the same person who dismembered two people two nights ago."

"Actually," Jacobson says, "*dismembered* means that a victim's limbs have–"

"So forget that idea," Lena says, cutting Jacobson off. "Because if Jimmy did kill them, he also decided to leave us with a snippet of text that's dead easy to track back to the source. That would be stupid beyond belief. And I don't think he's a total idiot."

"What if he's a genuine psychopath?" one officer wonders. "Perhaps he wants to be caught?"

"Which, as far as I'm concerned, would make him a total idiot. Enough guessing. Let's go and have a word with him."

Three minutes later, Lena stands just to the side of Jimmy's door. Jacobson and the other officers are positioned on her right, a few steps down the stairs, out of sight from the peephole. She knocks hard twice on the door and waits.

A moment later, she hears the faint scraping of slow footsteps, followed by the rustle of a curtain.

"Who is it?" asks a tired, nasal male voice.

"The police. Open up."

Seconds pass while nothing happens. Jacobson looks calm, but most of the officers behind him are tense, their gaze fastened on the door.

The metallic *clunk* of a security bolt being unlocked echoes in the stairwell, and the door inches open.

A man peers at Lena from under the hood of a jumper. He's somewhere between twenty and thirty; his skin is so riddled with acne scars it's impossible to tell his age. There's something vaguely vulture-like about his posture and pointed face, and his oversized hooded jumper and torn jeans don't help. All his clothes, including his socks, are black. His pulled-up sleeves reveal a criss-cross pattern of deep scars on his lower arms.

The man would be strikingly ugly if his features weren't offset by his unusually attractive mouth. He's also blessed with large, somewhat tilted eyes that draw attention away from his face. They are strikingly blue, but where Agnes's are the vivid hue of pure cobalt, this man's irises are so pale they border on white.

"Jimmy Franzen?" Lena asks.

"Yeah?"

"I have a few questions for you. Mind if we come inside for a moment?"

Jimmy looks between the police officers and Lena. His breathing and posture suggest that he's nervous, but his eyes are calm. For a moment, he looks as if he will protest or try to pull the door shut in Lena's face. Then he sighs and makes a defeated grimace.

"Fine," he says. "You got me."

Chapter 9

Felix watches the police cycle past his house. The officers do their best to look casual, but their stiffness betrays them. They are nervous. Sniffing around, poking in the dirt, looking for explanations.

Perhaps he should be worried; sometimes the police manage to unravel complicated crimes with surprising speed. One day they might be on his doorstep. Perhaps he will be bound, dragged back to a new cell, and forced to watch again. The police might be dressed in black rather than white, but they might shed their niceness and grow cold in an instant. Just like the nurses and the doctors.

"You're right," Timmy says behind him. "The cops are just as deceitful as the doctors. No one in a uniform can be trusted."

"The worst betrayers always wear nice guises," Felix says as he watches the cycling officers disappear behind a tall hedge.

"Precisely," Timmy says. "But they never have to pay for their crimes."

"Until now." Felix lets the curtain fall back and turns to Timmy. "Because we're turning the tables on them."

Timmy sits perched on the back of a kitchen chair like a bird, ready to dart into the sky at the slightest sign of trouble. He often does that at unexpected noises. One moment Timmy is in the middle of a long explanation, the next he vanishes like a mirage.

He always comes back, however. In a world of fake temptations, Timmy is a constant who can be trusted and confided in.

"But you need to be careful," Timmy continues. "That stunt with the note on the tree was dangerous. You mustn't leave any traces. We must not be stopped before we're done."

"My message fit the scene," Felix says and turns away. Timmy and he have argued over this many times since the night when they embarked on their first mission. Leaving the message completed the revenge. Some risks are worth taking.

Besides, Timmy is naïve if he thinks they can punish all the returned devils. Norra Ängby alone has too many of them. Sometimes, it seems as if the vile doctor lurks behind the face of every other man in the district. The best he and Timmy can hope for is to shift the scales as far as possible.

And tonight, they will push the weight of past crimes a little farther towards justice.

"Are you ready for our next revenge?" Timmy asks.

Felix nods. "Just show me where he lives."

"That's my champion." Timmy grins. "I have something special planned for this one."

Chapter 10

Lena places the coffee cup in front of Jimmy. Serving the despicable fluid to people taken in for questioning always strikes her as part warning, part punishment. *You think this is bad? Wait until you get to sample the prison variety.*

But offering a drink is protocol, and it also reassures many that things are not as bad as they thought. Or, sometimes, the coffee makes people skittish enough to slip up.

Jimmy stares at the cup as if it's a strange and possibly dead animal. He's uneasy but composed, his emotions sealed off behind a thick wall of arrogance.

"We placed bets on whether you'd go for tea or coffee," Lena says. "My money is on coffee. Black with lots of sugar. Am I close?"

"Spot on," Jimmy says. "You know, I got it all wrong." He smiles, laughs once, and looks up at Lena.

"How's that?" Lena asks.

"When I saw your card, I thought I knew why you'd come for me. Then I realised I was wrong. But it was too late by then."

"Too late for what?"

Jimmy smiles wryly. "Something tells me you wouldn't have liked it if I shut the door. Bloody hell, the way you look, you could've punched straight through it."

"Thanks for the compliment."

"This is what I mean," Jimmy says and points at Lena. "That look on your face. You were ready to take my door off the hinges with your bare hands."

"I don't have a 'look'. But yes, we would've entered your home, one way or another."

"And there was a fucking platoon of cops outside my door, too." Jimmy shakes his head. "That was intense. My neighbours must think I'm a mass murderer or something. But whoever you're looking for, I'm not him."

Lena watches Jimmy as he sips from the cup and pulls a disgusted face. That reaction at least is honest; she has shivered in the same way many times. But his throwaway remark about being mistaken for a murderer gives her pause. Most likely, it's a coincidence, but the remark can be an awkward attempt to play games with her.

"Just like you said," Lena says, "it's too late to go back. Remember those words you said when you opened your front door?"

"You got me?" Jimmy shrugs. "That seemed like the right thing to say. I didn't exactly plan to run, seeing as there were a dozen cops on my doorstep."

"Would you have tried to get away if there hadn't been?"

Jimmy laughs. "Nice try, officer."

"That's detective sergeant to you."

Lena closes her eyes, breathes out and opens them again. And she thought Jacobson would test her patience. Questioning Jimmy is making her sweat from the effort of keeping her voice level.

"What you said is enough reason for me to dig around in your file," Lena says.

"I don't really have a file, do I?"

"It's in the making," Lena says. "Which means that you have to cooperate a little."

"Not really," Jimmy says. "Unless you're going to charge me with something specific, I don't have to answer fuck all. So you can–"

Lena slams her stack of papers down in front of Jimmy so hard the table rattles. People in the nearby rooms will hear the crash, but enough is enough. Someone else might die while he's trying to act like some hard-boiled crook. She leans forward and locks eyes with Jimmy. He refuses to look away, but that doesn't matter; the boom made him flinch. His cool is less solid than he wants her to believe.

"I don't waste my time on berating belligerents for small-time thefts," Lena says through her teeth. "You are of high interest in a top-priority murder investigation that's running around the clock. Whoever goes down when it's over will spend several lifetimes strapped to a stretcher in a maximum-security prison, and believe me, someone will face the court before I take a break. Understood?"

"Jesus Christ, relax." Jimmy laughs again, but his voice is less steady.

"Besides, your website is crammed with images of locations to which I suspect you haven't got legal access. We can nip back to your little Gothic den and confiscate the laptop I saw on your bed as well as the cameras in your kitchen. The pictures we find might not have anything to do with my case, but perhaps they'll be of interest to other people."

"Hold on," Jimmy says. "You won't believe this, but I'd actually like to help. Not just to clear my name, you know. I'm serious."

For the first time, Jimmy looks troubled, but to Lena's surprise he also seems honest. She clears her throat and sits down. Protocol encourages casual conversation whenever it might get the interviewee talking. Perhaps that is a good strategy, but it should come attached with experts at talking shop. Few things rub her the wrong way as much as insubstantial chit-chat when there are more important issues on the table.

Still, bringing Jimmy in had been easy. He had agreed to let them search him, and he hadn't protested when they looked around his flat, only resorted to a sullen silence. Arresting Jimmy on the flimsy grounds of his website would cause Gren to have a fit, possibly in public, but Jimmy had offered to come with them to the station.

It means that he's either fairly smart or incredibly daft.

Jimmy's home had been surprisingly ordinary. A few unwashed cups in the sparse kitchen, some oversized pillows piled up in a corner, his bed linen crumpled and the blinds partly drawn. Cheap but not shabby mismatched second-hand furniture. No obvious traces of any other people. Certainly no signs of links to the murder scene. But such things are easily hidden, and his mere presence a short drive from Norra Ängby is enough to blip on any detective's radar.

She takes a moment to gather her thoughts while picking up her papers again. Getting the bead on Jimmy is more difficult than it should be. An almost down and out suburban kid in a rental flat. Some skill with a camera, and an obvious interest in music: his walls are covered with posters portraying bands with unpronounceable names and album covers smeared with abstract art in black and red.

Jacobson's rudimentary check on Jimmy's background had brought them a laughably poor catch. No job, no criminal record, and no taxable income. But his bearing is straight and his face is calm, even laconic. It's somewhat similar to Jacobson's permanent deadpan, but with a heavy shade of cynicism.

"If you want to be useful," Lena says, "tell me about this."

She places one of her printouts in front of Jimmy. The printer has left the photo from Jimmy's website much darker than it is on a screen, but at least it's recognisable. She can read the text from where she sits. It won't vanish from her memory in a long time, if ever.

Jimmy peers at the image and looks up at Lena. "Look deep and draw?" he asks.

"I know what it reads," Lena says. "Tell me about the picture."

"So this is why I'm here?" Jimmy sits back in his chair and frowns at Lena. "There's some connection between that image and your investigation?"

"Answer the question. Where was the picture taken, and what do you know about the motive?"

"I don't get it," Jimmy says. "What has my photo got to do with anything?"

"I don't understand half of this either, but I will get to the bottom of it. And you're helping me."

"This is about those murders in Norra Ängby, isn't it?" Jimmy sits up straight. "Damn, I should've guessed." He taps his fingers against the plastic cup and chews on his lip.

Unless Lena's instincts are off, Jimmy is more intrigued than unnerved. The brain behind his arctic eyes is hard at work, trying to figure out what this has to do with his photograph.

"You did guess," Lena says. "Which surprises me more than a little. How did you come to that conclusion?"

"The whole net's covered with rumours about the house there." Jimmy shrugs. "My feed is clogged with ideas on what went down in there."

"The media hasn't published any details," Lena says.

"Do you seriously think no one except the police knows what a coroner's van looks like?" Jimmy makes a pained face. "Everyone knows someone died in there, and in a bad way. Right in the middle of bloody Norra Ängby. It's like a volcano erupting in a local fun fair. Of course there's a lot of talk."

Sighing, Lena leans back in her chair. So much for the gag on the media. Perhaps the newspapers aren't camping outside the scene, but that's a small consolation when anyone with a social media account is pumping the Net full with inflated gossip.

"It all makes sense," Jimmy continues. "All those cops. You rushing me here and behaving like it's a national crisis. And it is so close to the text, too." He frowns into the distance in wonder. Rather than sarcastic, his tone is amazed.

Lena almost rises from her chair when she registers what Jimmy said. The ticking of the clock on the wall sounds too loud; then she realises it's her pulse that thuds in her head.

"What," Lena asks quietly, "is so close?"

Jimmy turns back to Lena. "The place where I took the photo," he says. "It's a short walk away from where those people were killed."

Lena drops her pen onto the stack of papers, takes out her phone, and calls Jacobson.

"We're going back to Norra Ängby," she says. "Right now. The man we picked up in Abrahamsberg is going to tell us where he took the photo. Apparently it's near the house. Tell Gren we'll need two cars – no, we need an emergency response team. Have one meet us at Runstensplan in Bromma."

The sight of a response team in Norra Ängby will draw an unpleasant amount of attention, but there's a chance that the murderer will be hiding in the location where Jimmy took the picture. If the killer is there and Lena doesn't bring reinforcements with her, Gren will never let her hear the end of it.

"I'll try to find Gren right away," Jacobson says.

"Meet me in the garage in five minutes." Lena hangs up.

"If I do this," Jimmy says, "I need some kind of reassurance. You have to guarantee I won't be prosecuted or fined."

"That depends on what you've done." Lena studies Jimmy while she shuffles her notes back into order. He might be making demands, but he's also uneasy.

"Some breaking and entering," Jimmy says. "Technically, just entering. I never destroy anything."

Lena switches the microphone off. Some parts of her work do not have to go on record.

"It depends on how helpful you are," Lena says.

"Am I under arrest?" Jimmy frowns.

"We can't hold you here for being a twat," Lena says. "Or because of a bunch of photos on a website, unless you've been dumb enough to state outright on your blog that you've actually trespassed." She can tell from his expression that he has done precisely that. Some people never cease to amaze her.

"You'll stay here until I've visited the site where you took that photo," she continues, "but whether or not we will knock on your door again is up to you. Help me out, and you can walk away later today. Be obnoxious, and you'll find your home turned upside down once a month."

"Are you serious?" Jimmy's eyes widen, but he looks just as amused as annoyed.

Lena shrugs. "Someone butchered two probably innocent human beings, and I am going to find out who did it."

"Fucking hell." Jimmy laughs harshly. "I guess I'm coming, then. Not that I have much of a choice."

"I just told you that you do. Perhaps you haven't broken any laws. I'll see when we get there. What's the address?"

"I can't tell you," Jimmy says.

Lena looks down at Jimmy. "It's not a matter of whether you want to tell me or not. You're giving me directions, right now."

"Impossible."

"How can this be difficult?" Lena demands.

"That place doesn't exist."

Chapter 11

"Today's news, sir."

Carl looks up at his assistant as he takes the tablet from the man's outstretched hand. The hint of concern in his assistant's voice suggests the day is about to lose some of its appeal. A pity, seeing as it had been so pleasant up until now. Clear skies over the city, hot sunlight through the tall open window, a twenty-year-old cognac in his hand. After his breakfast at Grand Hotel, he had retired for a lunchtime cocktail. The afternoon would have seen dinner on a yacht in the archipelago followed by drinks in a discreet club.

And now this. No matter how crisp the clouds, there is always an oily lining.

He reclines in the lounge chair on the veranda of the three-storey villa. In front of him is a large, immaculately trimmed lawn, and farther away glitters one of Stockholm's inner-city waterways. Behind and above him are twelve rooms, each lavish and decorated precisely to his taste. The villa is one of his four properties. All of them are maintained around the year, but this particular residence is his favourite.

Much, he admits to himself, because of the proximity of his peers. Most of the adjacent properties are owned by the upper crust of the richest. They are the country's *crema*, risen up through providence or hard work to float on the bitter masses. Kings and queens of a nation-sized hill.

And he has earned his spot at the top.

In truth, he deserves even more. Many of his neighbours consider themselves savvy businessmen when they rely on luck, or simply think they are superior by birth. He has secured his fortune by late nights and moves so bold regular people cannot even imagine them. And while he scaled Mammon's mountain, he saved thousands of people.

In contrast, his performance-car-collecting acquaintances have sacrificed others on the altar of careerism without discrimination, all in the name of gaining bigger stock portfolios. That is not, and has never been, Carl's way. This and his other houses are built on hard work.

Unfortunately, there are no ways to proof his life from the occasional crumb of bad news.

"What's wrong?" Carl demands. "Another financial crisis on the horizon?" If so, that would be a relief. Protecting his assets from the virtual vultures of global economic unrest is often just a matter of a few phone calls.

"It's nothing." The assistant clears his throat and puts on a blank face.

"I've dismissed staff for lesser transgressions than pretence. Speak up."

The assistant hesitates for a moment. "It's just the headlines, sir. A double murder in a suburb. They are rather graphic."

"The images?" Carl wonders. Explicit portrayals of victims are rare in Swedish media.

"Only the details, sir," the assistant says. "I filled in the blanks myself."

"Ah." Carl smiles. "Imagination is a double-edged sword. Thank you for warning me."

"Apparently the investigation is being handled by the detective who shot a businessman at the airport."

"I see." Carl pauses. "Wasn't it another officer who killed him?"

"You're right, sir." The assistant looks embarrassed.

"Don't worry. I'm not paying you to memorize such details. But I would appreciate if you don't guess when you aren't absolutely sure. It might lead one to jump to false conclusions. Don't you agree?"

"Absolutely, sir." The assistant's cheeks redden, but he keeps his face straight.

"Excellent."

Carl puts the tablet down to delay the inevitable moment. His thoughts have been unusually glum over the past day. He makes a firm point of barring negative, unconstructive or unrealistic considerations from his mind. His time is better spent on decisive actions and inspired whims. Yet a grey cloud hangs low over his mood this afternoon, despite the good morning and the promising schedule for the evening.

His glumness is both inexplicable and unbecoming. He considers not reading the news at all; the last thing he needs is information that might darken his mood even more. But keeping up to speed with current affairs is a vital habit. Insight makes for improvements. This truth has not changed in his lifetime, and he has lived for quite some time.

After a minute, Carl sighs and skims the tablet.

As the assistant said, two people have been killed. A man and a woman. No clues. Bestial murders, judging by what was mentioned and the journalist's breathless language. The houses in the background look familiar. He searches for a mention of the location.

Norra Ängby.

Carl looks closer at the picture. An archetypal house, not unique for the area, even if it is very common there. He doesn't recognize it. The murder is not the first one to take place in Norra Ängby, but in difference to most Swedish mainstream media outlets, this particular feed features images of the victims.

Below the picture of the house are two portraits. Both are pixellated and of poor quality, but enough to give an idea of what the man and woman looked like. The woman's face is unfamiliar.

His eyes linger on the photo of the man.

"Is that all?" the assistant wonders.

"Wait."

"Sir?"

"Keep an eye on how this story develops," Carl says. "I have old friends who live near where the murders took place." He hands the tablet back to his assistant with a rueful grimace. The lie is clumsy, but adequate.

"Shall I call them to make sure they are fine?" the assistant asks.

"They value their privacy. I wouldn't disturb them unless I was considerably more troubled. But thank you for asking."

The assistant nods and leaves. When the man has left the room, Carl turns back to the window. A string of apple trees line a path leading down to a penthouse next to the river. Not a single leaf or petal bothers the green lawn. His garden is an image of perfection, but like all things in life, its flawless state is upheld by constant maintenance. Every status quo requires effort. Advance comes only at even higher costs.

A line from the news report echoes in his mind.

No motive for the murders is known.

After a long moment, he leaves the window and walks up to his study on the top floor. A concealed drawer in his large desk contains a small red notebook. Each page holds a single phone number, their numbers rearranged in an order only he knows. Some information is too volatile to store in any electronic form.

He has no need for the numbers yet, but knowing they are safe and within reach soothes him. One day he may have to dial one of them. His life is like his garden: faultlessness requires maintenance.

And some types of maintenance come at high prices.

Chapter 12

"I have no idea what you're talking about," Lena says to Jimmy, "but I guarantee that whatever excuse you've cooked up, I'm going to ignore it. Give me the directions to the place so I can be on my way."

"You don't understand," Jimmy says.

"The address."

"There isn't one. If you'd just let me–"

"I can't even begin to tell you how much I haven't got time for this bullshit," Lena says, her voice rising. "What you're doing right now is called obstruction of justice, and it's punishable by prison."

"I'm not fucking around." Jimmy's voice climbs to match Lena's. "I can't tell you where it is because there's no fucking letter box with a street number. There isn't even a door."

"Oh, please. A moment ago, you said that you took the picture near Norra Ängby. It's an imaginary room now?"

"The room's real enough, and it's maybe a twenty-minute walk from the house. Going there isn't difficult."

"Then what is?"

"Getting inside. It's a labyrinth. I couldn't even write down all the turns I took."

"Damn it." Lena thinks for a moment. "If you were back at the location, would you remember how you got in?"

"I think so."

Lena fights the urge to throw her papers at Jimmy. A cocky semi-criminal in her car is the second-last thing she needs. It's an inconvenience surpassed only by the prospect of losing more time. But he has to come along. Gren will have a breakdown before the day is over; bringing Jimmy will violate a fistful of other regulations. As messy mornings go, this one is becoming a prize-winner.

"Talk while we walk," Lena says and opens the door. "You're riding with me."

Four minutes later, Lena shoots down the westbound arterial road. Jacobson sits next to her and taps on his phone. In the back seat are Jimmy and Gunilla Ahlgren, a patrol police officer in her early forties with a round face that reminds Lena of TV adverts for gardening equipment. Gunilla happened to be passing through the garage when Lena commandeered her on the spot. Someone has to keep an eye on Jimmy, and Jacobson, while reasonably bright, is about as intimidating as a timid poodle. Jimmy is not overjoyed at being part of the company and might decide to make a run for it at some point.

Behind Lena, the sun is struggling to gain a few more degrees on the heavens before starting to drift down. The sky is a gradient starting in crisp blue and ending in pale orange. Traffic is light; most of Stockholm is at work or are elsewhere enjoying the summer. If life were not such a perfect game of unwanted surprises, she too could be somewhere else. Out cycling, alone in the gym, or still in Gustav's bed.

Although even if someone gave her the opportunity to abandon the chase, she would not let it go. Just like going to the gym, policing is a source of adrenaline-inundated calm. Moving down the byzantine lanes of an investigation keeps her distracted in a good way. When not working actively on a case, the challenge sits at the back of her mind, urging her on, hinting at revelations and conclusions.

Downtime and inactivity open the worst kind of silence: the absolute quiet in which the wrong voices make themselves heard. Those whispers that point her to all the wrong decisions. For now, they are gone, shut up by determination and the presence of Gustav. He knows about her nature and can deal with it. With time, he might even accept it. She will not unravel before that happens.

Jacobson leans closer to Lena. "Why on Earth are you bringing that man?" he whispers.

Lena wishes that Jimmy couldn't hear the conversation; but the car is far too small for discreet chats.

"You mean Jimmy?" she asks. "Believe me, I don't have a habit of taking civilians sightseeing. This time, I have no choice."

"But he's technically not under arrest," Jacobson insists. "We have nothing on him. Gren will be furious if he finds out."

"And I will be just as pissed off if we lose more time running back and forth. Jimmy refuses – sorry, *can't* give me an exact location, so here we are."

"He must be able to give us at least a rough idea," Jacobson says.

"Good point," Lena says. "Jimmy, tell us where we're going."

The rushed departure from the police headquarters were filled with phone calls and interruptions that made it impossible to get a coherent story out of him.

"Beckomberga Hospital." Jimmy looks out the window as he speaks.

A cold ball forms in Lena's stomach. The name is well known to many: Beckomberga Hospital is a psychiatric hospital on the outskirts of Norra Ängby. Its name is still used throughout Sweden as a catchphrase for uncanny places.

The location was chosen for both its beauty and the distance from the city: over a thousand patients were relocated there, and some of them were considered extremely dangerous. If John Andersson had collapsed half a century earlier, he would have ended up in one of the hospital's cells.

Lena searches for the hospital on her phone and skims the results. Once upon a time the largest hospital of its kind in Europe, Beckomberga Hospital closed down its original operations decades ago, but the ongoing conversion of the oppressive facilities into expensive flats has not dispelled its unsettling connotations. She remembers glimpsing the entrance to the hospital the previous day, just after she stepped out of the taxi.

The link between the mutilated bodies and a former home for mentally ill people is open to all kinds of disturbing possibilities. It may be a coincidence, but flukes are an endangered species. Just like simple cases with obvious answers. To make matters worse, if the media spots the presence of the police at the hospital, rumours would crash servers left and right before lunchtime. All it takes is one idiot with a mobile phone.

And if the killer is hiding in the area, Lena is in for an enormous trial. Most hospitals come with a jumble of stowaways, disused rooms, storages and other spaces, all of them ideal for staying out of sight. More than one case has taken her into the bowels of abandoned warehouses and disused factories. Every large building seems to evolve the same way: over the years, it grows tunnels and alcoves out of control, like concrete vegetation spawning offshoots in every direction. The older the house, the worse it is. And Beckomberga Hospital is as old as they come.

"I'll call the hospital so they can evacuate." Jacobson reaches for his phone.

"Wait," Lena says.

Clearing the facility of people makes sense in case the killer is hiding there, but an evacuation is bound to generate ripples. Word will spread with blinding speed. Curious kids and adults who should know better will flock to the area. It may end with a repeat performance of the debacle when she tried to corner John Andersson in the city.

"Let's hold off with alarming the neighbourhood," Lena says. "We'll save that until it's really necessary."

"That's not protocol." Jacobson looks troubled.

"Neither is a sadistic murder in a pretty suburb. We will go in discreetly, find out more about this supposed room, and document it."

"The emergency response team is on their way," Jacobson points out. "Exactly how can we hope to be inconspicuous in the company of officers with machine guns and bulletproof vests?"

"We'll try to blend in?" Lena sighs. "Look, I don't have all the answers. But we have to keep a low profile. It's practically next door to the scene. Call the hospital and let them know we're coming. Reassure them we won't break down any doors or trouble their patients, if they still have any. We won't disturb the tenants either."

"What can we expect?" Gunilla asks.

"Jimmy here will tell us," Lena says. "And he needs to hurry up, because we're almost at the hospital."

Jimmy sighs and clears his throat.

"It's down in the hospital's subterranean complex," he says. "Inside some kind of old, abandoned ward. I don't think they've used it for years. Just a few large rooms, a few toilets and showers. There's something that might be the door, but it's been welded in place."

"What makes you think it's a ward?" Jacobson asks.

"Apart from that it's at a hospital?" Jimmy shrugs. "It reminded me of a sickbay. Lots of metal cabinets and a big rusted lamp. There were a bunch of beds there, too."

"How many is a bunch?" Jacobson asks. "Try to be more specific."

"Maybe a dozen," Jimmy says. "I didn't hang around to take notes. The place creeped me out."

"I saw your blog." Lena glances over her shoulder at Jimmy. "You do your photo shoots in all kinds of dark pits. That's not a hobby for someone easily spooked."

"These rooms were special. And before you ask me how, I don't know. They felt off. Wrong, somehow, as if they weren't meant to be there. Not to mention that there wasn't a door."

"Why would you build a ward underground?" Jacobson muses.

"They construct all kinds of strange shit under your feet," Jimmy says. "You know how Stockholm is supposed to be one of the most hollowed-out cities in the world?"

Lena nods while she turns off the arterial road and drives up a hill towards Runstensplan. Her hometown sits on top of countless secret train tunnels, walled-off bomb shelters, and miles of maintenance passages. Because of the advantageous type of bedrock on which the city rests, generations of engineers have dug and tunnelled ferociously for decades, scooping out so much dirt and rock that Sweden's capital balances on a honeycomb of hollows.

The basic anatomy of Stockholm is covered in the regular police training, since most officers have to descend into one depth or another during their careers. There are no reliable maps that cover all the passages. Many are forgotten, and others have been erased deliberately for the sake of security or for other reasons.

"I've seen quite a few of the tunnels you're talking about," Lena says. "Stockholm's a big rat nest."

"You haven't seen anything." Jimmy smiles at Lena in the rear-view mirror. "Triple what you've got on record and you might be close. The military alone have drilled out hundreds and hundreds of caverns, one weirder than the other. There's a whole world down there."

"So you crawl through soot and dirt to take pictures of the city's underbelly," Lena says. "Some would say you belong in a place like the one Beckomberga Hospital used to be."

"Some people have no clue." Still smiling, Jimmy turns to the window. "They trot around on the surface, clueless and blind, thinking all that matters is the colour of their kitchen tiles. No idea what's hiding right under their feet."

"Very poetic," Lena says. "Why should they care?" She curses as the traffic lights change to red, forcing her to brake hard. She let Jimmy distract her.

Jimmy is silent for a moment. "It's analogous," he says.

"I'm impressed you know what that word means." Lena raises her eyebrows. "As burglars go, you have a good vocabulary."

"Stop fucking calling me that," Jimmy says. "I'm an artist."

"So sorry," Lena says. "I didn't slot you in with Da Vinci and company. It must be your haircut. If you're done defending your hobby, perhaps you can get to the point?"

The car is becoming stuffy and humid. Being around Jimmy sets her on edge faster than should be possible; the man's questions float like needles around her delicate patience. It's as if he anticipates the memories that haunt her.

"When we hit the tunnels for a photo shoot," Jimmy says, "we're not just walking around for the sake of it. Exploring is about discovering. Finding new roads, coming across secrets, pushing open rusted doors four levels below the streets to see what's behind them."

"Without any permits or regards to safety, I suppose?" Jacobson asks.

Jimmy waves Jacobson's comment away with a faintly disgusted grimace.

"And at the same time," Jimmy continues, "we're looking inward. When you're climbing down a shaft into pure blackness, you question yourself. It's easy to start questioning your sanity."

"I can imagine," Jacobson says tiredly.

"Shut up," Lena says to Jacobson before she can catch herself. "Sorry, I – just let him finish."

"So I keep going out," Jimmy says, "to find the deepest, darkest and dankest stairs I can locate. And then I go down them to get to know myself better. When it's pitch black, it's easier to face what you hide when your eyes are open."

"And that's important?" Lena asks.

"Yes," Jimmy says and meets Lena's gaze in the mirror. "That's pretty important."

Lena realises she's gripping the steering wheel so hard her fingers are leaving white marks in the black plastic. Exhaling slowly, she releases her hold and sits up straight. Sweat prickles her back. Thankfully, they're only minutes away from their destination; the atmosphere in the car is becoming unbearable.

"I don't mean to interrupt," Jacobson says, "but this is a little off topic. How do we get in?"

"That's the problem," Jimmy says. "I'm not sure I can remember. The one and only time I've been there was after getting lost."

"Under the hospital?" Lena asks.

"First there," Jimmy says and nods. "Then in the ducts. We'll have to go through them and see if I can backtrack my steps."

Lena's mounting unease rises in her stomach like a slow wave. Having to walk around a former mental hospital is bad enough. She can do without having to crawl on her hands and knees in a cramped tunnel, especially if there's a risk of getting lost.

"We have no time for guesswork," Lena says. "We'll talk to the management and have them pull up a blueprint. Or better yet, find us a door."

"Won't work," Jimmy says. "I told you the room doesn't exist."

"Can you be any less clear?" Lena asks.

"I went looking for a map first thing after I got out."

"What, online?" Jacobson asks.

"It's easy if you know where to look and have the login details. I went over the charts again and again, hoping to at least pin down where I'd been, but there's nothing there."

"So he's involved in computer crime too," Jacobson says to Lena. "And we're bringing him to a potentially dangerous area without the superintendent's approval. I really don't agree with this."

Lena inhales slowly and stares at the road. If Jacobson stopped interrupting Jimmy, they might wring something useful out of the scrawny misfit today rather than next week.

"It might be a recent construction," Lena suggests. "An extension, maybe."

"The place looked really dated," Jimmy says. "It was covered with dust."

"Didn't you say it was practically cleaned out?" Lena asks.

"You'll see what I mean. If we actually find it. But if your constable buddy is going to dump a load of offences on me, I'm going to have a very hard time remembering the way."

"Are you seriously–" Jacobson begins, turning around in his seat to face Jimmy.

"No one's charging anyone with anything," Lena says, raising her voice a notch. "We're not collecting evidence for a break and enter case. Jimmy, is it likely that someone else uses that room as a hiding place?"

"Not unless he or she knows where it is," Jimmy says. "I guess you're thinking about the man you're looking for?"

"If there's a link between the murderer and the room you visited," Lena says, "there's a good chance the killer is aware of this mysterious room." She pauses. "I never said we're chasing a man," she adds.

Lena looks at Jimmy in the rear-view mirror. When he realises what he said, he seems taken aback. That's a good sign.

"I just thought–" Jimmy says quickly.

"Forget it," Lena says. "It's a natural assumption. In this case, you're right. Although you'll have to pretend you never heard that."

"Jesus Christ," Jacobson mutters.

"We're here." Lena slows down as she comes up to Runstensplan. "We'll park somewhere close and walk down to the hospital. I don't want to raise more questions or eyebrows than necessary."

The emergency response team has arrived before her. Their transport, a lumbering rhino of a van sporting ladders and bulletproof windows, is parked near a small roundabout. Partially hidden by a tall hedge, the response team are inspecting their equipment. Apparently the leader of the team is aware of Lena and Gren's desire for discretion. Or perhaps he or she just is intelligent.

Still, it's a matter of minutes before some kid spots them and starts uploading pictures to the Internet. Eight police officers in tactical protective vests and armed with sub-machine guns will not go unnoticed.

Lena walks around the hedge and spots the person in charge, a tall lean man with a red scar down the side of his neck. They've met before: his surname is Norling. He led the team that stormed the inner-city office where John Andersson had opened fire on the police.

"Franke," he says and nods in recognition. "I want a thorough brief before we proceed. This is related to that case, I take it?"

"Correct," Lena says. "There's a facility here that might be connected to the crime."

Lena repeats his words in her mind: *that case*. Everyone on the whole force must know about this investigation by now. Not to mention most of the people in the city.

"You're saying the suspect might be hiding in the hospital," Norling summarises. "Is he an ex-patient?"

"We've no idea," Lena says. "But we think the ward we're interested in closed shop decades ago."

"So you reckon it's being used as a hiding place?" Norling wonders.

"Possibly. It's a strange case."

Norling looks in the general direction of the hospital.

"Gren sounded nervous when he called," he says. "That's normal for him, but I don't like it when the brass gets jittery. They should know better."

"I can't disagree with that," Lena says.

"What are the odds that the target is present?"

"Pretty high."

Norling's taut, clipped language fuels Lena's misgivings. But she respects the team: they are efficiency personified, and they think on their feet in situations that would freeze her in indecision. In this instance, they may also end up being a shield between her and a killer. Fortunately, an individual armed with a knife is not a match for the team's combined experience and firepower.

At least that's how it should be. She thought the exact same thing about John.

Her own gun sits snug in her shoulder holster. She carries it as seldom as possible, preferring to keep it in a locker in the station and bring it out only for target practise or mandatory maintenance. The less she has to hold it, the better.

True to form, Gren noticed her apparent discomfort and in private asked her if she had any issues with her gun. The honest answer would have taken hours. She doesn't find it uncomfortable, and there's nothing about its capacity for damage that troubles her. The primary reason she keeps it tucked away whenever possible is the exact opposite: she wants to have it close at all times.

And that won't work. Her traumatic showdown with John showed her precisely how thin the membrane between right and wrong is. It also taught her what can happen if she has her finger on the trigger when push comes to wrestling in the snow. Only Agnes's intervention saved Lena from sliding down into the pit whose edge she kept skirting.

The team leader is about to turn when he pauses and looks behind Lena.

"Who's he?" the leader asks Lena. "That skinny man with the makeup."

Lena looks over her shoulder. Jimmy is waiting by Lena's car along with Gunilla and Jacobson. Until now, she hasn't noticed the mascara around Jimmy's eyes, but heat and sweat are smudging it into large circles. It gives him a panda-like look that probably would infuriate him if he caught sight of himself in a mirror. But the dark circles also make his eyes seem even paler, and there's nothing humorous at all about his gaze as he studies Lena. He's not hostile, but serious.

"He's a consultant," Lena says. "He's got vital information about the case, especially about this location. I'll keep him out of your way."

"Fine." The team leader nods, looks back at Lena for a moment, and then walks away to rejoin his team.

The meaning of the glance is unmistakable; he wants Lena to keep clear as well. Her dash into the city office where John hid is well known among the officers, and her mad sprint across the airport where they finally seized John is just as infamous.

"We're seeing the management first," Lena says to Jacobson and Gunilla. "Hopefully they'll point us the right way. Let's go."

The short walk takes them down a gentle slope flanked by a handful of the box-like houses. It's warmer than when she was here a few hours ago, but the air is still crisp and fresh. Birdsong spins and loops over the sound of traffic from a few blocks away. From somewhere among the trees comes the uneven hum of a lawnmower. A woman pushing a huge pram frowns and crosses the street at the sight of the police officers. Perhaps there won't be any cameras pointing at Lena this time. One can always hope.

They pass the hospital's old gatehouse, a mundane single-storey building in reddish brick.

"There's no fence," Gunilla notes.

"It was probably removed when they started to build residential properties on the grounds," Jacobson guesses. "It'd be difficult to sell flats here if there were too many reminders of the hospital's history."

"Show the way," Lena says to Jimmy.

"To the main building?" Jimmy asks. "Or to where I got in?"

"The offices," Lena says. "We're going to talk to the management before we get any other ideas. They already know we're on our way, so they'll be ready to help us."

In hindsight, she should have known better than to get her hopes up.

Chapter 13

"I'm not sure how I can be any clearer," the manager says. "The blueprints are right here in front of you, and there is simply nothing there."

Sitting slumped in his office chair, the manager glares at Jacobson as if the detective has insulted him. The middle-aged man is plump and sweating. It's clear he wants Lena and everyone else in his office out as soon as possible.

"Could the maps be outdated?" Jacobson asks.

"Those prints date back to the forties," the manager argues. "Every year's additions and demolitions are covered in the appendixes. There's a list of refurbishments as well."

"Someone could've removed the documents," Jacobson suggests.

"I've talked to the janitors," the manager says slowly, "the landscaping company, the security firm and the electrical contractors. No one has seen or heard about a ward in this particular location. Even the plumbers agree."

Lena paces back and forth on the carpet while Jacobson tries to reason with the manager. The response team waits in a nearby hallway. Jimmy languishes on one of the two large couches and stares at the ceiling in apparent boredom. So far, he has kept his mouth shut, which is surprising; his posture and constant sighing suggest that he's ready to explode.

She has gleaned a little more about the history of the hospital by skimming the captions of the framed photos on the wall. After the medical care was discontinued, the head of operations was replaced by a business-minded supervisor charged with maintaining every building and the extensive gardens. The job comes with a nice, spacious office and, judging by the current occupant of the role, a great deal of prestige.

The manager had been visibly disturbed by the presence of the police on his premises. When Lena explained that they needed access to a room, he demanded to see a search warrant. Given the nature of her visit, she could produce a warrant in no time, but there were even quicker ways. Instead, she suggested that they could do a preliminary superficial sweep. She went on to explain that such a sweep would include eight heavily armed and occasionally brusque policemen rushing up and down stairs and requesting directions from local residents.

As predicted, the manager saw the impact this might have on his weekend, as well as future real estate affairs for the hospital. He whipped his assistants into action, and some fifteen minutes later, his impressive mahogany desk was covered with large printouts of hundreds of rooms.

Thankful for some actual progress, Lena ordered Jimmy to point her to the place. Her gratitude turned sour ten minutes later when Jimmy declared defeat: the room was not marked on any of the maps.

The manager's mood had been black from the outset, but when he realised that Jimmy had breached the hospital's perimeter a few years earlier, his attitude slipped a notch further south. But Jimmy has no obvious reason to lie. The manager, however, may have plenty.

Lena walks up to the desk and looks at the map.

"Show me again," she says to Jimmy.

Jimmy rises, slouches over to the desk, and rams a finger down on a map.

"Like I said," he says, "the room's somewhere here, behind one of these walls."

"And its door is sealed?"

"Welded shut, even. Like a damn bunker."

"So you're definite that there's an opening down here," Lena says. "But the manager here disagrees."

"Yes," the manager says. "Because there simply isn't–"

"So one of you is mistaken," Lena says, "and this is a key piece of information in my investigation. Which means you two will stare at this map until one of you has an epiphany and tells me what's what."

"I'll try again," Jimmy says and draws a circle with his finger on the map.

The building he indicates is near the perimeter of the hospital. Lena vaguely remembers the location from when she walked across the grounds. Not too far away is a low, garage-like construction with a massive door. According to the map in front of her, the door hides a driveway that spirals down into the hospital's subterranean levels.

"I came in there," Jimmy says. "Made my way down, turned left here and here, and walked all the way down *here*. That's when the security came running."

He points at the far end of a long, narrow corridor. Set in the wall is a blue rectangle that the manager said represents the opening of a duct. This is where Jimmy claims he dove into the ventilation system. If he is speaking the truth, that is.

"And as I said before," the manager interrupts, "those rooms are storages. Our inventory suggests that they contained emergency supplies and other rarely needed goods, but nothing expensive or classified. They were emptied when the hospital ceased its operations."

"He's right about that," Jimmy says. "I checked most of them. All empty, save for a few crates and trolleys."

"I really hope you plan to prosecute this man?" The manager nods at Jimmy. "I must remind you that he broke into a private property. Just because he's cooperating now doesn't mean he isn't a criminal."

"Thank you for your succinct lecture on how the law works." Still looking at the map, Lena runs a finger along the outlined corridor. "If there isn't anything special in that part of the complex," she asks, "how come the guards showed up there?"

"We can tell from the report," the manager says. "The security staff who caught you wrote down a detailed description of the events that evening."

"Caught, my arse," Jimmy says and laughs. "They didn't catch anything that night."

"They prevented you from stealing our property."

"Why would I want to take anything from this stinking place?" Jimmy protests.

"Don't push it." Lena raises a warning finger at Jimmy. "Tell me what the guards said," she says to the manager.

"A member of the staff saw a suspected intruder and raised the alarm," the manager says. "The security officers weren't in that particular section, but went there to search for signs of the trespasser. That's why they ran down that corridor."

"Sounds about right," Jimmy agrees. "I heard them coming and needed a hiding place, so I ripped the grille away and crawled into the ventilation duct."

"Without using any tools?" Jacobson asks.

"The grille wasn't fixed to the wall," Jimmy says.

"That's strangely convenient," Jacobson notes.

Jimmy shrugs. "I deserved a little luck. Although I didn't have time to put it back in place behind me, so I dropped it on the floor."

"The guards must've noticed."

"Oh, yes. They waited outside the duct for what felt like hours. All I could do was hunt for another exit."

"Sounds like a claustrophobic nightmare," Jacobson says.

"No," Jimmy says. "The scares came later."

"In that room," Lena says, guessing what Jimmy means.

Jimmy nods. "I came across it by chance. But I didn't crawl for long, and I'm pretty sure the sealed door I saw faces one of the storage rooms."

"How many times must I explain that this door doesn't exist?" the manager bristles. "Every single shed and cupboard that has been built over the past century is on record."

"How can you be sure?" Lena asks.

"Because extensions and reconstructions cost money. In fact, some ideas for new facilities have been documented but never actually realised. Deals fall through, permits are denied, and budgets get changed."

"All records have gaps," Lena says.

"Not these ones." The manager spreads his hands. "This used to be a high-security hospital. There hasn't been room for errors or mistakes."

Lena chews on her lip and looks out through the window. This meeting is going in circles. There's only one way forward, and Jimmy has to light the path. Gren will have a meltdown when he finds out, but he'll have to file it away among the many other fits he has had over Lena's decisions.

"Take us there," Lena says to Jimmy. "All the way to the grille. Use the same route you did the last time."

"I'm not going into those fucking tunnels again," Jimmy says and takes a step back.

"You won't have to," Lena says. "The response team will take it from there. You'll hang back with us." She nods at Jacobson and Gunilla.

"Are you serious?" The manager looks incredulous. "I've told you in every possible way that this room doesn't exist. Why don't you believe me?"

"Because you keep repeating yourself," Lena says. "In my experience, that means it's worth digging deeper."

Lena's real motive is Jimmy's persistence; he is adamant and precise, when he instead could try to wriggle out of the whole situation. But the manager is so obnoxious that she doesn't mention this.

"That's downright insulting," the manager says. "I am going to have a word with your supervisor."

"You're welcome to, once you've given us a tour of the corridor." Lena switches her radio on. "Norling, round up your team and meet me outside. We're going in."

Chapter 14

The entrance is twice her height and wide enough for two cars to pass through side by side. It's set in a squat building of brown brick, surrounded by birches and thick shrubs.

Jacobson, Jimmy, Gunilla and the manager wait by her side. The emergency response team are preparing to move in as soon as the door opens. Farther away are groups of local residents and other people, most of which are looking in her direction. The rumour about the police's presence is spreading.

A slow wind rustles through the foliage while Lena waits for the evacuation to be complete. Apart from the distant whirr of traffic, all is quiet. She squares her shoulders and looks at the gates to the hospital's netherworld. Jimmy has gone through them long ago, in order to discover what rests below the gigantic lawns. Perhaps a deranged murderer followed in his footsteps. The room could be a shrine to whatever grotesque fantasy spurred the killer to his heinous acts or a stowaway for other bodies.

She reaches under her jacket to make sure her gun is there. The metal and plastic is cool and slick under her thumb.

The manager lowers his mobile phone and looks up at Lena. "The first and second floor have been cleared," he says. "There were only a few electricians doing repairs. The area should be completely vacated."

"That was quick," Lena says. "Did you call them over radio?"

"Good grief, no." The manager rolls his eyes. "Reception down there is patchy. We used the intercom. It's old, but it still works."

"You gave the order over a speaker system?" Lena asks.

"Of course," the manager says. "There's no quicker way."

"Well, fuck." The response team leader gives the manager a withering look.

"What's wrong?" the manager asks.

"If there was someone hiding in there," Lena says, "he knows we're coming. Jimmy, stay behind me. Keep quiet unless I take a wrong turn. Jacobson, Gunilla, close to my side."

"Move in," the team leader shouts.

One of his team members pulls the door open, and the response team rushes in.

Lena darts inside on their heels. Jacobson and Gunilla follow, herding Jimmy between them. For the first time, Jimmy looks palpably nervous; his eyes are wide and dark inside his smudged makeup. The manager, who does his best to look confident, walks a few steps behind Jimmy.

The driveway curves sharply right and twists down like a giant waterslide. Strip lights in the ceiling colour the concrete in a weak, buttery hue. It more resembles an underground parking garage than an entrance to a basement. All other hospitals she has visited before are pragmatic constructions with the odd decorative detail, but here the focus on a tranquil environment appears to have pushed all unsightly features out of sight. What cannot be seen will not disturb.

The response team zips down the subterranean road in a tight, caterpillar-like formation.

"Come on," Lena says to those walking near her. "We're going to lose sight of them."

The curved road ends in a wide intersection. Three near-identical corridors stretch away into the distance. Walls of smooth brick coated with yellow paint. More strip lights cast pools of warm light at regular intervals. Filling the air is a dense blend of detergents and disinfectants: lasting reminders of a century of washing out the dirt of patients and staff.

"Keep to the walls," Lena mumbles. "And stay back. Any sign of trouble, everyone turns around and gets out. Especially you," she adds and looks at Jimmy.

"At some point," Jacobson says quietly, "I would like you to explain what he's doing here in the first place."

"I still intend to talk to your superiors," the manager says. "This cannot be normal procedure."

Lena ignores the questions and concentrates on following the response team. They rush left and reach another intersection, where Norling raises his hand and gestures. The team breaks up and takes up positions to cover their advance.

Lena holds up her hand to tell those behind her to wait. All is quiet except for the scuttle of the team's heavy boots, echoing around them like a barely audible drumroll.

"Are we heading the right way?" Lena asks Jimmy.

Jimmy nods. "The ventilation duct is down the next tunnel on your left," he whispers. "I can't believe I'm back in this fucking place."

"I can't see what brought you here the first time," Lena hisses.

From around the corner comes a series of metallic bangs, each followed by a muffled shout: "Clear". The team is checking the rooms that lead up to the duct. According to the map, there are eight doors, so she waits for the eighth shouted confirmation and looks around the corner.

The response team is gathered at the far end of the corridor. They stand on each side of a grille, behind which is the gaping darkness of a large duct. One member of the response team shines a flashlight into the opening. Two others keep their weapons trained on the pool of light, the muzzles of their weapons held between the bars of the grille to avoid ricochets.

Lena walks closer. The square duct is half her height. More than large enough for someone to disappear into.

She orders Jimmy and the manager into one of the nearby empty rooms, which turns out to be an empty three-by-three metre space with a broken light bulb in the ceiling. A temporary safety room in case there's a dangerous guest in the tunnels. She leaves the door open to let some light in and instructs Gunilla and Jacobson to keep an eye on Jimmy.

The duct runs horizontally for a few steps before leading away left and right. So far, Jimmy is true to his word. Her next step is to find out if it is the rabbit hole Jimmy suggests, and what kind of unpleasant wonderland hides at its bottom.

"The grille is held in place by cable ties." A member of the response team points with a gloved hand at the strip of plastic.

"Where to next?" Norling asks. "We must keep moving."

"Jimmy?" Lena calls. "It's your time to shine. Stay where you are, just tell us how to get to the room."

"I haven't got a bloody clue," Jimmy calls back.

"So we're down to guessing from here on?" The team leader's face tightens with frustration. "That's risky."

"Wait." Lena runs back to the room where Jimmy is, and Norling follows her.

"Use your head," Lena says to Jimmy. "You must recall the last stretch. Didn't you say the room was close?"

"It's less than a minute away," Jimmy says and holds up his hands. "And I think the sealed-off door inside is behind one of these walls. But I took at least ten turns in the duct. There's no way I'll get them right by just describing them."

"So you have to see the tunnel again for yourself," Lena guesses.

"I'm afraid so." Jimmy runs a hand through his hair.

"This is absolute shit planning." Norling's voice booms in the confined space. "I'm not taking a damn civilian in there. We can't go either, because I can't bank on that we'll find the way. I've had people on my team hospitalized because of screw-ups like this."

89

"That won't happen this time," Lena snaps.

"How can you guarantee that?" Norling demands.

"I'm going first."

"That's out of the question."

"I didn't ask you one." When Lena realises she's shouting, she takes a deep breath and clears her throat.

"Like you said," she says to Norling, "it's my fault we're stuck here. So I will go first."

"I can follow you," Jimmy says.

Lena can't hide her surprise as she looks at Jimmy. She was about to say that she would do her best to navigate the duct on her own. If Jimmy comes with her, the chance that they find the room is much better. The risk is enormous; he might end up hurt or worse, which will see her ejected from the police force and hung from the rooftops of every media outlet in the nation.

On the other hand, Jimmy is volunteering. No one has yet ordered him *not* to enter the tunnel. If the manager agrees, the only thing stopping Jimmy from following is a direct order, which Lena or any other officer does not have to give. And there's no point in encouraging the manager to think he has a say in the matter.

There is a possibility that Jimmy is more involved than he's letting on, in which case a public dismissal might be the least of her worries. She has to stick her hand into the snake pit to find out.

"Remember to keep your voice down," Lena says to Jimmy. "Just whisper left or right. If I shout for you to back up, you crawl backwards like a rat on speed."

"This is insane," Jacobson says. "I have to object."

"Jacobson is right." Gunilla nods in agreement. "I'm jeopardizing my job here."

"This is my decision," Lena says. "We're out of options. And time's not on our side."

"What proof do you have that the killer will strike again?" Jacobson asks.

"Gut feeling."

"No offence," Gunilla says, "but your guesses have led to very difficult situations in the past."

"Anyone who can't deal with Jimmy and me doing this, call Gren or go back to the office." Lena looks around the group.

Gunilla gives Lena a look filled with equal parts irritation and pity, and then walks away. Jacobson scratches his neck and sighs.

"If Jimmy is injured," Jacobson says after a long moment, "you will carry the blame."

"Believe it or not, I have a conscience." Lena half expected Jacobson to leave as well, but he doesn't move.

"It's your call," the team leader says to Lena. "We'll be right behind you. Any hint of movement–"

"And we lie down flat," Lena says. "No stupid bravado ideas. I promise."

Lena notes the faint look of approval in the team leader's eyes. Perhaps there is a chance to scrub away her label as the force's number one firebrand.

"If there is a room in there," Lena says to Jacobson, "and it has a sealed door, I'll bang on it. If you hear me, try to figure out where it is."

She snaps her pocketknife open and cuts away the cable ties. A response team member catches the grille as it falls away and lowers it to the floor. Dust and grease fill the duct, but she can't make out any traces of other people passing through. She searches her pockets and finds a small but bright pen torch.

As she crawls into the duct, she holds her breath as if she were diving into a lake.

Chapter 15

Just as Jimmy had warned her, the duct is a labyrinth of intersections, sudden drops, and conduits sprouting away in every direction imaginable. Breathing is difficult; the air is stale and thick with particles. Her head is filled with the smell of steel and grime. The filth sticks to her hands as she listens to Jimmy's hesitant instructions:

Go left here. No, hang right. I think this way. Turn that corner, or the next one.

Clangs and muffled coughs come from farther behind where the response team is making their way through the duct. They are close, but out of sight. Just like the rumoured room.

After a few minutes, she crawls around a bend and enters a long tunnel so narrow she has to proceed on her elbows and knees. At the far end is a hint of another grille. At least she doesn't suffer from claustrophobia; that would have made her panic the moment she entered the duct.

"Hang on," Jimmy wheezes behind her.

"Keep going," Lena whispers. "We can't stop here."

"I remember this place. The room's straight ahead."

"Then let's hurry up."

Lena crawls up to the grille, shines her light through the bars, and presses her face against the metal for a better view.

Jimmy is right: there is a room beyond the grille. Judging by what is visible in her light from the torch, the space is many times the size of a normal living room, with tiles covering the floor and the lower half of the walls. Two large, old-fashioned strip lights are suspended in rusted metal wires from a high ceiling.

There are three doors, all of them metal. One leads left and two to the right. The opposite wall holds what looks like a window with smoked glass, unless it is an unusually dark mirror. The walls and the doors are painted in a greyish white hue, just like the tiles. Along the walls are a dozen metal bed frames. Each bed has metal hoops on its legs, possibly for transport, although something about the design suggests they are fittings for restraints.

The quiet is almost absolute, apart from a low, ambient drone. Its source is impossible to place. Perhaps water in a nearby pipe. Or the wind chasing around the ventilation system like a drawn-out breath passing through a buried flute. There is no sign of movement, but there can be someone in another room or watching from behind the dark window.

"How did you get through the grille?" Lena whispers to Jimmy.

"I pushed it out," Jimmy says. "It gave way easily."

"How did you get it back in place?"

"I used chewing gum."

"Seriously?"

"I don't carry a toolbox around when I'm working."

"How is breaking into buildings 'working'?"

"You wouldn't understand," Jimmy says, his tone growing edgy. "And by the way, you should see what's under the city hospitals. One can walk around there for days without seeing the sun. Those tunnels are treasure houses."

"Except for the treasures, I guess?" Lena asks.

"Discovering them is the reward."

"What's so fascinating with finding things that aren't on the map?"

"I think you already know the answer to that."

"I don't do riddles," Lena says. "And I don't like amateur psychology, either."

"Everyone who's a keen explorer has this special look."

"Give me a break."

"I'm serious," Jimmy insists. "It's the expression that comes from realising they're onto one secret or another. I probably have it, too."

"And I've got that face?" Lena asks.

Jimmy nods. "As if you're hunting around inside yourself. Don't ask me what you're looking for, though."

"Enough with the psychoanalysis. I need to think what to – hang on." She spots a speck of colour along the edge of the grille. "Was the chewing gum you used green?"

Jimmy pauses. "I think so."

"That's what I wanted to hear." Lena puts her torch on the floor of the duct and pushes tentatively at the grille.

"Why are you asking?" Jimmy hisses.

"It's still here," Lena says. "Which means no one's been through here since you left. Unless someone shares your taste in chewing gums, that is."

A shove sends the grille clattering down onto the tiles. Even though Lena is prepared for the noise, it makes her start, but the sharp echo fades quicker than she expects. The sound will alert anyone in the vicinity to their presence. Although given the racket Lena and the other officers have made so far, she won't be surprised if a platoon of journalists is waiting for them around the corner.

Shining her torch alternatively on the doors and the dark window, she wriggles out of the shaft and lowers herself down on the floor. A thin film of dust covers the tiles. The room is uncleaned, but not as grimy as she expected. On the walls are dozens of small holes in neat patterns: remnants of fittings for shelves or other items. The drone is louder here, distant but distinct, heaving and ebbing away.

Jimmy climbs down with a series of grunts. When his feet are on the floor, he looks incredulous as he takes in the room, as if unwilling to believe he's here again.

"Told you I wasn't lying," he says, his voice hushed.

"You don't get praise for being honest." Lena points at the dark, gleaming rectangle at the far end of the room. "Is that what I think it is?"

"A window," Jimmy says, confirming her suspicion. "You can walk in behind it through there. I can show you." He nods at one of the doors.

"We're not going anywhere until the response team catches up."

Which, she realises, they should have done by now, but the duct is empty and quiet. She walks up to the opening and squints into the black. No sign of Norling.

Cold sweat breaks over her back. She is alone with a civilian – or a suspect – at a potentially dangerous scene. It is the very thing that should not happen.

Just as she's about to call Norling's name, his voice reaches her, distant and distorted.

"We're stuck," he shouts. "We have to go back and take off the vests. Don't proceed until we've caught up with you."

"Make it quick," Lena calls back.

Lena inhales slowly and flexes her neck. The team leader's warning is sensible, but also too late. She steps away from the opening and hopes that no one is in the room. This is the most uncoordinated operation she has been part of. And she is leading it.

"We should go back," Jimmy says. "This place isn't safe."

Lena checks his face for sarcasm, but he looks sincere. She puts on a pair of single-use gloves she carries in her jacket.

"More people are in danger until we've found the murderer," she says "Stay here and be quiet. If I tell you to get down, hit the floor." She draws her gun, moves up to a wall, and gestures for Jimmy to do the same.

"This is unreal." Jimmy stares at the gun as he shuffles over to the wall.

"It's a damned mess," Lena says quietly. "And you shouldn't be in it."

"You blackmailed me into coming," Jimmy points out.

"That was before we were stuck here," Lena says. "Where's the wall with the text?"

"I don't remember." Jimmy looks troubled. "I got the chills when I found it and bolted. But I'll know the room when I see it."

Lena thinks back to her trek through the shaft. She tries to calculate how long it will take the team to crawl backwards, regroup, and make their way to the room. Her best guess is quite a while. And this time, Lena and Jimmy are unable to guide them. And if she and Jimmy try to go back, chances are that they meet the team halfway through.

"I'm going to check the other rooms." Lena walks up to the door Jimmy suggested leads to the space behind the window.

"I'm coming."

"You will stay right where you are. This is police business."

"Forget it." Jimmy shakes his head and raises his hands. "I'm not hanging around alone in here."

Lena opens her mouth to explain to Jimmy exactly how little say he has in the matter, then sighs and shakes her head. This is not the time for debating.

Besides, Jimmy's company is helpful, even if she never would tell him so. The arrogant budding artist might be a thorn in the side of any sane person, but right now the proximity of another human being is welcome.

"At least stay behind me," Lena says, "and keep your mouth shut."

As she suspects, the door is of white-painted steel. Its handle is fit for a vault rather than a hospital.

When she flicks a switch on the wall, there's a soft hum, but the room stays dark. She shines her torch at the strip lights in the ceiling. The sockets inside the covers are empty.

The door opens with a soft screech. The room on the other side is dark. She raises her gun and crosses her hands, aligning the torch with her line of fire.

96

"Hold on," Lena whispers to Jimmy.

She steps through the doorway and sweeps the light around in a wide arc to scan the room.

Another tiled chamber with suspended light fittings. It's almost identical to the first room, but this one holds three large wooden desks and a large, rusted metal filing cabinet. Its empty steel drawers are lined up on the floor.

On her left is a doorway partially concealed by a torn plastic curtain. Opposite the doorway is an alcove that gives access to the dark window. At the far end of the room is a large door in what looks like cast iron. The air is so rich with dust it clings to her skin like a gentle drizzle.

"That's the door they've welded shut," Jimmy says behind her.

Lena turns around and sees Jimmy point at the large door.

"I told you to wait," Lena says. Given the presence of Jimmy's old chewing gum, it's unlikely that they have company, but she will be damned before she gets him hurt.

"And I said that I wouldn't," Jimmy says. "Not in this place. What do you think has been going on here?"

"Maybe it's some kind of security ward."

"A ward so secret they didn't bother to put it on the map?"

"Stranger things happen. Close the door behind you."

She follows a wall and walks over to the curtain. It's transparent enough to let some of the light through. Making sure there's nothing human-shaped hiding behind the plastic, she tears it down and does a quick sweep. A crude shower cubicle and a toilet. The water in the bowl is murky and rancid.

She walks over to the dark iron door. The one she just opened is robust, but this one is massive, more a reinforced gate than door. Uneven smudges reach in like blackened fingerprints through the gap. Jimmy is right; the door has been welded shut from the outside.

Above the door is a wide metal box with a smashed green glass panel: a once-illuminated EXIT sign. It means the door should not be far away from the corridor where she entered the duct. A tentative slap on the door confirms what she suspected: the metal is thick enough to absorb the sound.

"Hold my torch and step away from the door." Lena pushes one of the desks away from its place and drags it to the middle of the room.

Jimmy moves out of Lena's way. "What are you doing?"

"Getting Jacobson's attention," Lena says. "This might get noisy."

She pushes the desk over the floor and slams it into the door so hard the bang makes her teeth ache.

"Jesus Christ," Jimmy cries and covers his ears.

"He's probably a long way away from this place," Lena murmurs. "Stay where you are."

She drags the desk backwards and rams it into the iron door two more times. Hopefully, it's loud enough for Jacobson to locate the exit. Chances are that the door opens into a different room or some other godforsaken uncharted part of the hospital, but the EXIT sign suggests otherwise.

"This place is scraped clean." Jimmy pokes one of the desks.

"No need to leave stuff behind if you're closing the room down," Lena says. "Especially not if you're going to seal it off."

"I mean literally scraped clean." Jimmy points at a corner of the desk. "Someone's peeled away the factory tag with the make and model."

"Could be wear and tear," Lena says.

But when she inspects one of the other desks, the information on its metal label has been erased by some sharp tool. The third desk has received the same treatment. She turns the file cabinet around and checks the back. The space where she would expect to find a serial number has been scorched and blackened. Someone has rendered the entire facility faceless.

No wonder the manager can't find these rooms in his treasured archives. Whoever locked this front door did not want any future surprise visitors.

"If you see anything with a number or letter on it," Lena says, "let me know."

"There's a drain over there." Jimmy points at a small rectangular hole in the floor near the bathroom.

"I'll get to that."

Lena takes a step back and looks up at the EXIT sign. Mounted on the wall just above it is a saucer-shaped form in white plastic. It's the size of a breakfast bowl but flatter and partially obscured by the sign. She climbs onto the desk and pulls the plastic away from the wall in a small spray of crumbling plastic.

It's a fire alarm. Perhaps state of the art once upon a time, but by modern standards, it looks like a prop from an old science fiction show. The alarm had been powered on mains; a bundle of wires dangle from the wall. Inside the cover is a small sticker that reads *Ignis*. The word is accompanied by a logotype she doesn't recognize.

Lena prises off the crumbling plastic that holds the sticker and pockets it. When she turns around, Jimmy is lying on the floor and fishing around in the drain.

"I think there's something down here," he says.

"Get your hand out of there," Lena says sharply. "You might cut yourself. I'm in enough trouble as it is for bringing you in here."

"Thank you for caring." Jimmy gives Lena a disdainful look and pulls his hand out of the hole.

"You're welcome. Move over."

Lena walks over and shines the torch down into the small pit. Its bottom is an arm's length down and almost completely covered by fragmented concrete. No sign of moisture. This place has been unused for a long time.

As she pulls her torch out, there's a glimmer at the bottom, so brief she almost misses it. A reflection, weak as a distant star. Using the torch to poke around in the filth, she uncovers a tiny piece of glass, with jagged edges and so delicate it's almost invisible. Grunting in disgust, she reaches down and picks up the shard.

"What's that?" Jimmy asks.

"Part of a smashed vial," Lena says. "Or so I think." She turns it around in her hand.

"What's it doing here?" Jimmy asks. He bends down and pokes around in the rubbish on the floor.

"It's a hospital, after all." Lena takes out an evidence bag, slips the piece of glass inside, and tucks it away.

"Are we leaving now?" Jimmy asks.

"There's another door. And I haven't seen the text yet."

Lena takes her torch back from Jimmy and walks back into the room with the bare bed frames. No sign of the response team yet. Making sure that Jimmy is following her, she crosses the room and moves to the side of the second door.

"Stand back," she says to Jimmy.

"I remember now." Jimmy taps Lena urgently on her back. "That's the room. The lamp's in there, too."

"What lamp?" She recalls Jimmy mentioning that detail earlier, but at the time she thought it was a random observation.

"A weird one. It doesn't look like any other I've seen. You'll see."

"Fine," Lena says. "But this time, wait until I tell you to follow me."

Lena holds her fingers over the handle. If the killer is here, this is where he will be hiding. Which is an unlikely scenario, she reminds herself, but she's more jumpy than she can remember ever being.

Jimmy was right: an aura of wrongness rests over these rooms. That dark one-way window. The sealed door. Signs of deliberate removal of traces. The hum she heard when she tried the light switch, like voltage trapped in the hidden wiring, looking for a way out.

"Maybe we should wait for the response team?" Jimmy asks.

"Quiet."

Lena pulls the door open a crack. Only darkness. She opens the door more, leans in, and shines her torch around the room.

Chapter 16

The room is large, almost the size of the first one she entered. The fittings for one single strip light gape empty in the middle of the ceiling. Rough concrete walls surround a floor covered with pale tiles.

On her left are three rows of metal but school-like benches, three in each row, each with a matching steel chair bolted to the floor. The chairs feature the same kind of metal hoops as the beds in the adjacent room. She can imagine reasons for why you would have to tie people down in beds, but hoops on chairs are a different matter.

On the floor to the right, mounted on a tripod and facing the benches, is a dull globe the size of a bowling ball. It's protected by a larger sphere of metal mesh. Somehow, the object looks like an old-fashioned camera, but this has never been a photographer's studio, and there is no visible lens.

There is no one in sight and no places where anyone can hide. The place is empty.

She sweeps the torchlight over the room again and spots the line of text she is searching for, neatly painted in black on the opposite wall.

Look deep and draw.

They are the only words she has encountered since making her way into this underground facility. So far, their meaning eludes her, but it is anchored to a point hiding just outside her awareness. Next to find the chain and start tugging.

She turns back to the dark globe on the tripod.

"What the hell is that?" she murmurs and squints at the strange apparatus.

"I thought it was some kind of lamp," Jimmy says behind her. "But now I'm not so sure."

Lena breathes out slowly. Jimmy has followed her again, even though he was told to stay put. The man appears pathologically unable to follow simple instructions.

"What part of–" Lena begins.

"– *stay behind* didn't I get?" Jimmy says, finishing Lena's sentence. "The bit where you walk into another room. There's a killer on the loose, and you're armed. I'm not."

"All the more reason to keep out of sight," Lena says, loosening her grip on her gun. "Besides, I'm not about to shoot at anything."

Lena holsters her gun, walks up to one of the benches, and looks underneath it. An engraving that may have been a serial number has been burnt to a patch of charred wood. Another deliberate erasure of possible traces.

She looks up and sees Jimmy trying to lift the mesh dome from the not-quite-a-camera machine.

"Don't touch that," she shouts. "Christ, it's like babysitting a five-year-old. This is a crime scene. Everything will be dusted down, and I don't want your prints anywhere."

Lena walks up to the tripod for a closer look. What she thought was a steel globe is a sphere of mirror-like glass. Rather than a lamp, the machine more resembles a small lighthouse. A thick power cord snakes its way from the base of the globe down into a socket on the floor.

Leaning close, she discerns inside the sphere a thick glass spiral interwoven with gleaming copper wire. A low hum emanates from the globe. It reminds her of the constant, low-frequency drone of a power station. She has never seen anything like it, but at the same time, the glass and copper spiral is oddly familiar.

"Any ideas?" Lena asks Jimmy.

"It looks like a camera flash," Jimmy says. "But it would be the biggest I've seen. And there's no camera."

"They might've removed it."

"And left this behind?"

"It's bolted down." Lena points at the large heads that secure the machine to the floor.

"Just like those chairs," Jimmy observes. "What kind of messed-up place is this?"

"Once we've got the exit open," Lena says, "I intend to ask the manager exactly that question."

On a thin base just under the sphere is a small switch. It's set to off. Its only other position is on.

"I wonder if–" Lena says to herself, and flicks the switch.

Light explodes from the flash in shockwaves. They flood Lena's mind with a hot, sudden brightness that forces her backwards as if struck by a blow. Blinding white fades to total black and slams back to sterile white, switching back and forth again and again like the pistons of a furious engine.

Lena stumbles backwards until she trips and falls over one of the immovable benches. The brutal transitions between darkness and light snuff out her conception of space and distance. Had she not known where she had stood when she switched the machine on, she could have been anywhere: on an open field, in a great cavern, or in a confined chamber.

There is no pause in which she can get her bearings. Even if she had been facing another direction, the rapid flashes would find their way past her eyelids and break her thoughts apart. And she had been looking right at the machine. Squeezing her eyes shut doesn't help; her vision has been reduced to a cascade of blistering reds.

A stroboscope, she manages to think, but no sound accompanies its manic flashing. There should have been raging thunder or a deafening hissing. This compact silence adds to the unearthliness of the indoor lightning storm.

She's dimly aware of Jimmy cursing and shouting somewhere in the inferno. Pressing her fists over her eyes, she rises from the ground and staggers in the direction where she last saw him.

"Turn it off," Lena screams.

"I can't see." Jimmy's shout is both close and distant.

Lena swears and reaches out, but her hands touch nothing. She has to risk a glance. Edging forward, she peeks between her fingers and freezes in place.

Another door has opened in the room.

On the wall behind the benches is an opening, less high and narrower than the other doors she has seen, but large enough to allow a person through. She must have missed it when she first looked around. The door may have been concealed; rather than being fitted in a frame like the metal doors elsewhere in the facility, there are no visible hinges or thresholds. It's as if part of the tiled wall has vanished and left behind a slim passage.

"Help me," Jimmy shouts. He's close on her right, bent over as if nauseated and holding his hands over his face.

Lena wants to help him, but she's transfixed by the newfound door. In the tornado of flashes, it's a consistent dark silhouette, more a hole than a passage. Her body is pulled towards the opening as if the floor is tilted.

The timing of its appearance is alarming; either she triggered some kind of mechanism when she switched on the lamp, or someone else opened the door just when the flashing started. Dazed and disoriented, she drifts up to the door and peers through the opening.

Inside is a set of wooden stairs, leading down. The landing below is either dark or too deep down to see.

Lena walks down the stairs. She reaches out to let her fingers brush against the cold walls while the steps squeak and tremble under her feet. A cool wetness brushes against her face, like the rush of frigid air from an underground train tunnel in winter or the stagnant mist of a cave.

After a while she looks over her shoulder. The doorway is a remote, blinking rectangle far above and behind her, smaller than a postage stamp. Jimmy is shouting incoherently in the distance, but the stairs carry her down as if she were standing on an escalator.

She keeps on going down. She has lost her torch, but this darkness is not unsettling; forming around her like a gentle caress, the gloom is welcoming, even relaxing. A moment ago, she was overwhelmed by the dreadful light. Now she is descending into the tranquil embrace of the earth, free from stress, shouts, or painful flashes.

She has no reason to go back up. There aren't any answers where she comes from, never any peace from news reports or nightmares. Continuing down is much simpler, and once she finds the bottom, she will discover all the answers she needs. There waits the prize that her job never delivers: an end to her need to repair all that is broken.

A fragment of her consciousness refuses to accept this unexpected, pristine peace of mind and demands that she stops. But she has paused too many times. She wants to explore the full extent of this mystery and find a way to live without ache or anxiety.

The stairs end, and she stumbles onto what feels like a level surface.

Before she has time to search for a door or an opening, she blinks in the sudden glow of a light bulb suspended from a power cord some thirty metres away. She stands on a floor of brushed concrete. The light is strong, but there are no walls in sight, and the ceiling is lost in shadow.

She peers into the silent night beyond the light. A giant room, twice buried beneath dirt and secrecy below the medical facility.

Perhaps it's an old bomb shelter, accessible through hidden entrances throughout the hospital. That makes sense: they must have needed lots of room to evacuate a whole hospital.

The ambient promise of answers to her unspoken questions is still sedating, but a forgotten network of tunnels means the ward might not be as abandoned as she believed. Someone can hide here and used the stairs to get in and out. Especially if there are more staircases that lead here.

The silence is absolute, except for an almost inaudible hiss from the light bulb. Slowly, she draws her gun and prepares to go back up the stairs again.

"Hello?" she calls. "This is the police. Anyone there?"

For a moment, Lena thinks she hears a brief, choked sound, almost like a quiet chortle, but it's so faint it might be the blood rushing through her head.

Looking around with every step she takes, Lena walks towards the lightbulb. A sharp smell hangs in the air. After a moment, she recognizes it as the reek of gunpowder and stops in her tracks. The smell is familiar, but so out of place here that it took her several seconds to place it.

On the edge of the light is a horizontal gleam. Step by cautious step, Lena walks closer and finds a plain steel table, empty save for a small paper box. On each side of the table is a tall, flat panel, making the table look more like a booth. A broad rail on the floor runs from the table and disappears in the gloom ahead.

"This can't be right," Lena says and lowers her gun.

It's a shooting range. The rail allows the shooter to bring the target up close for inspection. If she looks inside the little paper box, she'll find a pair of standard-issue earplugs. Far away, she glimpses the outline of a typical cardboard practise target.

She tries to take a deep breath, but the air seems to have turned into ash. All ideas of comfort and security melt away.

It is conceivable that a room like this might exist under Beckomberga. She can even believe that someone would use it for target practise; some of Stockholm's subterranean chambers are frequently turned into rehearsal studios, illegal clubs, or impromptu movie theatres. This one might be a sanctuary for a gun enthusiast.

But the table in front of her is not just archetypical: it is identical to those at the range where she did all of her practise as a police cadet. That is one coincidence too many.

She is being stalked. Someone is hoping to unnerve her to the point of collapse. This is a world-class sinister prank. And whoever the culprit is, he or she has gone through a lot of trouble to rig a scenario meant to break Lena for good.

Jimmy must be part of the set-up. Maybe he's obsessed with her media-framed reputation as an irate law enforcer following John Andersson's arrest. Most likely, he knows about the catastrophic raid in her past, too. It explains the obscure leads, his eagerness to help, and the accuracy with which he led her to this twisted, private prearranged stage.

It might be that everything she has encountered in this case has consisted of clever scenography and elaborate props. Perhaps even the murders are part of his scheme.

This is nothing but a game. She is being played. And the bets are about her sanity.

"Jimmy," Lena screams. "This ends right here, you sick fucker."

No answer.

"Have it your way," she says under her breath.

Anger rolls inside her like steam. When she finds Jimmy again, she will drag him back to the station and wring him so hard that he'll need a real sickbay. She turns back to the stairs, and stops.

The stairs are gone. Where the opening was is a smooth grey wall. It must be another of his concealed traps, designed to trap her with this petty reminder of her past. He must have spent a decade preparing this revolting show.

"Show yourself," Lena shouts and turns around. "The fun's over. Come out, and I'll do what I can to cut you a deal. You won't last a week in prison."

Only silence.

Lena's hands are cold and damp around the grip of her gun. Her chest is so tight she has to concentrate to inhale. Jimmy must be there, hiding outside the small patch of light, waiting for Lena to crack. She's a sitting target as long as she remains under the lamp, but she'll be blind in the darkness. It's better to wait him out; sooner or later, he will be compelled to give himself away.

Her eyes wander back to the booth. If the set-up completely mimics that of her old shooting range, there will be a button under the table for pulling the target closer. The target will be mounted on platforms with a pair of wheels that allow motorised wires to haul them up and down the track.

It's unlikely that Jimmy can have recreated a mechanism that complex, but given what he has accomplished so far, his madness seems both lethal and limitless. She moves up to the table and runs her fingers underneath the wooden top. The button is there, and it feels exactly like the one on a real range. She crouches down behind the table and presses it.

A soft whirr echoes from the darkness ahead of the booth. After a moment she sees movement: an approaching target slowly tugged out of the shadows and towards her.

It is not a cardboard target.

On top of the platform is a man. Ropes across his chest and chin tie him to the metal frame that normally holds the pretend target. The light is too weak to illuminate his face, but she can make out a cheap white shirt, stained beige chinos, and brown loafers.

The first surprise is that the man is not Jimmy. He is too old, taller and heavier, with tufts of thinning hair. She has been so convinced that the would-be photographer is responsible for arranging this macabre enactment that for a moment, she refuses to acknowledge what she is seeing.

The second shock is crueller.

When she realizes who the man is, she reels backwards and gasps for air. She has seen his face once in real life and countless times in her nightmares. It slides into her peripheral view every time she forgets to focus on her work. His name has vanished from her memory long ago, but his looks never will.

He is the paedophile she shot to death years ago in the disastrous raid.

Right in the middle of his countryside house turned hellish hideaway, she had taken out all her wrath on his useless body until she was certain he would never harm anyone again. He was as dead as a human being could be.

But now he has returned, strapped to a shooting target rack and hauled out of the subterranean night.

"I didn't expect you here," the man says. "Not so soon. But some people make the journey faster than others." His voice is surprised but smooth and precise.

Lena trains her gun on the man before she has consciously formed the idea to raise her weapon. Her hands are ice around the grip. He is gone. Bagged, removed, cremated, thinned out and forgotten. She stopped him. She ended his damage.

"You're not alive." Lena is breathing so hard her words come out as whispers.

"Neither are you," he says. "Living means feeling pity, or at least something. But feelings aren't your strong point, are they?"

"I don't care what your game is," Lena wheezes, "it's over."

The man shakes his head. Even though his face is partially hidden by shadows, his teeth are bright when he smiles.

"Our game has only begun," he says. "But I can speed it up for you. Go on, shoot me."

Lena feels the reins on her fury slip out of her hands.

Missing building plans and sealed-off rooms. Arcane machinery and chairs with fittings for restraints. Sadists returned from the dead. The full picture is still beyond her, but the implications are obvious: this has been a place of terror. And those responsible have never been punished. The understanding shatters reason as well as compassion.

History is repeating itself. Every time she tries to make things right, she flings open the wrong window and finds only a fresh view of the lowest reaches of the human soul. There is no respite or escape. Even empty spaces come with their own spectral weights, pulling her down until she will not be able to surface again.

Lena squeezes the trigger until her weapon goes inert in her hands. Part of her struggles to stop firing, but the voice of reason is snuffed out by the hot cloud of uncontrollable rage.

When she lowers her gun, the man has vanished. In his place is Agnes, hanging limp from the ropes, her body rent and torn by the bullets. She looks at Lena with vacant eyes and collapses while her blood ebbs away around her feet.

Lena staggers backwards and raises a hand to her mouth.

No.

It has happened at last. Her inability to restrain herself has extinguished an innocent life. She has been tricked, but that does not matter. Agnes is dead all the same.

Not real.

Clinging to the thought, she hits the floor screaming, and darkness closes around her like an ocean around a naked flame.

Chapter 17

Felix looks up from the book he's reading when a draught touches his neck. The wind is as subtle as a blown kiss and just as significant: it means he is not alone. Sighing in relief, he puts his book away and walks down the stairs.

Timmy waits for him in the kitchen. He sits perched on the back of the chair pulled up in a corner out of sight of the window. Not that anyone could see him anyway; unless the lights are on, the room appears completely dark from the outside, and the blinds let through only thin slivers of midday light.

"Well," Timmy says and rubs his hands together. "That was interesting."

"Are we in trouble?" Felix asks.

Timmy shakes his head. "But someone came too close for her own good, so I had to set an example. And you must never leave anything behind again."

"Why can't we talk to people about the laboratory?" Felix asks. "If we let the police know what happened, they can set things straight."

"It's pointless. We can't undo the bill. But we can pay the check, if you see what I'm saying."

"What if they don't understand what I'm doing?" Felix asks. "I know there's a woman looking for me. She's with the police."

He read the news on his computer earlier that day. Many articles featured an image circulated endlessly over the past twenty-four hours: a dark-haired woman in a dress, about to open the door to a house in Norra Ängby.

"Don't worry about the detective. I saw her in person a moment ago, and I almost got her." Timmy laughs. "She's a wreck. She'll crack long before she comes anywhere near you."

"Do you promise?" Felix asks.

Timmy nods and rubs his hands. "Next time, she won't get away so easily."

"You didn't hurt anyone, did you?" Felix wonders. Making their old tyrant suffer is one thing, but they must stay clear of innocent people.

"There's no need," Timmy says. "She's perfectly capable of injuring herself. All I have to do is wave the red curtain, and she'll run off a cliff in sheer stubbornness. The fall will leave her as unrecognisable as those she tries to catch. It will be a show to remember."

Felix turns away as Timmy laughs again. Sometimes the shadows fall in peculiar ways on Timmy's face and dissolve his features, as if his friend's face is nothing more than a layer of mist that hides another, very different person. It often happens when Timmy is annoyed.

That other, hidden Timmy is no one's friend. It's not even a real person, but a hungry, demanding nothingness, tugging at him with strings that only obedience can keep at bay. Worst is how Timmy's words have complete command over Felix's imagination. Timmy has the ability to rip away the barely healed skin over their mutual past and give the nightmares full rein.

Every time Felix suggests another way to get revenge other than taking someone's life, that threatening entity rears inside Timmy and looks out through his friend's eyes with disgust. It is a warning:

do as you are told, or suffer the consequences. The choice is always easy. There has been enough suffering, too many minutes and hours of hurt. Revenge is the only option.

And there are so many he must avenge. When Timmy first appeared, he revealed what Felix feared: those who Felix left behind are gone forever. All his friends, taken from him.

"When do we strike again?" Felix asks.

Timmy stops laughing and looks serious. "Tonight," he says. "And as long as we don't break the glass, this one will be easier."

"What glass?"

"I'll show you."

Chapter 18

"Do you have any idea what you've brought down on my head?" Gren asks.

Gren keeps his hands clasped on the folded laptop on his desk. Somehow, he looks like a man in prayer, hoping for a reply from his deity. Perhaps he's begging for mercy on his career and patience. Or perhaps he worries over Lena's future; even though he's venting his irritation, he cannot bring himself to pile all the blame at Lena's feet.

This time, though, Lena feels at least partially responsible for her commander's headache. He faces several difficult questions, and he expects her to give him answers he can pass on to his superiors.

On the table is a printout of the report Lena put together when the nurse released her from the headquarters' medical care unit. It took her two hours of intent typing and double-checking details to put together. She has included everything she can recall up until she passed out; the rest has been supplied by the response team leader. The gap between Lena losing consciousness and his arrival was filled by Jimmy.

It is not a pleasant read. Even less amusing are her memories from the underground facility. Many images remain fragmented, smudged by the urgent need to disbelieve and forget. All that took place after she turned on the damned lamp is particularly blurred.

But much is still clear and vivid, and what she can recall is enough to know that she was a hair's breadth from unravelling. She also knows she cannot trust her own senses anymore.

One moment, she was emptying her clip into a monstrosity that could not be real, the next she was convulsing on a bunk in the police headquarters, screaming and clinging to the mattress as if it were the only solid object in a reality on the verge of dissolving. Telling if she was awake or dreaming took almost a minute. She still isn't completely sure that Gren is real and not a figment of her imagination.

This is one of the many observations she did not enter in her report.

Jacobson came by to check up on her just as the nurse signed her out. He was in a hurry, but he had time to mention that the response team discovered Lena only a few metres from the lamp. No one had seen any more doors, let alone stairs or firing ranges. Jimmy was found unconscious on the floor next to her. The strange opening in the wall, and everything that happened after she passed through it, were a play enacted in her fantasies.

Which had not stopped her from firing her gun. Dream or not, her chamber was unforgivably empty. Lost in her private Never-Neverland, she tried to take out an imaginary adversary with a weapon of metal and lead, peppering the walls instead of a real target. Only a streak of rare fortune saved her from injuring or killing Jimmy. The event is the kind of nightmare that sends regular bad dreams scurrying for cover.

"Let's take it from the beginning again," Gren says. "Starting with how you brought a civilian to a crime scene."

"Technically," Lena says, "the hospital wasn't a crime scene. Although if we can prove that—"

"Oh, spare me." Gren waves Lena's excuse away. "You're perfectly aware of how blindingly stupid it was. There's a clear link between the murders and that room. And you brought a suspect there."

"It was a crisis," Lena says.

She shifts on the chair and resists the urge to drink from her glass of water. Perhaps she has misjudged Gren's position; he looks as if he's fighting the need to scream.

"An investigation," Gren says slowly, "is always an emergency. That's no excuse to stop caring about rules. Or laws, for that matter."

"Jimmy isn't a suspect."

"Not officially, but I'm of a different opinion. He's too implicated. You say yourself in your report that he disobeyed your instructions."

"He's a borderline antisocial who can't follow orders. It's not his fault."

"So acting against the direct command of a police officer is all right because he was born arrogant?" Gren demands, his voice climbing. "Are you trying to be funny?"

Lena flinches and blinks. She has definitely miscalculated Gren's mood. Unless she treads carefully, she might push him into a full-blown tantrum. That is not a problem in itself; Gren would feel better if he let off steam more often. But he might decide to take her off the case, which would be a disaster for everyone involved.

Her phone rings for the third time since she woke up. She doesn't have to check it to know who the caller is.

"Jimmy tried to help me," Lena says. "In fact, he's the one who prompted me to search the sewer."

"That might have been an attempt to distract you. He could've been waiting for a moment to go for your weapon."

"He had plenty of chances to do that."

"If Jimmy had turned on you," Gren says quietly, "no one could've intervened. It's hard to believe you let your guard down that easily."

Lena closes her eyes and exhales. Gren's trust in her is leaking away, and she cannot find the words that will plug the holes.

When she opens her eyes, she turns to the window. Somewhere in the distance is the high-security facility in which John Andersson is locked. At last, she is beginning to understand the strange affinity she feels for the damaged man: some day, she will visit him and let him know that he is not alone. She has visited his territory of uncontrollable anger twice. John slipped, while Lena still walks among the living. Perhaps only luck is what makes them different.

"You've read my statement," Lena says. "I thought that bringing Jimmy along was the only way to move the investigation forward."

"What if he felt pressed into compliance?" Gren asks. "He can take you to court."

"He volunteered, and the manager didn't protest. Also, we were alone in there because no one else showed up. It's not my fault the response team pack on so much gear."

"You should've waited with exploring until they got through."

"One can wait for only so long," Lena says tightly. "They bloody vanished. I even called for them."

"Apparently the team got lost. They said it's a real maze."

"Which is why I took Jimmy along in the first place." Lena leans forward and holds Gren's gaze. "We needed to find that room. Like I wrote in the report, when I saw that the grille looked untouched, I made a call and proceeded. Then things got confused."

"Yes, your report is more than a little confusing." Gren taps his fingers on the printed copy of Lena's outline of what happened at the hospital.

"So you proceeded to search all three rooms," he continues, "and bagged a few pieces of evidence. We're examining the glass now, but I can't see the point."

"Call it a hunch." Lena leans back again. "Someone has gone through great pains to remove every detail that would've indicated the owner or origin of the ward. If that's what it is."

"But they forgot a fire alarm?"

"It was mounted in a spot that's hard to see from the floor. They might've missed it when they closed shop. I'll check the factory name as soon as we're done here."

"Not tonight, you aren't." Gren shakes his head. "Jacobson will cover for you until you've rested."

"But–"

"You're off duty until you've slept." Gren shakes his head. "Nurse's instructions. Tell me about the lamp."

"I was hoping that you could explain it to me," Lena says. "Haven't the technicians pulled it apart yet?"

"They're as baffled as you are. Our best guess is that it's some kind of visual stimulation device for behavioural corrective treatment."

"Is it actually called that?"

"I'm paraphrasing. Let's go over this again, from the beginning."

Lena describes how she went to the hospital along with Jacobson, Jimmy, and Gunilla. She outlines her conversation with the emergency response team, the interview with the manager, how they continued to the tunnels and eventually relied on Jimmy to guide them. Her explanation ends with the mention of the lamp.

"What in God's name compelled you to switch on that machine?" Gren asks. "It could've electrocuted you on the spot."

"Gut feeling again. It stands out, so I reckon it's linked to the text, which means it has to do with my case. And I was curious."

"Curiosity–" Gren begins.

"– gets criminals arrested," Lena snaps. "But I admit that I wasn't prepared for what happened."

"You describe the effect as *a nightclub light show on speed*." Gren nods at Lena's report.

Lena shrugs. "It's the best I can do. But I don't do it justice. That flashing was out of this world."

"And this so-called light show bewildered you to the point that you drew your gun?"

Lena braces herself. This is the crossroads: unless she can convince Gren, she will be disconnected from the investigation and perhaps from the force.

"As I stated in my account," Lena says slowly, "I had the impression that I was being attacked. The light casts shadows in a way that resembles an individual coming at you. I fired a warning shot, and when I had no response, I aimed to incapacitate the aggressor."

"Using your entire clip?"

Lena nods. She longs to tell Gren what she truly feels, but doing so is tantamount to handing in her badge and her gun.

Yes, she would say, *I fired every single bullet. If I had stayed conscious, I would've reloaded and kept shooting. And when I ran out of ammunition, I would have used my fist on the bastard. Because I was aiming at a sadist returned from the beyond.*

Except that a moment later, the target of my wrath was Agnes. Which, in fact, was yet another hallucination, seeing as there never was a door in the first place, so let's discuss what this says about my mental health.

"The supposed attacker did not stop," Lena says. "Probably because it was a shadow. And shadows are notoriously bad at following instructions, no matter how much you shout or shoot at them. Who shut the machine down, by the way?"

"Jacobson did," Gren says. "He said it was a struggle to find the switch. In his report, he described the spectacle as pretty overwhelming."

"He's a champion of understatements."

"Possibly," Gren notes. "And then you passed out?"

"Like a candle."

Gren nods and studies Lena for a long moment before he answers.

"I believe you," he says. "And to my relief, Jimmy says that he too saw someone else in the room. So he's backing your report."

"There you go," Lena says, trying to hide her surprise. "Who debriefed Jimmy?"

Lena wonders where Jimmy is now. She needs to talk to him as soon as possible. Hopefully he hasn't gone off the grid, but given what he has been through, he's likely to want to stay under the radar for the time being.

"Jacobson sat down with him before we let him go," Gren says. "You better talk to Jacobson before you leave."

"What's wrong?" Lena asks. "I don't like that grimace."

"Sometimes," Gren says, "I wonder if I'm able to make an expression you don't dislike."

"I love when you look compliant and understanding. It's your frown that gets to me. Tell me what's going on."

"Jacobson requested an ambulance when he heard the shots. It was a sensible thing to do, but its arrival also drew in quite a crowd. As in people with cameras."

Lena rests her elbows on Gren's desk and buries her face in her hands. "Damn it," she murmurs.

"So you're doing the rounds on the Internet again," Gren says. "This time, you're unconscious on a stretcher at Sweden's most infamous former mental hospital."

"I could use a glass of wine," Lena says. "And something to eat."

She sighs and runs her hands through her hair. Add a shower to that list, and perhaps some sleep. The past day has left her more winded than a marathon run.

"The images haven't gone viral yet," Gren continues, "but some tabloid is likely to run an article. I've been recommended to take you off the case. Which is beginning to become a pattern."

"You know I can see this investigation through faster than anyone else."

"That's what I told the board. I have your back."

"So once again, I'm responsible for your career?"

Gren smiles tiredly. "Like I said, there's a pattern."

"Have they found the door into the facility?"

Gren nods and skims a paper on his desk. "It was hidden behind a layer of plaster inside a smaller room," he says.

"I knew it," Lena says. Finally, some good news.

"But we haven't made it through yet. That ward is sealed up tighter than a fortress. The technicians had to squirm in the same way you went, and from what I've heard, they aren't too happy about it. But they're going over the place as we speak."

"We should bring the manager in for questioning."

"There's no need," Gren says. "He's co-operating so hard he'd do cartwheels if we asked him to. Jacobson told me he was a bit uptight when you first saw him."

"That's another first-class understatement."

"Well, he's loosened up. When he realised there's a hidden room for which he's responsible, and that the room in question might be part of criminal activities, his attitude changed in a hurry."

"I need to show the manager the fire alarm."

"I'll have someone else do that," Gren says. "You should get some rest while we figure out what that room has to do with this case. That's an order, and it's one I expect even you to follow."

She has seen Gren in this state before: exhausted, pressed, and worried. Usually it means that he'll refuse to budge. But alongside his determination is a tenseness she doesn't immediately recognize. Only after a while does she realise what it is: the guarded anxiety of someone with a secret that demands to be voiced. She has seen the look on the faces of a hundred men and women, both during interrogations and casual conversations.

Gren is holding something back. A detail so scorching it shines through his mask of consternation, but at the same time too volatile to be let out of its cage. It's tempting to press him, although given his current mood, that approach is destined to backfire. The only way forward is waiting until her chief decides to open up.

"I'll handle the briefing while you're away," Gren says. "I know you've summed up your notions in your report, but round them up for me again so I don't get them wrong."

"Extortion," Lena says. "That's my primary suspicion for the murders. Even if those underground rooms had been on the manager's maps, there's still something off about them. Whatever happened there didn't work out, so they shut the place down. Now one of those involved is trying to intimidate another party."

"Someone with those intentions would want the message we found to become publicly known," Gren says.

121

"Unless he or she expects the words to find their way to the right person anyway. Or was left there by mistake. It could have been pinned there on whim."

"Those ideas don't sit right with me. What about the other possibility?"

Lena doesn't have to ask what Gren means. "It's possible that someone who was incarcerated at the facility is behind the murders," she says. "I haven't ruled that out."

"*Incarcerated*," Gren echoes. "That's a strange word to use for a patient in care."

"There were hoops for restraints on the beds and the chairs."

"I see your point. What's the reason this isn't your main theory?"

"Background checks of the victims don't show any ties to the hospital. And the couple were too young. Besides, given that the facility officially doesn't exist, we have zero hope in hell to chase down a list of so-called patients."

"Granted." Gren sighs. "So it'll be your secondary hypothesis, but one you'll work on actively?"

"I'll find a trace," Lena says. "I will turn every stone."

"Knowing you," Gren says, "you will bring the stones in for questioning. But I think Jimmy is as likely to be part of this as the manager. We can discuss that later, although we're keeping an eye on him."

"Don't freak him out," Lena says. "He's an asset."

"I agree on that. But I'll decide how we deal with him." Gren looks at Lena until she turns away.

"Understood," Lena says. As much as she respects Gren, pulling rank does not suit him.

"The brief is set to eight o'clock tonight," Gren says. "I promise to read out what you've written, word by word. By the way, Asplund asked me to let you know that he and his constables are working overtime patrolling Norra Ängby. That's all for now."

Gren opens his laptop by way of informing her that the conversation is over.

"I appreciate that," Lena says. "I'll be back in at seven tomorrow morning."

She rises and opens the door, then turns back to Gren.

"Why me?" she asks.

"Come again?" Green looks up from is laptop.

"I know you think I'm a loose cannon. And it's no secret that many others share your opinion. How come you wanted me for this case?"

Gren is silent for a moment.

"Some would say you're volatile," he says, "but you also have a tendency to hit the mark. And–" He pauses. "Well, you get the job done."

Lena knows what Gren does not dare to say. She would be the first to argue that her deductive skills are average at best, and also that she is successful only because of the combined forces of pig-headedness and long hours.

The superintendent has another reason for roping her in: the suspicion that she can glimpse a dimension of this crime that is out of sight to the other detectives. He thinks her well-known instability is grave enough to offer her a look into the psyche of a deranged murderer. The implications of the idea make her nauseated.

Although Gren may be right. Fight fire with fire, and so forth. The tactic is controversial but time-honoured. Still, in her case, it's more a question of battling flames with a barrel of petrol. If he knew just how close to the edge she limps every day, he would shrink back in his comfortable leather chair and dismiss her from the force without a second thought.

So she nods and leaves in silence.

Lena's phone rings as she walks towards her office. Gustav, calling for the seventh time. This is the part of relationships she struggles with the most: other people's need for constant communication. If only she could make Gustav see why words are too insubstantial to carry the weight of her day-to-day work. Kind gestures and physical closeness work much better. Conversation only breaks up her lines of thought.

She takes the call and prepares for the inevitable questions.

"Lena?" Gustav says. "I've been worried sick. Where have you been?"

"Working. There was a situation earlier today, so I've been cut off."

"The entire evening?"

"A pretty bad situation." Lena stops halfway down the corridor and rests her back against the wall. "I'm sorry I missed lunch," she says. "I know it's late, but would you like to meet up for dinner?"

"Has this anything to do with those murders?"

"Gustav—"

"I know," he says quickly. "No questions. Sorry, but it's hard not to care."

"I don't want you not to care," Lena says softly. "Only not to ask." She takes a deep breath and tries to calm down; her debriefing with Gren has left her edgy.

"I'd love dinner," Gustav says. "Can I come to yours? I'll shop on the way."

"Wouldn't you rather go out?" Lena asks.

"Correct me if I'm wrong," he says, "but I have a feeling that you'd rather do something low-key."

Lena smiles and closes her eyes. As different as their worlds might be, sometimes Gustav can read her perfectly.

"I'm a huge fan of your cayenne steaks," she says.

Jacobson turns around a corner farther down the corridor. When he spots Lena, he waves at her. He wants to talk.

"That's *Cajun*." Gustav laughs. "Prepare to be amazed."

"I miss you," Lena says softly.

"And I you," Gustav says. "See you soon."

Lena hangs up and looks at the phone in her hand. A few words are enough to shift the weights in the scales. When she left Gren's office, she felt dead on her feet; now she's awake and alert, as if skidding down the slopes of a serious caffeine rush. Being needed is still a new experience. One that is as comforting as it is addictive.

"Are you all right?" Jacobson asks when he reaches Lena. "You were in tatters when you left the nurse."

"He wouldn't have signed me out if he thought I were unable to work. That man fusses no end."

"That's his job," Jacobson says. "We should talk about what happened at the hospital."

"Everything's in my report."

"I'd rather hear it from you." Jacobson pauses. "I'm on your side, you know."

"That makes you part of a very small minority in this building."

"Look, I still think bringing Jimmy was irresponsible. And taking him along in the duct was even worse. But I can see the logic. And the fire alarm you discovered helps the case. That's what matters."

Not seeing any sign of mockery on Jacobson's face, Lena decides to take what he says at face value.

"We just might get along pretty well," Lena says after a moment. "Any leads yet?"

"Possibly. But we have another problem."

"I heard about the pictures. Too late to stop them now."

"It's something else."

Jacobson switches on his phone and gives it to Lena. When she turns it around and looks at the screen, the sense of relief she had felt after speaking with Gustav fades.

The phone displays part of a feed from a social media channel. Centred on the screen is a photo of the note she discovered next to the eyes of the victims. Below the image is a caption that describes the note as a clue in the murder. Farther down is the number of times the article has been shared. At the moment, the count stands at over thirty thousand.

"Who the fuck posted this?" Lena pinches the bridge of her nose. A new setback is the exact opposite of what she needs.

"Some kid with a good camera," Jacobson says. "We traced the postings back to her Facebook page."

"A woman?" Lena asks. "Is she in custody?"

"She's a fourteen-year-old Girl Scout who happened to be out taking photos for a school project. Bringing her in would have us burned at the stake for the worst public relations move of the decade. A patrol went to her home and had a word with her parents."

Lena rubs her face in frustration. Gren's comment about the note rings in her head. He had suggested that anyone interested in getting under the skin of another person connected to the hidden facility would want the message to spread. Now the words are out there.

"Do you think we're dealing with a killer who wants to be in the spotlight?" she asks Jacobson.

"He wouldn't be the first," Gren says behind Lena.

Lena jumps and spins around. She didn't hear Gren leave his office. Her weapon is tucked away in her locker, but that doesn't stop her from reaching for her empty holster. At the last moment, she raises her hand and scratches her chin. Gren is right; she needs to wind down.

"As I said," Gren continues, "you're taking the evening off. Leave the footwork to someone else for once." He looks at Lena pointedly and walks away.

Lena swallows the curse on her lips and walks in the other direction.

"Where are you going?" Jacobson calls after her.

"To a dinner date," Lena says over her shoulder. "And you're invited."

Chapter 19

Carl jerks awake and looks around his office.

He has dozed away most of the evening in his swivel chair. On the desk, his slim laptop has gone into sleep mode, tired of waiting for him to check his email. He had planned to go through his weekly overview of his stock market transactions and drifted off like some drooling vegetable at a care home. It is absolutely unacceptable.

His phone buzzes in the inner pocket of his suit jacket. He suspects its ringing pulled him out of his unplanned oblivion. Tonight, he's meant to have drinks at an acquaintance's rooftop terrace. He needs a solid espresso before leaving the house, or he might fall asleep during the event. A hit of caffeine, and perhaps a few grams of some even more potent substance.

Carl rises gingerly from the chair and takes the call.

"Sir?" his assistant asks. "I have some news."

"Be quick about it. I'm on my way out."

Carl crosses his office floor and takes his coat from a hanger. There is an excellent café a five-minute drive from his house. His kitchen is closer, but the company of other people will do him good.

"It's regarding the murders," the assistant says. "You asked me to inform you about how the case progresses. Of course, I can only relay what the media reports."

"I'm fully aware that you aren't a member of the Swedish police force," Carl snaps. "But I trust you've come across something of interest?"

"I'm sorry, sir." The assistant clears his throat. "The news story you asked me to keep an eye on is getting a lot of coverage, and there's an image that has been shared quite a lot. It's rumoured to be associated with the murders. There's no proof, although that hasn't stopped it from spreading."

"Does the image show the victims?" Carl asks.

Carl awaits the answer with trepidation. What little sleep he had was filled with faces and voices, and some of the more unpleasant ones were related to his work. He woke up surprised; decades have passed since his last nightmares.

"It's just a photograph," the assistant says. "It shows a piece of paper with what allegedly is a message from the killer. It was pinned to a tree, near the eyes."

Carl slows down in the corridor outside his office. "Whose eyes?"

"I thought you knew, sir. Rumours say the murderer took the eyeballs of his victims and hid them in a nearby forest. The note was found close to where they were discovered."

Carl stops. The Internet tends to amplify whispering games and turn trivial incidents into immense dramas, but stories with precise and quirky details can sometimes be true. No wonder the media is all over the case.

He turns around, walks back into his office, and wakes up his laptop. The night is not old yet. He can afford a few minutes to read up on this piece of news; it's likely to be the talk of the town soon.

"Why do people think a random note in a forest has anything to do with the murders?" Carl asks while the laptop starts up.

"My guess is that someone said it was," the assistant says. "Usually, that's all it takes. But we can make an effort to find out, if you would like us to?"

"Maybe later."

The agency from which he hires his assistants is impressive. They provide discreet and reliable drivers, secretaries and other kinds of support staff to those who can afford their services. For an additional charge, they deploy specialist teams that deal with more delicate tasks, such as fact-finding or cleaning up after parties that go off the rails. Nothing too advanced, but useful for everyday hiccups.

"Tell me what this note reads?" Carl asks. "My laptop is taking too long to boot up."

"Just a few words, sir. It might be a snippet from a poem."

"I really am on my way out," Carl says tersely.

"*Look deep and draw.*"

Carl's mind goes blank, as if his thoughts are plucked away by a spectral hand. The room tilts around him: the walls become ceiling, then floor, then opposite walls.

He throws out his hands to support himself, but he is too slow and slumps sideways down into the chair he woke up in just minutes ago. As he sits down, he knocks his laptop off the desk and onto the floor. It hits the floorboards in a burst of cracked plastic, but he registers the sound only as a distant thud.

"Are you all right, sir?" the assistant asks. "I thought I heard a crash."

"My computer," Carl mumbles. The room grows dim, the air darkening like thickening smoke.

An impossibility has become reality. No, a near impossibility. His entire being screams denial, but he has not climbed the ladder this high by giving in to wishful thinking. The scenario has never been completely incredible; the risk has always been there.

For many months, it existed at the very centre of his existence: a loose end, flailing free in the wind, threatening to unravel all his work at any moment and without warning. Every knock on the door made him sweat in fear, each phone call unnerved him to the point of breaking down.

But nothing happened. The project was shut down immediately, of course, but no policemen came for him in the night. Months turned to years, which stretched into decades. Still not a sign of the calamity he expected. Eventually, the whole episode became dreamlike, a bold vision compromised by a slip-up too ridiculous to be real. New ideas and fresh ventures waited. Success upon success helped to erase the memory of a fateful mistake.

But the past has a tendency to leak through the fabric of the current at the strangest of times. Sudden recollections triggered by scents, pictures of long-gone moments resurrected with the help of a laugh. The darker aspects of history are especially cunning. Like mould or rot, they always find a way inside.

And now, a blunder he thought suffocated by the weight of uncountable days is holding a suburb in fear.

"Sir?" The assistant raises his voice. "If your computer is broken, I can call for the cleaners and–"

"Fuck the laptop," Carl breathes. He presses his free hand against his brow and forces the office back into focus.

The assistant pauses. "I'm sorry?"

"Keep tracking the story. Call me back as soon as anything happens."

He ends the call, stands up, and pulls the curtains apart; the oppressive darkness fills the room like a filthy liquid. He needs new perspectives.

Outside the window, the branches of his apple trees are heavy with fruit, but not a single one lies on the grass. The gardeners swoop in to snatch away any stray apples that might blemish the perfection.

The garden's grandeur is upheld only because of Carl's attention. The view from his office is superficial eye candy. Peel away the lawn, and it will reveal a patch of dirt and roots. So much effort is spent on maintaining the sheen of excellence, but without the work to smooth over the ugliness of unkemptness, nature wins. One must smooth every wrinkle if perfection is to be upheld.

Carl slowly places the phone on the desk and exhales. There is only so much he can ask his assistant to do. For tasks that require increased discretion, there are other agencies operating in groups or as individuals. Contact details to such individuals are passed around between trusted friends who need to protect themselves and who have the money to do so.

Such services come at a dear price. Sometimes, their toll on one's conscience can outstrip the financial price tag.

He has collected a handful of these numbers for many years. But while he keeps them within easy reach, they have remained a resource too extreme to consider putting into use. Merely a day ago, he took them out just to be reassured that in a world growing wilder by the second, there are ways to deal with the worst kinds of crises. As if he stored a lion in his basement, a beast whose presence infused him with comfort but which never could be turned loose.

It seems the time has come to set the beast free.

With shaking hands, he retrieves the notebook for the second time in forty-eight hours. He finds the right number, raises his phone, and punches in the sequence that will open the cage.

He is not surprise when a voicemail answers on the other end. The friendly female voice explains that the garage port installation firm is closed, but that they are happy to take a message.

"My name is Carl Adlerberg," Carl says after the beep. "I have a situation."

"Go on." A calm voice, this time male.

"The investigation into a double murder in Norra Ängby is headed by a detective called Lena Franke. I want her movements reported back to me continually via email."

"Do you want the contents of the actual case?" the man asks.

"I only need to know her location." Hopefully, this will be sufficient to give him ample warning if the detective is getting too close.

"Is it likely that the assignment will get more advanced?" the man wonders.

Carl closes his eyes and leans his brow against the cool windowpane. *More advanced.* The two innocent words describe the shift from surveillance to assassination.

For the second time in his life, he faces imminent catastrophe, and all he can do is move as fast as possible. That way he might be able to dictate fate, rather than the other way around. Even if doing so requires bloodshed.

"Yes," Carl says. "That's quite likely."

Chapter 20

Central Stockholm

Thursday

22:29

Lena drives over Tranebergsbron, a long, winding bridge that empties its load of traffic into Stockholm's sprawling carpet of southern suburbs. Jacobson sits next to her and taps at his phone. He followed Lena to her car with an expression that almost could be read as sulking; he would prefer to be somewhere else, but just like her, he is too invested in the case to leave it alone.

Suggesting that Jacobson come with her was an impromptu excuse for working for as long as she can without directly contradicting Gren's instructions. Only when she turned the ignition did she realise that Gustav might not appreciate the added company. Then again, Gustav is both intelligent and understanding. His job must have made him used to quick changes, and the investigation is at a critical phase.

"Finally," Jacobson says and swipes at his phone. "A little progress."

"If I lean over to look," Lena says, "we'll go off the bridge, which will be annoying and probably leave us very dead. So please tell me what you've found."

"I put an assistant on checking the factory name of the fire alarm," Jacobson says. "It took him three minutes to find that the company folded in the early nineties."

"Any luck with the paper trace?" Lena asks and changes lanes. "There's a serial number on the piece I took. If we get hold of a record of the shipment, we might be able to track where it was delivered."

"The business has been deregistered," Jacobson says, "but the files still exist. I spoke with the current owner of the trademark earlier today. Every tax return and invoice is stored in a storage facility just outside of the city."

"Oh, joy."

"But the assistant who's on the job got hold of the keys," Jacobson continues. "He's on his way there now."

"Impressive. Remind me to get him a coffee one day."

"That might come across as a threat rather than a reward."

"What's that supposed to mean?" Lena asks.

"Some days I wonder if the automatic coffee machines at work are meant to test our resilience to oil spills."

"I mean a real coffee, obviously. As in one from a café." Lena looks at Jacobson from the corner of her eye. "Was that an actual attempt at a joke?"

"No wonder you made detective at twenty-eight." Jacobson glances at her, smiles drily, and continues to scroll on his phone.

Lena frowns at the road while she overtakes a car. As far as she can tell, Jacobson is thoughtful, but also keen to be more informal. Hence the unexpected pun.

"What about the glass?" Lena asks.

It's a long shot, but until they have any idea who bought the fire alarm, she's ready to put every iota of dust from the hospital under the microscope.

"Nothing yet," Jacobson says. "The lab wasn't exactly pleased to run a full analysis on what they think is broken tableware. Why did you pick it up?"

"To be honest, it was almost by accident." Lena sighs. "Jimmy was rummaging around in the grime. I was worried he would cut his hands open."

Jacobson is silent for a moment.

"You take a civilian – a possible suspect, even," he says slowly, "into a room in which a murderer might hide, and you're concerned he might hurt himself on a shard of glass?"

"What's so strange about that?" Lena asks.

"Your work ethos is likely to leave you without a job one day."

"Or it might leave me without something I'd miss much more." Lena sighs. "I'm not a robot, Jacobson. Jimmy went through a bad ordeal down there. That was my fault, and I feel awful for it."

To make matters worse, Gren wants to come down hard on Jimmy. Bring him back for more questioning, perhaps even arrest him. He thinks Lena's trust in Jimmy is misplaced, and try as she might, no rational excuse to protect him comes to her mind.

Her sole reason is that inexplicable as it is, she likes the sardonic misfit. And Jimmy does not fit in the puzzle. By now, he should either have tried to kill her or confessed.

"I heard you spoke with Jimmy before Gren released him?" Lena asks.

"Only briefly," Jacobson says, just as his phone beeps. "One moment. It's the lab."

Jacobson takes the call, murmurs for half a minute, and hangs up. Lena can sense his surprise when he turns back to her.

"The lab found traces of chemicals on the vial," Jacobson says.

"Anything surprising?" Lena asks, already anticipating the answer.

"It's a drug. Some kind of hallucinogenic, and an extremely addictive one. They're running more tests to pin down the exact type. That isn't what I would've expected."

A tremendous weight rolls off Lena's shoulders. When she had dreamed up long stairs and shooting ranges, her visions felt real. But a narcotic substance in the air explains everything. It also might mean she has inhaled something that will prove dangerous in the long term, but knowing that there is a reason for the bizarre phantasms is a dizzying relief.

"Can they match the stuff against any particular product?" Lena asks.

"They're trying to." Jacobson taps his fingers against the glove compartment. "What do you think that facility was?"

"Some failed experiment." Lena slows down at a red light. "Fifty years ago, Sweden had some pretty nasty ideas on how to treat mentally ill. It isn't a secret that lobotomies were all the rage a while back."

"The rooms sure felt old," Jacobson says, still frowning.

"But not old enough?" Lena asks. "I agree. I'd say the seventies or eighties."

"Can I ask you a personal question?"

Lena laughs sharply. "Most think of my personal life as a funny meme."

"Is that a yes?" Jacobson asks, frowning.

"For God's sake, out with it."

"Won't your date be uncomfortable with me joining you at the table?"

"We're going to my place," Lena says, "so the table in question is my rickety almost-large-enough-for-four-people desk in my cramped kitchen. Also, we're cooking at home."

"That's not really an answer," Jacobson notes.

"You're quite the detective too. Don't worry. He'll understand." Lena's phone buzzes in her pocket just as she negotiates a busy crossing. "Hold on, someone's calling."

She takes the call without checking the display. "Franke."

"We have to talk."

A few seconds pass before Lena recognises Jimmy's voice. His words are clipped and muffled.

"I'm glad you called," Lena says. "I have a few questions for you." She mouths *Jimmy* to Jacobson.

"Not as many as I've got." Jimmy laughs, but his voice is tight. "Can we catch up?" he asks. "Maybe back at the station. Somewhere not in the open."

"Questions first," Lena says. "Let's start with this one: how the hell did you get hold of my number?"

"You're in the phone book," Jimmy says after a short pause.

"Not any book you have access to."

"Fine," Jimmy concedes. "I might have looked over Jacobson's shoulder when he tried to call you at the police station. Can we get back to how we sit down and talk?"

"This is a bad time. Why did you cover for me in your statement?" She decides to save the more mysterious question for later: how come Jimmy knew exactly what to say.

"I'll tell you later. Look, I saw the pictures of you online. They're on every channel."

"That's my headache."

"And I've also seen the photo of the note," Jimmy continues, almost hissing as he speaks. "Do you know what happens if you type those words into a fairly well-known search engine?"

"Obviously," Lena says, "that's the reason we came knocking."

"That's what I mean. But in difference to you, I *am* in the bloody white pages, so anyone who wants to pay me a visit can just look up where I live. That includes murderous fucking psychopaths with kitchen knives."

Lena shakes her head in irritation. Jimmy is understandably nervous and has answers she needs, but she can't see him right now.

A solution comes to her. It's obvious, straightforward and painful, and Gustav will think that she has gone mad. Finding time alone with him seems to be a puzzle harder than any she has encountered so far.

"Meet me at home," she says.

Jacobson's eyes widen as Lena rattles off her address and the code to the building's front door. When she hangs up, he presses his fingertips to his temples.

"Did you just invite a suspect to your own residence?" he asks.

"Calling my flat a residence is like referring to a tree hut as a palace." Lena shoves her phone down into her pocket. "Besides, Jimmy is Gren's suspect, not mine."

"He'll go ballistic. Gren, I mean."

"Only if he finds out. And you're not going to rat me out."

"Why?" Jacobson wonders. "Will you cancel our date if I tell on you?"

Lena glances at Jacobson in mild surprise. She was right; there is an edge to her otherwise dull, textbook-shackled colleague. That's a relief.

"No, but you had every chance to interrupt and stop me," Lena says. "And I think you're too curious not to talk to Jimmy."

Jacobson sighs. "He's a rude, loudmouthed smartarse, but if he is embroiled in the murders, he would've come clean by now. So I think he's telling the truth."

Lena nods. Hopefully, Jimmy is the troubled, threadbare artist he appears to be and not a conspiring killer. If he is, the evening is bound to become interesting.

Chapter 21

Carl paces along the bottom of his garden while he waits for an update. On one side, his immaculate lawn stretches away up to his house, while the canal flows on his other side like a bared vein. Crossing the grounds from fence to fence takes thirty-three seconds on average.

He has timed the distance over fifty times over the past hour. If any of his neighbours are watching him, they must correctly think he's going through a crisis, although they cannot imagine its scope. But the walking helps, and there's no one within earshot.

After explaining his problem to the man on the phone, Carl received a set of curt instructions. Payment in cash is to be delivered within an hour to a downtown location specified only minutes before the drop-off is due. A task easy and innocent enough to be handled by his regular assistant. All contact will take place via phone numbers, updated after every call. No face-to-face meetings, no written communication, no questions outside those which concern the assignment.

He reaches the end of the garden and turns around to walk back. Leaving the house would be more sensible. He could secure enough money to see him through the next twenty years and go into hiding, perhaps on the French Riviera or the Italian countryside. But then he would be distanced from the developments. He always goes toe to toe with problems. Meet every doubt head-on and choke it with logic.

This approach is the joker waiting up his sleeve. The tactic has never failed him. It helped him amass a fortune and revolutionise a small but lucrative niche in medicine. It also enabled him to survive in the wine cellar when he moved into the house.

Perhaps he will go there again. But not until the state of affairs is truly cataclysmic.

His phone rings. An anonymous caller. The call is a blessing and a curse: while he craves news, it means something vital has happened. He stops next to an antique sundial and takes the call.

"Carl speaking."

"We have the name and address of the individual who first posted the photograph of the note. Please advise on further action."

The man calling is the same person Carl spoke to earlier. He walks slowly around the sundial while he thinks. So they have managed to trace the image back to its origin. Directing his anger that way is tempting but pointless; the damage is already done, and the person in question might not know anything beyond the note itself. And every action Carl requests will cost him more, both in terms of money and stress.

Of course, the one who posted the images may be the actual murderer, but that is unlikely. The crime scene and the subsequent discovery in the forest are not warnings or messages. They are twisted expressions of memories. This is Carl's area of expertise. The killer does not want to be found; he is unable to resist framing his creation in what he felt was a fitting manner.

And the killer is without question male. Were it not for the ability of time to dilute and distort his memory, he would even be able to put a face on the perpetrator. After all, there is only one candidate.

"Please advise on further action," the man on the phone repeats.

"Watch him," Carl says, "but keep your distance."

"The individual in question is a female teenager."

"Ah. Never mind, then. Have you found out anything else?"

"We have discovered the same words on a different website, although we're not sure if it's linked to the picture you asked us to research."

"What kind of website?" Carl stops.

"A photography blog. The words in the photo match the caption of one of the pictures. They look drawn or painted, possibly on a wall."

Carl closes his eyes. Were it not for the image that currently flies around the Internet, he would disbelieve what the man is telling him. First a murderer on the loose. Now an intruder who has delved into Carl's greatest secret. One demon from the past, and one from the present.

"We have the address of the individual who runs the website," the man says. "It appears to be a one-person project. Please advise."

Carl opens his eyes. He will meet this problem too head-on. And as with all challenges, one must pick out the most painful snags first.

"Remove him," Carl says. "As quickly as possible. But make sure it's definite."

Chapter 22

Some fifteen minutes later, Lena stands in the doorway to her kitchen and watches Jimmy inspect the barely controlled chaos that fills most spaces in her flat.

Jimmy was waiting outside her entrance when they arrived. *I was in the neighbourhood*, he said. *Thought I'd lay low for a while at a friend's. That's why I got all the food, see?* It was an odd coincidence, but not so strange it screamed outright lie, so she let him in.

The loaded plastic bag Jimmy brought turns out to contain a great number of smaller bags filled with fresh vegetables, multi-coloured pastes, ground spice, brown rice, large potatoes, and other foodstuff Lena doesn't recognize. Jimmy doesn't seem the type to splash money on luxurious food. Jacobson even demands to examine the contents, in case Jimmy brought any drugs.

Jimmy proceeds to unpack a crisp chef's apron, which he puts on with a flair that suggested a lot of practise. He switches on all the hotplates on Lena's stove, opens a drawer, and closes it.

"What in the world," Lena asks slowly, "do you think you are doing?"

"Soup." Jimmy rummages among the food on the table and looks up at Lena. "You don't mind, do you?"

"Seeing as you've already started, go ahead and help yourself."

Lena rests her head against the wall. This was meant to be a quiet evening. She has even been ordered to keep it that way.

"Dinner will be ready in a moment," Jimmy says. "If I can get started, that is. Has there been a burglar here, or is your kitchen really this underequipped?" He opens another drawer and rams it shut with a sigh.

"All the cooking tools are in that cupboard." Lena points behind Jimmy. "I don't use them much."

"You don't look like a fast-food kind of person," Jimmy says while he rummages in the cupboard.

"I get my dinners from restaurants near work."

"Every single day?" Jimmy's face is mock-aghast. "That's just gross – what the hell is this?" He taps his foot against a huge plastic jar on the floor.

"Protein supplement. Probably won't go well with your soup, so leave it alone."

So far, letting Jimmy into her home has not revealed him as a frothing murderer, but his transformation into hyperactive chef is disturbing in itself. For a while she almost thinks it's an act meant to distract her, although if he is faking it, he's putting on a superb performance.

"How about telling me the real reason you're here?" she asks after a while.

"I saw the pictures of the note and decided to call you," Jimmy says over his shoulder. "Someone can track that right back to me. Actually, I think I was being followed for a while, but I shook them off."

It's an odd coincidence, but not so strange it screams outright lie. The nature of Jimmy's supposed stalkers are easy to guess: they are the officers Gren has charged with monitoring Jimmy after he left headquarters. Apparently Jimmy managed to lose them, or they would be on her doorstep by now.

She should call Gren and let him know that Jimmy is with her, but Gren might want Jimmy brought back to the station, which would kill off any trust Jimmy has in her. Hopefully, Jacobson will keep quiet about Jimmy's presence.

The doorbell rings. Lena prepares to explain why she's not alone and opens the door.

"Hey," Gustav says, beaming at Lena. "I hope you're hungry, because I brought–" His smile freezes in place when he looks over Lena's shoulder.

"Oh," he says. "You have company." His tone is not unfriendly, but openly tense.

"I'm sorry." Lena makes a pained face. "Work followed me home today. I had no idea it'd happen when you and I spoke on the phone. It's complicated."

Gustav slowly lowers the bags to the floor. When he looks back up, his attitude is easy and relaxed, but she has known him long enough to tell that he's irritated.

"To most people," Gustav says with a calm laugh, "overtime means a few hours in front of a laptop. Not having two detectives in your kitchen."

Jimmy fails to keep down a chortle, which earns him a stern look from Jacobson.

"This is Detective Jacobson," Lena says and gestures at her colleague. All stiff professionalism, Jacobson rises and shakes Gustav's hand. "And the brooding man in the apron is Jimmy. He's helping with an ongoing – well, job."

Jimmy waves his spoon at Gustav by way of greeting and goes back to stirring his soup.

An unexpected insight strikes Lena as she watches the three men eyeing one another as they wait for someone to speak. She has always been irrationally drawn to alpha types. Men who take shortcuts and break rules to have their way, stopping for few and respecting fewer. Some have been blatantly pushy and forward. Others have been more modest, but just as driven.

Tall, physically intimidating and gunning for a management role at his company, Gustav is a prime example: a tight bundle of ambition with a sprinkling of gentleness. And as he looks between

144

Jacobson and Jimmy, Lena expects both her colleague and the scrawny photographer to back down. Not in a dramatic or even obvious way, but on the hushed level that signals deference to a stronger specimen: changed body languages, some nervous smiles, a few cleared throats.

But Jacobson and Jimmy run right against her expectations. Jacobson returns Gustav's look with the cool air of a scientist who has happened to come across an unusual creature. And while Jimmy is more skittish than Jacobson, he studies Gustav with bemused interest, as if keen to see what happens next. There are no traces of nervousness on either man's face.

Trapped in the middle, Lena wishes she could run out of her flat and head straight back to the office. The stillness in her kitchen as the three men size each other up is familiar: it's the kind of tension that can spiral out of control, even in the most civilized circumstances.

This evening is promising to be an absolute garage fire.

Just before the atmosphere becomes unbearable, Gustav takes a step back and motions at Lena to come closer. Lena leaves the kitchen, closes the door behind her, and joins Gustav in the small hall.

"Look," Gustav says.

Lena closes her eyes and nods slowly. She knows what he will say.

"Don't worry," Gustav continues. "I get it. Sometimes, my days are the same." He opens his arms, inviting her.

"I know." Lena leans her head against his chest. She would bet her teeth that Gustav's days are nothing like hers.

"You're leaving," she murmurs.

"Only for now." Gustav hesitates as he searches for words, but eventually settles for a textbook excuse. "I don't want to get in the way of your work. I'd feel awkward, and I wouldn't be able to contribute. Unless you're dealing with a design agency exec on a rampage, that is."

Lena's plea for him to stay dies on her lips. Gustav is right: he would feel uncomfortable, and she needs to hack away at the case. There will not be a moment of rest in her life until the bastard is locked up.

"I thought not," Gustav says, trying to end their one-minute date on a humorous note. "See you later. Hopefully soon."

He gives Lena a light kiss on her cheek and closes the door behind him.

Lena stands motionless while the sensation of Gustav's touch fades from her skin. It's a pale shadow of the intimacy she hoped for. Half a year is barely enough to see the outline of most people, but Gustav is familiar enough for her to lose herself in his company when the evening sinks into night. His physical presence is heady. Near him, she can escape the constant churning in her head.

Now he has left. For understandable reasons, and perhaps for good.

She snaps out of her downward spiral. There will be a better time to deal with her mounting frustration over her inability to manage a normal relationship, let alone a regular life. In any other situation like this, she would head for the basement gym and let the steel drain her of all thoughts, but her present company makes that impossible.

She takes the bags Gustav left behind and returns to the kitchen. If she cannot have a moment's pleasure or peace of mind, she will at least have answers.

"Do what you can with this." Lena drops the food at Jimmy's feet. "When we've eaten, you will tell me what happened after I switched on that lamp."

*

After thirty minutes spent in tongue-tied near-silence, Lena and her two impromptu guests finish their meals and push their plates away. It had been a series of dishes fit for any decent restaurant. Jacobson raises his eyebrows and looks at Jimmy.

"Young and male," Jacobson says. "Lives alone, dresses in black and spends his spare time in tunnels. I thought you'd be limited to microwaving leftovers."

"I nearly screwed up the steaks." Jimmy sniffs at the stove. "But I blame the tools at hand. And I guess I'm a bit distracted, too."

"Are you a hobbyist chef as well as a photographer?" Lena asks.

She ate too fast to register any actual taste, and the absence of Gustav hangs over her like a leaden blanket. Still, she did notice Jimmy's skills at the cutting board.

"One of the few useful perks the army left me with," Jimmy says. "Is there any more wine?"

"You're an ex-soldier?" Jacobson asks.

"Not in Sweden," Lena guesses. If Jimmy has a military background, it would have been flagged in the background check.

"Very much past tense," Jimmy says. "Two years in a Finnish regiment. I worked in a field kitchen. And no, I'm not traumatized or on the run."

He sighs, sits back in his chair, and looks tiredly between Lena and Jacobson as if expecting them to bombard him with questions.

"But you went through basic training?" Jacobson asks.

"Only the mandatory parts. I needed a job, and there was an opening."

Jacobson shoots Lena a quick look. Finland's military force is renowned throughout Scandinavia and many other parts of the world for its rigorous, unforgiving training. Its body is not made up of sickly reeds like Jimmy, who more looks like someone in dire need of a solid meal as well as a ground-up health check.

"So you left for a career in night-time photography?" Lena asks.

"I got ill." Jimmy finishes his wine. "Lost a lot of weight and needed more than five hours of sleep every night. A chronic condition. Not lethal, but enough to leave me winded from walking up three storeys."

"That must be a challenge when you're out shooting pictures," Jacobson says.

"Only when I have to climb. Which happens more often than you might think."

"You're full of surprises, aren't you?" Jacobson asks.

"Says the detective who plays jazz." Jimmy puts his glass down and looks at Jacobson.

"Who plays what?" Lena asks.

Her thoughts were rushing back and forth between the case and Gustav's departure, but the new turn in the conversation brings her back to the present.

"Your friend in arms here is a pianist," Jimmy says, smiling at Jacobson. "Ask him."

"It's just a pastime thing," Jacobson says. "For unwinding and relaxing. But I'm curious to learn how you're aware of what I do outside of my job?" He gives Jimmy a look that suggests that he had better answer the question.

"Wait." Lena holds up a hand. "Can someone fill me in here?"

"He taps out beats all the time," Jimmy says and points at Jacobson's hands. "I know a polyrhythm when I hear one, which kind of narrows down the options. Pianos are rare in metal. Hence, he plays jazz."

Jacobson nods slowly. "I guess the bands in the posters on your wall are a bit more advanced than I would've thought."

"Colour me impressed," Lena says. Jimmy appears to be much more observant than she has given him credit for.

"It's none of my business," Jacobson says, "but I'm sorry that your boyfriend chose to leave. I assume he didn't expect us here?"

Lena considers telling Jacobson that her private life is exactly that: private. Then again, Jacobson looks genuinely apologetic. Even Jimmy manages to keep his sardonic expression in check.

"He'll come around," Lena says. "Now that I can think about anything other than food, tell me what happened when the light came on."

Lena focuses on Jimmy. His explanation might not sway the investigation, but she must know how quickly she passed out and why he backed her story.

"Things went crazy." Jimmy says curtly and looks out the window.

"I'm hoping for more specifics," Lena says.

"Those flashes made me stumble around the room like an idiot. I've no idea how much time passed in there. For a moment, I thought I saw – things. Unpleasant things."

"Go on," Lena says, hoping she doesn't look as anxious as she feels.

"Then everything went totally black. And just after that, he shows up." Jimmy points at Jacobson.

"He shut the lamp down," Jimmy continues. "You were on the floor right next to me," he says to Lena. "And you were out cold. Before I had time to remember where I was, there were cops all over the place, barking orders and shoving me around."

Lena studies Jimmy as he speaks. His face is the perfect blank of someone working hard to keep it that way. He is holding back, just like Gren. I have become a hazard best handled gently.

"I need to know what you saw," Lena says slowly. "You supported my statement, even though you had no idea what I'd said. Tell us what happened. Please," she adds after a moment.

Jimmy opens his mouth to speak and sighs heavily. He rubs his face with his hands and peers between his fingers at Lena.

"You'll think I'm nuts," he says quietly. "All right, but I need to know that you won't charge me with anything or drag me back to the station."

"We don't make that call," Lena says. "But I'll do what I can."

She thinks back to Gren's grim look when they discussed Jimmy. Then there were Jimmy's might-be stalkers. The photographer is still on her superintendent's radar, but there is no need to raise that here and now.

"Fair enough." Jimmy steals Jacobson's wineglass and sits back on his chair. "When you switched on that damned machine, I tried to find the exit, but the light was too strong. It was like being inside a sun gone insane. Then I started to see things."

"What kind of things?" A cold wind travels down Lena's back.

"Shadows, mostly." Jimmy shrugs. "They looked like people, only they moved wrong. Gracefully, like dancers, although I knew I was as good as dead if they got their hands on me. This sounds right off the planet, I know."

"Less so than you think," Lena says quietly. "Those flashes made it easy to imagine things," she adds when she sees Jacobson glance at her.

"I must've spent several minutes staggering around looking for the door," Jimmy continues, "thinking that I'd be stabbed in the back any moment."

"Did you find the way out?" Jacobson asks.

"Eventually, and I was sure that you'd found it too," Jimmy says to Lena. "So I threw myself through the doorway and pushed the door shut. That's when I realised I had no light. Right after that, I heard you scream and fire your gun. I reckoned you thought you were being attacked. Or that there was someone in there after all."

Lena nods. She had thought exactly that, but not because of vague silhouettes on the concrete walls. Her shadows had perfect voices and lifelike faces. The darkness had worn masks and spoke of secrets. As soon as the lab figures out what kind of insidious drug she inhaled, she'll ask them if there's any risk of flashbacks.

"We heard the shots all the way to where we were standing," Jacobson says. "In fact, the bangs helped the response team find their way through the duct, which was a good thing. Otherwise they'd still be crawling around down there. I charged Gunilla with watching over the manager, then went in and followed the response team. I was through in less than a minute."

"So you stayed outside the room in case you'd get shot?" Lena asks Jimmy.

"Actually, I went back inside." Jimmy looks uncomfortable. "And wasn't that a mistake. I thought being prepared for the flashes would help, but it was just as bad the second time around. Before I could see you, I passed out. I'm glad you turned up," he adds to Jacobson.

"The response and I found both of you just behind the metal chairs," Jacobson says. "It took me a while to shut the lamp off. Norling came close to shooting it to pieces."

Lena digests the new information in silence. Only luck saved Jimmy; if he still had been in the room when she opened fire, he could have been resting on a metal stretcher now.

"Hey." Jimmy sits up and searches one of his trouser pockets. "Can't believe I almost forgot. I found this in the rubbish on the floor where you came across that broken glass."

Jimmy places a strip of gleaming brown plastic on the table. It's as narrow as a pencil and as long as his lower arm. Jacobson and Lena lean in for a closer view.

"It's from a cassette," Jacobson says. "Why didn't you hand this over when you were interviewed?"

"I was so stressed out I forgot." Jimmy frowns at Jacobson. "Seriously, I could barely remember my street address back then. I'm giving it to you now, so give it a rest."

"We need to play it," Lena says. The snippet of tape is another hard lead.

"There's a cassette player at headquarters," Jacobson says. "Or at least there should be. I can't say that I've seen one, come to think about it."

"I am not going back there tonight." Lena rises from the table. "Gren will lock me in a cell if he catches me working now. He was wearing his serious face when he spoke to me." She gets her phone from her jacket.

"I can probably chase down a friend who has one," Jimmy says.

"We appreciate that you want to help us," Jacobson says, "but this is police work."

"Funny how that seems to depend on whether or not you *need* my help." Jimmy leans back on the chair and crosses his arms.

"Don't worry," Lena says. "I've got this."

She scrolls through the list of contacts on her phone and tries to shut out the two bickering men in her kitchen. Both Jacobson and Jimmy are right: Jimmy has already been dragged far enough into the investigation to have Lena sacked. But after their visit to the hospital, Jimmy deserves to know how this ends, and Jacobson or Gren can disagree as much as they want.

"Have you got a cassette player here?" Jacobson asks.

"I got rid of my last one fifteen years ago." Lena finds the number she's looking for and dials it. "But I know just where to borrow one."

Chapter 23

There is a gentle knock on Lena's door less than two minutes later. When she opens the door, her view is filled with the Herculean frame of Hugo, her downstairs neighbour. Cradled in his arms is a battered portable stereo that had been cutting edge in the early eighties.

Articulate, calm and crowned with the wispy curls of a frantic orchestra conductor, Hugo's meek looks are offset by the hulking physicality of an ambitious bodybuilder. Most people file him away on sight as a mid-forties potential lunatic. Having known him for half a decade, Lena knows he is fond of sparkling wine and uneasy around spiders. She has also been under his careful supervision for the past three years in their shared makeshift basement gym.

"I came as soon as I could," Hugo says with a wide smile. "Why the phone call?" He holds out the portable stereo to Lena.

"It was faster." Lena smiles back and takes the stereo. "We would've come over to yours and saved you the hassle of unplugging it, but–"

Hugo raises a hand and winks at her. "It's about secrecy. I understand. And not everyone can say they've helped a detective. By the way, I also brought an old cassette you can destroy. Is that what you asked for?" He hands Lena a cassette in a plastic case.

"Perfect. Thanks, Hugo. I'm happy you still had the stereo. I remember seeing it in the gym a while back, but I wasn't sure if you'd thrown it away."

"I'm selling it. Collectors pay a lot for these. Let me know when you're done, and I'll pick it up. Oh, hi there." Hugo waves at someone behind Lena.

Lena looks over her shoulder. Behind her, Jimmy leans out of the kitchen and stares at Hugo.

"One of your colleagues, I take it?" Hugo nods and smiles at Jimmy. "Nice to meet you, Detective. Right, I'll get out of your hair. Good luck with whatever you're doing."

"He's not a coll – never mind," Lena says. "I owe you one."

"Just keep practicing your squats. I'll catch you later."

Lena says goodbye, closes the door, and opens the plastic cassette.

"I have some sticky tape," she says to Jacobson. "Let's see if we can edit in what Jimmy found and play it."

"This block must be a burglar's nightmare." Jimmy looks incredulous. "That guy is a monster."

"He's an athlete." Lena hands Jacobson the tape, a pair of scissors, and a roll of sticky tape.

"Like a brick wall on legs," Jimmy insists. "And then there's you, too. Must be something in the water around here. What's that you said about the basement?"

"We have our gym next to the boiler room," Lena says. "A bench, a few bars, three dozen plates and a permanent smell of mould. Everything the body needs."

She scoops coffee into the brewer. This is set to be a long evening, and she is far too wired to sleep anyway.

"How much can you actually lift?" Jimmy asks.

"On a good day?" Lena shrugs. "Around one hundred and sixty kilos."

"And on a bad day?"

"A little more. Let's get down to the matter at hand. How's that tape coming along, Jacobson?"

"Shouldn't take long," Jacobson says.

Just as the last of the coffee drips down into the pot, Jacobson hands the cassette back to Lena.

"We can try," he says. "With a little luck, the new strip Jimmy gave us won't break. It must be quite old. I can't even promise I put the tape in the right way, so we might be hearing the recording backwards."

"Here goes." Lena snaps the cassette into place, makes sure the volume is turned up, and hits play.

The cassette starts to spin. Given the length of the tape, the piece Jimmy found will only last for a few seconds, but what they hear might be vital to the investigation.

She is prepared for a range of sounds: some old tune, the voice of a doctor, recorded instructions for a medical procedure or anything in between. The sound will be an echo of actions long gone, but it might hold an important clue.

What she is not ready for is the harrowing screech that blasts from the speakers.

The wail shoots through the tense silence in her flat like a knife through cotton. Jimmy scrambles away from the table and presses his hands to his ears. Jacobson jerks backwards so fast he almost topples the chair. Lena stands still, but only because shock has pinned her to the kitchen floor.

Sharp and deafening, the scream rises in pitch and grows almost animalistic, but it's not a horse or a pig that makes the agonizing sound. She is certain of one thing: as impossible as it seems, the noise comes from a human being. Someone in tremendous pain or who is terrified beyond words.

"Fucking hell," Jimmy shouts. "Turn it down."

Lena lowers the volume, but the damage is done: her nerves are set on edge so sharply a cold sweat breaks along her neck. All chances of sleep over the next twenty-four hours are thoroughly gone.

Without warning, the scream fades away and is replaced by a calm voice.

Now use your pen, a woman says. *Hurry, before the images fade. Show me what you see. Pay attention to detail.*

The voice is placid and methodological, but at the same time strict and commanding. It sounds to Lena like an old-fashioned schoolteacher, distanced and severe. She does not recognise it.

Next is a hushed whisper, whimpering incoherently, followed by a soft, irregular scratching. The murmuring is too quiet for Lena to make out any words. She can't even tell if it's a man or a woman, but the scraping sound is familiar.

"What's that noise?" Jacobson mumbles and moves closer. "Clawing? Or footsteps?"

Lena's mouth is dry. Her head is light and hot: two sure harbingers of a severe headache. Pieces of the puzzle slam home so quickly she reels with the insight.

"It's a pen," she says. "Someone is drawing on paper."

"Why would they–" Jimmy begins, but his question is cut off by a new howl, this time so wild and uninhibited that Lena reflexively back-pedals out of the room. The scream lasts for a few seconds before it abruptly turns into an upbeat mid-eighties disco track.

Jacobson slaps the stop button, and silence rushes back in. After a moment, he unplugs the power cord.

"I see," Jacobson says after a long moment. He looks at the stereo as if it might decide to start up again of its own volition.

"I really don't." Jimmy swallows and shifts on his chair. "That was the worst sound I've ever heard. Can someone tell me what the hell's happening here?"

"This is a guess," Lena says, "but I think that's a recording from the hospital. And they're making people draw pictures. Don't ask me why."

She runs her hands through her hair and tugs it back, trying to force her concentration into submission. The path is laid. She must just walk down it.

"So far," Lena says, "we have a walled-off facility. Add in the removal of the labels on the furniture, the metal hoops on the chairs and that damned lamp, and it's safe to say that those rooms weren't meant to be found. Then there are the drugs, plus possible residual chemicals."

"What drugs?" Jimmy's eyes widen.

"Probably nothing dangerous," Lena continues. "Well, I hope they aren't. But they were enough to tip us over the edge when the flashing started." Or at least it had done so to her.

"Perhaps that's why they evacuated and sealed off the facility?" Jacobson suggests. "There could've been an uncontrollable leak."

Lena shakes her head. "That steel door was not put up in an instant, and they wouldn't have had time to tidy up. Besides, anything airborne would've spread through the ventilation to other parts of the complex."

She pauses. If the unknown substance in the smashed vial is behind her hallucinations, it could have escaped the rooms into the corridors where Jacobson and everyone else were waiting, as well as members of the staff. And it should have done so over decades. The more she considers the idea, the less plausible it seems.

"Now we've got this recording," Lena says, "of a person scared out of his or her mind, and who is told to make pictures. Maybe while sitting at one of those benches. What does this add up to?"

"Some form of bizarre hypnotherapy," Jacobson ventures. "A hushed-up experiment, maybe."

"My thought exactly. I'm going to wring that manager until he squeals." Lena shudders at the memory of the scream on the tape. No wonder those rooms were meant to be kept under wraps.

"I'm not sure the manager knows anything," Jacobson says. "He's new in his role, but the recording is old. Just like the facility."

"We'll see. I know his type. Rattle the possibility of a few months in prison in front of his pasty face, and he'll unload his dirtiest laundry without thinking."

"I feel like throwing up." Jimmy is still staring at the stereo. "I've never heard a scream that creepy."

"That's because it's genuine," Lena says. "But what we *haven't* got is anything that'll help us find the murderer."

Her phone buzzes. She picks it up and checks the display.

"It's Gren," she says. "Perhaps he has some good news." She takes the call. "Franke."

"Get in your car," Gren shouts. In the background is a cacophony of sirens, agitated voices, and roaring engines.

Lena moves the phone away from her ear and winces. Jacobson and Jimmy frown when they see her expression.

"What's going on?" Lena asks. "I thought I was on mandatory leave?"

"Drive to Jimmy Franzen's address as fast as you can. There's a nationwide warrant out for him. If he gets in touch, set up a meeting so we can nail the fucking bastard."

Lena almost lowers the phone to look at it in disbelief. It's the first time she has heard her superintendent forget his safe-for-work vocabulary.

"A warrant?" Lena's head grows light. "Since when?"

"Since just now."

"I told you he's not a primary suspect." Lena can't help glancing at Jimmy, who looks stunned.

"And I disagreed. Are you on your way yet?"

"I'm almost at my car," Lena lies. Gren's tone is making her wary. "Has Jimmy done something recently that I should know about?"

"Yes," Gren says. "He's killed a police officer."

158

Chapter 24

Lena backs up against a wall while she processes what Gren has said. She feels as if the floor gives in and leaves her floating down, unable to move fast or sit down. Her hand reaches for her gun, but it's still at the station. She can't leave the kitchen; if Jimmy grows suspicious, he might go for a knife, and Jacobson is unaware of what Gren just said.

"Repeat that," Lena says.

"She's not officially declared dead, but I spoke with a paramedic on the scene, and she said there's no hope. Her name was Gunilla."

"Ahlgren?" Lena asks. "Who went to the hospital with Jacobson and me?" Her own voice sounds distant.

"Affirmative. Apparently it was quick, or so I've been told."

Lena draws a shuddering breath. When she had been driving to the hospital, Gunilla had not been much more than a convenient presence chosen at random to help supervise Jimmy. Knowing she's dead makes details of her flash past: the curls in her tied-back hair, her bright voice, the almost invisible makeup.

"How was she killed?" Lena asks. Jacobson looks up sharply, but she holds up a hand, asking him to wait.

"An explosive device. The injuries were bad." Gren pauses. "Not much is left of her."

Lena looks at Jimmy, who is using his fork to chase a leftover piece of steak across his plate. When he sees Lena staring at him, he turns his palms up and frowns: *what is happening?*

"Hold on," Lena says to Gren. "You're suggesting that he used a bomb to murder an officer?"

"No, I'm telling you that he did kill her." Gren struggles to keep his voice under control. "He'd set a trap. Gunilla was part of the team that investigated his flat, when–"

"They did what?" Lena spits.

"Jimmy Franzen is a suspect," Gren snaps. "I've told you several times, and it turned out I was right. Stop talking for once and listen to me."

Lena takes a deep breath and looks at the ceiling. It's all she can do not to throw her phone through the kitchen window. Gren is understandably upset, but his imagination has the better of him.

"He had rigged his car," Gren continues. "The team found the keys in the residence. Gunilla volunteered to look for it in the parking lot. We suspect that the bomb was triggered when she sat down in the seat to check the glove compartment."

Lena tries to get her thoughts back on track. Things are happening too fast, and the new variables do not fit into her emerging picture. Or rather, they change the entire scene, making the puzzle bigger.

But this is not Jimmy's game. He has no reason to prepare and fit a bomb while at the same time seek Lena's protection. There is a different and simpler explanation. Less complicated, but much more frightening.

"I haven't seen Jimmy since we were at the hospital," Lena says.

Jimmy and Jacobson stiffen as if a venomous snake has appeared on the dinner table. After a moment, Jimmy opens his mouth, but snaps it shut when Lena makes a cutting motion. Jacobson grows a shade paler and gives Lena a warning look. He doesn't yet know what she's playing at, but can tell that the game is far outside his comfort zone.

"He'll do everything he can to stay low," Gren says. "The little rat knows every tunnel in the city by heart, so my guess is he's skulking in a cave somewhere. But we'll find him and flush him out."

"Perhaps he's left town," Lena says. Her suggestion sounds hollow and artificial; lying has never been her forte, especially to people she likes. Or who put their trust in her.

"His kind gets nervous in the woods." Gren pauses. "I'm not the only one who wants Jimmy brought in, Lena. I've had orders from high up to hunt him down. The kind of orders that don't allow for questions or compromises. Our jobs are on the line here."

"Understood."

"I'll see you at the site," Gren says. "You need to have a look, but then you're going back home again. I'm not having you back on duty until you've recovered. It's for your own good," he finishes and hangs up.

Lena pockets her phone and stares vacantly at the wall while the world spins around her. One day, she will stop thinking that the croupier of life will deal better cards only because the last round was bad. The world is not a set of scales rocking from one side to the other. There is no balance, plateaus, or games of give and take. There is only a spectre of increasing madness, growing bigger every day.

And its tendrils are coiled tight around Jimmy.

"What the hell," Jimmy breathes. "Did you just lie to the police?"

"Not all of them." Lena turns to Jacobson. "Maybe I haven't done anything to deserve this," she says to him, "but I need you to trust me."

"What I need to do is keep my job," Jacobson says. "What has happened?" he asks. "Why on earth did you tell Gren we don't know where Jimmy is?" His face is drawn and tight, much like his voice. It's the closest to angry Lena has ever seen him.

"An officer has been killed by a bomb. A team was searching Jimmy's flat, and she was examining Jimmy's car when it exploded.

Gren thinks that Jimmy rigged the trap." Lena glances at Jimmy and looks away. "I'm sorry."

"You're joking." Jimmy's voice is barely more than a whisper. "I mean, I know you aren't, but – Jesus Christ."

"Is someone else living with you?" Lena asks. "Perhaps a flatmate you haven't told us about?"

"No," Jimmy says, his voice faint. "Someone died in my car?"

Lena can see him trying to gather his thoughts; the news she broke has overwhelmed him. She's about to explain the situation in more detail, but Jimmy cuts her off by slamming his palm onto the table.

"And you think I'm a murderer?" Jimmy demands. "That I killed a cop?"

"I don't," Lena says. "But people with a lot more clout than I have do, and they've ordered a search for you. I need to go and see the scene."

"You back-stabbing bastards." Jimmy slumps in his chair and buries his face in his hands.

Lena motions for Jacobson to follow her into the hallway, where she gives him a hushed rundown of what Gren told her. When she's done, Lena and Jacobson look at Jimmy, who hasn't moved since Lena explained to him about the phone call. She can tell by Jacobson's expression that he has come to the same conclusion as she has: Jimmy has no apparent reason to set traps for anyone. The consequence is straightforward.

"You think the bomb was meant for Jimmy," Jacobson says quietly.

"It's logical," Lena says. "No one told Jimmy that his flat was going to be raided. I didn't even know myself."

"I'm still confused why you weren't honest with Gren."

"Because someone's leaning on him to get Jimmy." Lena lowers her voice even more. "He's being pressed hard from above to find him. How often does Gren get instructions that specific?"

"Not very often," Jacobson says, but he still looks troubled.

"And when Gren is whipped by the board to pin someone down, how often does it happen this quickly?" Lena raises her eyebrows. "I'll answer that myself: once in never at all."

Lena keeps the other reason to herself: Gren is nervous, just as he had been when they spoke at the station. Something other than losing an officer has thrown him badly.

"So you're saying that Jimmy is a target," Jacobson asks, "and that those who're after him have contacts inside the police?" He looks in disbelief at Lena.

"If you have a better theory, I'd love to hear it."

A few seconds pass while Jacobson studies Lena. He sighs and looks back at Jimmy.

"This is unbelievable," Jacobson mutters. "And frankly, this case is moving so fast I struggle to keep up. But I can't think of another reason at this point."

"You'll have my back?" Lena exhales and relaxes slightly. She was not aware she had been holding her breath.

"I do," Jacobson says. "For now." He nods at Jimmy. "We can't turn him loose, though. If you're right, they'll be looking for him."

"Correct," Lena agrees. "And I think we can agree on who 'they' are."

"Someone linked to the facility," Jacobson says.

Lena nods. "Who has access to explosives or at least the right connections. And maybe a plant in the police force."

Jacobson is silent for a moment. "Have you any idea," he says softly, "how big this is?"

"I'm doing my best not to think about it. And I'm also trying not to think about what we must do with Jimmy."

"What do you mean?"

"If he leaves, he'll be unprotected. He can't stay here, and we can't take him to headquarters."

Jacobson reads Lena's face and understands. "Jesus wept," he groans. "Gren will disown us if he finds out."

"We have no choice. Besides, those who want Jimmy locked up or dead probably have a list of names. No prize for guessing who's next."

"Then let's get to the bottom of this," he says. "For Gunilla's sake."

Lena nods. For their lost colleague. For Jimmy as well, whatever his agenda, and for those forgotten souls who were shackled and tortured beneath an unsuspecting suburb.

And for themselves.

"Why are you just standing there?" Jimmy calls from the kitchen. "Aren't you going to arrest me or something?"

"Get your jacket," Lena tells Jimmy. "And bring the cassette tape. We're going for a ride."

Chapter 25

The last time Lena walked up to the tower block where Jimmy lives, it was late morning and the area was almost deserted. Tonight, as she parks her car on a lawn and walks along with Jacobson towards the building, the scene is transformed into a pandemonium of blue lights and noise.

She slows down when she gets closer to the cordon tape. The reek of burnt rubber and molten plastic fills the air. Signs of destruction litter the area: strips of charred metal, pieces of shattered glass, and shreds of grimy textile. Police officers, paramedics, firemen and spectators mill around the base of the block. There has to be several hundred onlookers. Perhaps a thousand.

To the right of the building is a small parking lot, currently illuminated by several portable floodlights. One of the cars is reduced to a twisted framework of blackened metal. The neighbouring vehicles look as if they've been hit by a giant sledgehammer, pushing them sideways into other cars. A large pool of soot spreads out on the ground from the centre of the explosion.

"My God," Jacobson says. "This can't be intentional. They could've killed a dozen people."

"I'm guessing they don't care." Lena stops some ten metres away from the remnants of Jimmy's car.

"Maybe it was a tank mine," Jacobson guesses.

Lena nods absently. It's a reasonable idea, and one with unpleasant implications. But what worries her more is the speed with which the bomb was planted.

Nothing remains of the seat in which Gunilla had been sitting when the bomb went off. If Lena's guess is correct, her colleague had been torn apart because of a long-gone crime that still sends ripples throughout the city. At least Gunilla's death had been instant; given the wreckage, any other possibility is unlikely.

"They won't stop at this," Jacobson mutters. "To be honest, it's hard to imagine that anyone would do this just to get to Jimmy."

"That depends on how much they want to silence him," Lena says.

Stockholm's history is lined with attempts to warn or silence people by grotesquely violent means. The more valuable or great the secret, the more brutal the methods to protect it. Jimmy must have stumbled on the worst kind of information: one prized highly enough to render the lives of innocents unimportant.

"We shouldn't have brought Jimmy here," Jacobson says.

"You and I agreed that it was the only way," Lena says.

"He's unreliable. If we take him along and he leaves the car, I'll have to tell Gren the truth."

"Let's hope it doesn't come to that. And he has enough brains to sit tight."

Or at least so she hopes. Jimmy seems intelligent, but also pathologically impulsive. He also runs around abandoned tunnels for amusement, for one thing. It might not be a sign of a fully rational person.

"Besides," Lena continues, "I locked the car down. There's no getting out without the key fob."

Jacobson looks at her sideways. "He might not appreciate that."

"It's for his own good. And ours, too. Let's get this over and done with." She points at Gren, who is sitting in a police van and talking on his phone.

Lena is back in her car less than ten minutes later. Strained beyond coherent thinking, Gren outlined the disaster and told her he is directing all incoming reports to Lena's case file. Once he was confident that Lena was up to speed with the circumstances, he commanded her to return home. Jacobson hung back and took notes.

She didn't mention the tape. Until she knows more about the situation, it will stay secret. Even Jacobson is reluctant to hand it over, perhaps in fear that he would climb higher on the possible lists of other targets.

Thankfully, Jimmy didn't try to leave the car. If he'd found out that he was locked in, he might have had a tantrum. Hiding him under a blanket on the floor in front of the back seats had been a desperate snap decision. Taking him along in the first place had been another. Sometimes, improvising is all one can do, and it always beats inaction.

When they've driven for a few seconds, Jimmy unfurls from the blanket and peers at Lena in the rear-view mirror.

"How bad is it?" Jimmy says.

"As bad as you can imagine," Lena says.

"I'm sorry," Jimmy says. "For your friend."

Lena is silent for a long moment. "I didn't really know her," she says eventually. "But thanks."

Apart from the visit to Beckomberga Hospital, Gunilla was a set of scattered memories from meetings and passing-bys in corridors. Her death fused what little Lena knows into the image of a complete person. A breathing, thinking woman plucked away by a cocktail of volatile chemicals.

Lena accelerates onto a four-lane road. Only after a minute does she realise that she's driving home. An unread text message from Gustav waits on her phone; she doesn't trust herself to come up with a sensible reply right now. The sight of Jimmy's ruined car and knowing what happened to Gunilla have left her furious but unfocused. Gren is right: she needs to sleep, or she will be useless tomorrow.

"It's the room, right?" he asks. "Someone wants to kill me because of the pictures I posted."

"I'm not going to argue against that," Lena says.

"This is insane." Jimmy's voice is choked. "What if they're following us? At least I'll be safe at the police station."

Lena clears her throat. "There's a hitch," she says.

"How can this get any worse?" Jimmy shrinks down a fraction in the seat.

"It's complicated. But you should stay somewhere else for the time being."

Lena hopes Jimmy will think her decision is because of administrative reasons, but he sees straight through her ploy.

"Jesus Christ," Jimmy says weakly. "You don't think I'm safe with the police?"

"Let's just say it's possible that you'll be safer in a different location," Lena says.

"And where exactly would that be?"

"Anywhere else."

A long silence passes while Jimmy thinks about this. Jacobson is on his phone, listening to either a speech or a recorded message. She looks at the sky as she drives and wonders how much sleep she'll be able to get; a halo of pinkish orange spreads from the western horizon where the sun has set, momentarily out of view before it will rise again. In theory, she has already rested today, but whatever state she entered after collapsing at the hospital was not solid sleep.

Jacobson hangs up and turns to Lena. "That was the lab," he says.

"Give me some great news," Lena says.

She glances at Jacobson and sees that her wish will go unfulfilled. No surprise there.

"They've got more conclusive results from the shard you found." Jacobson scrolls on his phone. "I'll forward everything to you."

"What's the gist?" Lena asks. "You spend a lot of time on the phone."

Jacobson hesitates. "There are traces of a very strong psychedelic and addictive drug."

"That's already been established."

"But there are only traces. And the drug is powerful only when concentrated. What you found is nowhere near enough to affect you in any noticeable way, even if you'd licked the glass."

"Tell them to test it again."

"They've been pretty thorough. Also, it's a common component in quite a few prescriptions. Nearly a tenth of Norra Ängby uses it in one form or another."

The tendrils coil again in Lena stomach. She had filed away the surreal experience at the hospital as a drug-induced episode because it is the only reasonable explanation. But precise science and hard facts are against her.

Her hands clench around the steering wheel. She has been deluding herself: drugs weren't the only coherent reason for her experience. It's only what she wants to hear. Given that she was wrong, she's left with only one last alternative, looming on her inner horizon like a thundercloud.

"I'm not insane," she says under her breath.

"Pardon?" Jacobson says.

"Never mind." Lena shakes her head, both in dismissal and to clear her mind. "We need to have a plan." She looks over her shoulder at Jimmy. "How long will it take you to find a friend who can set you up?"

"Won't happen," Jimmy says. "I've been in Stockholm for less than a year, and everyone I know by name is an explorer. No one will offer up a space."

"What kind of people do you run with?" Lena asks.

"The careful kind."

"Family?" Jacobson asks.

"A few distant relatives out in the Finnish countryside."

"Right place, wrong country." Lena sighs.

"Can't I stay at your place?" Jimmy asks Lena.

"Ask him instead." Lena nods at Jacobson.

"Unfortunately," Jacobson says, "I have family. It's too dangerous."

"Would you actually take him in otherwise?" Lena looks at Jacobson sideways.

"Well," Jacobson says evenly, "seeing as there's an unknown person or group, with access to advanced explosives, who wants to murder a man you and I are hiding from our superiors, I would, in fact, let him stay in my home. In fact, I wish I could. But the risk is too great."

"Damn it." The light shifts, and Lena accelerates hard. "My place it is, then."

So she will host a fugitive who is wanted by both criminals as well as the police. The perfect end to a disastrous day.

It also means having Gustav over is out of the picture, perhaps for considerable time. The realisation is infuriating enough to take her mind off the case for a moment.

"Thanks," Jimmy says uncertainly, making it sound like a question.

"Hold on." Jacobson swipes at his phone. "I just got an email from the assistant I put on chasing the fire alarm producer. She's attached a lot of files. Bear with me." He peers at the screen as he scrolls through the documents.

"Any more negative information now," Lena says, "and I will ask everyone to leave the car."

Jacobson looks up, and this time he's smiling. "We have a lead," he says. "We've found the invoice for the alarm you found. The addressee is a defunct company."

"What kind of business?"

"A medical research company."

"This is the best news I've heard this week. Any luck with tracing the management?"

"The assistant got hold of an out-of-hours assistant at the tax authority who pulled the register for us," Jacobson answers. "We have the names of the board. It had twelve members."

"Finally." Lena punches the seat, making Jimmy give up a startled gasp. "Sod sleep, then. We'll round them up tonight. I'll call–"

"Wait." Jacobson holds up a hand. "All the people in the company are gone. And everyone except two is dead."

Lena purses her lips. "I should've seen that coming." She frowns at the road. "Wait a moment. Some are just gone, not dead?"

Jacobson nods. "The two founders don't have any record of their deaths. Carl Adlerberg disappeared in nineteen eighty-six, just after the company folded. The other, a woman by the name of Kristina Stenberg, vanished soon after that."

"Vanished how?" Jimmy asks.

"Both walked away from their homes," Jacobson says. "Left all belongings and assets behind. They were thirty-one and thirty-three years old respectively."

Jacobson reads their birth dates out loud. Lena enters them in the police console and watches the records appear on the screen. Kristina's image is from her driving license: blonde, classic eighties-style curls, round face with a tight mouth and nonchalant blue eyes. An ideal high-school beauty queen, albeit with a less than radiant smile.

Carl has the giveaway wooden face and green-collared shirt of a military service mugshot. Most people in such photos appear nervous, but he looks unruffled and defiant. His short-cropped brown hair makes the lanes on his already angular face seem almost artificially sharp. Handsome, if in a strangely featureless way, as if any real characteristics were unable to find a foothold on his skin.

"Hold on." Lena taps at Carl's face on the screen. "Look at this." She loads the case file and brings up the driver license photos of the first victims.

"Look at the man." Lena opens the picture of the second victim. "And now this guy."

"He kind of resembles Carl when he was younger," Jacobson says after a moment.

"I'm starting to believe that our killer isn't too fond of Carl."

"You're saying he's killing his old tormentor?" Jacobson asks.

"It's a theory." Lena shakes her head in wonder. "And it's a decent one. Let's see what else we have on Carl."

A quick check reveals a past as an army engineer. His rank had been the highest available in his department, which in turn had supported one of Sweden's elite units. She brings up more recent documents and finds a photo from a press conference in 1985. One year before he slipped off the grid. At the time, Carl was still good-looking, and his confidence seemed intact: his smile competed with the spotlights on the stage on which he faced the press.

Lena switches off the console. Twelve months after the photo was taken, Carl was less happy. He had gone to ground for some reason. If it isn't the lab, she will resign.

"No one reacted when they took off?" Lena asks.

"I checked," Jacobson says. "There were only routine investigations. Both were dropped after a couple of months."

Lena is not surprised. People vanish every year, and in this case, there had not been any reasons to suspect foul play.

"But based on what we've found," Jacobson says, "I think it's safe to assume they'd been involved in sensitive activities."

"You mean sadistic," Lena corrects. "Go on, tell me how there aren't any traces of the missing pair."

"I'm happy to disappoint you."

"More good news?" Lena asks. "You're spoiling me."

"No one has reported any sign of Carl," Jacobson says. "But Kristina may have done a runner. She was under investigation for tax fraud when she disappeared. As she didn't take her property or make any withdrawals, she was believed deceased."

"But not confirmed," Lena says. "So she might just have decided to lie low."

"Possibly, but the fraud case was very small, and she was wealthy. As in seriously rich. In fact, all members of the company were very well off."

"And she wouldn't have abandoned all her assets just to dodge a rap on the knuckles by the tax authorities," Lena says, continuing Jacobson's line of thought.

"Exactly," Jacobson agrees. "But there was a tentative sighting on an airplane. It was a fluke, really. A police officer who'd been on vacation saw a picture of Kristina at his station. He remembered her as an irritable, skittish woman on his outbound flight."

"What was the destination?" Lena asks.

"Malaga," Jacobson says. "But this was thirty years ago. Vanished or not, the missing pair may have passed away by now."

"We have three dead bodies who'd argue differently." Lena shakes her head. "One of them is alive. Hiding out there, watching us."

"I'm inclined to agree," Jacobson says.

"So one man who turned into smoke," Lena says, summing up the facts. "And a woman who might have eloped to Spain."

"Doesn't it take two people to elope?" Jimmy asks.

"I suspect she had her bad conscience for company," Lena says. "And it must've been a pretty nasty companion."

She slows down as she nears her flat and parks in a space two blocks away. A side entrance to the basement will let them reach her flat without stepping through the building's front door. Some extra caution won't hurt right now. At least no one has followed them; the road behind her car has been empty for several minutes. Which, of course, doesn't matter if they have her address, which anyone on the force could look up.

"Do you want to act on what we have?" Jacobson asks. "Or would you rather continue to question the hospital manager and his staff?"

"We go after the board," Lena says. "They were immediately involved in whatever went on at the hospital. If Carl's alive, we'll chase him down. I'll get Gren to raise hell in every office. He's surprisingly good at that when he's upset, and I've never seen him more pissed off than he is right now. I'll ask him to send off a copy of the warrant to Spain as well, just for good measure."

"But they would be old," Jimmy says. "Even if they're alive, they won't look anything like those pictures."

"We won't know unless we ask." Lena stops and switches the engine off. "And there are workarounds."

"Age progression software," Jimmy says, knowing where Lena is going. "I thought that stuff was myth. Can you really tell what she'd look like today?"

"It'll be an educated guess," Lena says. "And plastic surgery, scars or other disfigurations make it almost impossible to be sure. Wigs and beards make it even harder. Although I've been told that the program does a decent job."

Jacobson sighs. "Lena, remind me again why we're sharing this information with a civilian?"

"Because I've helped you," Jimmy says tiredly. "Also, someone killed your friend by accident while trying to finish me off just because of you. In short, my life is shit because of you. And by you, I mean the police in general, so don't get all riled up."

"We might still need your help," Lena adds. "As it stands, I don't trust my own people."

She looks over her shoulder at Jimmy. Their eyes meet, and she knows he understands what she cannot say out loud.

This is also because you were there with me, Jimmy. You shared the moment when the light came on. You backed my story, even though your version was a pretty collage of lies. Gren might have bought it. I don't.

But for whatever reason, you risked your hide for me. So I owe you.

"I'll make sure Kristina's driving license photo is run through the software," Jacobson says, "and I'll see to it that the images are passed on to the Spanish police force. For what it's worth, I still object to Jimmy's involvement, but you already know that."

"Your scepticism regarding my professional conduct is noted." Lena yanks the keys out of the ignition. "Now keep quiet and follow me. First we'll eat; then we can discuss how to best squeeze more useful information out of the manager." She notices Jacobson's incredulous look. "I get hungry when I'm under stress."

"And then what?" Jimmy asks.

"Then we sleep." Lena swings the basement door open and ushers the two men inside. "The photos are likely to be dead ends, so I'm putting the manager on the anvil first thing tomorrow."

A few hours later, she is reminded that her plans are doomed to always go wrong.

Chapter 26

"Define *unsuccessful*," Carl says to the man on the phone.

A crowded sailing boat passes on the river along the border of his property. From his office window, the vessel looks like an ugly undersized tub, brimming with fashion dolls in garish clothes and equally garish sunglasses. Stockholm's would-be elite usually disgust him, but the annoyance the sight causes him is dwarfed by his outrage over the failed assassination.

The nosy blogger is alive. A police officer is not. What should have been the end of this unfortunate affair turns out to be a possible start of a much greater crisis.

"The target was absent from the property," the man on the phone says, "and we couldn't secure an operative inside the flat."

"Why the hell not?"

"The neighbours were getting suspicious. So we chose a standard secondary method."

"A bomb," Carl says tightly.

"Of course, it is unfortunate that someone else disrupted the scheme."

"*Unfortunate?*" Carl sinks down on a garden chair. He lowers the phone and presses it against his chest to avoid shouting at the man on the other end.

All the major news websites feature stories about the explosion in Sundbyberg. A blast that powerful in a densely populated area is very unusual, and several witnesses claim to have seen a police officer enter the car moments before it was disintegrated by a so far unidentified device. Reporters swarm around the bomb site. Quite a few in the comments to the news articles guess that it was a tank mine.

Judging by the devastation Carl has seen in the pictures, he would hazard that it was more than one. And the contraption failed to rid him of the overly inquisitive photographer. Instead, it killed a member of the police force. The law will pull in resources from every corner to hunt down the perpetrator.

The nameless agency Carl is using comes with many recommendations by close friends. Always efficient, never leaves a trace, complete discretion. Apparently, this is not a guarantee against inaccurate hits and massive collateral damage.

He should have guessed. But he is in the arena now, and his opponents are fielding their forces as he speaks. There is no room to back down.

"If you are displeased with our services," the man says, "we can always terminate the agreement. That option is always open. Simply let us know if this is the case."

"No," Carl says quickly. Disentangling oneself from the agency is impossible. Rumours suggest that some have tried, only to have a close member of their family pass away prematurely and in headline-grabbing ways.

"Can you locate him and make another attempt?" Carl asks.

"We are monitoring the target right now. His location became known to us only a few minutes ago. He doesn't seem to be in possession of his phone anymore."

"Wonderful." Carl sighs in relief. "Then go ahead and take him out. Preferably in a fashion that doesn't result in as much wreckage as your first try."

"A more precise incision might be problematic."

"Good lord, what now?"

"We have sent you an image that illustrates the problem."

Carl's phone beeps as it receives a multimedia message. Carl opens it and angles his phone away from the glaring sun for a better view.

The image is sharp and has the peculiar focus of advanced telescopic lenses. In the centre of the picture is a young, slouching man dressed mostly in black. His expression suggests that he is frustrated with something.

Next to him is a woman Carl knows by sight. Her face is familiar to a sizable chunk of the Swedish population: it is the female officer who leads the murder investigation in Norra Ängby. The two stand next to a car against a backdrop of boxy, anonymous three-storey blocks.

"Is the one in black the blogger?" Carl asks.

"Affirmative. It seems he's travelling with Lena Franke."

"What the hell is he doing with her?"

"We're not sure. She might be hiding him. Perhaps he is deemed to be a key witness."

"Then they would've tucked him away in their headquarters."

"A reasonable assumption," the man agrees. "But that doesn't seem to be the case. Please advise on further action."

Carl lowers his phone and stares into the distance. The full scenario is too large for him to see, and it's not about to shrink. Unknown variables and blank lines fill his view no matter how he turns and twists the problem. And all hell might break loose if the detective manages to find the killer. Still, the detective has no reason to home in on Carl or the murderer. Regardless of Lena Franke's alleged ruthlessness, she must be grasping for a handhold on a perfectly smooth cliff.

This whole debacle could come to an end if only he recalled the name of the murderer. To be tripped up by the shortcomings of his own intellect is the greatest insult imaginable.

"Watch them," Carl says. "Keep me posted constantly on their movements. And be prepared to intervene."

"Even if the target is in the company of the detective?" the man asks.

"It's unfortunate, but I have to adapt to the scenario."

"We can monitor the police's activities via an inside source, but it will incur a significant increase in the fees."

"Whatever it takes. I have the money."

Chapter 27

Southern Stockholm

Friday

09:23

Lena's phone is in her hand before she realises that it's ringing.

Her blinds slice the morning light into rectangles that fill the wall opposite the bedroom window. Jimmy and Jacobson sleep on the sofa and a foam workout mattress in the living room. Both refused to leave Lena's flat; Jimmy because of the possible threat to his life, Jacobson for less clear reasons. Lena suspects he doesn't trust Jimmy yet. Which, all things considered, makes sense.

She rolls over in her bed and holds her phone over her head. The display reads *Gren*. She hoped it would be Gustav. Making up for her negligence will be a superhuman task. When this turbulent case is closed and she's back on her feet, free from nightmarish fits and sleepless nights, she'll suggest that they go on a trip. A week away, or at least a weekend escape.

She takes the call. "Franke."

"Are you at the office?" Gren asks.

"I'm at home. You sent me home from school, remember?" Lena sits up and blinks. Gren sounds as taut as a metal wire. "Has the manager decided to speak?"

"There's been another murder."

The news burns away her drowsiness. Holding her phone jammed between her ear and her shoulder, she hops out of her bed and starts to dress, pausing to ram her shoulder into the door to the living room. Jimmy and Jacobson wake up with a chorus of startled exclamations. Lena raises a finger to hush them and turns away.

"Is it connected to my case?" Lena asks.

"I wouldn't contact you if it weren't. The scene is a minute's walk away from where the double homicide took place. And a witness has reported excessive violence."

"Give me the details."

"I have only bits and pieces, so you're better off getting them from the officers on the scene. The profile of the victim is in your case file. I heard that the woman who found the body is frantic."

"Just like last time," Lena observes. "Are the technicians on the scene?"

"Only the local police so far. They've cordoned the site, and they're looking after the hysterical woman." Gren pauses. "I understand that the house is already under siege by onlookers. I'd be surprised if you beat the TV crews there."

Lena curses. "If there are people in the area, the media has already arrived. This will have gone viral in minutes."

"Also," Gren continues, "the manager is still cooperating. He's jumping to get us whatever we want. Put him out of your mind, and focus on Jimmy instead."

"You really think he's behind this?"

"I'm positive. He's still on the run. How better to taunt us than to strike again right next to his first crime?" Gren makes a disgusted sound. "He's making us look like idiots."

Gren is right, but not in the way he thinks. The killer is eluding them, although this murder proves that Jimmy is innocent. And she can't tell Gren that she knows. The irony is enough to drive anyone insane.

"Anything else you can tell me?" Lena pulls on a T-shirt, pauses in the doorway to the living room to get Jimmy and Jacobson's attention, and jerks her thumb at the front door. The men nod and start to dress.

"The local constables will bring you up to speed there," Gren says, "and the technicians will give you their preliminary as soon as they can. I want you to run a full brief before lunch. There'll almost certainly be members from the board present."

"Got it."

Lena flings the fridge open and pockets a handful of emergency chocolate protein bars. Jimmy, bare-chested and drowsy, pads into the kitchen and points questioningly at the coffee machine. Lena fights the urge to punch him. She shakes her head and gestures at his shoes.

"Call me as soon as you've visited the scene," Gren says. "I'm sending Jacobson there now."

"Don't bother," Lena says. "I'll tell him." She regrets the words as soon as they leave her mouth.

"Is he with you?" Gren sounds surprised.

"He's been – Jacobson came this morning to check up on me."

"I see."

Lena sighs while she puts her jacket on. Gren's response is a fraction too slow. He knows he hasn't got the full story, which means he will watch her even more closely.

"In the meantime," Gren continues, "I'll get every available officer to look for Jimmy. With luck, I'll be authorised to broadcast the warrant and get the public to help us. We'll have him soon."

"I need the dog team," Lena says. "As in today, not next month. I don't care about their priorities. With two scenes this close, I bet my kidney the murderer is local."

"They're out of town. We'll have to make do without them." Gren gives Lena the address to the scene.

"I'll call you back," Lena says and hangs up.

Chapter 28

Norra Ängby

Friday

10:18

Lena's apprehension turns to disgust when she arrives at the scene. A crowd blocks the street from side to side, and a dozen cars are parked both on the street and the sidewalk. An ambulance and two police cars are lined up on her left. There has to be at least seven hundred people milling around the barely visible blue-and-white cordon tape.

Many hold their phones raised high in hopes of getting a good angle at the house and police officers. The blue light on all vehicles are switched on, but rather than keeping people at bay, the swirling lights appear to have vacuumed in everyone in the immediate neighbourhood.

She parks some distance from the turmoil and zips up her jacket. Stopping by headquarters to pick up her revolver delayed her at least ten minutes, but she cannot afford to go unarmed; this case twists and turns so fast it can spiral out of control at any moment. If or when that happens, it will occur when she least expects it. And the next bend in the road might see a collision.

Jacobson looks over his shoulder at the floor behind his car seat. "Your shoes are showing," he whispers.

"Shit." Jimmy shuffles around on the floor and pulls the blanket down to hide his Dr Martens.

"Better?" Jimmy asks.

"It's perfect," Jacobson says. "Now it only looks as if we're trying to hide a dead body in your car." He gives Lena a withering look.

"Like I said before," Lena says, "I'm open to better ideas. Jimmy, not a sound or any funny ideas. Stay quiet and still. Even if someone bangs on the window."

"I'm not suicidal," Jimmy hisses under the blanket.

"Good to hear. Now shut up." Lena takes out her phone and skims the details of the victim again.

His name was Martin Valin. Male, forty-four years old, unmarried and no family. Only resident on the address. Record cleaner than polished glass. No driver's license and no debts. Someone has unearthed a ridiculously blurry photo that hints at a thin man with black thinning hair radiating from his head like an uneven halo. He had been a pianist, with some freelance gigs, but making most of his living from teaching suburban teenagers the finer aspects of classical music. As jobs go, his must have been stressful.

For some reason, Martin is the "suspected" victim. Apparently the body's identity has not been determined yet.

"He's as different to the other victims as one can be." Jacobson shakes his head as he studies the same information on his phone.

"Wait here in the car until I call," Lena says. "I don't want to run into any surprises." She pockets her phone, braces herself, and opens the door.

The air is velvet-like and rich with scents of Norra Ängby's gardens. Not a shred of cloud in the blue sky. The rising sun washes over the suburb with a crystalline light. It is shaping up to be a hot, humid day. Not to mention a long one.

She sizes up the house as she walks closer. Two storeys, green façade with white corners, light ochre tiles on the roof, and those oddly small windows. A low hedge surrounds an unkempt garden. The property is typical for the district, although it is not visibly extended, and its peeling paint is a rare sight in this renovation-intense suburb. So are the untrimmed trees and the overgrown flowerbeds.

Just as Gren said, the house where the previous murders took place is a quick walk away. And he mentioned that the same level of violence had been used. A possible connection between the two incidents would be likely, even if they had taken place farther apart. This kind of proximity rules out every ghost of a chance.

The crime scene technicians' white van arrives just as Lena and Jacobson push their way through the crowd. Two men and a woman, both dressed in white protective suits, leave the van and make their way to the gate. Most curious onlookers have enough sense to give way to the trio, even if it's only to make sure they get a good camera angle.

Five officers staff the perimeter: Gunnar and four others. She recognizes two of them from when she inspected the gruesome findings in the nearby forest.

Lena walks up to Gunnar. "Who found the–" She glances at the crowd, many of whom are within earshot. "Who was the first officer on the scene?" she asks.

"I was." An officer next to Gunnar clears his throat.

Gunnar nods. "Constable Michaelson here made the discovery," he says. "I was there too, but I'll leave it to Michaelson to outline the scene."

"Follow me."

Lena guides the officer halfway down a driveway riddled with weeds. Gunnar follows behind the officer. They stop at the foot of the stairs that lead up to the front door.

"Sum it up for me," Lena says to Michaelson.

"A woman walked past this house just over two hours ago." Michaelson struggles to sound neutral, but his voice is trembling slightly. "Apparently her dog started to bark and ran inside. The owner was using a lead, but in her own words, her dog went berserk."

"Another dog?" Lena asks.

"There are quite a few of them in the area."

185

"Where's the owner?"

"At the station," Gunnar says, "with a nurse. She was almost catatonic by the time we got to her. Several neighbours called when she ran down this street screaming incoherently."

"Have you managed to get anything useful out of her?" Lena wonders.

"Good heavens." Gunnar looks pained. "She's in shock, Franke. We weren't about to press her on details. The dog's at the station too while we're waiting for the pound to come over."

"Then what happened?" she asks Michaelson.

"I did a quick search when I arrived. All five of us were at the station, so we drove here straight away. Another officer came and helped us secure the woman."

"Why 'secure'?"

"Like I said, she was hysterical." Michaelson swallows. "I don't blame her. The door was wide open, but no one answered when I called out. I proceeded inside, went upstairs, and saw a – the body. He – I mean, it's in the tub." He pauses. "There's a lot of blood."

"I haven't had time to read a line of anyone's report yet," Lena says, "but Gren mentioned significant violence?"

Michaelson nods and clears his throat again. "The head has been severed from the body."

Lena shifts her feet as she braces herself against the surge of unease. The same degree of violence, indeed. No wonder they haven't yet determined the identity.

And perhaps there are more similarities to the first murders.

"Don't say the head is missing?" Lena asks.

"Yes, it – how did you know?" Michaelson asks.

"Jesus." Lena shades her eyes and looks down; the sun's rays seem to grow stronger. A severe headache looms on the horizon.

"Why didn't you call in backup when you found the body?" Lena asks.

"The bathroom upstairs was the last place we looked," Michaelson says, "so we'd searched the whole house by the time we found the victim. And there's no trace of – well, the missing body part. But there are signs of a fight in the bathroom."

"Get someone to search the forest," Lena says to Gunnar. "I have a feeling the killer is arranging a new exhibition. We need to find it before anyone else does."

She doesn't know why the murderer has decapitated the man, but there can be only so many reasons. Gren had better call on some major favours to get those dogs out here. If he has any favours left after keeping her employed for the past two years, that is.

"We're on it already," Gunnar says. "I have three men combing the woods around here as we speak. There are a few off-duty constables from nearby districts on their way in, too. They've offered to check as many forests as they can during the day."

"Thank them from me." Lena looks at the house. "Did you know him?" she asks Gunnar.

"Not at all," Gunnar says while Michaelson shakes his head. "We've had statements from the neighbours, but few could tell us anything at all. Apparently Martin was a recluse. As far as you can be one around here."

"The neighbourhood watch kept tabs on him?" Lena guesses.

"There aren't many oddballs in Norra Ängby," Gunnar says. "It's not the cheapest district. Three decades ago, you'd find more characters here. More scruffy types, too. So I wouldn't be surprised if people watched Martin."

"Show me the way," Lena says.

Chapter 29

Norra Ängby

Friday

10:27

The body in the tub is savaged almost beyond recognition. Martin – if the dead man really is him – had been wearing a light shirt, dark chinos, brown slippers and, strangely, some kind of reinforced leather gloves resembling those of a motocross racer. Beige floor-to-ceiling tiles cover the walls. Most surfaces are smeared with blood, as are Martin's clothes.

With some imagination, his arms and legs fit those of a middle-aged man, but his neck ends in a white and purple mess. The floor is almost completely hidden beneath smears of blood.

Lena stands on the threshold to the bathroom and surveys the scene. The square bathroom is large enough for a tub, a toilet and a sink, but not much else. She memorises as much as she can and turns away. There isn't much more she can do at the moment. Given the extreme circumstances, the technicians will file an official complaint if she so much as breathes too carelessly.

To her own surprise, she doesn't feel sick, only mildly queasy. She puts the reaction down to the sheer absurdity of what she beholds. There might be a delayed impact waiting in the wings. That had happened before.

As she made her way up to the bathroom, she noted details about the rest of the house. An old piano in the living room. Three violas on a wall. Bookshelves burgeoning with folders and volumes on musical theory, history, and biographies of composers. Stacks of specialist magazines on pianos and violins. A small bookshelf dedicated to literature on animals, judging by a glance at a few covers. An expensive sound system in a dust-laden living room, four speakers surrounding a seventies leather recliner chair. Hints in the air of food gone off.

Upstairs is just as bad: a single unmade bed in a small, dank bedroom, a worn sofa, and a decade-old TV set. A Swedish flag pinned to the ceiling just outside the bathroom. Four flowers fighting for their lives on a windowsill. All rooms are hot and stuffy, and all have an aura of withdrawal. The unhappy home of an unhappy man.

Maybe this is how her home looks to other people: the dwelling of a soul obsessed with a thin slice of life and disconnected from all its other aspects. She can't even remember when she last vacuumed, let alone cleaned out her fridge. It's a marvel that Gustav, a perfectionist down to the core of his being, has not fled for his life. Or at least descended on her flat with a bagful of disinfectants.

At least her space cannot smell this bad. There's a sharp, foul tint to the air here that makes her want to hold her breath. It might come from the corpse, but she doesn't think so.

Downstairs, the technicians are walking up the stairs in a quick rush of rustling suits and careful steps.

"Why you, Martin?" Lena says under her breath. "What did you do wrong?"

Lena moves to give room to the technicians, who survey the bathroom and begin to unpack their equipment without breaking pace. No one so much as pauses at the sight of the headless body. Their unflinching attitude is a reminder that some on the force regularly face worse encounters than she does.

"He was rushed this time," one of the men says.

"How can you tell?" Lena asks. She recognises him as one of the technicians that examined the previous scene.

"The edges." He points at the body. "He went at it fast. Probably with a regular saw."

"Is it that easy to tell?" Lena avoids looking at the corpse and stares at the technician instead.

"Are you suggesting I can't do my job?"

"If I thought that you couldn't, I wouldn't ask for your opinion."

"Well, it's not rocket science." The man nods at the blood on the walls. "This was a violent affair, and judging by what I see here, a lot of force was used when removing the head. Now if you'll excuse me, I have work to do. You'll get the extensive report when we're done."

Lena's phone rings and stops her from demanding more answers. It's Jacobson. She takes the call.

"What's the status?" he asks.

"It's a right mess," Lena says, "but no other trouble in sight. Come up when you want."

Standing just outside the bathroom, she looks at the technicians as they discuss how to best remove the body. The amount of blood is almost incomprehensible. Almost all of it is contained in the bathroom, but large blotches stain the floor near her feet as well.

There are, she realises, a lot of stains close to where she is standing.

"We should wrap up here as soon as possible," Lena says. "Gren will want me to look for Jimmy instead. I almost wish that Jimmy was–"

She trails off as her gaze wanders back to the bathroom. The largest smudges end just outside the doorstep. The killer may have paused there, perhaps to stuff his trophy into a bag, but that couldn't have taken very long. And the technician believes the murderer was stressed. There had to be another reason why the killer had been standing still on this spot.

"Lena?" Jacobson asks. "Are you still there?"

"Something's not right." Lena steps away, accidentally shouldering one of the technicians aside, and looks up.

The Swedish flag above her is attached to the ceiling with a pin in each corner. It's the kind of decoration she would expect to find in a teenager's den, not in the home of an introvert high school teacher. Especially as there are no other paintings or posters in the entire household.

"What do you think you're doing?" The technician whom Lena pushed frowns at her. "Just because you're some kind of hotshot detective, there's no need to be rude."

"Quiet."

Lena shoves the phone in her pocket, steps up on the sofa, and pulls out one of the pins that holds the Swedish flag to the ceiling.

Part of the flag falls away and reveals a trapdoor, painted white and secured with a small but robust combination padlock. She puts one foot on the armrest and pushes herself up for a closer look. In one of the cracks between the trapdoor and the ceiling is a dark, glistening smudge.

"What's that supposed to mean?" the technician demands. "In difference to you, we actually have to–"

Lena raises a finger in the technician's face to direct his gaze upwards. She finds a piece of tissue in a pocket and touches it to the crack. When she lowers the tissue, it's stained by a wet, red line.

"Oh," the technician says.

Lena nods. The single word sums up her feelings fairly well. She takes out her phone again.

"Hurry up and get here," she says to Jacobson. "We have a situation."

Chapter 30

After a quick conversation between the members of the crime scene technicians, a ladder is brought in from their van and positioned under the trapdoor. Lena dons a pair of borrowed plastic gloves and climbs the step for a closer look at the lock. The technicians have relocated downstairs, while Jacobson stands next to the ladder.

He keeps his pistol aimed at the floor. The odds that the killer has locked himself into the attic from the outside are small, but Jacobson is nervous. Perhaps the latest victim being a musician has rattled him.

The lock is sturdy for its size, but it will be easy to break with a bolt cutter. One of the police cars is bound to have one in their trunk. If not, Gunnar will have to produce one. Out of curiosity, she tugs at the lock experimentally, and it snaps open.

"Someone closed the padlock, but didn't scramble the code." Lena blinks in surprise.

"This is bad," Jacobson whispers. The technicians have moved halfway up the stairs and watch Lena in silence.

"But no one could have closed it from inside the attic," Lena says. "Whoever left it here was probably in a hurry."

Judging by the structure of the ceiling, the attic is as long as the roof, but nowhere near standing height. At best, one might be able to crawl or stand on one's knees. But it is enough for someone to hide. Or to hide part of someone else. Wincing, she removes the lock and lets the trapdoor swing down.

A lightweight ladder extends from the door as it opens. The contraption allows for easy passage up to the cramped space. Nothing else falls down through the opening, except a bright, reddish light so intense it casts the room below in a golden glow. Heat washes over her face as if she were standing close to a bonfire.

"Has he got a solarium up there?" Jacobson wonders.

"The attic's too small for that. Wait here." Squinting in the glare, Lena climbs the ladder and looks around.

On each side of the horizontal opening is a short stretch of floor covered with what looks like gardening tools. Beyond the floor are stacks of large, rectangular glass containers the size of fish tanks, all brightly lit by arrays of halogen lamps. Most boxes are empty except for scattered patches of sand, small stones, and gravel. Some contain empty, overturned terracotta flower pots. There have to be at least a dozen containers in total. The room is as hot as a sauna.

In one of the containers is the severed head of a man.

It faces ninety degrees away from the trapdoor and directly at a large spotlight, whose molten light illuminates every feature of the skin. Broad swatches of blood cover the floor that leads up to the container. The features on the face of the head are distorted, but match those on the blurred photo. They are also relatively similar to those on the picture of Carl Adlerberg.

Careful not to touch the blood, she climbs all the way up to get a better look. As always is the case when she is confronted with a crime that reaches far outside what she understands, she is filled with both anger and cool dispassion. Part inevitable rage because of the suffering, part forced calm to funnel her attention down to the details, the leads, and the evidence.

There is writing on the might-be fish tank that contains the severed head.

A few lines in black smudged felt pen, scribbled hastily or by someone nearly illiterate. The writing is on the short side of the rectangular container. It faces the head, just like the lamp, as if the unseeing eyes have been left to stare at the words. She knows what has been written on the glass even before she makes out the individual letters.

Look deep and draw.

"Talk to me," Jacobson calls from down below.

"The victim's head is up here." Lena moves backwards to climb down. "It's inside some kind of display case. The attic looks like a vacated mini-museum. Don't ask me how he got this junk up here."

She looks away from the head to take in the full extent of the room and pauses in mid-step.

She is wrong; the attic is not an exhibition. These glass containers are terrariums. The image of the snake on the cover of the magazine downstairs springs to her mind. Martin's attic is filled with habitats for reptiles. Fortunately, all of the terrariums seem empty. Perhaps Martin had planned to populate them, or maybe the animals are dead or given away.

Or –

A sharp bang on one of the glass panes makes Lena twist sideways. She presses herself against the drooping ceiling, whips out her gun, and turns around.

Behind one of the terrariums, a shape moves under the light, unfolding and elongating as she watches. Two black eyes gleam in the light. A snake, heavy and bulky, its head wide and triangular. Dark hourglass markings run down its pale grey body. Its smacks into the glass again and hisses loudly, displaying fangs as long as matches.

She knows very little about animals in general, but the snake is definitely foreign and probably venomous. It is also extremely agitated. Perhaps by the intrusion or by having its nest converted into a macabre impromptu showpiece. Either way, the creature wants revenge and hopes to take it out on Lena.

Lena leans closer. She should try to shoot the beast or at least scurry down the ladder, but fascination and surprise have her paralyzed as if she were encased in concrete. The snake watches her with eyes as inert as polished marble. It's a beautiful creature, but wholly void of compassion or care.

Lena squeezes the trigger halfway, but the effort makes her sweat. She has no right to kill this creature.

On one hand, its limited animal senses cannot comprehend the scope of events unfolding around the house. Yet its impassive stare is omniscient and cuts through every layer of pretence. The snake and she are equals: one executioner facing off another, both of them stuck inside a confining universe.

"What's going on up there?" Jacobson shouts.

Lena gasps and moves her finger off the trigger. Her breathing is fast and shallow. The snake flinches, slithers away from the light, and recedes into the darkness as far as it can. After a few seconds, it is lost in the jumble of reflections and mirror images among the terrariums.

Her legs threaten to give in as she climbs down the ladder. A cold sweat has broken over her entire body. The lights have left her dazzled, and her vision is so blurred the walls resemble curtains of smoke.

When she reaches the floor, she slumps down on the sofa.

"For God's sake," one of the technicians shout. "You can't sit there. We haven't checked the furniture yet. I wish we could work undisturbed for once."

"You have to–" Lena falls silent as she realises she has no idea where to report poisonous animals. It's the first time she has faced this kind of threat. And, she hopes, the last.

Jacobson approaches her slowly, as if any sudden movement might make her dart away. He glances at the gun in her hand: she's gripping it so hard her knuckles are pale, and she is trembling badly.

"There's a snake up there," Lena says.

"Are you sure?" The technician who scolded Lena looks up at the open trapdoor.

"More sure than I'd like to be. But the remaining part of the victim is there too, so the attic has to be cleaned out."

"Is the snake domestic?"

"Hardly," Lena says.

"But do you think it's dangerous?"

"Put it this way," Lena says as she struggles to her feet. "I'd rather eat shattered glass than go back up there. Call it in."

She holsters her gun on the second attempt and walks towards the stairs. Jacobson follows close behind her.

"Are you just going to leave?" the technician calls after her.

"You wanted me out of the way," Lena says. "Wish granted."

Chapter 31

Norra Ängby

Friday

10:52

Lena rests her head against the car seat and looks at the crowd farther down the road. Two TV teams have joined the onlookers, as have at least another hundred people. Jacobson sits in the passenger seat and waits for her to speak.

She provides Jimmy with a twenty-word rundown of what she found in the house, knowing that otherwise he will leave the car to go and find out for himself.

"Bloody hell," Jimmy whispers from the back seat. "That's horrible. And look at all these idiots blocking the road. Looks like the whole suburb has come here."

"Get your head down," Jacobson hisses.

"I'm just curious. Are you sure it's the same guy?"

"That's none of your–" Jacobson begins.

"Affirmative," Lena snaps. "And he's not finished."

"I give up," Jacobson sighs and shakes his head.

"We know Jimmy's not our man," Lena says. "So I prefer that he's up to speed with what's going on." She takes out her phone and turns it over in her hand.

"Are you going to ditch me somewhere?" Jimmy's voice is dangerously loud.

"You can hardly stay in the car forever," Jacobson says. "Or anywhere near us, for that matter. It's only a matter of time before someone spots you."

"It's only a matter of time," Jimmy says, "before that bastard comes for me. Or any of us. Don't you think he's watching right now?"

"I'm convinced he is," Lena says. She doesn't mention that those who want Jimmy dead might not be behind the murders in Norra Ängby.

"Really?" Jacobson asks.

"If I were him, I'd keep an eye on the scene. He wants his installations to be found. It makes sense that he's following the developments." Lena glances at the dark windows in the villas along the street.

"He needs only a web browser to do that," Jacobson argues.

"That's not the same as seeing it live." Lena starts the car. "I suspect that the murderer lives nearby, perhaps only a block away. Actually, I'm sure of it. For now, we're going to follow the only lead we have, and wring it dry."

"I take it we're going to see the manager, then?" Jacobson asks.

Lena nods. "Jimmy, I'll drop you off at–" Her phone rings.

"Hold on." She frowns at the unknown number on the display. It doesn't look familiar, or even Swedish. She takes the call.

"Who's this?" Lena starts the car and accelerates away from the scene.

"Is this Señora Lena Franke?" A woman, speaking English with a southern European accent.

"How can I help?" Lena remembers the photo she asked Gren to send to the Spanish police force. "Are you calling from Spain?"

Jacobson looks up at her in surprise.

"Yes," the woman says. "This is the Cartagena office. We may have found your missing person."

Lena brakes hard and pulls over. Jacobson uses his hands to brace himself against the glove compartment, while Jimmy curses on the floor behind her seat.

"Go on," Lena says.

"We have received a tip from a village nurse. She recognized the woman in the photo you sent us. A rich, elderly Swedish lady?"

"Possibly," Lena says. The description is promising.

"She has a property here. I have sent the address to your office, and we have obtained the telephone number."

"Don't call her," Lena says. "The woman has no reason to talk to us. It's a complicated case. I'm afraid she'll run before I've said three words."

Lena taps her fingers against the steering wheel. Getting an arrest warrant in Sweden can be frustrating enough, and trying to have one issued in another country won't be any easier. She has never done anything like it before. It's a whole new ballpark, and not one she wants to enter.

"But you are interested in talking to her?" the woman on the phone wonders.

"Of course," Lena says absently.

"So you don't mind if I put her through to you?"

"You have her on the line?" Lena sits upright in the car seat.

"She rang us ten minutes after the nurse called, and she's still waiting on the switchboard. Would you like me to connect you?"

"Quickly," Lena says. "Before she changes her mind and hangs up."

Lena makes a hushing gesture at Jimmy, makes sure no one is near the car, and turns on the speakerphone. Letting Jimmy take part in the conversation is less than ideal, but Jacobson needs to hear what is said. The fact that Kristina is calling the police herself is not necessarily a good sign.

The line goes silent except for a few whirrs and clicks.

"Hello?" a voice says after a moment. A different woman, speaking in Swedish. She sounds apprehensive and tired.

"Is this Kristina Stenberg?" Lena asks.

"I'm afraid so," Kristina says. "And you must be Detective Franke." She laughs lightly. "Your voice isn't as dark as I expected.

In the photos, you look like a proper vigilante, just like the papers hope to portray you. All anger and intent. Well, apart from the pictures in which you're wearing a dress."

Lena chooses her words carefully. She must make the most of this conversation. Kristina's banter can be interpreted as an attempt to rile her, but the woman's tone is not sarcastic, only tired and weak.

"Is it correct that you founded and jointly managed a medical research company around thirty years ago?" Lena asks.

"Straight to the point." Kristina sighs. "Exemplary tactics. No wonder you're making such headway with your investigations. I should've known they were getting louder for a reason."

"Who's being loud?" Lena cannot resist asking. Jacobson looks at Lena and shrugs: he is as bewildered as she is.

"No one you know." Kristina pauses. "Well, I might be wrong in that. I've read up on your past."

"Please answer the question," Lena says. Kristina sounds thoroughly unhinged. At some point, she might decide to hang up or just wander off.

"I knew you'd found the lab when I saw you carried out on the stretcher," Kristina says. "But I must admit I'm puzzled by how you linked the facility to me."

"The fire alarm."

"Ah." Kristina chuckles. "How sloppy of us. To forget such a trivial thing, after we went through the trouble of erasing all those serial numbers. We scrubbed or scorched everything we didn't have time to move out. But then, I knew we could've done a better job when we closed the lab down. It was a shoddy affair. The clock was ticking, you see. Rumours were spreading."

"If you tell me what you were doing in there, I might be able to negotiate a deal for you," Lena says.

It's good that Kristina can't see her face, or the woman might be able to tell that Lena is lying. Brokering extenuating arrangements for criminals of Kristina's calibre is almost impossible. It is also out of the question because of simple principle, but Kristina doesn't have to know that.

"It's too late for that," Kristina says. "As it turns out, I've already signed a different kind of contract. One I can't break free from. And I'm ready for my sentence, so save your cajoling for some petty thief."

"Fine," Lena says. "I've more urgent matters on my hands than your dirty past and your sadistic experiments." Jacobson makes a calming gesture, as he fears Lena might lapse into a fit of rage.

"Of course," Kristina says. "You're busy solving the murders."

"There's a link between the facility you built and the incidents," Lena says. "I need to understand what it is."

She must also find out about the connection between Kristina and those who rigged Jimmy's car, but one thing will lead to another.

"What if I told you who the killer is?" Kristina asks.

"Come again?" Lena wonders if she misheard.

"You're looking for a man in his forties. His hair was dark, I think, and his eyes were green. I suspect that he's rather short, although that's a guess."

Lena and Jacobson look at each other in disbelief. Jimmy slowly sits up, but she is too distracted to tell him to hide. The temperature in the car seems to have dropped.

"What's his name?" Lena asks.

"He didn't have one. As I said, we made sure the records were destroyed."

"Then tell me how you know he's the man we're looking for."

Before Kristina continues, Lena presses the mute button on her phone.

"Make sure the case is updated with those details," Lena says to Jacobson. "And spread the word to Asplund and his people."

"I'll call him straight away." Jacobson steps out of the car as silently as he can.

"Go on," Lena says to Kristina when Jacobson has left.

"Carl and I ran the business together. I assume you're aware of what we tried to achieve?"

"Humour me."

"We were gunning for the Nobel Prize. Or, failing that, fame and fortune. Laugh if you will. I certainly have since the day our work fell apart."

"By creating some revolutionary medicine?" Lena guesses.

"Precisely. We were about to cure a host of mental illnesses, or so we thought. Carl had devised a complex treatment that appeared to wipe out certain unwanted tendencies in the psyches of our subjects. In short, a one-stop medicine. Gold in a beaker."

"A drug," Lena says. "Used in combination with that flashing lamp."

"Well guessed. So you turned it on, then."

Lena swallows. "That's not important."

"I'll take that as a yes. We were stupid to leave it for last. I suggested we take it out first thing when we moved, but like I said, closing down was a hectic affair."

Lena shudders and swallows. More and more pieces are served up by Kristina's unexpected confession. There is no one in sight outside the car apart from Jacobson; however, she feels observed, as if Kristina's words hide the power to transport Lena back to the abandoned lab.

"However," Kristina continues, "there was a third component. We had to make the subjects face their worst fears. Only then, when they confronted their phantoms, could we tell whether or not our products were effective."

"This is all very fascinating," Lena says, "but I need to know more about the man you think is behind the murders."

"It's not a theory. There's only one possible candidate."

"Then help me identify him."

"I'm getting there. As I was saying, Carl and I tried countless ways over the years to get our subjects to meet their nightmares. Eventually we settled on pens and papers. The subjects didn't need any skill with drawing; they managed to channel their ideas well enough to trigger the responses we wanted."

"You speak about these poor people as if they were animals. Or even something less."

Kristina laughs, but there is no warmth in her voice.

"They were a handful of broken souls," Kristina says. "Damaged beyond repair by birth or accident. Unable to function outside the hospital, and barely manageable inside. No one missed them. On the contrary, the staff was quite happy when we took the cretins off their hands. A win-win situation."

Lena counts down from ten while she breathes in and out. Her temper hangs on a thread, and Kristina is doing her best to tear it apart.

"When our treatment worked," Kristina goes on, "it did marvels for violent behaviour. All hints of such tendencies were gone. But the success ratio was only one in four."

"Three out of four people weren't affected?" Lena asks.

"They ended up worse. Some were reduced to homicidal lumps of meat. That wasn't ideal, but it got them sent straight to isolation, which back then was a cheaper way of storing patients than it is today. So again, it was a mutually beneficial agreement."

"Hospitals don't store patients," Lena says quietly. "They treat them."

"Call it what you want. We wanted to be rid of problematic subjects, and so did everyone else. Better a restraint shirt and a cell than walks in the park with teams of expensive staff."

"But word got out," Lena guesses. "There's no way everyone involved could have turned a blind eye to what you were doing. And there are no records at all about those rooms."

"No one knew anything," Kristina says. "The hospital helped arrange the facility. We said we were studying a new type of medicine for the patients, which was perfectly true. Then we arranged for suitable subjects to be relocated to us on a regular basis. Not all of the management was involved. Only those who knew better than to babble and who could pull the right strings."

Jacobson quietly opens the door, sits down in his seat, and gives Lena thumbs-up. He has contacted Gren.

"What happened then?" Lena asks.

"Word never got out," Kristina says, "but a subject did."

"The murderer," Lena says, finally understanding where Kristina is going. "He escaped."

"Against all odds, one of them slipped through our fingers. A male picked the lock that secured him to his bed. Then he disabled the alarm, stole a key to the main door, and fled through the tunnels."

"It was a high-security hospital," Lena says. "How did he make it off the grounds?"

"By shutting down all the lights. He opened a power box and ripped out the right cables. Quite impressive, given how young he was at the time. Your murderer has a knack for these things."

"And then he vanished?"

"Into thin air," Kristina says. "As did we. Shutting down our operations was the only option. But as you've noticed, we weren't particularly thorough. All the other subjects were moved to another project. I think its name was Glömminge, although I wasn't involved in that."

Lena searches for something to say, but her mouth has gone dry. Knowing what went on in the rooms she visited, and what the killer suffered through, clouds her thoughts like ink splashed in water. She has managed to uncork the bottle, and the genie is threatening to swallow her whole.

Lena mutes her phone temporarily and leans close to Jacobson. "Check if there are any orphans in their forties living nearby," she whispers. "Have them send us a list if there's anything promising."

Jacobson nods and leaves the car again.

Jimmy looks up from between the seats and catches Lena's eye. She knows what he thinks: no one sane would reveal this much. If Kristina's story holds true, it's an express ticket to several lifetimes in prison.

Lena raises her phone to her ear again. "Why are you telling me this?" she asks.

"Because I'm tired of hiding," Kristina says. "I cannot bear the voices another day."

"You mentioned those before. Who's doing the talking?"

"All of them. And they're singing day and night. It's the choir of my departure."

Lena hears them: a low keening in the background, like a hard wind outside a cabin. Kristina is slipping as they listen to her speak. She might be coming clean, but she's not planning on answering for what she has done.

"Did you plant the bomb in Abrahamsberg?" Lena asks.

"Of course not," Kristina says. "What am I, some kind of barbarian?" She laughs. "I'm going now."

"Wait," Lena says.

"My waiting is over. I have spent three decades trying to shut the voices out. It's enough."

"Then help us," Lena says. "Tell me where Carl is."

"I have no idea."

"But you think he's still alive."

"It's irrelevant. Even if Carl is around, you'll never find him. He knew how to evade the authorities even when he was young. Now he's rich enough to buy all the privacy in the world. No one can catch him."

"Watch me," Lena says.

"As entertaining as it might be to see you try–" Kristina sighs "– I have to pass. The dance is over for me. As for the murderer, go to the Nordea bank office at Hornstull. I've honestly forgotten what I left there, but if you're lucky, you might retrieve something of use."

"What dance?" Lena asks. "What's at the bank?"

"They say some sins come back to haunt you, and it's true. I've stayed alive by not paying attention. Year after year, I've coped with the damning whispers, the lamenting choir behind my back, and I've spent every waking moment shutting them out."

Kristina's voice climbs as she speaks. Lena tenses and grips the phone; the woman on the phone is losing her composure.

"Don't do anything rash," Lena says. "We can still negotiate–"

"I'm too tired. The murmurs have worn me down."

"Stay on the phone," Lena shouts.

"At last," Kristina says with profound relief in her voice, "it's time to give them my undivided attention."

The call ends.

*

A few minutes later, Lena turns onto the large arterial road and drives towards the city. She overtakes a truck and zips past a crossing moments before the lights turn red. Jacobson studies a page on the police console while Jimmy crouches on the floor in the back of the car.

The bank is located on the western tip of Södermalm, the large island that makes up Stockholm city's south. About thirty minutes. Less if she uses the blue lights, but traffic is light.

"Finding any orphans in Norra Ängby will take time," Jacobson says. "We're getting a record from the tax agency, but we have to check it against the local address registry."

"What's so hard about that?" she asks. "Have a computer do it."

"The formats of the lists aren't compatible. We have to convert all the spreadsheets, and they're more complex than you'd think."

"Why am I not surprised?"

"Do you think Kristina arranged the bomb?" Jacobson asks.

"You heard her," Lena says. "I doubt she can tie her own shoes."

Tying a noose was a different matter, however. Kristina had done something stupid after she hung up. She had spoken like someone balancing on a ledge and not looking for a railing to hold on to. Jacobson had called the Spanish police and asked them to send a unit to Kristina's address, but they haven't reported back yet.

"Which means there's another party involved," Lena continues. "Stay hidden on the floor while we're at the bank. We might be followed."

"I looked up Carl." Jacobson shakes his head. "No one's seen him since nineteen eighty-six. Over a week, he shifted a fortune in bonds into untraceable assets abroad, withdrew a mountain in cash, and vanished."

"Doesn't sound like your average suicide candidate," Lena says. "How much is a fortune and a mountain?"

"More millions than I can add up." Jacobson drums his fingers on the seat. "He made an absolute killing from his company's medicine patents. I'd say he either ran from trouble or decided to go dark. Or both."

"Is that even possible?" Jimmy wonders. "Can people just disappear because they want to?"

"That kind of money enables everything." Lena squints at the glaring sun and turns onto the bridge to Södermalm.

"Everyone's got a price?" Jimmy suggests.

"Correct," Lena agrees. "But the currency varies. We're almost there. Soon, we might know what Kristina tried to escape."

Chapter 32

Cartagena, Spain

Friday

11:13

When Kristina hangs up on the detective, the voices are louder than ever before.

Decades have passed since the first time she heard them. Back then, they had been only a hint of a name, quickly dissolving like smoke in a breeze. The occasion had marked the end of a better phase in her life. Perhaps a time that had *been* her life; the thousands of hours that have passed since cannot be called a proper existence. On the contrary, the past thirty-odd years are better described as a prolonged detachment, pulling her ever farther away from the shores of reality.

And today, she must abandon her failing ship.

Life had been easy before the sounds began to invade her privacy. It was an era of curiosity and problem-solving, filled with work and progress as Carl and she wandered down the corridors of the human psyche. Money rolled in at a rate other researchers could only dream of.

Some experiments were demanding, especially those that required tests on living subjects; she often had to remind herself that some human beings were more animals than persons. But advancing the knowledge was the only way forward, so she ignored the voices as long as possible. They were, after all, impossible, and she dealt only with facts. Guesses were for feather-brained amateurs. Proof was her bat, theories her balls, biology her playing field.

She helped Carl build an empire on the foundation of her unshakable assuredness. For years, she thought that the words that called to her from around corners and empty chambers were mostly due to her workload. A taxing sign of fatigue and pressure, but nothing worse.

Then doubts began to corrode her armour of firm ideals. Her resolve thinned as her research continued, and the look on the subjects' faces became more difficult to ignore. Some begged her to end their lives with such fervour that the pleas sounded almost genuine.

It dawned on her that perhaps she had made a mistake with some of the subjects. *Or maybe,* the voice only she heard suggested, *you have been mistaken all the time.*

She needed to understand what was happening to her. Some time off would do her good. But before she had time to raise the topic with Carl, that boy had escaped from the facility at Beckomberga Hospital, and Carl decided to close down the laboratory. A few days of intense bribing and cleaning later, Carl said goodbye and left with all the remaining subjects stuffed into a truck. He had a new project lined up, he told her.

That was the last she saw of him.

The trials conducted under Beckomberga had been their most lucrative project to date. They had all the results they needed to produce the key substances: microscopic doses of chemicals that boosted the efficiency of many other medicines. Getting the compound right took hundreds upon hundreds of tests, but those long nights proved priceless.

Carl patented the drug and netted millions in the first quarter. Many more millions followed the same year. Kristina's shares in their company made her rich, and she was set up for a life in exceeding comfort. If it had not been for the voices.

She never knew what Carl's next project was, although the look on his face when he said goodbye gave her misgivings. He was a changed man. For him, there was no end to the questions, and no way of finding the answers he wanted was too extreme.

Kristina realised that even she might get in his way one day, and if that happened, Carl would not hesitate to crush her. His behaviour prompted her to get the safety deposit box. If worst came to worst, she might use its contents as leverage.

But Carl never got in touch or moved against her. Instead, the voices grew in volume and in number.

Kristina took a management role in a new company, but held it for less than a month. The single whisper soon multiplied into a group. Incoherent mutters became distinct words that spoke of terrors, threats, and promises of unimaginable torture. They detailed all the experiments she had conducted in the name of progress. The voices knew about every injection, incision, and jolt she had inflicted on the subjects under her rule.

She heard them at night and during the day, at home and at her workplace, while watching TV or brushing her teeth. There were no sanctuaries. She could not sleep or think, let alone manage a job. Her wealth meant she never had to worry about finances, but she lived to work, and the voices seemed to thrive in the still waters of inactivity. Eventually, she fled to Spain in hopes of outrunning her unseen pursuers, but they followed her. All she could do was settle down and try to ignore their ceaseless accusations.

Three decades passed. Then today, her nurse woke her up by banging on Kristina's front door.

"My brother works for the police," the nurse said. "They are looking for a Swedish woman. He showed me a picture. She looks just like you, *senora*."

The nurse was breathless and sweating as she spoke. Presumably, she thought there had been a family crisis of some sort in Kristina's family.

Kristina had smiled, shut the door, and called the Spanish police who transferred her call. There was no point in prolonging the inevitable. She knew what had led the police to her; out of habit, she kept an eye on the Swedish news, and she had seen the photo of the message pinned to the tree.

Look deep and draw.

Long ago, she'd painted the same words on an underground wall, hoping they would serve as a visual reminder for their research subjects during her and Carl's experiments. The police's interest meant they found a link between her and the murders. Which, of course, was correct.

Everything is coming together.

The conversation with the neurotic detective relieved Kristina. So much time has passed that she had almost forgotten about the papers she hid at the bank as a precaution in case Carl turned on her.

Now she has pointed the police the right way, and with a little luck, the hurried stash of information she had tucked away in the vault might contain some detail that could pull Carl down from his mighty height. Untroubled by his past, her former colleague swam with the swans of Sweden's elite, while Kristina was held hostage by voices that never stopped accusing and condemning her. That ongoing unfairness always pained her.

But her and Carl's shared history has risen to cast a shadow over the present. Given their sins, it was bound to happen. She imagines the runaway boy as a bird leaving his nest and returning as a larger, much more deadly specimen, leaving behind a trail of destruction as it bears down on its prey. He must have Carl shivering in fear.

Kristina rises and walks over to the bedroom door. A great calm has settled inside her. The race is over, and her chosen track has taken her to the edge of a cliff. Now remains one last bid for escape, but this time, she will not move country. Her next and final journey will take her to what she longs for the most: a quiet place.

The voices scream from her bedroom so savagely that the door shudders. She has never heard them this restless. It's a marvel her neighbours haven't noticed. Neither has the nurse, but then again, the cries always stop whenever Kristina has company. They know how to best make her suffer. It is, Kristina suspects, the very point of their existence.

It ends today. She is ready to confront her tormentors.

Slowly, with a strange sense of ceremony, Kristina swings the door open for the first time since she started to hear the whispers. When her eyes adjust to the gloom, she grows as cold as if she were caught naked in a blizzard.

Her bedroom is packed with men, women and children. Everyone is dressed in the green gowns of Beckomberga Hospital. They are curled up on the floor, pressed to the walls, and sprawled on her bed. One young boy clings to an empty wall as if he were a fly. A woman looks up at Kristina from under the bed, and a man hangs upside down from the lamp in the ceiling.

The cries vanish and leave behind an echo too long for the small room. All eyes are fixed on her.

She recognises the intruders immediately: they are her subjects, every single one, gathered in her own home. They are not people but impostors, creatures taken human form, unfit for the better world she helped to build.

When the voices come again, they speak as one.

"You had a *secret*," they hiss.

Kristina backs away. She doesn't know what the voices are referring to, but the terror that floods her drowns out the brief confusion. The pitiful, monstrous creatures are unbound, and they are intent on her, advancing like a swarm of malice towards the door.

"I had such plans," the voices spit in a deafening chorus. "Such glorious, lovely schemes. You have ruined them all."

"This cannot be real," Kristina croaks. "You're all gone."

She backs out on the balcony. It has always been her plan to leave from here, but the shock of facing these obscene so-called human beings nearly makes her forget her ambition. Six storeys below is the irregular oval of the large outdoor pool, currently drained for maintenance. It will be her way out. A perfect curtain to close over her suffering.

"We are here," the voices snarl. "All and one, just as we always have been. You finally opened the door and let us in. Now you are our plaything. And we have endless fun in store."

Kristina leaps over the balcony railing.

During the several seconds she falls, she longs for the unyielding ground to meet her. This way, her end will be quick and painless, and she will finally have the silence she has craved for so long.

But as Kristina's body breaks against the cold tiles, her long-awaited silence eludes her.

Instead, all the women and men Kristina once used for her experiments are waiting for her. Hundreds upon hundreds they rush in, ready to catch her with outstretched arms, eager to teach her everything they know.

Above all, they will show her how to sing.

Chapter 33

Carl locks the door to his office and pulls out the top drawer of his desk. It is empty apart from a thick and expensive notepad filled with calculations and quick scribbles. Most would write down even casual notes on their laptops, but he is a traditionalist, and for good reason. Computers can be hacked and digital files can be copied endlessly. Papers are easy to tear out and, if necessary, burn or flush down.

Pity he was not as cautious in his youth.

His empty leather gym bag waits by his feet. He must decide what to pack. Decades have passed since he last did so himself; he always delegated the boring task to assistants or housekeepers. This time, however, he cannot alert his paid staff that he might leave.

If he goes, he can't tell them where he's staying. Contact over email is out of the question. He will have to throw away his current phone. Complete secrecy is paramount, and escaping without leaving at least an electronic trail is next to impossible in this silicon-permeated society. Unless one has a safe house prepared.

The key is hidden inside a concealed space underneath the desk. He turns it over in his hand and smiles. Useless to anyone unaware of where to use it, invaluable to one who knows to which hideaway it grants passage.

He pockets the key and holds his breath when his phone rings. An unknown, anonymous number. Quickly, he looks out in the corridor to make sure no one is near, then sits down and takes the call.

"Carl here."

"The detective has left the second crime scene. She's currently in the city centre."

The man from the anonymous agency. His voice is level and calm, despite the fact that this whole ordeal is a driverless catastrophe about to swerve off the road.

"Any sign of the blogger?" Carl asks.

"Our operative at the location is confident there are three people in the detective's vehicle. Lena Franke, a man who appears to be her colleague, and a third individual in the back seat."

"Is the third person him?"

"Probably. He tries to stay out of sight, but our operative caught a flash of dark hair. Please advise on how you wish to proceed."

Carl looks out the window and considers his options. The blogger might guide the police to the room where he took his cursed photos. That's an unpleasant thought, yet the lab is a dead end, scraped clean of all potentially compromising details. A tomb that can raise questions but offer no answers. Its past stays buried there.

Only one loose end remains: the murderer. To find him, Carl must tail the detective, so that he can step in if she manages to corner her quarry.

"Follow them," Carl says. "They're probably bound for the police headquarters, although let me know if they head somewhere else."

"I don't think they're going to the police station," the man replies. "The detective is currently at western Södermalm. Her car has stopped outside a bank at Hornstull."

"Just keep watching her, and–"

Carl pauses as a thought comes to him. The notion is so outlandish he almost rejects it out of hand, but the past days have spun countless impossibilities into moments of devastating reality. He can no longer dismiss even the most outrageous ideas.

"What is she doing at the bank?" Carl asks. "Quickly, where exactly is she."

"Our operative says that she has entered the bank office. Apparently she drove fast, as if she were in a hurry to get there."

Carl closes his fist by his side. Everyone uses banks, even unhinged detectives, and this particular office is located between her office and her flat. It may be a coincidence that his old company used the same bank office decades earlier while they conducted their successful but fateful experiments at Beckomberga Hospital.

He moved all their assets to other banks long ago. Some of the staff had their accounts and safety deposit boxes there, but everyone is confirmed dead or have long since fled abroad. Most likely, the detective's visit means nothing.

But chance is quickly becoming an endangered species.

"Here are my instructions," Carl says. "If Lena Franke or anyone in her company leaves the bank with so much as a piece of paper, engage and remove them."

"Are you sure?" The man sounds mildly surprised.

"Absolutely," Carl says.

"This will triple the current cost."

"I'll get you the money. Just make sure you don't leave anyone alive."

Chapter 34

The interior of the bank is as bland as Lena expects, but much larger. Two groups of large sofas, a wall with five counters opposite several office doors. Grey tiles, bright halogen lights, stairs leading up and down behind reinforced glass doors.

Lena has time to inspect the uninspiring décor for several minutes while she waits for Jacobson to finalise the search warrant. Given that the person of interest was both reported missing and supposed dead, processing the warrant takes longer than usual.

When Jacobson is done, she walks up to the nearest counter and taps the woman who is being assisted on her shoulder. The woman turns around and frowns.

"We need a word with the officer," Lena says.

"Why don't you queue like everyone else?" the woman murmurs. "This is misuse of authority."

Lena opens her mouth, but Jacobson inserts himself between the two women.

"Apologies," he says. "Urgent police business. I'm sorry for the intrusion, but we won't be long."

The woman leaves reluctantly. Lena walks up to the counter, where a young male clerk looks wide-eyed at Lena's ID card.

"How can I help?" he asks.

"Fetch your manager," Lena says. "Please," she adds when Jacobson glances at her.

"I'm afraid she's on lunch, but she should be back any minute. Can I be of assistance?"

"If you perhaps–" Jacobson begins.

"Yes, you can." Lena raises her voice a fraction. "Call your boss and tell him or her to get back here right now. Otherwise we might have to call in a locksmith and enter your archives by force. This is an investigation, not a cash withdrawal."

"Archives?" the man asks weakly as he fumbles for the phone. "Do you mean the vault?"

Lena looks at Jacobson, who nods thoughtfully. She had been about to ask for Kristina's account information. If the branch has safety deposits, there might be much stronger leads within reach.

Two minutes later, a fidgeting, suit-clad woman in her thirties emerges from the stairwell. She crosses the floor with impressive speed, considering her high heels. The man behind the counter nods at the approaching woman.

"There she is," he says.

Jacobson presents the search warrant to the manager, who tries to smile at Jacobson and read the information on his phone at the same time.

"We need access to a safety deposit box in the name of Kristina Stenberg," Lena says.

"Of course." The manager clears her throat and lowers her voice. "Can we handle this as discreetly as possible?" she asks. "I don't want to distress the customers."

Lena looks at the manager blankly, but then she understands. The woman is afraid that Lena will turn her neat office into a disaster zone. As if disasters inevitably follow in Lena's footsteps wherever she goes. Her reputation is becoming a major nuisance.

"This is as subtle as we get," Lena says.

"Wonderful." The manager beams nervously at her. "I'll get the keys and take you downstairs immediately."

The manager retrieves the keys from one of her employees and opens the door to the stairwell. She guides Lena and Jacobson down the stairs into a dining room-sized chamber that smells of dust and old paint. Its grey walls are bare except for the massive vault door in matte steel. It looks much more robust than Lena expects, even for a bank vault.

"That's a very imposing door," Jacobson notes. "Fit for a fortress. Quite old, isn't it?"

"Over sixty years," the manager says. "Once upon a time, these were the central vaults for the entire company, so they got the best protection there was on the market. That's also why there are so many corridors."

The manager punches in a code on the keypad next to the door and uses a long key to open a series of other manual locks. A loud clank is followed by the dull whirr of a retrofitted electric engine, which slowly swings the door open. The manager steps inside and flicks a switch.

Lena pauses on the doorstep to take in the sight. In her experience, vaults were tiny spaces, but behind the door is a corridor so long she can barely make out the end. Blue metal boxes are set into the wall on both sides. Thick but worn carpet, white-painted ceiling. Bundles of pipes and cables hang suspended over her head in metal hoops. Bright strip lights bathe the corridors in a clinical white glow. The air is warm and stuffy. Far away, the corridor branches off in new directions.

"There must be thousands of deposit boxes here," Lena says. Her back itches and her hands are clammy. The sooner they are out of here, the better.

"Six thousand three hundred and eleven," the manager says. "The vault was constructed in a former air-raid shelter, so there's plenty of room. It's one of the biggest in the country."

Lena stands still on the broad metal doorstep. Another step forward and she has entered the vault. A few more and she will be at the box. In less than a minute, they can find out whether or not

Kristina sent them on a wild goose hunt, or if there is anything useful in the old woman's hideaway.

But the air seems to thicken in front of her. Entering the vault feels less like a small movement and more akin to descending a set of stairs or throwing herself into an unlit shaft. The tunnels ahead are well lit and used daily. They are a far cry from the rank culverts below Beckomberga Hospital, and nothing like the claustrophobic disused laboratory.

What gets to her is the silence. The complete lack of sounds from traffic, voices, even machines. In its absence is not calm, but an opportunity for other voices to make themselves heard. Once such voice belongs to an aspect of her persona she hopes will stay quiet to the end of her days.

That voice had reared its head twice: once on the botched raid, when her reputation as a ticking bomb was founded. Later, it almost got the better of her when she finally caught up with John Andersson. Only Agnes's intervention had stopped Lena from falling prey to her persistent desire to inflict pain in the name of retribution. Another moment, and she would have been a different person. If a person at all.

The voice is still there. Reduced to a distant whisper, but not gone. Work, distractions and determination shut it out, while this kind of gagged atmosphere turns the whisper into a loud murmur. The sensation is enough to make her legs weak, but she must go on. Agnes is no longer around to have her back.

"I could really use you here right now," Lena says under her breath.

The manager frowns at Lena. "Are you all right, Detective?"

"Lena?" Jacobson looks at her sideways.

Lena swallows and nods. "I'm right as a drizzle," she says. "Just thinking out loud."

"I can go alone if you're uncomfortable," Jacobson suggests.

Lena shakes her head and walks into the vault. "I've just seen one tunnel too many over the past couple of days," she says. "But I can handle one more."

Kristina's deposit box turns out to be located at the far end of a corridor, three turns from the entrance to the vault. The box is the width of a standard office paper and as high as Lena's hand. Its only label is a series of numbers.

The manager unlocks the box, pulls out the drawer, and stands back. Inside the drawer is a thick brown paper folder filled with documents. Lena takes the folder and frowns at a faint whiff of crayon.

"This won't take long," Jacobson says to the manager. "We'll have a quick look, but we will need to bring its contents with us to the station. I'll see that you get a receipt. Please make sure no one else enters the vault while we're here."

"Of course." The manager smiles. "I'll wait outside until you're done."

Lena waits until the manager has turned a corner and is out of sight, then chooses a page at random and opens the folder. She expects graphs and statistics, rows and columns with data, lists with cryptic jargon and machine-typed medical notes.

She does not expect drawings.

Inside a yellow plastic folder labelled *samples* is a stack of sheets that holds at least a hundred illustrations. Each paper features a tornado of jumbled lines in black crayon. Every drawing portrays vaguely organic forms: the suggestion of a spine, hints of faces, curves that could be the outlines of bodies. But even in their ambiguous state, the shapes are asymmetrical. They are twisted around, stretched out, pulled apart and put together wrong.

Lena fights the impulse to drop the paper. While the drawings are crude, there is a restless, violent energy to the works, as if they might come alive without warning and seek to escape the papers.

"What's that?" Jacobson frowns at the page. "A spider?"

"Fingers, I think." Lena turns the paper upside down. "Don't ask me what they're holding."

"These must be the illustrations Kristina talked about," Jacobson says. "The ones their patients made."

"After they were drugged and forced to watch that flashing lamp." Lena nods. "I guess this represents their worst nightmares. And now those dreams are mine." She closes the folder with trembling hands and puts it on the floor.

"Listen to this." Jacobson has opened another folder and reads out loud from a machine-typed sheet.

March 17. Some subjects display positive responses to the latest batch, but we need more conclusive results before we step up the trials.

Our new approach to let the subjects themselves visualize their traumas, imagined or real, continues to give good results. Moreover, Carl's optical catalyst has enabled us to trigger the reactions almost instantly. The screams are distracting, even through the door, but we are testing solutions such as earplugs.

There is general unrest among several of the subjects. This complicates the tests, so we have increased the sedations as much as we can, and experimented with corrective penalties; however, the risk for permanent injuries is great. Some have broken their ankles and wrists whilst trying to escape from their restraints.

"I feel sick," Lena says. The folder is a record of heartlessness and human suffering reduced to detached jargon.

"There are hundreds of pages," Jacobson says. "Here's another one."

The male subject that calls itself "Timmy" is increasingly uncooperative and disturbing. It is charismatic, and the other male subjects have formed an unhealthy attachment to it. One might describe their relationship as "friends", if the subjects were capable of such complex emotions, but we cannot fool ourselves to think that they have such aptitudes.

This week, we will return three subjects whose neurological responses have been too damaged. We hope the hospital will have replacements ready, or we will be behind schedule.

Jacobson slams the folder shut. "I really hope the Spanish police round up Kristina. She has to go to court for this."

Lena nods absently. She wants to believe that the police will rush to Kristina's home and take her into custody, but the woman is already beyond punishment. Her defeatist voice had been telling: Kristina is not going to let herself be caught. She will flee, one way or another. And while her victims were already past saving, her files might hide a lead that will lead Lena to those who tried to assassinate Jimmy.

"There's too much here to go over right now," Jacobson continues. "We'll have to continue at the station."

"We can take turns in the car. I'm heading back to Norra Ängby."

"You want us to go back to the scene again?"

"We might as well examine Kristina's papers there, in case we need to check something out at the hospital. Who knows, perhaps there are more hidden rooms out there that we have to find."

"Heaven forbid," Jacobson mutters.

"What's in that one?" She points at the last folder in the box.

Jacobson flicks it open and thumbs through the papers. "Receipts and invoices. Might be interesting."

"Wait." Lena stops him at a yellowed legal paper.

"A land instalment contract?" Jacobson looks wonderingly at Lena.

"For a property at Glömminge." Lena points to a field on the form. "Kristina mentioned that name when we spoke on the phone."

"Maybe another laboratory," Jacobson says. "I'm beginning to dislike when you're right."

"Let's hope it isn't." Lena pushes the deposit box closed. "Bring the lot to the car. I'll have a closer look while you drive, and–"

A shadow moves in the corner of her eyes.

Lena steps in front of Jacobson and puts her hand on her gun. The movement had been swift but distinct. There are three openings in the corridor ahead: on her right is the main passage back to the door. Some twenty steps away, the corridor ends in a T-junction. It was there something flitted past.

"What's wrong?" Jacobson's voice is soft but troubled.

"We aren't alone." Lena walks down the corridor and takes a quick look around the first corner. No one there. Far away, the door is a bright circle in the strip lights.

"Are you sure?" Jacobson asks.

"Someone moved past at the junction ahead."

"Could be a customer."

"The manager said we were alone. And the door was locked."

"Perhaps she forgot someone was here."

Lena looks back at Jacobson, who glances at Lena's hand where it rests on the grip of her gun.

"For God's sake," Lena hisses. "I'm not going to shoot some old lady tucking away her favourite earrings. But I have to take a look."

She pads down the rest of the corridor. Jacobson follows close behind. There are no sounds apart from a muted ticking from the pipes in the ceiling. Her hands are growing sweaty, but she keeps her gun holstered. There are limits.

Perhaps she imagined the shadow after all. With the exception of her basement gym, confined spaces make her uncomfortable. And her recent experiences underground at the hospital are bound to have left some form of imprint.

She walks around the corner as soon as she reaches it, countering her growing unease with decisiveness.

There is no one in view, but the corridor is also longer than she would have guessed. Lined with deposit boxes on each side, it runs on until its features become blurred. It must continue far past the vault's door in a parallel passage. For some reason, the lights are more dimmed here, but that impression might be due to the adrenaline surge.

"All clear," Lena says to Jacobson. "Sorry for being this jittery, I'm suffering from tunnel overload. I owe you a beer once this is over."

When she turns around, Jacobson is gone. She didn't hear him leave, and there is no sound of footsteps.

"You could've waited," Lena says loudly. Jacobson must have walked down the other corridor towards the door.

She jogs back, turns the corner, and stops. Another corridor, this one too is so long its end is lost in the halo of the brilliant strip lights.

"No," Lena whispers.

This should be the way out. The door must be just ahead; she saw it a few seconds ago. Still no sign of Jacobson. There is nowhere he could have hidden unless he squeezed himself into one of the biggest deposit boxes, which he would not be able to open in the first place. The idea is irrational as well as impossible.

Another insight hits her: the corridor where Kristina's box is located is also longer than it should be. There had been a concrete wall less than ten steps from where Jacobson and she examined the folders, but now its far end is nowhere to be seen. In fact, the corridor is exactly identical to the other ones, as if they were the never-ending reflections of a funhouse mirror maze.

Or a dream.

"Jacobson," Lena shouts.

It's happening again. Just as the laboratory reshaped itself, the geometry of the vault is distorted, its doors gone and the floors stretched into infinity. She is having another episode. Her reality has evaporated, its rules left up for grabs like an unscripted theatre. Only she has no way to control the play.

"As prisons go," says a voice behind Lena, "it's almost perfect."

Lena pulls her gun, spins around, and finds herself face to face with Agnes.

Chapter 35

Lena's arms grow so weak she can't hold her weapon up. The room spins until she has to lean against the wall for support. Part of her notices that the metal is dangerously cold, but seeing Agnes here makes the chill easy to ignore. It is such a relief that Lena almost reaches out just to touch her. She has spent days and nights wondering why she left, and now she can ask.

But Lena does not move.

As much as she wants it to be true, the woman who stands before her cannot be Agnes. The young officer is gone, in hiding since months back, despite Lena's spoken requests and unmentioned wishes that Agnes contact her. Agnes's absence is an inexplicable enigma; she had been the model officer, diligent, ambitious and loyal.

Gren was clearly uncomfortable even touching on the subject of her disappearance, but Agnes has to have a good reason to hide. She cannot be here, prowling the vault like some predator. Which means that she isn't.

It's happening again.

"Won't you say hello?" Agnes asks with a slow smile. "It's been so long."

"You're not real," Lena tries to say, but her mouth is parched.

"Thick door, solid walls, no windows." Agnes takes a step forward. "No wonder you stuffed me here. As far out of sight as possible, but never out of mind."

"Shut up." Lena backs away.

"I thought I could trust you. You were meant to guide me. And instead you pitched me straight into the line of fire, only because you couldn't keep yourself from hurting someone else."

"Don't come close." Lena staggers backwards to keep out of the other woman's reach.

The woman who cannot be Agnes looks just like Lena remembers her colleague. The stray strands of her hair, the hue of her skin, the lines around her mouth. Every feature is right, all details photorealistic.

But the eager confirmation of Lena's senses run headfirst into stark rejection. While Agnes looks lifelike, her sudden presence and menacing behaviour howl discordance.

The conflict jars Lena so viciously she sways on her feet, but it also gives her an unexpected breathing space to gauge the situation and rally her determination. Agnes is anything but resentful. Maybe Lena never had the chance to know her former colleague as well as she would have liked, but she is sure about this.

She is having a conversation with an illusion. Most likely, the apparition before her is conjured by a rogue splinter of her own psyche, broken free by the burden of her ceaseless worrying. The creature in front of Lena is only a puppet brought alive by self-deception. But she will not succumb to this trap. She cannot allow herself to slip now, when they are so close to finding the murderer.

Lena moves forward. Her arms find their strength again, and she raises them.

"Will you shoot me too?" Agnes laughs. "Do you want to add me to the mountain of people you've injured? Lead, bile or betrayal, you always find a way to get under their skin. It must be a useful talent."

Lena takes another step. There is no sign of concern on Agnes's face, but she has stopped moving. She is so close Lena can reach out and touch her. When Lena moves again, Agnes flinches and makes a disgusted grimace, as if offended by Lena's proximity.

Agnes never pulled that face. The expression is as false as a brush of cold air in a desert.

Lena throws her gun away and reaches out with her fingers. Fury shoots through her as if she were standing on a live wire. Not only is she hallucinating; her imagination is corrupting her most precious memories and turning them into grotesque caricatures. The sight is enough to wash away the weakness. If she is bound for inevitable madness, she will at least have revenge on the delusions that mock her from the roadside.

"*Get away from me.*" Lena springs forward and closes her fingers around the other woman's neck.

Her hands find only empty air.

Stumbling, Lena tries to find her balance, but her momentum carries her forward and down until she crashes on the floor. Only the carpet saves her from worse damage than bruises.

"What on earth is happening?" Jacobson says behind her.

Lena groans and rolls over on her back. Jacobson stands a few steps away and looks at her as if she were a strange animal. He has his hand on his revolver.

As Lena rises from the floor, she glances along the thick carpet. Deep footprints lead away in the other direction. They fade while she looks at them. After a few seconds, they are too faint to make out.

Crouching, Lena presses her thumb into the carpet and studies the impression in the textile. After a few seconds, the cavity is flattened out as the fibres in the carpet rearrange themselves.

"Are you hurt?" Jacobson crouches by her side. "Or–"

"Or am I going crazy again?" Lena finishes the sentence. "That's what you want to ask, isn't it?"

She stands up, leans against the wall, and looks down the corridor. Its end is clearly in sight. A second ago, the carpet had run on into a bleak haze in the distance.

"Lena," Jacobson says softly, "I'm asking this as a colleague – no, as a fellow human being: how are you holding up?"

"Not too well," Lena says after a moment.

His concern is genuine, and she wants to be honest for once. The charade of pretending that she has only accidental blackouts is tiring. Two hallucinations in two days. Both so intense she still cannot tell them apart from reality, and unsettling enough that only luck prevented her from damaging herself or someone else within firing range.

"What did you see after I went to look behind the corner?" she asks.

"You stepped out of my line of sight. Then I heard you shout. Or snarl, I should say." His eyes are unreadable as he looks at Lena.

Lena nods and swallows. This has gone on for too long. She has to tell Gren. And she needs to come clean to Gustav before she does something so erratic that she scares him away.

"I need help," Lena says. "I keep seeing things. And I think being underground triggers the episodes."

"Can it be stress?" Jacobson wonders.

"That, or some kind of condition. At any rate, it's getting worse. Feel free to join the office choir that crows about my slipping sanity. As it turns out, they've been right all along." She sighs and closes her eyes.

Jacobson studies Lena for a moment.

"Did you know that I asked Gren to work with you?" he asks.

"I thought Gren was joking." Lena looks up at Jacobson. "Why?" she asks. "Wasn't normal police work challenging enough?"

"Many cases take too much time." Jacobson peers at her. "Do you get enough sleep?"

"Officers never rest as much as they should," Lena says. "Insomnia is part of our job. You didn't answer my question."

"Yes, I did. Some say you aren't the tightest bundle in town. Others call you a walking disaster with a bad temper." Jacobson shrugs. "But I looked at your track record, and your cases are closed faster than most others."

"The general consensus is that I'm efficient, but only because I don't have any feelings."

"I suspect you have them too much."

Lena looks at Jacobson for signs of sarcasm or a hint of wanting to get under her skin, but his face is as placid as always.

"Thanks," she says after a while. No other word comes to her mind.

"However," Jacobson says, "you do need a break. And it wouldn't hurt you to see a doctor."

"I'm booking an appointment as soon as we're back. Gren will probably ask you to lead the investigation, and I'll back the idea. He'll find you a partner inside of five minutes, too. You have a good rep at the department."

Lena walks back towards the exit, and Jacobson follows.

"It sounds reasonable," Jacobson says, "but I want to ask you a favour."

"That I don't have another fit on the way there?" Lena asks.

"I want you to stay on the case until we've found this man." Jacobson looks sideways at Lena. "Please?"

"I can't manage an investigation if I fall apart every five minutes."

"Then don't. This case needs you. I know you can hold yourself together. You're as strong as she says."

"Who?"

They reach the massive door to the vault. Jacobson pauses with his hand on the huge handle. "Not everyone thinks you're a sinking ship," he says. "You've got friends."

"Who's 'she'?" Lena asks again.

Jacobson hesitates. "I spoke with Agnes some time ago. She thinks very highly of you."

"When did you talk to her?" Lena asks quickly.

Her hopes shoot high before she can hold them down; maybe someone has heard from Agnes at last. She might be safe. Perhaps she's even in town.

"Back when she was around," Jacobson says. "Sorry."

"I see." Lena tries to hide her disappointment, but she can't help letting her shoulders sag.

"But Agnes looks up to you. She told me she's never seen anyone so insanely hell-bent on righting wrongs. Those were her exact words."

"You want to make that past tense. I'm responsible for letting her take a life."

Lena runs Jacobson's words through her mind again. She can imagine Agnes talking to Jacobson in confidence, discussing Lena behind closed doors. The image jars her like a searing wind on an already hot day.

"I suspect that Agnes doesn't agree with that view." Jacobson taps his fingers on the handle. "And she's no idiot. She understands the risks of the job."

"Pity we can't ask her in person," Lena says. "Fine, I'll give it another day before I check out. But the slightest whiff of anything weird and I'm off to the office sickbay. And a vacation."

"I'll take you there myself," Jacobson says with a small smile.

*

The manager waits outside the door. "Is everything in order?" she asks.

"All good," Jacobson says. He guides the manager back up the stairs to the ground floor to fill out the paperwork.

Lena follows, but each step feels as if she were trudging through mud. The incident in the vault exhausted her. Thankfully, it didn't last long, and it was different to the nightmare she had at the abandoned laboratory. And she had been aware of the delusion. That is a first, and it might be a good sign. Or a very bad one. She'll leave that to a psychiatrist to answer.

231

A few minutes later, Jacobson and Lena exit the bank. Jacobson carries the folders under his arm while Lena concentrates on ignoring the sensation that she's being watched.

The sky is still blue and the warm air borders on hot. She can pick out the brittle freshness of the nearby river, but it's tainted by the fumes from the traffic that crawls through Hornstull.

"That's a nice ride," Jacobson mumbles just as Lena opens the door.

Lena looks up, and her stomach sinks.

Slowing down outside the bank is a new, blocky yet sleek BMW. It is indeed a nice car. Understated enough to blend in with Stockholm's trademark greyscale colour scheme, but sophisticated enough to stand out anywhere. Much, Lena thinks, like its driver.

The car stops, and Gustav steps out.

Jacobson follows Lena's gaze. "Isn't that," he begins, and stops when he sees her face.

"I didn't ask him to come here," Lena says both to Jacobson and herself.

"Don't worry." Jacobson looks between Lena and Gustav. "I think he wants to talk to you. I'll wait in the car."

Lena walks up to Gustav, but rather than crossing the final distance and leaning against him, she stops at arm's length. Her mind is filled with the drawings in the folder. There is no space for her feelings for Gustav.

But at the sight of him, her emotions press against her focus, demanding to be let in and take over the controls. The conflict leaves her vacant and apprehensive, like the no-man's-land between the trenches of a battlefield.

"Hey," she says.

Gustav reaches out but notices when Lena stiffens. "No pashing in public?" he asks and smiles. "I don't remember that bothering you before. Am I embarrassing you?"

"Don't be stupid." Lena forces herself to smile back at him. "My mind is elsewhere, that's all. What are you doing here?"

"Want to get some lunch?" Gustav asks. "My office is just five minutes away." He is much too handsome to pull off a sheepish expression, but he makes a good effort.

"I've arrested better liars." This time, Lena's smile is genuine.

"That'd look horrible on my CV." Gustav grins. "Actually, someone in the bank posted that you were here, so I thought I'd swing by to say hello."

"Have you got friends in this office?" Lena gives Gustav an incredulous look." I know you're mates with half of Stockholm, but this is ridiculous."

"Not as such, but I follow a few feeds that gossip about police activity."

"What, for inspiration?" Lena can't see what such channels have to do with advertising.

"I'm interested in what's going on. You're out there, every day and some of the nights. I like to imagine what you're up to."

Lena has an unpleasant feeling that she can fill in the lines Gustav left blank.

"Someone in the bank decided to tell the world I was there?" she asks. "That's how you knew I was in the neighbourhood?"

Gustav looks apologetic. "I'm afraid so."

"That's it," Lena says. "I'm getting a ski mask."

She closes her eyes and shakes her head. Someone is probably uploading this very moment as a film clip. The thought is maddening. Privacy in public places has become a luxury out of her reach.

"Can I help somehow?" Gustav asks. "You look miserable."

"I have to apologize for the other night," Lena says. "My unplanned guests."

"I'm tired of things going as planned anyway." Gustav shrugs lightly. "Honestly, where I work, every hiccup is a drama. Bigger surprises are treated like pest-ridden rats."

His comparison makes Lena relax, but the comment is a jest. Gustav revers smooth perfection and solid plans. He can't write a shopping list without using an ideal font or outlining the best route inside the store. And when it comes to more major undertakings, he is manic about deadlines and timetables.

He's probably the same about relationships. There's no telling how he'll react when she breaks it to him that she has visions so bizarre they put any medieval prophet to shame, but she can't keep her situation secret any longer.

"We need to talk," she says. "Or rather, I need to speak to you."

"That sounds ominous." Gustav's smile fades.

"There's something you need to know."

"Whatever it is, I can deal with it. I promise. If not lunch, how about dinner tonight?"

Lena almost says yes; the temptation to hold off revealing her damaged psyche is overwhelming. But stalling has done her no good so far.

"Can you drive me to Bromma?" Lena asks. "I'll explain in the car."

"What are you doing in – oh. I remember."

"I'm not asking you to take me to that place. Just drop me off nearby, and my colleague will meet up with me."

"Won't you get in trouble if you ride with me?"

"Please?" she asks. "I have to get this off my chest."

After a moment, Gustav nods. "I'll wait in the car."

Lena sighs and nods. That was the smallest hill: the true challenge awaits her. She calls Jacobson.

"I'll ride with Gustav," she says. "Stick close to us, or go ahead if you want."

"You're not actually taking him to the scene, are you?" Jacobson sounds startled.

"I haven't gone fully insane just yet," Lena assures him. "We'll stop several blocks away. I'll walk the last bit."

Chapter 36

Felix turns on the shower and closes his eyes. The water is so hot it's almost insufferable, but as it hits his face, the heat momentarily eclipses the images of the previous night. The last punishment they carried out left him numb. While Timmy seems to find great pleasure in their victim's begging and pleading, the blood and the violence makes Felix exhausted.

It is a lonely and difficult mission. Only he seems able to identify his enemy. Perhaps his friends could have done the same, but they are gone. Everyone except Timmy. And there are so many who must be destroyed: the more Felix scrutinizes people around him, the more numerous his enemy appears. He cannot rest until each and every one is subjected to their own treatment. They must be made to see what he has seen.

Although he must constantly remind himself that his acts are retributions. Alternative descriptions such as *murder* are used in media and by the police, but they do not apply to him. He is not a mindless killer. If anything, his mind is larger than most: it encompasses all the unavenged lives of his lost friends.

When he turns around to reach for the shampoo, Timmy is there.

"We have to move," Timmy says.

Felix is so startled by Timmy's appearance he almost trips and falls. Every previous time, Timmy's arrival has been signalled in subtle shifts in the environment: a frigid gust of wind, the creak of an opening door, or a shadow growing too dark.

"What's wrong?" Felix asks. "Is it because I let the snake out?"

"That's got nothing to do with this. I told you to release her because the poor thing was suffering. No one traps snakes if I can help it."

"Then what's the problem?"

"I met up with that detective."

"The woman who's looking for us?" Felix asks. "Why would you want to see her?"

"To spook her a little. A well-aimed bump is all it'll take to derail her completely. And I'm something of an expert at nudging."

"But this meeting didn't go as planned?" Felix has never seen Timmy look so disturbed.

"I brought the wrong costume to the party." Timmy sighs. "All I managed to do was tick her off even more, and she wasn't happy to begin with."

"Is that an issue?"

"I need her to be scared." Timmy throws up his hands in desperation. "That's my window, the hole in the mosquito net. Just angry doesn't work. And even worse, she's homing in on us."

"How is that possible?" Felix asks weakly.

"Because she's been helped by someone else. There was a stubborn waste of flesh and bone who kept secrets even from *me*. I tried to shut her up for years, but the pig-headed fuckwit refused to listen to my instructions until today."

"What instructions?" Felix tries to catch up with Timmy's barrage of spat words.

"To end her miserable life, of course. Year after year of cajoling to no avail. It irked me so much I never realised what she was hiding in the back of her head. Can you believe I didn't even know about the vault?"

"Which vault?" Felix asks. "Are we in trouble?"

Timmy sighs. "Oh, my sweet, damaged little tool. Yes, you're in a bad spot. So now, you have to run."

Felix nods weakly and turns off the water. This moment had to come sooner or later, but his legs are still trembling. All hunts have an end. He just didn't expect it to come so soon.

"You really must hurry up," Timmy says. "The self-righteous hounds are bearing down on us. They're hoping to cage us again."

"Can we still make them pay?" Felix asks, hoping for a glimmer of hope.

"Not all of them." Timmy smiles. "Only the woman."

Chapter 37

The traffic is still light as Gustav drives back across the bridge. Far below, broad streams reflect the sun in a cascade of bright shards. Tower blocks in distant suburbs dominate the horizon like monuments of polished rock. Summer washes through the car's state-of-the-art air conditioning. Lena's mood could not be more different than the fantastic weather.

Gustav looks at the road, but she can tell his attention is on her.

"Is it about that raid that went wrong?" he asks.

Lena suppresses a twinge of unease. Once, she mentioned in passing to Gustav that one of her assignments had taken a catastrophic turn, and he had quickly linked her censured story with the high-profile news piece from a few years earlier. It's the downside of seeing someone who works with media for a living. Unfortunately, her problem is even more serious, at least for her.

"That's in the past," Lena says. "I've archived everything."

"Some ghosts don't die easily." Gustav gives her an encouraging smile. "We all have demons. Although I think yours are several degrees worse than the odd skeleton rattling away in my wardrobe. Still, they're only imaginary."

Lena swallows and nods. If only she were as convinced as Gustav seems to be.

"By the way," Gustav continues, "before you say anything, I want to apologize for showing up without warning today. Even I can tell that you didn't want to be interrupted. I hope you don't think it's creepy?"

Lena's phone buzzes just as Gustav stops at a red light. It's Jacobson. His call is welcome; it saves her from telling Gustav that being tracked by idiots on the Internet is far worse than creepy.

She takes the call. "What's going on?"

"I've got something," Jacobson says. "Among Kristina's papers is a list with numbers of so-called subjects, but the sequences are pretty long. I think they're real patient numbers."

"Can we link the numbers to actual names?" Lena asks.

"I'm not sure how, but the hospital might know."

"Call them and ask. By the way, are you driving and looking through the folders at the same time?" That kind of audacious multitasking sounds unlike Jacobson.

"Actually, it was Jimmy who found the list."

"Please tell me you aren't serious," Lena says.

"He pinched them when I wasn't looking. I'm not sure whether to thank him or whack him over his ear."

"Toss a coin. Where are you now?"

"We just left Hornstull," Jacobson says, "so you're ahead of me. I was distracted by the might-be patient numbers."

"Understood. Call me back when you've talked to the hospital. I have an idea."

"Sounds good, give me five minutes and I'll have an answer – *look out*." Jacobson's warning is followed by the screech of tyres skidding on asphalt.

"What was that?" Lena asks. "Are you all right?"

"Sorry, I had to give way. Some lunatic sped past me as if I were standing still. A big white Saab, heading north at twice the speed limit."

"Did you catch the plates?"

"I didn't have time, but I'm calling it in. You might spot the car. It's coming your way."

"I'll keep an eye out. See you in Norra Ängby." Lena hangs up.

The lights turn green, and Gustav accelerates onto the great bridge that will take her back to the western side of Stockholm.

"Trouble?" Gustav asks. "Not that it's my business."

"Just a speeding driver." Lena sighs. "It's the least of my problems right now."

"I'm listening." Gustav looks at Lena and waits for her to speak.

Lena takes a deep breath. For a brief moment, she pictures herself back outside the cursed countryside house where she prepared for a bust that would change her life. Even though there are no physical threats involved now, she feels more exposed than ever.

"There's something wrong with my head," Lena says. "I get disoriented and imagine things. Most of the time, pretty unbearable things."

"Waking nightmares?" Gustav asks. Far away is the sound of several car horns.

"It's worse. The walls change around me, and I see people who aren't there. And there are voices, too. But I have some control of what I do."

"In difference to when you're dreaming?"

Lena nods. "Although I can't break free. And I think it's getting worse."

"I thought you believed your temper was your biggest problem," Gustav says. "Not that I think it's an issue." He glances at the rear-view mirror.

"Not my temper," Lena corrects him. "Only the fact that sometimes I lose the reins. But that's a different mess. This is much more – are you paying attention to what I'm saying here?"

Lena struggles to keep her voice down. This might be the most personal piece of information she has ever shared, but Gustav keeps frowning at the mirror as if inspecting his eyebrows.

"Sorry," Gustav says. "There's a car coming up really fast behind us."

"Where?" Lena turns around and looks through the rear window.

The bridge is made up of two lanes in each direction. Next to the rightmost lane, behind a tall chicken-wire fence, is the underground train track. A few hundred metres away is a large white vehicle darting between cars as it overtakes them.

While she watches, the driver finds a window between two cars and guns the Saab forward, rapidly closing the gap between its headlights and Gustav's rear bumper. Its black-tinted windows gleam like slick oil in the sunlight.

"It's that speeder who almost hit Jacobson." Lena raises her phone. "Just keep driving, I have to call and let–"

Lena looks up at the sudden roar of the Saab's engine. It's so close it almost touches Gustav's car.

"Jesus," Gustav shouts. "What is the bastard playing at?"

The Saab swerves right and accelerates until it's parallel to Gustav's car. Nearby drivers lean on their horns and break hard to avoid crashing. One of the black windows slides down. The car's interior is dark, but she spots movement and a hint of metal.

A freezing wind travels down Lena's back.

"Hit the brakes," she screams to Gustav. "Now."

Gustav slows down, but the Saab matches his speed. The flash of metal inside the Saab's interior turns into a black pinpoint. Lena catches the pale glint of a squinting eye.

She flings her leg sideways and rams her foot down on the gas pedal. The BMW jolts forward as if struck by a massive wave. Gustav shouts in pain and surprise while Lena twists the wheel to avoid crashing into an adjacent car. The blare of engines and horns sends bolts of white heat through her head.

"Let go," Gustav yells. "You're going to get us kill–"

A series of rapid bangs hammer against Gustav's car, and the side window behind Lena disappears in a hail of crystals. Stuffing from the back seat explodes from dozens of holes in the textile and whirls around in the air.

Lena lifts her foot, holds on to the seat, and yanks up the handbrake.

The tyres of Gustav's BMW lock up, causing the car to turn ninety degrees and come to a screeching stop. The shift in speed makes the metalwork creak in protest.

Lena is thrown first against the panel, then into the door. Oncoming cars dart left and right to avoid colliding with the motionless vehicle that blocks the way.

She looks over her shoulder. Clusters of holes have shredded most of the back seat. Some kind of sub-automatic machine gun. Possibly armour-piercing ammunition. Useless at a distance, almost certain death up close.

First Jimmy. Now me. Then Gustav.

Fear fills her mind like hot embers. The reek of scorched rubber oozes through the air conditioning. She tries to quick dial Jacobson, but her hands shake too much.

She looks up and sees the Saab do a smooth U-turn, expertly avoiding other cars as if it were alone on the road. A professional driver. The shooter will be just as skilled. Only luck saved Lena from ending in a rain of small-calibre bullets. Images of Jimmy's obliterated car come to her.

The Saab accelerates fast towards Gustav's car. It will close the distance in seconds.

There is no way off the bridge apart from the car lanes. Climbing onto the train tracks will take too long. Lena draws her gun and forces herself to move. If she stays in the car, the attackers will gun down both Gustav and her.

She pulls at the handle to open the door, but it's locked. Before she can tell Gustav to unlock it, the engine booms to life and the BMW takes off, slamming her back in her seat.

"Stop the car," Lena shouts. "They're after me. You have to get away."

"We're going in the wrong direction." Gustav's voice is so hushed Lena barely hears him. "This is bad. I shouldn't be doing this. We're breaking all kinds of laws." As he speaks, the BMW picks up speed.

A glance at Gustav tells Lena the full story: he is panicking, and in a bad way. Some go catatonic when they're stricken. Gustav belongs to a different and more dangerous category: his senses have shut down, but his body is set on survival. He ignores anything and anyone around him. She cannot snap him out of this state.

"We must hide," Gustav mumbles. "Out in the country, where it's quiet. This stress is too much." He grins through tears streaming down his cheeks.

A familiar shape swishes past in the opposite direction: her car, with Jacobson behind the wheel, his eyes wide as they meet Lena's for a fraction of a second. The BMW speeds up and sways from side to side. They will crash at any moment. She catches a glimpse of white in the rear-view mirror. The Saab is closing in.

She scrambles between the seats and down on the floor behind Gustav, then crawls up in the back seat and peers through the window. The Saab is just behind them. Farther ahead, several cars have stopped and block the bridge. The attackers risk being trapped in a jumble of vehicles. They will have to get away, or their Saab will be surrounded.

But this is not retaliation for arresting some low-grade street dealer. They are professionals who want to finish their assignment. Their car will pass slowly, and they will unload everything they have to make sure the job is done. Unless Gustav outruns them.

Although he won't make it. Despite the BMW's state-of-the-art engine, the SAAB closes fast. The assassin's car must be so tricked out there's not a single original part left under its hood.

There is only one route left.

Lena fires a shot through the rear window. A web of fine white lines appears around the small hole. She leans sideways and kicks at the window once, twice, a third time. Shattered glass falls away behind the BMW in a string of jagged pearls.

She raises her gun and aims through the opening at the Saab's windscreen. It will almost certainly be bulletproof, but she is out of options, save for perhaps prayers.

Gustav turns left sharply to evade an oncoming truck, then right as he crosses a roundabout. Lena hisses as her hands brush against the edge of the ruined window. Blood drops down on the seats.

"Keep the car straight," she screams, even though Gustav is beyond listening.

They have passed the turn onto the bridge towards Hornstull and continue east, towards the police headquarters. Cars swish past in quick blurs of black and silver. Soon they'll reach a large crossing. There will be traffic lights and queues. The attackers will want to end this now.

When the BMW stops turning, Lena aims again, only to be flung to the side when Gustav swerves right. She snatches her hand back reflexively, but the grip of the pistol is snagged by the broken window, which rips the weapon out of her fingers. The gun bounces on the trunk and vanishes behind the car.

A moment later, three heavy thuds shake Gustav's car. The neck support in the passenger seat is cleaved in half. A fist-sized hole materializes in the windscreen close to Gustav.

"Fuck." Lena ducks down and curls up to make herself more difficult to hit.

Not a sub-machine gun this time; something much larger, maybe a hunting rifle. Just as she predicted, the soon-to-be murderers are far past using stealth. They are unleashing whatever they have in store to finish her.

The BMW slows down and veers left. Gustav slumps sideways in the driver's seat. A frozen chasm opens up inside Lena's chest.

Screaming at the top of her lungs, she lunges between the front seats, grabs the wheel and gets the BMW back in the lane. Another five seconds are lost as she climbs into the driver's seat and works her feet down over Gustav's legs to reach the pedals. Gustav bleeds from a cut on his head, but looks otherwise unhurt.

The SAAB is almost upon them. Another bang echoes from behind. A traffic sign ahead folds in half as a bullet punches through the metal.

Red lights hover in the distance. The crossing at Fridhemsplan. Hundreds of cars, cameras, and witnesses. The shooters will be stuck if they follow Lena and Gustav up there.

But Gustav is going much too fast. The BMW's engine is pushed to its limits and complains with a shrill howling that makes her teeth ache.

Lena dislikes driving with a passion. Many of her colleagues enjoy being on the road, but the pleasure of navigating a multitude of strung-out egos who block the path between her and her destination is beyond her. For years, high-priority cases have let her avoid taking the mandatory advanced driving classes. Other drivers always test her patience, and she has better things to do.

Now she wishes she had gone to at least one of those sessions. Preferably one that covered how to stop a car going at ballistic speeds. Braking is a given, but they are too close to the cars waiting for the green light. Flooring the pedal while going straight will at best make it easier to remove her dead body from the wreck.

She has to turn. The question is how much. Too little and she will hit another car. Too far, and the BMW will flip and roll.

Pressing herself back against Gustav's unconscious shape, she brakes hard and steers left sharply, hoping to stay level with the ground.

The BMW snaps into a fast spin while it barrels towards the crossing. Stockholm flashes past in snapshots of windows, lampposts, railings, storefronts and offices. Screaming over the rumble of protesting metal and squealing tires, she untangles a foot to press herself away from the side door.

The car pirouettes past the hard shoulder, slams over the curb, continues across the sidewalk and through a row of parked bikes. Bent pieces of metal spray away as the BMW continues onto a side street and slowly comes to a stop.

At the last moment, the car loses the battle against gravity and tips onto its side, falling over almost leisurely, like an animal of steel and smoke lying down to sleep.

Lena breathes in loud gasps and looks around. She lies on her back on top of Gustav. Her feet point toward the smashed passenger-seat window. The jagged outline of glass shards frame the blue sky above.

She is bruised and bleeding, but all bones are intact, or at least the critical ones. Gustav is mumbling incoherently as if he is speaking in his sleep. A car engine roars nearby. People scream and run past the BMW. No one stops.

They're not dead, but not safe either.

"Wake up." Lena twists around and touches Gustav's cheek. "Please, talk to me. We have to get out."

Gustav stirs and opens his eyes. "Am I dying?"

"If you don't move, you will." Lena releases Gustav's safety belt. More seconds lost because of her trembling hands.

"I can't walk."

"You have to," Lena shouts. "Get up." She climbs up along the vertical front seats and looks out through the broken window just as the Saab reverses into view between two cars. It's half a block away. Between Lena and the assassins is the underbody of the BMW, but that will not protect them from the weaponry her hunters are using.

"It's pointless," Gustav says. "They'll get us. We should talk to them, really. Make them see sense."

Lena ducks down and looks at Gustav. His eyes are closing again, as if he's falling asleep. Terror has the best of him. He will not rise. The attackers might be driving away, or they may be coming closer. Her way forward is still slimmed down to one choice.

She leans against the sunroof and shoves at the glass pane. It doesn't budge. Conscious of every moment she wastes, Lena takes a catalogue from the glove compartment, puts the catalogue between her hands and the glass, and pushes away with her feet from the floor of the car.

The sunroof gives in with a loud crack and tumbles down onto the street outside. That had been the easy part. She reaches down and pulls at Gustav's arm.

"Snap out of it," she shouts. "Please, Gustav."

Gustav shakes his head and smiles ruefully. His psyche has fled to a less chaotic place at the fringe of his mind. With a guttural curse, she drags Gustav's arm up and around her neck, and pulls him upright.

He is heavier than anything she has ever lifted before, an asymmetrical weight that only wishes to fall back down. Lena's arms and back scrape against the roof and the gearstick. Pain shoots through the muscles in her back and her side. A man screams behind the car. It sounds like *gun*.

Screaming to counter the agony in her tendons, Lena tilts Gustav forward and out through the sunroof. When he falls forward, she bends her knees again, tugs his legs up, and topples him through the opening. Landing might knock some of his teeth out, but it won't kill him.

Gustav slumps down on the asphalt outside the car. Lena follows, climbing feet-first through the sunroof-turned-window as fast as she can. Just as she clears the window, a bang rattles the BMW so hard she thinks it will fall down over them. Another boom follows, and the air close to Lena's face is superheated, as if touched by a miniature sun. A large hole gapes in the BMW's roof.

The assassins have not given up.

The single scream multiplies into a cacophony of cries and shouts. Lena throws herself down flat on the street an instant before a third boom splits the air. The car shudders again. Shredded metal and pulverized glass spray over her hair. Farther down the road, an old man in the line of fire drops his shopping bags and stumbles to the ground. The BMW catches fire with a dull thump.

"Fucking *bastards*," Lena screams.

Rage runs wild through her awareness, but she cannot succumb to the desire for retribution. Gustav is down. Her weapon is gone. She is injured, outgunned, and too shaken to think straight. Only fleeing is important.

She hooks her hands under Gustav's armpits and drags him away from the BMW. Flames envelop the car and spread away like flickering tongues along the street. A bullet must have pierced the fuel tank.

She takes care to keep the car between her and the Saab as she backs away. Gustav's car is not stopping the hellish bullets the assassins are using, but at least the burning wreck keeps her out of her would-be murderers' view. The black smoke spewing from the fire helps, too. Although if the shooters come at her past the BMW, she will have nowhere to hide.

An engine roars somewhere in the distance. A flash of white rips past beyond the flames. The Saab, escaping the scene. Her instincts urge her to run forward and try to stop the shooters from getting away, but the impulse is as futile as it is suicidal. She would only make her assailants' job easier.

A quick series of brittle and familiar bangs cracks between the houses. The police force's standard-issue handgun. After a few seconds, a figure in a rumpled suit jacket darts around the burning car, spots Lena, and rushes towards her. It is Jacobson, his gun drawn. He stops next to Lena and looks around as if expecting another assassin to pop into existence behind his back.

"Are you wounded?" Jacobson asks. His face is pale and his voice trembles.

Lena looks down at Gustav, who shakes his head from side to side as if trying to clear his head. After a moment, he rises to his elbows and looks around in confusion.

"I'm fine," Lena says hoarsely. "Check him over there. I think he was hit." She points at the still shape of the elderly man who had fallen over farther up the road.

"I feel ill." Gustav frowns and shakes his head again. "Am I dreaming?"

"It's shock," Lena says. "Just keep still."

Gustav rolls away and throws up on the asphalt as soon as Lena's words have left her mouth. Jacobson runs up to the man who might have been gunned down by a stray bullet. Sirens filter through the din of shouts: police cars homing in on the site like wasps. Ambulances and fire trucks follow close behind. Soon the noise is deafening.

Lena rises up and checks her limbs. Shallow gashes run along her hands from when she cut herself on the smashed window. The muscles in her back smart after pulling Gustav from the car. Dozens of bruises ache from her feet to her neck. Her head pounds, both from an escalating headache and the racket.

She climbs up on a bin to spy past the burning BMW. Her position makes her an easy target, but the Saab is most likely gone, at least for now. Firemen dash past her, hoses trailing behind them. She is so dazed she didn't notice when the fire engine pulled up just behind her.

As she guessed, the shooters' vehicle is nowhere to be seen. It will have a tough time leaving via any major bottleneck; Jacobson will have put out an alert. Then again, unless the police get a helicopter in the air soon, the assassins might slip away. There are many ways to make a car disappear, even in the city.

A crowd is forming around them: thousands of people streaming in from all directions, everyone keen to capture a piece of the drama. Rumours of what happened tear through the town. Soon Fridhemsplan will be packed.

Gustav struggles to his feet and looks in disbelief at his ruined car. Lena climbs down and moves closer to Gustav. She wants to hold him, but he shies away like a startled hart.

"I was on lunch," he says numbly.

"You need to sit down," Lena tells him.

Gustav's expression saps her of what little strength she has left. He is winded and scared, but also repulsed. His precious safety has been violated. To him, losing control of a project is a major disaster; almost being murdered by a team of faceless hit men does not fit on his scales at all. He is profoundly shaken. And he wants someone to blame.

"I thought being with you would be easy," he says. "Exciting, even." Anger creeps into his voice as he speaks. He is too shocked to understand how his words hurt, but that does nothing to soothe the pain.

Lena closes her eyes. Her hands, which had just stopped shaking, start to tremble again. She cannot handle this. Not here, and not now.

"I said to myself, how hard can it be?" Gustav tries to laugh, but it comes out like a choked cough. "Of course, I knew life would be different. But this?"

His face is still, every line as sunken as a downtown statue weathered by wind and fumes. He looks ten years older than he did thirty minutes earlier. An involuntary adventurer, plucked from routine and hauled through an unfamiliar wilderness at reckless speed. And the backwoods of his beloved city had almost finished him.

"I have to go," Gustav says. "I'm sorry. It isn't you. It's just – this." He nods at his BMW wreathed in flames and smoke.

After a moment, Lena nods. No more words are needed. The nervous indifference in Gustav's eyes is more obvious than a message carved in her skin.

She turns around and walks away before she has to witness Gustav do the same.

Chapter 38

The paramedic secures the bandage around Lena's hand.

"Make sure it stays on," she says to Lena. "And you need twenty-four hours off, minimum. But I have a feeling you'll ignore that."

Lena doesn't answer. She sits in the back seat of a police car with her legs through the open door. A thick blanket is wrapped around her, but a cold has spread throughout her body and refuses to go away. The police vehicle is one of nine that has arrived. Parked around them are three fire engines and four ambulances. A fifth has left with the seriously injured man who was hit by the shooters.

An emergency response team transport waits nearby. Parked farther away are the vans of half a dozen news teams. Add over two thousand people who have stopped to document the scene in trillions of pixels, soon to be shared with added captions and special-effect filters. More people will arrive before the wreck is cleared away. Every news report tonight will begin with a low-down of the calamity in central Stockholm.

Jacobson stands next to the car and briefs Gren over the phone on what has happened. There is no trace of the shooters so far, and she doubts they will be found. The web in which she's trapped is pulling in the worst kind of spiders: those who scurry away too fast to be caught or who refused to enter the light at all.

"At least take it easy," the paramedic continues. "And no more driving today. You could've killed someone when you went off the road."

The paramedic pulls off a stern, commanding voice, which is impressive given that Lena has at least ten years on the woman. But it's not the brief scolding that leaves Lena searching for a reply. Emotions roll around inside her in a perfect storm.

"Next time I'll opt for getting shot instead." Lena gives the paramedic a dismissive look, but the woman is unfazed.

"Did you really drag a guy out of that car's sunroof?" the paramedic asks.

Lena nods slowly. "I was in a hurry," she says absently.

"I'll be damned." The paramedic raises an eyebrow in what might be disbelief or approval, then walks away.

Lena rests her face in her hands. The temporary darkness is bliss; it gives her a chance to reorder her thoughts. She is alive, despite all odds. But someone is bent on stopping her from finding who is behind the murders, the laboratory, or both. And they will not make the same mistake twice.

Or *he* will not. There is no doubt who is behind the attack.

"Carl Adlerberg."

Lena whispers the name into the dark sanctuary of her palms. Thirty years ago, he tortured helpless patients. Now he has turned his attention to her. He will be watching her movements, waiting for the next opportunity. And next time, he will be discreet, or at least more accurate. What this team of assassins failed to do can be done in a thousand more effective ways.

But Carl had come at her recklessly for a reason. His hand must have been forced, which in turn made his henchmen expose themselves. It smacks of panic. That means she's getting closer. She still has time to reach down the foxhole, if she can find it. For that, she must stop thinking about Gustav and the solitude that already pours in to fill his absence.

Jacobson hangs up and turns to Lena.

"Is your boyfriend all right?" he asks.

Lena looks straight ahead to avoid Jacobson's scrutinizing gaze.

"Depends on how you see it," Lena says. "He left."

"In an ambulance?"

"In disgust."

Lena sucks in air while her eyes grow hot. She stands up, throws the blanket inside the car, and slams the door shut. Gustav's words are fixed in her head. He was right: his life is different, on the other side of a fence that separates the mortally mundane from the actually lethal. He isn't even a police officer, but he still wound up almost dead simply by being too close. No one sane would choose to be around her.

This is yesterday's news. She opted for solitude years ago when she joined the force. Her job is not only about righting wrongs; it means exclusion, distancing, selecting a side and turning her back on the rest. Gustav cannot have been more different or more likely to end up hurt. Her loss is of her own design.

Jacobson waits for her to speak. He notices her mood, but he's unsure what has happened.

"What did Gren say?" Lena asks. She must keep moving.

"He wants you to get in touch as soon as you can. Did you really pull Gustav out of that?" Jacobson glances at the BMW, now wreathed in dense smoke as the firemen work to put out the fire.

"Will he order me to take time off again?" Lena asks, ignoring Jacobson's question.

"That's highly likely," Jacobson says. "But I never said that."

"Then he'll have to wait. Was it you who fired shots after we crashed?"

Jacobson nods. "I tried to get their tires, but I wasn't even close. Sorry about that."

"At least you didn't run away like I did."

"Did you have another option?"

"There are always alternatives. I just didn't have time to think of any. And I lost my gun, too. Can you drive?"

"There's a stack of paperwork waiting for me. Well, you're leading the case, so technically it's for you. But I don't think Gren minds if I take care of it, seeing what you've been through."

"Did you have time to talk to the hospital about the numbers before this pretty hell broke loose?"

Jacobson nods. "They were patient records, just like I guessed. I should have the names in my inbox by now. Apparently, they have only the surnames, but that's better than nothing."

"It's all we need. Dump the forms on someone else and take me to my car. We're still going to Norra Ängby."

"Do you have another lead?"

"With a little luck," Lena says, "I can have the address of the murderer."

Chapter 39

After a quick run through the thickening crowd to the car, Lena and Jacobson are heading back over the bridge towards Norra Ängby, retracing the chase as they navigate the gridlock. Jacobson had found and mounted the blue light after seeing the avalanche of cars hoping to get past Fridhemsplan. It helps to clear a way, but not much.

Jimmy continues to hide in the back of the car. Surprisingly, he hasn't said a word since Lena sat down in the passenger seat.

Lena inspects her hand while Jacobson drives. It hurts, although she can move it without a problem. The paramedic insisted on patching up two grazes on her face as well. Those were the visible wounds; more hid under her clothes, not counting large bruises, aching muscles and smarting tendons. But she was operational.

"Plan A," Jacobson says. "Can I hear it?"

"Did you get those names from the hospital?" Lena asks.

Jacobson nods. "They were on the ball. I have the list in my mail."

"That's all we need."

"But we can't use it to search for people with matching surnames in the area," Jacobson continues. "I had a quick look before the Saab appeared, and the names are rather generic. We'll get hundreds of results."

"Perhaps, "Lena says, "but the lab said that chemical on the vial we found is extremely addictive."

"They also explained that it's present in too many medicines to pin down – ah, I see." Jacobson taps on the wheel. "We've got the names, so we can cross-reference it against the record of residents with prescriptions."

"There's your plan A," Lena says.

Against her expectations, her phone still works despite being banged around in her pocket when trying to evade the assassins. She calls headquarters and instructs an assistant to open the case file and run a match between the two lists of names.

"That should leave us with fewer candidates," Lena says after she ends the call.

Jacobson nods. "But only if the suspect still uses his real name."

"He was probably old enough to remember it when they took him to the lab," Lena says. "His name might be the one real thing he has. My guess is that he's clinging to it."

"Is that idea founded in actual psychology?"

"It's a hunch. That's the best I can do right now."

"It's also a long shot."

"Wrong day for that proverb." Lena gives Jacobson a sidelong glance. "I can still hear the sound of those bullets when they tore up Gustav's car. By all that's fair, I should be an obituary now. Whoever hired those bastards must be desperate."

"We both know who paid them."

"Can someone fill me in?" Jimmy looks up between the front seats.

Jacob sighs. "I'd hoped you were asleep," he says and looks at Lena.

Lena nods in silent agreement with Jacobson's unspoken opinion: they can't travel with Jimmy much longer. It's a great enough offence for everyone in the car to end up in prison, and they're making a bigger target for those hunting them.

Then again, she can't jettison Jimmy and hope he manages to stay under the radar. For all his dourness and supposed street smarts, there's a bumbling, hapless quality to him that makes him a natural sitting duck. Turning him loose would be like dumping a clueless puppy in a crocodile pit. Even the police might be involved. And he is in danger because of her.

Their best bet is finding the murderer. Once he's in custody, it'll be too late for anyone to try to shut her or Jimmy down. Or at least doing so will be pointless.

"Asleep?" Jimmy says to Jacobson. "Are you serious right now? I won't sleep for a week. First you turn around on a bridge, then race against traffic at two hundred miles per hour. Then, before I can ask what the fuck is going on, you're out the door with your gun in your hand. Talk to me. What is happening here?"

"I summed it up for you when we drove back to Fridhemsplan." Jacobson glances down at Jimmy as he stops at a red light.

"You were cursing like a rabid parrot," Jimmy says.

"That was the summary," Jacobson says and looks at Lena. "We're coming up to Norra Ängby in a minute. Where do you want to go?"

"Some place where I can get a coffee while we wait."

Chapter 40

A few minutes later, Jacobson parks behind a petrol station at Islandstorget on the outskirts of Norra Ängby. The dirty brick-and-metal building is close to the main road and the underground train tracks. Not the most scenic spot in the area, but it allows them to wait out of sight of both passing cars and trains.

Jacobson ventures to get supplies while Lena waits by the car. He returns with a loaded takeaway tray and hands Lena a steaming polystyrene cup, followed by a plate with a hamburger on top of a small mountain of chips. The burger looks greasy and tasteless, but the mere sight reminds her that she's famished.

"Any news?" Jacobson asks.

"Nothing yet." Lena takes the coffee and the burger. "I don't remember telling you I'm hungry," she notes.

"No offence, but it's unusual to see you not eating." Jacobson opens the door and tosses a pair of chocolate bars and a large soft drink on the back seat.

"We might have to move again soon," he says to Jimmy. "Stay hidden, and do exactly what we say."

"No burger for me?" Jimmy asks.

Jacobson closes the door with forced calm and gives Lena a pointed look.

"I know," she says. "He's asking for it. Thanks for the coffee."

Her hands are still trembling badly. She's colder than she should be and also irritatingly light-headed. They are familiar signs. Caffeine might not be a recognized antidote to shock, but at least it's an established shortcut to temporary lucidity. She needs to dilute the adrenaline and sharpen her mind.

Side by side, Lena and Jacobson lean against the car and wait for headquarters to call with the result of the cross-referencing. Every passing second adds to the tension. She tries to push away the memories of the car chase, the gunshots and the look on Gustav's face, but the events are too recent. It would be easier to ignore standing in a campfire.

Norra Ängby is visible as a patchwork mess of tiled rooftops above the fence around the petrol station. Lena studies the picture while she eats. Thousands of families packed together and isolated inside bubbles of timber. Sheltered from the non-stop din of the city as well as the concrete melancholy of bigger, less affluent districts.

Under the small sea of roofs in front of her, people are going about their daily lives, but they are not oblivious to what's happening in their midst. The murders must have the entire suburb on edge. Most people will be checking the news feeds every two minutes.

She looks at her wristwatch. Seventeen minutes since they requested the list to be compared. They will have a result soon unless there are any technical problems.

"Do you really think it'll be this easy?" Jacobson asks.

"It never is." Lena finishes the last of her chips and leaves the plate on the hood. "But with luck, we can start banging on doors."

"But first we would call for backup." Jacobson pauses and looks at Lena. "Right?"

"As soon as we think we have a definite lead. I'd love to bring in the response team, but seeing how that went the last time, I can't imagine them being overjoyed to back us up."

"If Gren pulls a string, they don't have a choice."

"Which takes us to the next problem."

"You still think Gren will take you off the case?" Jacobson asks.

"The way I think the sun will set at dusk. He'd have me off duty, and probably hospitalized to boot."

"Would that be so bad?" Jacobson shrugs off Lena's glare. "You were nearly killed less than an hour ago. Repeatedly, I should add."

"I'm going to get this murderous bastard." Lena slams her hand down on the roof of the car. "And then I will find the sadistic shit who started this. If Kristina is gone, and I hope she is, I'll make sure Carl wishes he were dead."

"You don't mean that." Jacobson's expression is neutral, but he shies back from Lena's outburst.

Lena opens her mouth to answer, but the words refuse to come. *I really do mean that,* she thinks. *And I don't know what that says about me.*

She exhales slowly and presses her fingers to her temples. When tears well up in her eyes, she wipes them away with the sleeve of her jacket and hopes Jacobson doesn't notice.

"I'm sorry," Lena says. "I'm not the tightest of bundles right now."

"You've had a horrific day." Jacobson touches her arm. "It's all right to—"

Lena's phone rings. With trembling hands, she takes the call and hangs up after a brief conversation.

"That was headquarters," she says. "They're done. The results are in the case file."

Lena and Jacobson climb into the front seats and bring up the file on the console.

"Two hundred and seventy-three residents with similar names," Jacobson says as he skims the report. "But the prescription matching brings it down to twelve. Seven women, five men."

"Get the men up on a map."

Jacobson taps on the console, and five addresses appear as bright dots on a map of Norra Ängby's uneven grid of streets and woods. Three of the addresses are close to the murder scenes.

Lena pushes Jacobson's hands away, brings up a different screen, and searches for the five names in the taxation registry.

"Software engineer," Lena says, pointing at the first name on the list. She moves to the next name. "Surgeon."

"Could be a lead," Jacobson says. "One of the first victims worked at a hospital."

"We'll check him out first," Lena says. "I still think the killer is going for lookalikes, but it's worth looking into." She moves through the rest of the names. "Attorney, electrician, real estate agent."

Her finger slides back up to the fourth name on the list.

"That guy," she says. "Felix Nyman. The electrician."

"Why him?" Jacobson asks.

"It's a loner's job. And Kristina said the man who ran away from the lab was good with wiring, at least when he fled. Bring up his full profile."

Jacobson taps a button. "Forty-two years old," he says. "No criminal history. Lived his entire life in Stockholm. No siblings or living relatives."

"Where does the record say he was born?" Lena asks. The information will be fabricated, to protect him from unwanted questions in interviews, but it might add to the picture.

"Home birth." Jacobson raises his eyebrows. "Right here in Bromma."

"I wouldn't be surprised if that's a convenient lie to cover for an orphan. That way, the hospital won't have to fake an entry in their registry. We'll try him first."

She flicks back to the map. Felix's address is next door to the first murder scene.

"I'll be damned." Jacobson looks up at Lena. "This is when we call for backup," he says.

"And it's when I get the hell out of here," Jimmy adds. "I'm not going anywhere near a suspected murderer."

"This isn't the same people who blew up your car." Lena starts the car.

"He's still a madman," Jimmy protests. "I've read the news."

"Someone is looking hard for you," Lena says. "So out there, you'll be a rabbit in the field." A thought comes to her. "Are you following this on your phone?"

"No, on my portable plasma screen. Of course I'm using my phone."

"Get rid of it," Lena says.

"Can it be tracked?" Jimmy looks stunned. "Who could do that?"

"I hope to find out at some point." Lena pushes a button and rolls down the rear side window. "Come on, wipe the memory and toss it out."

"I paid a lot for this phone."

"Is it more valuable than your skin?" Jacobson asks. "Do as she says."

Cursing under his breath, Jimmy throws his phone out and lies back down with his arms crossed. Lena reverses out from the parking behind the petrol station and heads north, into Norra Ängby. The address is only a few minutes away.

"Can we please go back to discussing backup?" Jacobson asks.

"Just a quick look first," Lena says. "I'll call Gren after we've sniffed around. That's a promise."

"But that – oh, I get it." Jacobson looks at Lena suspiciously. "You want to be so entrenched Gren can't order you to pull out."

"I don't understand what you're saying." Lena shrugs. "Although it wouldn't make sense to dismiss a detective who's actively monitoring the scene."

"This is not according to protocol," Jacobson says and sighs.

"Nothing about this whole investigation has been done by the books. I'm just cultivating the trend." Lena peers at the numbers on the façades. "I'm parking here. The house is over there next to the scene. It's the one with the tall hedge."

The house is painted in the hue of wet autumn leaves, but the paintwork is flaking in several places. Two storeys, grey slates on the roof. Brown curtains and blinds drawn across every window. No car in the driveway. The garden is noticeably unkempt.

"Looks kind of deserted," Jacobson says. "Don't ask me what gives me that impression."

Lena nods. There is a desolate feeling to the property, the way summer houses can come across as hollow in winter. And her notion of who lives inside its walls is bound to colour her impression.

She takes a deep breath and exhales slowly. Her muscles are tight. It feels as if she balances on a threshold, one step from crossing back into the moment when she entered the office where John Andersson was hiding. A single move away from shutting the lid on a case. As long as she sticks to the plan.

Chapter 41

"We've waited long enough." Lena takes out her phone. "I'm calling the response team, then Gren. My guess is he'll come here himself. Possibly just to keep an eye on me."

"There's a familiar face," Jacobson says and squints along the road.

Two uniformed police officers are cycling towards them. Lena had been so preoccupied with watching the suspect's property that she missed them. One of the officers is Asplund, and behind him is one of the constables who accompanied Asplund when he alerted Lena about the victim's eyes.

"Keep cycling," Lena whispers under her breath.

"They'll stop," Jacobson says quietly.

"Don't jinx it."

"We've parked illegally."

"Oh, for fuck's sake." Lena closes her eyes when she realises Jacobson is right.

The two officers slow down as they approach Lena's car. Asplund scowls as he disembarks and walks up to the driver's window, but his face brightens when he recognizes her.

Lena rolls down the window and musters a smile. Asplund is a nice enough character, but he has to move on. To anyone looking for Lena or Jimmy, their presence is like a lighthouse in a swimming pool. It's bad enough that she's still using her own car.

"I'm glad you're all right," Asplund says. "The report about what happened in the city came in not long after we heard the news on the radio. What a nightmare. Shouldn't you be at the hospital for a check-up?"

"I'm on my way," Lena says. "This is just a detour."

"Through Norra Ängby?" Asplund looks along the street at the house where the first murders took place. "Have you found another lead?" he wonders.

The other officer leaves his bike and joins Asplund, standing a respectful half step behind his superior. He radiates the eager intent of an ambitious recent police academy graduate. Agnes had been all calm and focus, but this man shines with desire to impress. She's glad he's not her partner; he would grate down her nerves to powder within hours.

"You don't happen to know if they've spotted the Saab?" Lena asks. She has been so intent on pinning down the murderer that she forgot about tracking the hit men.

"Not that we've heard," Asplund shakes his head.

"I'm sure we'll find them," the younger officer says quickly. "A vehicle like that can't slip away easily. It was an assault on a member of the force, so everyone will be looking out for them."

Asplund rolls his eyes, and Lena offers an understanding nod. She tries to will Asplund and his protégé back on their bikes and out of sight.

"You've got lots of packing," Asplund notes. "Camping equipment?" He nods at the rear side window and Jimmy's crumpled form under the blanket on the floor.

Lena's face heats up as if she were back in high school. This is going from an inconvenience to a farce. And if Jimmy so much as moves, the next stop is serious trouble.

"Good catch," Lena says and smiles at Asplund. "I'm off on a hiking trip in a few days. When I'm out of the hospital, that is."

"We've got movement," Jacobson hisses.

"Are you sure?" Lena looks at the house but sees no sign of life.

"I'm positive." Jacobson opens his door and steps out slowly. "In the backyard. Blue jacket, low profile, heading down the garden."

"God *damn* it." Lena pushes her door open and forces Asplund to step back.

"Is there an intruder on the crime scene?" Asplund looks confused, then stunned.

"I'll go left," she says, "and see if I can cut him off. Jacobson, watch the driveway." She points at Asplund. "You stay here."

"I thought you were on your way to the hospital?" Asplund blinks and looks around nervously. His colleague's expression tightens, and he puts his hand on his gun.

"If anyone wearing blue approaches you or the car," Lena says, "order them to stop. If they don't, make them."

She closes the car door quietly while Jacobson jogs up the street towards the house. Her legs feel as if she ran here from the city, and her thoughts feel sluggish. The chase has exhausted her to a point she thought impossible.

Asplund looks at Jacobson, who slows down and draws his gun.

"My God." Understanding dawns on Asplund's face. "The neighbour. He's a suspect. You were doing recon. Why didn't you tell me?"

"Call for backup," Lena calls over her shoulder as she jogs towards a house. "First degree murder suspect sighted. And look out for–"

"He's on the move," Jacobson shouts. "Coming your way."

Jacobson points in among the houses while he runs back towards the car. Lena looks left and catches a flash of blue behind a greenhouse. Definitely a person sprinting hard. The shape crashes through the greenery and disappears into an adjacent garden.

"I got this." The younger constable runs into one of the gardens.

"Stop," Asplund bellows. "Don't follow him. That's an order, damn you."

The officer ignores the command and races in behind a house. He is impressively fast, but also likely to get in the way, especially if he catches up with the fleeing suspect. Asplund's junior colleague has leapt into waters much deeper than he anticipates.

"Just get the backup here," Lena calls to Asplund, and runs after the constable.

She dashes over a manicured lawn and tries to force her way through a wall of barbs and sinewy branches, only to have to give up and try a different route. After a few seconds, she pushes past a bush and stumbles into a bigger garden littered with inflatable pools and trampolines.

Up ahead, a man vanishes behind a cluster of trees. He's wearing a blue jacket, dark jeans, white trainers and a black beanie. The constable is right behind him.

Lena opts for what looks like a shortcut, but her jacket is snagged by vicious thorns that force her to stop and disentangle it. When she's free, there's no sign of the suspect or the constable in pursuit. A moment of panic passes.

Far away on her left, someone screams *stop*.

She runs again. Every hedge in sight is either ridiculously tall or dense. The sun's glare makes her eyes water. Her radio is back in the car. The phone she carried in her pocket is gone, probably dropped in someone's garden. She's cut off, unarmed, and winded.

At least the shout gives her an idea of where the suspect is. He will be gone forever if they lose him now. Hopefully Asplund has called for backup, but even if he has, it'll be several minutes away. Time she doesn't have.

Lena bursts through a lilac bower and stops in the middle of a herb garden. No sign of the suspect or Asplund's hotheaded colleague. Jacobson is nowhere to be seen.

She gulps in air and rests her hands on her knees. Running is not her passion, and she's even weaker than she anticipated.

A radio plays behind a fence. Far away, a child laughs. More echoes reach her: saws digging into timber, footsteps on gravel, chirping birds. Everyday sounds on an afternoon that might be someone's last.

A new scream sounds farther down the block. This time, it's a horrified shriek, followed by the unmistakable crash of a smashed window.

"Felix," Lena shouts and runs. "Stand down, damn you."

Lena runs sideways through a gap between two bushes, sprints past rows of raspberries and skirts around a playhouse. A wide trellis separates this lawn from the next.

She tackles it down and finds herself in a garden larger than the other ones she has passed. Along one of the hedges is a big, partially smashed greenhouse. She spots a pair of legs in dark trousers underneath a mound of shattered glass. The constable.

"You idiot," Lena breathes. "Please be alive."

She runs up to the injured man. The jagged pieces of glass are the size of palm leaves. Many of them are smeared with blood. A shaft protrudes from his stomach: some kind of tool, maybe a screwdriver. One of his hands moves. The glass shifts, and the constable groans.

Lena rises up and looks around.

A large but otherwise typical Norra Ängby villa surrounded by cherry trees and redcurrant bushes. No trace of Felix. He might have run on, hid behind a hedge, or sought shelter inside a house. The officer at Lena's feet will die unless she helps him, but more innocent lives might be lost if Felix gets away.

She crouches down and hesitates. Removing the glass without hurting the constable or herself will take minutes. Felix slips farther away with every passing moment. Soon, the chance of finding him again will fade to zero.

"Jacobson," Lena screams at the top of her lungs.

No reply.

She wipes away sweat and grime from her face. Her eyes burn as if they were being stung by needles. She can save a human being now, or prevent more from being lost down the line. A single life versus many others. Both roads build on compassion, but only one is lit up by logic.

She looks down at the wounded constable.

"I'm sorry," she whispers, then prepares to run.

"What are you doing on our property?" someone behind her calls.

Lena looks up. A middle-aged woman frowns down at Lena from an open window in the house.

"Stay inside the house," Lena shouts. "Lock your doors and call for an ambulance."

"I'm calling the police." The woman slams the window shut.

"No, an ambu – listen, damn you."

Jacobson appears from behind a garage. He spots Lena, runs up to her side, and leans against a tree. His breaths come in pained rasps.

"Any idea where he went?" Jacobson asks.

"I lost him," Lena says. "He stabbed Asplund's man."

Jacobson looks down at the constable. "Merciful Christ," he says weakly.

"We need an ambulance. Can you raise an alert?"

Jacobson nods. "Officer down," he barks into his radio and rattles off the address.

Lena leans down again and removes the pieces of glass as fast as she can. The injured officer has started to shake feebly. If he rolls over now, he will slice himself open in a dozen places.

"Help me get the shards off him," Lena says. "I have to fixate the screwdriver before it causes more damage."

"Have you secured the area?" Jacobson asks.

"The constable's more important. Felix is far away by now."

"How can you tell?"

"He's a murderer, not a lunatic."

Lena pricks her finger on one of the shards, but she's too furious to register the pain. The useless woman inside the house delayed her for several invaluable seconds. Felix will be long gone by now.

269

They'll have to kick off a major manhunt, and once they do, he's going to be caught. He is too uprooted and unhinged to pull back into the shadows.

Finding him isn't the problem: the challenge is to contain him before he goes on a rampage. He's cornered and short on time, and he knows it. Felix will aim to wreak as much havoc as possible before the noose snares around him. It's a textbook pattern.

And the carnage will be on her shoulders.

Chapter 42

Felix and Timmy stumble past a group of pines and stop in a tiny clearing. The forest is dense but small, not much more than a block full of boulders and unkempt trees. Behind them, the sun is drifting out of view, slowly nesting among roofs and treetops. The cooling air is filled with scents pared down to faint whiffs by Norra Ängby's greenery: mowed lawns, grilled meat, and the sharp tang of resin.

Felix leans against a rock and gasps for air. He hasn't run in years, and fear is constricting his already aching lungs. There are several exits. All of them take him back into the suburb. He should be able to escape before they find him. This area is his backyard. It has no secrets from him. If only Timmy would tell him which way will take them to safety.

"That woman moves faster than should be allowed." Timmy looks around the clearing in dismay.

"Where do we go?" Felix asks. He wishes Timmy would focus on getting away. As long as they're free, they can still get away, find shelter, and perhaps even continue their work.

"I'm done here. My work isn't, but that can't be helped." Timmy shakes his head. "What a mess. I should've pulled down the wretched cretin a long time ago."

"The detective?"

Timmy nods. "I have to up my game. She'll drop her guard sooner or later, and that's when I snag her." His smile is as slow as a setting sun.

"Can't you take care of her now?" Felix asks. He's unsure exactly how his friend deals with problems or keeps them at bay; Timmy's allusions are too vague and obscure. All he knows is that Timmy fixes, manages and sorts out.

"Not today," Timmy says. "Oh, well. You've played your part. With some flair, I might add. You've certainly made a mark."

"Don't leave now," Felix pleads. "I'm lost without you."

"Some would argue the opposite," Timmy says and laughs. "No, you're on your own. I need to think."

"Let me come with you."

"In time, you will. That was settled long ago. Bye for now, Felix. I'll be seeing you."

Before Felix can speak another word, Timmy whips out of sight, quick as the beat of a wing. Sounds of the forested suburb rush in to fill the absence of Timmy's voice: creaking trees, rustling leaves, distant cars. And, farther away, sirens.

Felix stands on a blank map. No route is safer than the other, no passage more likely to lead him to safety. Pitfalls and traps can hide anywhere. Going home would be the worst option: if Timmy is right, his house will no longer protect him. The police know where he lives.

But remaining still is the worst option. If he does nothing, he becomes the prey.

He must mourn his loss later. Right now, he has to act, look for a sanctuary where he can think and plan. The safety of a deeply familiar place. A hideaway out of sight.

Chapter 43

"The ambulance will be here in five minutes," Jacobson says and pockets his radio. "The response team is due in fifteen. Every patrol in western Stockholm is inbound, and most of the other ones are coming too." He swallows and looks away from the wounded constable.

"What about the dog patrol?" Lena asks.

She lifts away the shards immediately around the stab wound. The screwdriver is buried to its hilt in his body. Fragments of glass pepper the blood that pools on his stomach and trickles down on the crushed flowers around him. Blood covers her hands and her wrists. Cleaning the wound is out of the question, but she must stop the bleeding.

"They're on their way," Jacobson says, "although they'll be at least half an hour. But Gren is closing down the roads out of Norra Ängby, so Felix must be panicking. We'll find him."

"Not soon enough." Lena curses as the constable shudders violently. "I need a bandage. Over there." She points at a white shirt on a clothing line on the other side of the garden.

Just as Jacobson turns away, a woman and a man come running across the garden. Both are in their early twenties and wear matching joggers' outfits. They stop in their tracks when Jacobson whips out his police ID.

"I'm sorry." The man shields his eyes from the sun and backs away. "We heard screaming and thought there was trouble. We'll go right away – oh, my God." He looks down at the groaning constable.

"You need to leave the premises," Jacobson says.

"They're staying here." Lena looks up at the two joggers. "Get that shirt from the laundry line and bring it here," she orders them.

"Have you lost your mind?" Jacobson hisses to Lena.

"I need you to help me. Felix is still on the loose."

"I am not leaving a wounded officer behind."

"I'll go alone. You can stay here to coordinate with the response team and the rest. And you must keep Gren up to speed."

"Look," Jacobson says. "You're shaken. This is irrational. It'll get you fired." He raises his hands a little, as if approaching a nervous horse.

"I'm going to find Felix," Lena says quietly, "no matter what it takes. And at least I know in which direction he was heading. Getting sacked doesn't compare with what he might do next. It's a matter of time before they kick me out anyway."

Jacobson closes his eyes and mutters under his breath. The two joggers return with the shirt, but share an anxious glance and edge backwards when they hear the two officers arguing. Lena takes the shirt and carefully winds it around the screwdriver.

"Press like this," Lena instructs the joggers. "Keep it in place. His life depends on you. There'll be an ambulance here in a few minutes."

As Lena rises up, she notices a patch of black in the grass near the broken greenhouse. The constable's pistol. She picks up the weapon and slides it into her empty shoulder holster under her jacket. The constable is lying on his radio, so it has to stay; moving him might kill him outright.

"Please," Jacobson insists. "Don't go. It's pointless."

"I'll find a way to get in touch." Lena looks around. "Where would you go if you wanted to hide around here?" she asks the jogging couple.

"Maybe the forest?" the woman says. "The edge is right behind this house. It's the one where they – I mean, where you found the eyes."

Lena squints in the sunlight and nods. "I'll try the woods first, then the underground trains. Maybe someone's spotted him."

She takes two steps and stops.

The sun.

Slowly, she turns around in a circle and recreates Felix's path in her mind. From his house, across one adjacent garden, then the next one.

There had been many opportunities for him to dart out through a gate and onto the street. Perhaps he had stuck to the gardens in hopes of not being spotted, but stressed people are primarily concerned with speed or shelter. He would either have hid or looked for a way to run as fast as he could. Instead, Felix stuck to the gardens, where the vegetation is bound to slow him down. That doesn't add up.

Unless he is compelled by a different urge. Felix ran in an almost straight line from his house, and he may well have continued to do so.

"I'm asking you for the last time," Jacobson begins, but Lena waves him to silence.

"What's that way?" Lena asks the joggers.

The pair looks up from the wounded constable. Both the man and the woman look pale, but at least they're doing a good job with the makeshift compress.

"Runstensplan," the male jogger says, his voice unsteady. "Farther west, you have Råcksta, then Vällingby."

A moment of vertigo washes through Lena. She sways, staggers, and finds her balance again. Of course. She should have known.

"Are you all right?" Jacobson asks. "Lena, talk to me."

"Get in touch with the hospital," Lena says and straightens up. "Tell them to keep an eye out for Felix. Meet me there once the ambulance has arrived. And tell Gren to converge on Beckomberga."

"Why would he go there?" Jacobson asks. "He must hate that place."

"Even so, he chose to live here, just a ten-minute walk away. I think he has an affinity to the hospital. And right now, he wants to hide."

"The lab must be the darkest place he can think of."

"Which might be exactly what he wants. He'll be there. Trust me on this one."

Hoping she's not too late, Lena runs towards the sun.

Chapter 44

Lena passes through the forest as fast as she can. Felix is nowhere to be seen. Paths crisscross the wooded hill, splitting around boulders and old trees. Fortunately, the sun provides all the orientation she needs. Sweat pours down her back and into her eyes. Her clothes are far too warm, but her jacket offers some protection in case Felix decides to ambush her.

Not that he will. Felix is bound for his childhood prison like a fox bolting to its hole. Jacobson's doubts are understandable, but his tidy mind is a world away from Felix's harried soul. She can anticipate his line of thinking as sure as if his thoughts were her own.

Can you, now? And why do you think that is?

Lena shakes her head and leaps over a log. She can't afford to doubt. Better to chase a lead to its end and make sure nothing hides at the final stretch than to turn around halfway down the road. The hesitation doesn't even feel like her own: its soft, cajoling tone is unfamiliar, as if she brushed against someone else's thoughts.

Not a great sign of a healthy head. Then again, she has already established that she's tumbling down a rabbit hole from which she might not escape. She even tried sharing the experience with someone else. Some mistakes will not be repeated.

The path ends at the corner of a road that continues down a long slope. Still no sign of Felix. If she's right, the hospital is only a few minutes away. Her impression back in the garden had been correct: Felix is heading straight for Beckomberga. Sirens wail from several points in the distance.

A couple of minutes later, she jogs past the gatehouse and enters the hospital's premises. A security car is parked diagonally across the road just inside the main gates. Two men in brown uniforms lean against the vehicle and study Lena as she comes closer. Probably private security contractors roped in by the manager or the local residents' association.

"This is private property," one of the men says. "I'm sorry, but entry is restricted to residents and members of the staff."

Lena slows down in front of the man who addressed her. Bearded and plump, he could be Norling's less fit cousin. She reaches for her ID card and realises it's gone. Another victim of her madcap race through Norra Ängby's gardens.

"Have you seen a man in black jeans and a blue jacket?" Lena asks. "On his own, probably running or walking fast. He would've passed through here in the last ten minutes." She rests her hands on her knees and gasps for air. Today has seen more running than she has done in the past six months added up.

*"If your husband's gone missing," the man's shorter and leaner partner man says, "you need to contact the police. In the meantime, please look somewhere else."

"I know her," the bearded man says, surprised. "She's the detective who shut down the airport."

"Are you sure?" The other man looks unsure.

"I'm positive," the first man says. "And I don't think she's looking for her other half. Listen to that." He nods towards the road that leads up to Runstensplan, from where an escalating cacophony of sirens is rising.

"What's going on?" he asks.

"A police operation," Lena says.

"Can we help?"

"Just tell me if you've seen the man I described?"

"It's been twenty minutes since we let someone past. And that was a family. We would've turned the man you want away unless he could prove that he lives in one of the flats here."

He holds up a list of names, probably of the local residents. The manager is trying to protect the reputation of his profitable neighbourhood.

"I'll be damned," his partner says. "This is about those murders, isn't it?"

Lena looks around. Normally, she would get rid of anyone who is not on the force, but the grounds of Beckomberga Hospital are vast. Every available hand is needed.

"You know the big entrance to the tunnels just up ahead?" she asks.

"The one where cars can drive down?"

Lena nods. "It has to be shut."

"We locked it up yesterday. The manager wanted that area sealed off. Weren't you part of what happened down there?"

"So there's no way anyone can get in?" she asks.

The man shakes his head. "We closed the doors ourselves."

Lena nods. At least they won't have to extract Felix from the basement, but he might flee somewhere else. If he does, he may decide to go anywhere, and no police force in the world can monitor every patch of a huge suburb full of forests.

"Could you do a round along the major roads?" she asks. "Check for anyone in the clothes I just described."

"And if we spot him?" the bearded man asks.

"Call the police. They'll put you through to the right people. Don't try to apprehend him."

The men nod to each other and drive away. A few seconds later, the first police car arrives and stops next to Lena. Behind it is the emergency response team's massive transport. Three ambulances and at least a dozen more police cars are on the way down the road from Runstensplan.

Officers stream out of their cars and converge around Lena. Norling waits at the back. He looks at her with an unreadable expression as he shifts his sub-machine gun behind his back. Lena waits until all the officers are gathered around her and raises her voice.

"We've reason to think the suspect is nearby," she says. "Spread out in teams. If you see him, be cautious. He's a high-level risk. Apprehend him using any means necessary, but be prepared for a violent response."

"Can you make a better guess than 'nearby'?" Norling asks.

"He's likely to try to access an abandoned underground facility. You know which one I mean."

"So he was hiding there all along?" Norling raises his eyebrows. "I thought that mission was a complete dud."

"The suspect never stayed in the lab," Lena says. "He had a property next to the scene of the first murder."

"So why is he here?" Norling asks. "Our last assignment here was a fucking travesty. I'm not going in blind again."

"It's complicated." Lena says. "But we can assume that the suspect knows the area well, including good places to stay out of sight. Stay on your toes."

She gives them a rundown of how Felix looks and watches the officers move out. For the first time in months, there is a general lack of comments and scornful glances. The seriousness of the situation overshadows every idea of sarcasm. There will be time for jabs and glib remarks later on, especially when her colleagues find out why the suspect is on the run in the first place.

Jacobson appears a moment later. He parks Lena's car near the gatehouse, slams the door shut, and jogs over her. He looks flustered and winded.

"They're taking the constable in," he says. "He's alive, for now. Any sign of Felix?"

"Nothing yet," Lena says. "But he's here."

"Don't tell me you have a gut feeling or can sense his presence?"

"It's a little more complicated than that."

"I'd definitely come up with a better excuse for Gren."

"Is he coming?" Lena asks.

Jacobson nods. "He'll be here in thirty minutes or so. You won't be surprised to hear that he's pretty unhappy. I had a hard time explaining why we spooked Felix instead of waiting for backup and surrounding the house."

"But we planned to," Lena says. "You heard me say that."

"Yes, I know you would've called it in, but we shouldn't have been outside the house in the first place. Now Felix is on the loose." Jacobson's face is red, probably both from anger as well as his earlier sprint.

"Then let's find him," Lena says. "Is Jimmy still in the car?"

"Against all odds, he hasn't bolted yet. Do you think Felix will go back to the laboratory?"

"He might try, but the garage door's locked."

"So he can be anywhere, then?" Jacobson asks. "If he's even at the hospital at all. This is madness. We should focus on cutting off the routes out of Norra Ängby."

"Felix might take a hostage. Or go on a killing spree."

"He's unarmed," Jacobson insists. "How much damage can he do?"

"Ask the constable." Lena looks Jacobson in the eyes. "Work with me here. I need you to have my back. Especially when Gren gets here." For all she knows, the superintendent might be planning to retire her on the spot.

"I want to support you." Jacobson rubs his forehead and lowers his voice. "But apart from your hunches, we haven't got any proof that Felix is here. He may be–"

The ringing of an alarm bell blasts through the quietness. Its suddenness and volume make Lena and Jacobson flinch and cower. The sound comes from somewhere close to the hospital.

"How's that for proof?" Lena draws her gun and nods at Jacobson. "Let's go."

Chapter 45

Beckomberga Hospital

Friday

15:37

Finding the origin of the alarm is easier than Lena expects. A quick dash takes her and Jacobson to the entrance to the tunnels. Mounted on the brick wall is a large, old-fashioned shielded bell that rings incessantly. The members of the response team fan out and take up positions to secure the area.

After a moment, the private security contractors' car veers onto the road and comes to a screeching stop in front of Lena. The two guards step out and run up to check the massive padlock on the door.

"It's still locked," the bearded man says.

"Are there any other entrances?" Jacobson wonders.

"Lots, but they've all been sealed off. The manager keeps tabs on the keys. Unless your man has a copy of the skeleton key, there's no way he could have made his way inside."

"If your suspect is down there," Norling says, "all the better for us. In that case he's trapped. We can go in and scoop him up."

"Unless he goes walkabout in the ventilation system," Lena notes. "You know how fun that is."

"Fuck." Norling's face tightens. "All right, unlock this door."

"What about windows?" Lena asks the security guards.

"There's one on the back of the building," one of the guards says. "But it's too small."

"Show me."

The two security guards run around the corner. Lena follows, Jacobson trailing behind her. Norling and his team follow close behind her. As the guards said, a window runs along the rear of the entrance, but it's high up and so low only birds and rodents can enter. It's also closed and intact.

"What triggered the alarm?" Lena asks.

"Must've been one of the motion sensors underground," the bearded guard says. "They're old, but do the job. They cover most of the corridors in this sector."

"Are you sure?"

"I've been patrolling the hospital for two years. It's our job to know our way around here, especially concerning alarms. Trust me on this one."

Lena runs her hand through her hair. In theory, Felix could have ventured inside the hospital's main complex, stolen a set of keys, gone down to the basement and managed to navigate the corridors all the way to the lab.

But not enough time has passed. And Felix must be too distraught. He'll have gone for a more straightforward way.

She peers into the dense wall of bushes, elms and birches that spreads out behind the building. Leaves and trees limit the range of sight to a few steps.

"There must be another entrance," Lena says. "What's inside this grove?"

"No idea," the security team says in unison.

"Come again?" Lena says. "You just said it's your responsibility to know what's what here."

"This specific area is completely overgrown." The bearded guard shrugs. "I heard the manager wants it cleared for more properties, so I guess it's been ignored. The gardeners haven't touched it for years."

"In other words," Lena says, "you haven't got a clue if there's another door in there."

283

"No," the security guards say after moment's silence.

"Norling," Lena calls, "we're searching these trees."

"Copy that."

The response team leader signals to his men, who run to Lena's side. Guns drawn, Lena and Jacobson walk into the tangle of branches.

The area is only the size of a basketball court. The vegetation is so dense one could safely hide a car, but the spot of untended wilderness is too small to conceal a construction as large as a stairwell. One sweep will be enough to reveal any hidden building, no matter how small.

"There's nothing here," Jacobson says when they reach the other end. "We should open the main entrance, go down, and hope to block his escape route."

"If Felix knows about another way in, he might sneak away that way."

"True, but we need to check. So my point stands."

Lena nods tightly. Jacobson is right. They're losing time.

"Change of plan," she calls. "Move back and look around the main buildings."

Someone on Lena's right gives up a startled cry. She dodges in behind a tree and raises her gun, but there's no one in view. After a moment, a member of the response team appears, seemingly crawling up out of the ground.

She runs up to the man and finds him climbing out of a square hole in the dirt. Some four metres below him is a brightly lit concrete floor. An open trapdoor hangs down into the corridor and swings back and forth.

"I got hold of a root just in time," the man says. "I think the hatch was propped up with a twig."

"This must be where he got in," Jacobson says.

"Another damn trapdoor." Lena circles the opening to make sure Felix isn't waiting below just out of sight, but she can't see anyone.

"Why does it open inwards?" Jacobson asks. "That's idiotic."

"Perhaps a safety measure if it happened to be covered with snow."

"Never mind that." Lena looks at Norling. "After you. We'll follow."

"We're going in," Norling shouts, and his team takes up position behind him.

Lena turns to Jacobson. "Have the rest of the men look out for Felix," she says, "in case there's another way out of the tunnels. He might be able to unlock a door from inside."

"We can show you where the main exits are." The bearded private guard points at the hospital. "At least the ones we know about."

"Guide the other officers there, and keep those doors shut." Lena turns back to Norling. "On your mark."

Chapter 46

Lena lands unsteadily next to Jacobson. Her balance is off, and her vision is blurred at the edges. Any normal human being would be trying to recover after the crash. And that had been the lowest point in a generally traumatic day. She's running out of steam.

The response team splits up in two groups to cover each direction. As Lena expects, the area immediately below the trapdoor is clear. Felix knows he's being followed, and he isn't interested in standing and fighting. He's flushed out, hunted, outnumbered and trapped. All that remains is to box him in.

Norling flicks a signal to his team and advances on the first corner. Lena and Jacobson follow. The sense of déjà vu is overwhelming: she retraces her own steps, flanked by the same walls and faces and passing through the same rank air. It's as if the turbulent hours that passed between the two occasions were a feverish dream.

They turn the first corner. The tunnel ahead is empty. Scuttling forward in a disturbingly insectoid way, the response team storm down the corridor and stop at the next junction. Lena and Jacobson stay at the back of the group.

"Are you all right?" Jacobson whispers. "You look dazed."

Lena nods. "I think he's near."

She hopes Jacobson doesn't ask from where Lena gets that idea. Telling him there's a hint of a presence in the complex won't boost his faltering trust in her judgement. But she can't ignore the sensation that Felix is very close, as if she were holding her hand over a naked flame.

Norling looks around the second corner and raises his weapon in one fluid motion.

"Police," Norling barks. "Stay where you are, and step away from the–"

A loud bang rings between the concrete walls, and Lena's vision turns black. For a second she thinks she has been shot, but there's no pain and the noise was wrong. Still, all she sees is compact darkness.

Bright lights flash into being around her: torches attached to the response team's weapons. The corridor ahead is illuminated by wavering patches of pale white. She switches on her own torch, but it's much weaker than those carried by the response team.

"Bastard killed the strip lights," Norling says. "I think he short-circuited a power box."

"Again," Lena whispers. "Just like when he escaped. He's coming full circle."

"What was that?" Norling frowns at Lena. Behind him, Jacobson shakes his head at her.

"Nothing." Lena shakes her head in irritation. "Why aren't you going after him?"

Her legs are shaking, and she leans against the wall for support. Jacobson shifts his feet and wipes sweat from his eyes. Even the response team looks hesitant: this should be a routine task, but Felix is prolonging the chase, as if he wants to goad his pursuers into more dangerous territory.

"I'm trying to figure out how these tunnels are laid out," Norling says. "The target disappeared behind another bloody corner, and I don't want to run after him in a circle."

Lena looks around. There are few landmarks in these anonymous corridors, but she recognises the area.

"You won't have to," she says. "He's heading for the lab."

Norling and his team dart around the corner and move down the corridor at near-running speed. Lena follows as fast as she can, but she's losing her focus, her thoughts drifting apart until she almost forgets to move her feet.

She hates these confusing, never-ending tunnels. This warren is like a mirror image of the sunlit parks above: confined spaces, no light, and barely breathable air. The walls and the ceiling glisten like wet wallpaper, decorated with fluttering shadows cast by the torchlights, as if she were surrounded by giant moths.

On the wall ahead is a stack of water pipes she remembers from her first visit. They have reached the corridor that leads up to the lab. Norling takes point, kneels down, and peers around the corner.

"Clear," he calls. "Check all the side rooms."

The response team swarm down the corridor and search the smaller rooms on each side. Lena and Jacobson follow them. When the team reach the end of the corridor, they line up their sights on the large air duct. The grille lies on the floor.

"Wait here," Norling says to Lena and Jacobson. "I'll leave two men with you, in case the target managed to dodge us. I'll take the others and sweep the lab. Don't leave until we get back."

"Be careful," Lena says. "I have a bad feeling about this."

It must be a phenomena caused by the torchlights, but the walls continue to look frail and artificial, as if she could press her hand right through them. The shadows seem to move a fraction too slowly as they dance around her.

Even worse is the smell: the first time she entered this underground complex, all she noticed was a hint of disinfectants and paint. Now that scent is replaced by the tinny stench of burnt-out electrical circuits.

She pushes her finger against the paintwork. The wall is solid, but she can't shake the idea that she's strong enough to budge the concrete. She leans closer and presses harder. To her eye, nothing happens. Her senses tell her a different story.

Norling looks at Lena as if unsure whether or not to take her advice seriously, then raises his weapon and walks into the room where the police found the door to the lab. Five members of his team follow him.

"Didn't the technicians put that back?" Jacobson points at the rusted grille on the floor.

"I was unconscious the last time I left, remember?" Lena says.

"They did," Norling says as he returns to the corridor. "And that's not the biggest problem. The front door is locked."

"Are you sure?" Jacobson steps past Norling to look inside the room. Still frowning at the walls, Lena follows the two men.

The large metal door occupies one wall inside the small, undecorated room. She recognizes it immediately: on her previous visit, she saw it from the other side. It's the entrance to the laboratory. The plaster that hid the door has been chipped away and brushed up against the opposite wall.

"I guarantee it's locked," Norling says. "Or barred from the inside."

"This makes no sense." Jacobson shines his torch at the handle. "From what I read, the technicians cut through the metal and propped the door open. They wouldn't have shut it again."

"I was told the same." Norling shifts his weapon behind his back and looks at Lena. "Looks like we're going back through the duct. What a bloody joke."

Lena grows numb as she turns to the opening behind her. She cannot think of anything she wants to do less than going back to the lab that way.

"You first," Lena says.

"I still don't know the way to the lab," Norling says. He eyes the opening as if it were lined with teeth.

"I can try to lead the way?" Lena suggests.

"And get yourself stabbed in the neck?" Norling asks. "Forget it. I'll find the damned place. After all, we can't do worse than last time." He raises his voice. "Everyone, to me. We're going through the duct again."

Chapter 47

Beckomberga Hospital

Friday

16:02

One by one, the response team strips off most of their protective gear and climbs into the large ventilation duct. The sounds of their boots and belts scraping against the metal fades, then disappears.

Lena and Jacobson are alone. There are no sounds except for the faint drone of the constant wind.

"I don't have to tell you how much this feels like déjà vu," Jacobson says quietly.

"That's why I'm happy the response team went in first this time," Lena says. "I'm not leaving this spot until they return with Felix. Hopefully through the front door." She wraps her arms around herself; the temperature is definitely dropping.

"You think Felix blocked it from the other side?"

"I can't think of another explanation."

At least she cannot come up with one she wants to share with anyone else. The last time she was here, an opening had appeared in a tiled wall, and she had passed through it. Or so she had imagined. Later, Agnes appeared in a fleeting but inhuman hallucination that had vanished into thin air, but also left a brief imprint in the carpet on the floor.

These moments have widened the perimeters of her imagination. She can suggest a range of alternative reasons for why the door is locked again, but none that would make sense to Jacobson. Or any other human being, for that matter.

"I don't like this." Jacobson brushes away sweat from his face. "Something in these tunnels makes me queasy. It might be the paint."

"Are you hot?" Lena asks.

"I'm being boiled alive. Aren't you steaming in that jacket?"

Lena shakes her head. Running after Felix had left her soaked with perspiration. Now she's shivering with cold. She could use a woollen blanket, but decides not to mention this. It occurs to her that Norling look uncomfortably warm too.

One minute passes.

Two minutes become five, then ten. The response team is still gone.

Lena and Jacobson look at each other in the light of their two flashlights.

"I know," Lena says. "They should be back. That lab is only a minute away, and it'd take only one more to sweep it."

"Totally unbelievable." Jacobson shakes his head. "They're supposed to be experts at this."

"The ducts are hard to navigate," Lena says, although she's increasingly sure that isn't the problem.

"This is still shocking. I'm going out to report back to Gren. We'll have to get another team in here or find a way to break down the door."

"It won't work." Lena shakes her head. "I have to go."

Jacobson looks at Lena as if she has turned her gun on him.

"What the hell is the matter with you?" he asks.

"I can't explain, but you have to trust me on this. Felix is waiting for me."

"That's what I'm worrying about."

"Not like that. I have to go and get him. He won't come out otherwise."

The longer she waits, the more convinced she becomes: they are going about this the wrong way. Other rules are in play down here, at least for her. Under the sun, finding Felix had been a matter

291

of deductions and conclusions, but she has left that arena and its constraints behind.

Norling and his team have not gone astray because they're incompetent or unlucky. Perhaps that was the case when they got lost the first time, but this is different. They will never find Felix. And neither will Jacobson. Only she has a shot. She understands the geometry of this place, or perhaps it recognizes her.

But Jacobson too is attuned to the menacing ambience that surrounds them, at least to some extent. That means he's stuck in the same delusion or that she imagines his presence. She knows that her assumption is delirious, but so is the entire situation. And everyone knows how to best fight a fire.

"You can't do this," Jacobson says, but his sternness is faltering.

"It's my case." Lena doesn't challenge him; she simply states a fact. "Felix is my suspect. I'm getting him out of here."

She's right; Jacobson senses the twisted mechanisms at work. He opens and closes his mouth but finds no words.

"What should I do?" he asks eventually. His face is a picture of defeat.

"Watch the entrance." Lena shines her light down the corridor. "We could be wrong. Felix might be hiding somewhere else, waiting for a chance to sneak up on us."

"But you're convinced he's in there."

"I've never been surer."

"I wish I could say that I think you're wrong," Jacobson says. "This whole situation is a waking nightmare."

As Lena climbs inside the duct, she wonders if Jacobson is more accurate than he understands.

Chapter 48

The duct is less confusing than Lena remembers. She reaches the first crossing, and after a few moments, the path is as obvious as if it were lined with a red carpet. But that doesn't dispel her fear that she will lose her way and wriggle through this dirty honeycomb until her body caves in. Just like last time, her hands are sticky with filth and grease, and the stale, frigid air is difficult to breathe.

When around two minutes have passed, her flashlight finds the opening to the lab at the end of a long, narrow duct. The grille once held in place by Jimmy's chewing gum is still gone. The response team is nowhere in sight. They may already have scoured the lab, but the silence is absolute, and there are no lights beyond the opening. It's unlikely that Felix got the better of Norling and the others, but the complete quietness is just as improbable.

"Norling," Lena hisses, trying to keep her voice down.

Nothing except the wheeze of a slow wind washing past her while she stares at the dark square at the end of the duct. It's even colder here than in the corridor: the draught makes her shiver, and the metal under her palms is chilly. Felix may be lurking just out of sight, ready to bring a knife down on her as soon as her head is out of the tunnel.

Jacobson is right: she should not go on. The response team is here for a reason. She'll back up until she reaches a place where she can turn around and crawl out of this cold maze as fast as she can.

"Screw this," Lena murmurs and shuffles backwards.

She stops when her shoes touch air, as if one of the metal panels of the duct has disappeared. Expecting to feel the walls of the duct, she moves one of her feet sideways, but there is no resistance. Not even when she stretches her leg out can she feel any part of the duct. It's as if the confined tunnel ends just behind her and opens into a gaping room.

There should not be any such spaces here. And even if the duct for some inexplicable cause had been constructed inside a giant chamber, there is no reason for why the air should be so bitter. She scrambles forwards and squirms around until she can look behind her.

There is nothing there.

As her senses had told her, the duct stops just behind her. Her flashlight doesn't touch upon anything in the darkness. The tunnel through which she has crept is simply gone, replaced by a gloom so compact her way back could be sealed with a vertical pool of oil.

"This can't be," she breathes.

Her mind is betraying her again. It holds up a silver screen of horrors that obscures the real world. She fights the panic, but the insight is too much. One sob racks through her body, and soon she curls up and cries, knowing that she has reached an end.

She is coming undone. Stairwells in walls, friends in vaults, and now a vanished way out. Whether the sights are conjured by a latent madness or some residual chemical, their impact and significance are the same: lucidity is a thing of the past. From here on, she can slip only farther south.

A minute passes while she manages to get her crying under control. Slowly, she raises her head and looks around. The duct is still gone. Her flashlight flickers and loses some of its strength; its batteries will last only a few more minutes. After that, she will be both blind and stuck in this delirium.

She turns to the dark opening to the laboratory. Perhaps this is an end, but one door remains to explore, even if it turns out to be one that gets her killed. Whatever happens, it's better than to submit to these treacherous illusions in complete darkness. Every chance to fight her curse is a mercy.

"Felix," Lena shouts, "I'm coming in."

She doesn't expect him to reply, but the sound of her own voice fills her with a shade of resolution. Bracing herself, she moves towards the opening.

Just before she reaches it, a weak voice drifts out of the darkness ahead: "I can't run anymore."

Hearing the voice is such a surprise she almost stops, but she can't afford to hesitate. As soon as she reaches the opening, she shines her flashlight around the room and spots Felix lying on one of the bed frames at the far end of the room. It would take him at least three or four seconds to run up to the opening. Enough time for her to reach the floor safely.

Awkwardly but carefully, she climbs down and looks around. The laboratory looks the same as the last time she was here: a film of grime on the walls and floors, metal bed frames lined up against the wall, empty armatures hanging from the shadowy ceiling. Small clouds of dust swirl past the cone of light from her flashlight.

At the same time, the room feels different. Its derelict atmosphere is replaced by an elusive restlessness, as if its shape is only temporary and might contort into a new, unsettling form without warning. Then again, she could be imagining this entire facility, including Felix. Whatever the truth, she has a mission to finish.

Keeping both her flashlight and her gun trained on Felix, she walks closer to the bed on which he lies.

"Felix Nyman," Lena says, "you are under arrest."

He looks crumpled, as if dropped from a height. Pale, sweating and dressed in smudged, ill-fitting clothes, he also looks like a man who has stumbled through a warzone and survived due to sheer luck. Red grazes cover one side of his face; maybe a result from his attempt to escape. His eyes are large but alert. They seem fixed at some point far above the ceiling.

She pauses to cough and reads him his rights. The formality feels pointless and impotent, as if someone is laughing behind her back, and she has to concentrate not to dwindle off.

"Stand up and turn around," she says when she's done. "I'm not going to tell you again, Felix."

"I tried for so long." Felix exhales with a shudder. "Year after year, I convinced myself that I had to be mistaken. Carl would not be hiding in plain sight."

"You'll have plenty of time to elaborate on all your mistakes when we're at the station. And the poor bastards you killed weren't Carl. You're confused."

She shifts her fingers around the grip of her gun and walks closer. Images of the crime scenes hover at the back of her mind. It's nearly impossible to imagine that the ragged, scrawny figure slumped before her is capable of such brutality.

Nearly, but not impossible. She knows people better than that. Thankfully, her handcuffs still hang from their clip on her belt.

"But Carl is out there," Felix insists. "Pretending, acting, smiling. Eyes bright and blue, even when they used to be black. And he keeps coming back, no matter how much I make him look."

"You can write all of this down at the station." Lena walks around the bed to make sure Felix isn't hiding any weapons.

"I had to show him what he'd done to us," Felix continues. "Everything he forced us to face, I wanted him to see too. That's only fair. Don't you agree?"

The question catches Lena unaware. She is so intent on getting Felix out of the laboratory that she almost answers it reflexively. When she realises what word is forming on her lips, she swallows it.

"Get off the bed," she repeats.

"I'm not going anywhere. Coming back was a mistake."

"One of your many. Stand up, or I'll drag you out of here."

Felix lowers his voice, as if speaking in confidence. "I was expected, you see."

"Is there someone else here?" Lena looks around. No sign of movement, but her flashlight is on its last breath. This is taking far too long.

"Not yet," Felix says. "But soon."

"We're leaving now," she says. "Did you bar the door from the inside?"

Felix shakes his head slowly. "It was locked when I came here. I didn't understand why until later."

"Can you open it or not?" Lena snaps. Felix does not make much sense, and her momentary sense of triumph is quickly being eroded by unease.

"This place wants me to stay." Felix smiles at Lena. "That's why I had to go through the ventilation, like a tadpole down a bottle."

"Have it your way."

Lena takes one of Felix's arms and pulls him off the bed. She has spent enough time listening to his babble. Even though he speaks nonsense, his rambling carves out a pit in her stomach. Imagined or not, the man is in her custody, and she's taking him in.

She stops after only a single step. For some reason, Felix is suddenly immobile, as if someone else were dragging him in the opposite direction. Felix looks up at Lena and raises his other arm.

A shackle links his wrist through a heavy chain to a hoop on the bed frame. On the shackle is an old, rusted padlock.

"What have you done?" Lena looks at the lock in total incomprehension.

"I needed to rest, so I lay down." Felix looks almost apologetic. "That was another mistake. I let my guard down. But he did it so you have to stay, too. He really wants to meet you."

"Who?" Lena demands. "Tell me who did this?"

She swings around and shines her failing light at the walls. The room with the giant flash and the steel benches is only a few steps away. While Felix is secured and not an immediate threat, she still cannot find the willpower to open that particular door. She will crumble in an instant if the flash comes on.

"You feel it too, don't you?" Felix nods eagerly when Lena looks back at him. "This place has thin walls," he says, "like old brittle skin. They can barely hold the hunger out."

Lena yanks at the chain while Felix babbles on. The metal is old, but as thick as her thumb. Sweat stings her eyes as she looks around for something that can help her break one of the links. The urgent need to get out is not only due to her dying torch: a presence is closing in on her, invisible but still tangible, like a thundercloud rolling over the ground.

"I thought Timmy would help me," Felix says. "Or at least that he'd stay by my side."

"What did you say his name was?" she asks.

"Timmy Patreus." Felix draws a shuddering breath and struggles to his knees. "My friend. Only it wasn't really him. I get that now."

Lena gives the chain another explorative tug. *Patreus.* The name was on the list she and Jacobson found in Kristina's safety deposit box. Maybe Felix has a collaborator. She files the idea away for now; there will be time to consider that when they interrogate Felix. One challenge at a time.

"He looked like the real Timmy." Felix speaks quietly, as if explaining the situation to himself. "But he wasn't. It was only a mask."

"Come again?" Lena looks up sharply at Felix.

"One day he was just there, in my house. I hadn't seen him since I ran away. He was still about twenty years old, just like when we first met. At that time, I was so lonely I forgot that he should've been much older and that the real Timmy was nice."

"But he'd changed," Lena says.

"This Timmy was pushy," Felix murmurs. "Kept telling about terrible things that had happened or could come to pass. He said I had to get even with those who hurt me. So he made me break into their homes, and–"

Lena shifts her hand around the chain. Felix's description captures exactly how Lena felt when she met Agnes at the bank. An elegant, intimidating fraud, wrapped in a perfect disguise and armed with a voice tailored to slip past all disbelief. When the apparition spoke to her in the vault, its words had sunk in like blows.

It would have been easy to pay attention a little longer and let the cruelties hit home, to accept the scorn until the lies became true. After all, it had been Agnes. A woman Lena would have trusted with her life. Perhaps she still would. Only the outrage at seeing Agnes perverted by the hallucination had stopped her from being completely transfixed.

But Felix had not been furious when he saw his old friend. To him, the appearance of a long-lost comrade had been a blessing, and he had opened his heart without thinking twice. Because of that, Felix had been violated. And Lena had come close to sharing his fate.

Two people suffering from an identical delusion. Perhaps it is possible.

Maybe, the detective in Lena notes. *But the evidence suggests otherwise.*

"My God," Felix whispers. "What have I done?" He looks at Lena as if seeing her for the first time. His face is the sickly pale of profound astonishment.

"You've listened to the wrong people," Lena says. "Turn your face away."

Lena holsters her gun, puts a foot on the edge of the bed frame, and grips the chain with both hands. It's so cold she cries out in surprise. She tightens her hold, straightens her back, and pulls.

The chain does not break.

"Damn it." Lena drops the chain and rubs her hands together. Blisters from the icy metal spring up on her palms.

A low scraping echoes around the room. A moment later, there is another. Within a few seconds, the sounds grow into a recognizable pattern: footsteps, unhurried but relaxed, and coming closer.

The response team would be noisier or more silent. This is the approach of a single individual who has all the time in the world and no qualms about discretion. Someone with confidence and complete authority.

Lena picks up the chain and pulls again. She pushes away from the bed with her legs until the frame creaks. The veins on her arms press against her skin. Her tendons shoot out jolts of pain in protest.

She pulls harder. Words come from her mouth, but she is only dimly aware that she is speaking.

"Give in," she snarls under her breath. "I'm not letting go. Felix is mine, you scheming, tricky, malicious bastard. So just – give – *in*."

The chain snaps.

Lena tumbles backwards and crashes down onto the floor. She manages to twist sideways and land on her side, narrowly avoiding cracking her skull open against the tiles, but the impact knocks the air out of her. Her torch clatters to the floor.

The footsteps come closer. Striding assertively now, like a head teacher descending on a classroom to correct a pair of belligerents. Or a prison warden marching towards a cell where the inmate waits to be taken away.

Swaying, Lena climbs to her feet and draws her gun again.

"Hands on your back, and turn around."

Felix turns slowly. Lena cuffs him with some effort; her hands tremble so much it takes three attempts before the metal rings snap in place.

"To the exit," she rasps and waves with her gun.

Felix shuffles into the adjoining room, and Lena follows. He moves uncertainly, as if sleepwalking, but at least he does what she tells him to do. The door is still there. It's a welcome surprise: nothing can be taken for granted anymore, at least not in here.

She tries the large handle, but it doesn't turn. She leans on the handle with her full weight and manages to shift it a fraction.

"Help me," she says to Felix. "Push down, like this."

Felix turns around and finds the handle behind his back.

"If I go with you," he asks, "will you keep Carl away?"

He looks at Lena, and for the first time, she glimpses the sign of a human being in his eyes. An unravelled, bruised and maltreated person who never will fully heal, but a person nonetheless.

If you don't come willingly, Lena thinks, *I'll drag you screaming and kicking out of this pit. You don't belong here. You have to pay for what you've done, but you never asked to come here in the first place.*

"Sure," Lena says. "Now push."

Felix presses down, and the door clicks open under their joined weight.

Chapter 49

The sudden appearance of half a dozen strong torches blinds Lena. Shouted commands bounce off the walls and blend into a cacophony. She shields her eyes with her hands, staggers backwards, and waits until she can see again.

Jacobson stands just outside the door and aims his gun at Felix. Behind Jacobson is Norling and the rest of the response team. They pounce on Felix and force him down on his stomach before Lena has time to speak.

"He's already cuffed." She coughs; her lungs are filled with dust. "Don't break his bloody back."

"You heard her," Norling shouts. "Get him off the floor. Franke, what's the status?"

"There's no one else here." Not anymore, at least; the footsteps stopped the moment she opened the door.

She walks over to Jacobson, who stares at her and shakes his head.

"You scared us," Jacobson says. "We were trying to agree on what to do, then all of a sudden you burst out through the door, no warning or anything."

"Didn't you hear me shout?" Lena asks.

"It's been dead silent. What happened in there?"

"I'll brief you later. Get us out of here." She coughs again, and Jacobson reaches out to hold her arm.

"Do you want me to get the medics?" he asks.

"I'm only winded. Just point the way, and walk on."

A minute later, Lena staggers out through the same huge doorway she used the first time she was here. Outside is a congregation of police cars, ambulances and fire trucks. Fifty-odd people, everyone on her side. It is the best sight Lena has seen in years. Even the sun seems to have positioned itself to cast the scene in an exquisite light.

"Felix goes with me," Lena says. "I want to start debriefing him straight away."

There's no telling how Felix's arrest will affect the broken cogs and wheels inside his head. At the moment, he is lucid and cooperative, but it might be a temporary phase.

"I'll drive," Jacobson says.

The response team joins Lena around her car. Two members steer Felix by his shoulders. Both men eye him as if he might hide an arsenal under his tattered jacket. Norling's face is stiff and pasty.

"Where the hell did you go?" Lena murmurs to Norling.

"I made a tactical error." Norling refuses to meet her eyes.

"Meaning what?"

"We got lost."

"Again?"

"I take full responsibility," Norling snaps. "Drop the subject."

"My pleasure."

Lena opens the door to the back seat of her car and turns to Felix. Pale and shivering, he looks so miserable that she struggles to believe he is responsible for the horrific crimes.

He ran for a reason, and he confessed to her, all of which makes him obviously guilty. And she wants him to feel the pain he brought upon others. But at the same time, she cannot think of him only as a callous killer. He was cast in a broken form and moulded by Carl into something even more damaged.

"Get in the car," she says to Felix. "You're safe now."

And right then, Felix is shot.

Chapter 50

Felix wonders why the detective stopped pushing at him. A moment ago, she was guiding him inside her car, her face torn between rage and concern. Now she stands still and watches him with an expression of disbelief.

Her colleague, the short man in the brown suit, is just as still, mouth open and eyes wide. His white shirt is stained with blood, and the detective has streaks of wet red across her face.

It is quiet, too. The discord that rang in his head is gone. At least everyone has stopped shouting at him; he was buckling under the screamed commands and curses. Silence is better. Now he has a chance to find his bearings.

Then the detective fades away. The other police officers go with her, dissipating slowly but steadily, like thick smoke washed away by a gentle breeze. After a moment, the police cars vanish too, as do the ambulance and the ground on which he stands. Even the trees lose their form and melt away, as if dissolved by a draught moving at glacial speed.

Before long, he can see right through the people and objects around him. The day itself is bleeding away into darkening grey, as if sinking into dirty ice.

Only one shape stays solid. A man lying on his back next to Felix's feet. Spreading from the man's savaged head is a shadow that pools around his hair. But Felix knows the man is not really *there:* his shape is only a cooling husk, empty of meaning.

Felix recognises the man's shirt. The shoes are familiar too. So are the untrimmed beard, the sunken eyes, and the straight, freckled nose. He knows how all those details look up close. He has inspected them hundreds of times in his hallway mirror, after waking up, before leaving his house, or when preparing for another night of uneasy sleep.

The shock is forceful enough to distract him from the evaporating surroundings. Possible explanations come to him as he backs away from the sight. It is a twin, a mirror image, a mirage. Someone wants to startle him, perhaps warn him of the consequences of continuing his mission. It cannot be him. He is one person, not two.

He feels the sudden presence of his only friend. Turning around, he finds Timmy standing next to the body on the ground.

"Well, isn't this a conundrum," Timmy says ruefully. "You spend lifetimes worrying over appearances, but you can't cope with seeing yourself from the outside."

"That's not me," Felix says. His voice is too loud, as if shouted inside a confined space.

"It is and it isn't." Timmy sounds both sad and annoyed as he looks down at the body.

"But I'm *here*," Felix insists.

"I know it's confusing. Not even celebrities can deal with seeing themselves this way, even though they've spent their whole lives fretting over their images. But I admit this wasn't according to plan. I wanted to greet her inside the lab, where I could've picked her apart. Damn her galling temper."

All the police officers are gone. The hospital and the trees have vanished too. His double-body has disappeared. The darkness gains texture as it closes in and crystallises into cliffs of damp rock, approaching purposely, as if hoping to crush or funnel him to somewhere else. He has a sensation of slipping down, like the vertigo of tripping across the border of sleep, but prolonged and escalating.

His body tells him he is falling far. His soul agrees.

"I want to go home," Felix says weakly.

He needs the comfort of hard floors and thick walls, soft blankets and old routines. He must wake up and find a foothold, a grip on his dissolving life, before he cannot climb back.

"You're in luck," Timmy says. "Your real home is actually your next stop. And you won't be alone. There'll be one or two who want you to explain what happened to their eyes." He crosses his hands behind his back and paces around Felix.

"The torturers?" Felix asks after a moment. "The ones we took revenge on?"

"Precisely." Timmy laughs. "As well as the creatures we drew in the lab. Everyone's here. And they're desperate for company."

"But they hurt us, Timmy. It was only payback. You were the one who told me to–"

At last, Felix understands.

Decades of confusion had nurtured a rage and poisoned his mind until it leaked into the outside world. But Carl was gone, and in want of his actual nemesis, Felix directed his anger elsewhere. He made do with the second-best alternative to real reprisal: retribution against those who bore the unsmiling doctor's face.

The young doctors. The lonely man with the snake. Felix made them symbols and destroyed them. His acts had felt reasonable at the time, and Timmy had reassured him, guiding his hand and urging him on in moments of doubt.

The realisation coils around his waist and pulls him down faster, dragging him away from the surface of his past life like an anchor sinking into the sea. But Felix knows that he will not be allowed to drown. Horrors far worse than oblivion wait at the bottom. Their voices reach him from below: eager whispers and gleeful promises.

"You tricked me." Felix turns to face Timmy. "I had already realised you weren't real, but you made me as bad as you are. This is your fault."

"Please." Timmy rolls his eyes. "If I had a coin for every time you idiots say that, and so on. This blame isn't shareable. Who do you think I am?"

"My friend."

"This *face* was your friend's," Timmy corrects. "I needed one to make you listen to me. And it worked gloriously. If only you hadn't left that fucking note in the forest, we could have achieved so much more."

"Take me back up." Felix takes a step forward, but Timmy glides away gracefully.

"No one escapes," Timmy says. "Believe it or don't, but I am a big friend of laws, just like that thrice-damned detective. But she too will ride the elevator one day. And trust me, it won't take her to an ethical north."

"You made me kill them." Felix's scream comes out as a whimper.

"As I say to everyone, it was your call. I only held the door open."

The voices grow stronger. A bright light explodes into view below and illuminates a pale concrete floor. In the middle of the floor is a metal bench and a matching chair. Leather cords spread away from the bench like writhing snakes. Just outside the circle of light are hints of movement, darting in and out of view. The light flutters once, then twice, and begins to flash.

"Please," Felix manages. "I'm sorry."

"Not yet," Timmy says, "but you will be. "We'll keep drawing, you and I. We will waltz with every horror hidden in the farthest recess of your mind. And when we're done, we will start over."

Timmy fades away, leaving behind only an afterglow of his canine, too-wide smile. Then Felix is back in his chair. And this time, he knows, his shackles will never come off.

Chapter 51

Felix shudders as if jolted by an electric current, topples forward, and slumps into Lena's embrace. A distant boom washes through the garden and fades away. Lena blinks in surprise and looks down.

A large piece of Felix's head is gone, as if raked away by a great, invisible claw. She tries to hold him upright out of sheer reflex, but as soon as her arms are around him, he drags her down on the ground.

Gun, a voice screams. Someone else shouts *down, get down*.

Lena does not hear the words. Her head is filled with a white, fiery noise that mutes the world to a subdued buzz. A river of shattered expectations storm through her. Her hands are floodgates, hinged on her next decision. She needs to swing them wide open.

The tyre on her right disintegrates in an explosion of foul air and shredded rubber. A fraction of a second later, another distant thunderclap rips through the air. High-velocity bullets. Just like those that pushed through Gustav's car. Her hunters have returned.

She rolls over on her stomach. The shooter can be anywhere. Until she knows where, every direction is as good as the next one. Most likely, the sniper has climbed up to get a good vantage point; the first shot was precise.

Her body burns with the need to stand up and run.

"The blood's on the roof," Jimmy screams.

Lena looks over at Jimmy, crouching next to Jacobson behind her car. He makes a cutting motion with his hand along the road.

"His blood," Jimmy shouts again. "It went that way." He points at the top of Lena's car.

Lena shakes her head in confusion. Jimmy is right; almost all of the tissue torn away from Felix is sprayed over her car, but she can't see why that matters. Only the noise is important. It threatens to suffocate her.

She must let the river out.

All the officers who were standing around her are lying prone. The members of the response team crawl towards one of the trees. Lena rolls sideways behind the front of her car. She searches the treetops for a sign of the sniper, but the curtain of leaves obscures everything.

"It's a shit angle." Jimmy screams so loud his voice breaks. "The shooter's on the ground. *Stop looking at the fucking trees.*"

At last, she understands. Just as she cannot make out the branches because of the leaves, a shooter would not be able to see the ground. Felix was hit straight from the side. The assassin is not on high ground. He is somewhere on the lawn. A glance at the blood on her car tells her in which direction. The response team is going the wrong way.

The noise in her head gathers in strength.

Lena pushes herself up from the grass and runs. She heads north, at what she hopes is sideways from the viewpoint of the sniper. Another shot might come any moment. If she's hit, her death will be silent. No warning boom or flash of fire. Only a sliver of lead, light as a feather and just as quiet, passing through her being like a spear though cotton.

But the sniper will not want to stay. There are too many people in the area. Hiding behind a tree won't work for long. Retreating makes more sense. All large buildings are far away, but the shooter will still head that way. There is no other usable cover anywhere else.

She looks back at Jimmy but sees only Jacobson. A second ago, Jimmy was hiding next to him, but he's nowhere to be seen. Police officers are hugging the ground or cowering behind trees and benches.

The noise in her head shifts to a flat drone. Her visual focus shrinks down to a pinpoint.

She rushes towards the largest of the buildings, a three-storey colossus in brown brick. A former hospital wing converted into an office. Open archways cut through the ground floor. Dozens of doors open to what looks like a long corridor. Perfect for hiding or slipping away. Bushes and twigs whip past her legs. Her limbs are on fire and her head pounds, but the purpose that fills her snuffs out the warnings.

She reaches the corner of the building. Holding her gun pointed at the gravel, she takes a quick look around the corner. Twenty-odd people in sight, most standing still and talking on their phones. Residents on their way to the gathering of police officers. Many stand still or look at each other. The sound of the rifle must have given them second thoughts. No one is running, but a few are walking away hurriedly.

Anyone can be the shooter.

Lena runs towards the most conspicuous individual, a woman who is jogging away from the building, but slows down when she notices her orange reflex vest. Not the choice of a sniper.

As Lena turns back, she spots two men sitting on a blanket. They stare at Lena and lower a roll of textiles on the ground. She takes a step towards them, then realises that they're tending to a baby.

Lena turns again and stops. Near the other end of the building are a man and a woman with a pram. They walk fast and look over their shoulders, but they're not gazing towards the police cars. Something else has spooked them.

She rushes up to them and blocks their way.

"What's wrong?" Lena asks.

"Nothing at all. We're fine." The man glances wide-eyed at the gun in Lena's hand and pulls the pram backwards.

"You're freaked out. Why's that?" Lena takes a step towards the couple. "For fuck's sake, talk to me."

"Jesus, calm down." The woman nods over her shoulder. "It was just a man in a hurry. He nearly hit us."

"In a car?" Lena asks.

"On foot," the woman says. "He went in there." She points at the three-storey building a few steps away.

Lena runs up to the nearest door and yanks it open. A kitchen back-door entrance. Two cooks look up in surprise. She brushes past them, flings the next door open, and dashes down a white-painted corridor.

No one running outside the windows. The shooter might still be inside. Perhaps he hopes to hide. But that plan is illogical; he must know the police will turn the area upside down. He will want to get away. What had the private security guards said? Something about access to–

The tunnels.

She crashes through a set of double doors. Stairs up and down. A door leading outside. Footsteps come from below. She raises her gun just as a man in a blue overall turns a corner and comes into view. He's climbing the stairs from the basement slowly and with difficulty.

Not the shooter – too old and wrong clothes again, even if they would blend in here.

Lena lowers her gun. Perhaps it was the female runner after all. She could have ditched the rifle in a bush, put on the orange vest, and simply jogged away. It wasn't a bad strategy.

She moves towards the exit and pauses with her hand on the door.

The man coming up the stairs is staggering rather than walking. On his cheek is a smear of dark red. He's bleeding.

"Are you hurt?" Lena asks.

"What a bastard." The man shakes his head and rubs his face. "Punched me for no reason. My teeth hurt."

"Where?" Lena demands.

"Down there, in the basement."

Lena is down the stairs in four long leaps. She stumbles on the landing, but uses her momentum to shoulder open a closed door. It swings inwards and opens to a long, windowless corridor clad in green tiles and lit by yellow strip lights.

In the far end of the corridor, a man tries to insert a key into the keyhole of the opposite door. By his feet is a long, slim canvas bag. He looks at Lena and curses.

Got you.

"Police," Lena shouts and raises her gun. "Stay where you – damn it."

The man grabs his bag and darts through a side door Lena hadn't noticed. Judging by the sound of his footsteps, he's running upstairs.

Lena sprints down the corridor. He's about ten seconds away. Getting the rifle out of the bag will take him at least a few seconds, longer if he's also running up a set of stairs. She hears his footsteps. The man is above the ground floor.

She holds her gun raised and takes the stairs three steps at a time. Her legs soon burn with the effort, but she moves fast, and the man she chases is carrying a sniper rifle. The ones she has seen are heavy. It will slow him down.

The footsteps end. Lena turns the last stairs: she has reached the end. They must be three storeys above ground. At the topmost landing is a red steel door standing slightly ajar.

She moves the final steps and lies down on the steps just below the landing. The shooter looked stressed. Perhaps he's so nervous his reflexes are doing the thinking. Pressing herself flat, she reaches out and pushes the door open.

The rooftop is wide and flat. There is no railing or chimneys. The assassin is only a dozen steps away. His rifle is lined up at the door.

This time, Lena anticipates the shot.

The boom reaches her a moment after the bullet passes through the air above her head. A piece of the wall behind her shatters and falls down in a brief cascade of mortar and plaster.

Every sniper rifle she has seen also has manual bolt action. For a trained shooter, reloading takes only a second, but someone who is hunted might need another moment. That is all the time she needs.

Lena springs up and takes aim. "Drop it," she screams. "Do it now."

The sniper gapes at her. He stands with one knee on the ground and the rifle lowered, as if he can't believe that he missed his shot.

"You have no idea who you're up against," he says. "I'll be out in an hour again."

He balances on the edge between two decisions. His eyes follow her movements, gauging her posture, her face, the finger on the trigger of her gun.

Lena moves closer. There are people on the ground below, but everyone is hidden by the angle. The need for retribution drowns out all thoughts.

"And you're as good as dead already," he says. "You might as well–"

He whips up his rifle mid-sentence, hoping to catch her off guard. It's an old tactic: catch your opponent when she or he is distracted.

Lena sees it coming.

The bang of her gun is much quieter than the roaring crack of the sniper rifle, but in the relative hush on top of the roof, the shot rings out like an amplified whiplash.

The man's face is incredulous as he stumbles backwards. He clutches his stomach and looks up at Lena with a venomous gaze.

"You fucking–" he begins.

Lena fires again, this time hitting the man in his legs. She brings up her other hand to steady the gun and fires a third round in the assassin's chest.

The man doubles over, but remains on his feet. He drops the rifle and staggers backwards towards the edge of the roof. As he backs away, he leaves behind a smudged trail of blood.

Lena lowers her gun and walks after him.

When the man's shoes bump against the low ledge where the rooftop ends, he stops and looks up. His eyes are bloodshot with pain and rage. He tries to spit, but manages only a red-frothed drool.

"They'll get you," he wheezes. "You'll pay for this."

Slowly, he straightens up and tips backwards over the edge. His eyes are still on hers when gravity hooks him and pulls him out of her sight.

"Not today," Lena says to the empty air in front of her.

Chapter 52

Carl sits in his car and watches the day fade into another brief lull. He is alone in the driver's seat, isolated from the world behind tinted windows in a vehicle too expensive for the vast majority of the beautiful citizens currently making their way to Stockholm's glittering core of restaurants and clubs.

Once, he was one of them. Today he cannot be more removed from the mindless crowd bent on entertainment. He needs escape, but not through fluids and substances.

He lowers one of the windows and inhales. The air carries hints of grass, jasmine and salt. A horn echoes from downtown. Like the scents, the city's sounds change as night approaches: Its bright buzz of traffic and commerce shifts to a soundtrack of clinking glasses and reflection on hours, weeks and lifetimes gone past. The light changes too: slowly, as if weighing its options, the sun sets behind the city's western skyline, a shallow rise of black angles against the reddening sky.

Stockholm never had much of a profile. Prevailing architectural trends choke all ideas that can catch someone's eye rather than blend in and disappear. Any form of progression is met with the same treatment. Stand out and make a mark, and conformity will come at you with scissors of regulations and trim you down to mediocrity.

An inevitable fate wired into the culture and the buildings in which it thrives.

He has saved thousands from uncountable hours of pain. Because of him, an entire scientific field has been advanced. Now one of his few mistakes, perhaps his only real blunder, has risen like a spectre from the tombs of time to haunt him. It is typical. And so immeasurably, infuriatingly unfair.

Leaving is a nuisance he could do without. Then again, this city does not deserve him. The capital is too small for souls as large as his. He will miss the house, even its dreaded cellar, but perhaps he has needed a break for longer than he thought.

His phone buzzes next to him on the leather seat. Another anonymous call. He doesn't need to hear what has happened: the news coverage has told him everything of importance. Dozens of residents were only seconds from the events at the hospital grounds, and some teenager had caught several dramatic moments on video and uploaded it on the Internet.

The film includes the moment when a supersonic bullet hits the long-lost subject and wipes out the last living memory of a promising experiment gone wrong. Carl launched many other ventures after that, some even more daring, but those had all been conducted with more care and greater emphasis on security.

It takes only one pebble to start an avalanche, and this one is still in motion. That damned detective will keep scratching away at the dirt of history until some faint scent leads her to his doorstep.

In another person, he would admire such stubbornness, but Lena Franke is a threat. She has to be dealt with. At heart, she is no different than the viruses he has spent his life eradicating. He will regroup in peace and quiet. The storm has to pass before he makes his move, or he might draw too much attention to himself.

Carl takes the call after the third ring.

"The mission has been accomplished." The caller is the same man who has been Carl's contact person throughout the past days.

"I noticed," Carl says, unable to keep sarcasm out of his voice.

"Quite an impressive finale. It's making a splash on every news channel in the country."

"The method we used was our only option."

"If you say so. It was very definite, I'll give you that. Pity the police caught up with your shooter."

One of the shakier video clips doing the rounds shows a man falling from a rooftop. Rumours suggest this man was the assassin, and that the police shot him. The video also features a glimpse of a woman on the rooftop. He is willing to bet part of his fortune on that it is Lena Franke.

"We realise that our assets are lost from time to time," the man says. "But our operatives never reveal any sensitive information about our clients."

"In my experience, 'never' is a placeholder term for many other words. Such as 'practically never'."

The bullet holes in the fallen man's chest and face suggest that he is very deceased. But he did not die the moment the detective spotted him, and no one except she knows what transpired between the two before she killed him.

"Are you displeased with our services?" the man asks.

Carl laughs sharply. As if he will stumble into such an obvious trap.

"You did all you could," Carl says. "And ultimately, you handled the most important task with adeptness. As for the various hiccups, I think this episode has been too chaotic for anyone to ride out smoothly."

"I am pleased to hear that you are content," the man says after a moment.

Carl shakes his head as he considers the true meaning of the man's words. *I'm happy we don't have to hunt you down and riddle you with bullets.* Or something to that effect.

"There's a good chance I can use you again," Carl says. "Once I'm convinced that I am free to do so. The police are likely to take great interest in many aspects of this affair."

"We understand."

"I will be in touch."

Carl hangs up and looks at the sun again. It has slipped below the horizon, just as he is about to do. His house will wait for him here, sheltering its secrets. He will return soon. Perhaps in the company of the detective who is causing him so much trouble. If paid enough, the anonymous agency might help him take her down.

She and he are less different than she wants to think. They are ambitious, uninhibited, and uncontrollable. Both he and the detective are ready to cross battlefields to succeed. But she shies away from doors he flung open as a child. He has mastered the game, while she still refuses to accept the rules. That will be her downfall.

And given her past, it will be quite a fall.

Carl starts the engine and lets the night of the eastern sky swallow him.

Chapter 53

Central Stockholm Police Headquarters

Saturday

22:35

Gren's office is normally an oasis in the twenty-four seven turmoil that pervades the headquarters. His room is located next door to the large room where Lena and fifteen-odd other officers spend their days and occasional nights at their desks. The superintendent's private space consists of two uncomfortable office chairs, a bookshelf crammed with folders and magazine holders, and a desk nowhere near large enough for the paperwork that weighs it down.

The room is also unbearably hot. On another day, the warmth could have been a blessing; the average temperature in the headquarters typically borders on illegally cold. But the heat makes Lena's back itch, which in turn does nothing to help her mood.

She dimly recalls how Jacobson guided her back down from the rooftop and drove her back to the station, where she slept for almost a full day. After waking up, she spent the remainder of the day writing a seemingly endless report, parts of which sent her back to scenes she wants to forget. Then, over the past two hours, Gren has grilled her on every imaginable aspect of her latest case. It's enough to break a lesser woman.

She explains the events chronologically, racks her mind to recall the smallest details, and answers every question. Responding to Gren's non-stop requests for more information is a superhuman effort.

Adding to the challenge is the need to keep Jimmy out of the narrative. A day and a half have passed since Lena gunned down the assassin at Beckomberga Hospital, but she's still exhausted.

And Gren isn't done. He has been building up to an explosion that he holds back by a hair, and his seams are ready to burst. The tipping point appears to be Lena's lack of a good reason for not reporting back to him after she was assaulted on Tranebergsbron.

"I should file an official warning," Gren says. "But Norling says you made all the right decisions at the hospital."

"Really?" Lena says. "That's a first."

Norling is an uptight knucklehead who tolerates few and approves of an even scarcer number, but he is good at what he does. Getting lost in the duct two times straight must be robbing him of his sleep. There is, of course, a possibility that he never stood a chance of finding the lab, but that is food for thought for another day.

"Although," Gren continues, "I've fielded several calls from people upstairs who want you off the force. Norling's statement and Jacobson's report saved you this time. But you're making enemies." He pauses. "Even inside this building."

"So what's changed?" Lena asks. "I've been unwanted for years. My answer is still the same: fire me if you want to. It'd be your loss. Otherwise, let me do my job."

"This is serious. There's a limit to what you can get away with, even in murder cases. There are other detectives on the force who could've stepped in after you were attacked."

"I had the situation under control."

"Then why didn't you report back after turning Fridhemsplan into a war zone?"

"Our damn car crashed. I was a little dazed."

"Which is exactly why you were unfit for continuing to lead the investigation," Gren says. "Not to mention that you were in no state to approach a suspect. Jacobson could've handled it."

"It's my fucking case." Lena raises her voice. "Am I some kind of blunt tool you want to hide away once we're done?"

"You could've been hurt," Gren says.

"And fucked up your career? Is that it?" Lena rises from her chair and pushes a stack of folders off Gren's desk, sending letters and receipts flying around the room. "I nearly lost my life, you egotistical prick."

"That's the problem," Gren shouts. He stands up and glares back at Lena.

Seconds pass in silence. The papers she swept from Gren's desk settle on the floor. A phone rings far away. Doors open and close. No voices come from outside the room: everyone within earshot is eavesdropping on the argument.

Lena stares at her superintendent, then looks away. She lowers the folder in her hand and places it on Gren's desk.

"I'm sorry," she says quietly.

Gren clears his throat, adjusts his shirt, and sits down.

"As it happens," he says, "I care about you, despite your fly-by-night attitude. Next time, call it in."

"No suspension?" Lena can't help sounding surprised.

"I can't afford not having you around. I've been instructed to give you an official reprimand, but I'm going to wriggle out of that too. Take a week off. Then I expect to see you back at your desk."

"On one condition."

"Probably not," Gren says. "But let's hear it."

"Something's eating at you. Please don't lie; you're a terrible actor. Just spit it out."

A long silence follows. Lena can see Gren struggling to reach a decision, and she helps him along by never taking her eyes off him. After several seconds, he clears his throat.

"Agnes is back on the force," he says. "As of last week, she's a constable at a department in northern Sweden. In her hometown, as it happens."

Lena looks at Gren sideways. She must have misheard him; Agnes went to ground and has stayed there. Not a single report on her whereabouts has come in since she left with only a brief note by way of goodbye. If Agnes were back, she would have got in touch.

"Impossible," Lena says after a long moment.

"I remember a newly promoted detective who once told me she hated that word." Gren shrugs.

"Don't get smart with me."

"Well, it's true. But it isn't the whole story."

"Why hasn't anyone told me?"

"I just did. But I waited, and that's part of the story."

"Then start talking, for God's sake."

"Sorry, I can't. I made a promise. And I'm sure you'll appreciate that I keep those."

Lena raises a fist to slam it down on Gren's desk. After a moment, she folds her hands behind her back instead and tries to look calm. Her superior might be moody and obnoxious, but he's also a block of principles that grew legs. He will not speak more about this.

"It's because of me," Lena says, "isn't it?"

"Like I said," Gren says, "I made a promise."

"Can I at least get in touch with her, or is that off bounds too?"

"Of course you can. She's in the official address book. But I'd give it a while."

"I want to ask you why."

Gren sighs. "And I would like to tell you."

After a moment, Lena nods and leaves the room.

Chapter 54

Jacobson is waiting for Lena when she returns to her desk. In his hand is a large, steaming takeaway cup.

"A proper coffee," Lena notes. "What's the occasion?"

"Being alive, maybe?" Jacobson gives Lena the cup. "One for the road."

"And where would I be heading?" Lena takes the cup and sits down.

"I should've known a simple 'thank you' was too much to hope for." He smiles and sits down on her desk. "Word in the corridor has it that you're taking a break."

"I don't have a choice." Lena sighs. "Thanks for the coffee and for not flying off the handle. I know this case put you through a lot."

"Come again?" Jacobson looks astonished. "You're the one who flipped a car and shot a man."

"Technically, the car didn't flip."

Jacobson looks at Lena and shakes his head.

"Why this constant bravado?" he asks softly. "Some might doubt your brains, but no one thinks you're weak."

"I'm not being flippant. Shooting that man is something that'll stay with me forever. So will the rest of the madness."

"It's all right to talk," Jacobson notes. "If you want to, that is."

"Most say I talk too much."

Lena puts her coffee on the desk and runs her hands through her hair.

"Look," she says. "It's been a hellish weekend. I'm still processing what we've done here."

"You managed to talk down a serial killer. That alone has redeemed you in the eyes of a lot of people.

"Including yours?"

"I already believed in you. It was my idea that we work together, in case you've forgotten. What I'm saying is no one blames you for having to neutralize the killer."

Lena nods to hide her face; she's unsure what Jacobson will read from her expression. She had indeed neutralized the assassin. It had been him or her. But if there had been time, she would have done so much more. The need to exact revenge on his body, on the worthless collection of ideals and ambition that had been his excuse for a soul, had been overpowering. She had wanted hours to put him through the hell out of which she had pulled Felix.

She looks down at the floor and pretends to think. Most likely, her face is haunted, as can be expected of someone who dodged the scythe several times over a few days. Finding Felix had been exhausting. Losing him was harrowing. But taking the sniper's life had been a thrill, intoxicating and addictive.

And just beneath the surface of her frayed nerves is the temptation to smile.

Good God, what have I become?

Felix fled one nightmare only to enter another, and on his long, painful journey towards his end, he became one of the monsters he once feared. She is still alive. Her ride goes on. But just like Felix, she might be changing.

When Lena looks up again, Jacobson appears hesitant. She notices a thin black folder on her desk.

"What's that?" Lena points at the folder.

"More bad news. In fact, Gren asked me not to break this to you yet. He wanted me to wait until you'd had some time off."

"Totally unbelievable. One moment I'm a precious asset, the next I'm a porcelain doll. Let's hear it."

Jacobson places a hand on the folder. The gesture is gentle, almost reverent.

"Remember the legal documents we found among Kristina's papers?" he asks. "The ones about a property?"

"In Glömminge," Lena says. "I had in mind to follow that trace. Something about the name rings a bell."

"It's the name of the project to which Carl moved his patients. Or subjects, as he called them."

"Please don't use that term. It turns my stomach."

"It turns out Glömminge was only a destination, not a new research project." Jacobson pauses. "For the people Carl took there, it was a final destination."

Jacobson's tortured look is all Lena needs to fill in the gaps.

"That mother*fucker*," she whispers. "How did you find out?"

"I sent a team there to look around last night. There's only a ramshackle barn at the property. There were shovels in their patrol car, so they decided to poke around in the ground."

Lena buries her face in her hands. "How many?"

"They aren't sure yet, but I suspect they'll find the remains of everyone except Felix. The technicians reckon it'll take weeks to complete the examinations. If we don't find more graves, that is."

She wonders what Carl's so-called subjects thought during their last moments. Perhaps they were relieved to be free from the shackles and the oppressive chambers. Or maybe they knew Carl well enough to know he would offer even worse torments.

"Cause of death?" Lena asks.

"To be determined." Jacobson sighs and taps the folder. "The reason I'm going against Gren's instructions is that I read your report."

"What did I miss?"

"Nothing you could've seen. They've done an initial dental check of the bodies, which came up with a few names. One of them is the name Felix mentioned before you brought him out of the lab."

"Timmy Patreus," Lena says. She can recall every word from her and Felix's short conversation. "Felix thought Timmy was alive. He claimed that Timmy was the mastermind behind the murders.

"Perhaps for some people, insanity needs company."

"Or a spokesperson," Lena says quietly. "Like a ventriloquist uses a puppet."

Felix had described Timmy as false and hollow, just as the perverted image of Agnes that tried to intimidate Lena in the bank had been.

"A puppet?" Jacobson asks. "Are you sure you're all right to drive home? You don't make much sense, to be honest."

"I need you here to keep an eye on the case," Lena says. "This time, I actually plan to do as Gren suggests and lie low. I'm not in his good books right now. It's a marvel I still got my job."

"You're the worst workaholic known to mankind. What will you do at home?"

"Rest and recover." Lena stands up and takes her jacket from her chair. "Nurse's orders."

Chapter 55

Lena is walking through the garage when her phone rings again. She doesn't recognize the number.

"Franke," she says. "Who's this?"

"I never thought I'd say this, but it's good to hear your voice."

"Jimmy?" Lena stops in surprise. "Are you all right?" she asks. "Where are you?"

"This might be a shock, but I'm hiding as far away from Norra Ängby as I possibly can without access to a private jet."

"Consider me not shocked. Although you had me worried when you disappeared."

"Someone tried to kill you, and you were worried about me?" Jimmy asks.

"I meant later on. You could've been kidnapped."

"What am I, a wayward teenager?"

"Near enough."

Jimmy chuckles. "I'm sorry about the Houdini act. When they shot the guy you'd arrested, I decided that enough was enough, so I made a run for it."

"I would've done the same in your boots." Lena pauses. "Thanks for pointing me at the shooter. I was disorientated."

"It was just a lucky guess."

"You kept your head cool when everything went south. And you can cook, too. Remind me not to screw around with the Finnish military."

"Good call."

"I wasn't entirely serious."

Jimmy snorts. "If someone would decide to go up alone against an entire army, it would be you."

Lena smiles to herself. Jimmy's banter is thinning the greyness that hangs over her mind. It's a temporary relief, but better than nothing.

"Watch your back," Jimmy continues. "Whoever hired that sniper isn't done."

"How can you tell?"

"Perhaps the guy they shot could've led you to their doorstep or witnessed against them. But they tried to get to you first."

"Any idea why they went for Felix the second time around?" Lena asks.

"They didn't know where he was until you hauled him out of his cave. He was the biggest threat, but if the shooter had had a chance, he would've done us in as well."

Lena nods to herself; Jimmy is right. Carl will be looking for a window for revenge, especially if she lets anyone knows she's trying to locate him. He will be careful not to attract the wrath of the entire Swedish police force. But whatever path she chooses next, she has to be cautious.

"If you ever think about applying for the police academy," she says, "you'd do pretty well. But please don't. They don't go easy on bigmouths."

"It can't be that bad. After all, you made it through."

Lena shakes her head ruefully. She is being honest: Jimmy would probably sail through some of the tasks, although the other aspirants would give him a hard time.

"Look after yourself," she says. "You aren't safe."

Jimmy makes a disgusted sound. "I got that," he says. "I haven't slept for the past two days. Don't worry; I'll stay under the radar. Or off it completely."

"Going back to the underworld?" Lena asks. "More projects?"

"You'll understand if I won't tell you." Jimmy pauses. "Take care. I'll see you around."

The call ends.

Chapter 56

A few minutes later, Lena leaves the garage and crosses Fridhemsplan, past the destroyed bike rack and the scorch marks left behind by Gustav's burning car.

She rolls down the window as she crosses the bridge to Södermalm. The evening is cool, but the wind is still free from hints of autumn. Winter is a long time off. Her week off will be warm, with mild evenings lit by the restless sun. A good time to rest.

And rest she will.

I will sleep for days, she thinks. *Cook my favourite foods. Brew coffee, lift iron, and stretch for hours.*

I won't think about Gustav or Agnes. I won't dwell on the drawings we found or the trapped, innocent children who are no more.

Because what I feared was madness might instead be a lens, or a key. I have glimpsed behind the curtain that envelops us all. And there's more to the world than I thought.

Exactly how much remains to be seen. Another investigation for a different day.

So come night, I will venture outside, assassins and murderers be damned. I will not be a prisoner. I'll slip away and walk the woods, alone and unseen.

Maybe there, I can figure out where I'm truly going.

Chapter 57

Gren waits until the door has closed behind Lena. After a moment, he rises to check that she isn't waiting outside, but she's nowhere in sight. Police officers sit hunched over their laptops or stride through the office. No one meets his eyes.

He closes the door and sits back down behind his desk. His phone is close to his right hand. In front of him is his laptop. On its screen is the crime scene technicians' full report about the lab underneath Beckomberga Hospital. Over the past four hours, he has read it three times. After the first reading, he tagged it confidential and excluded it from most other members of the force, including Lena Franke.

Gren picks up the phone and looks at the display one last time.

He must call the police force's central laboratory to double-check the information they've given him. Most likely, there's an error or some oversight on behalf of the technicians. But neglecting to follow up on what he has read would be misconduct, and the question would fester like a tick on his mind for months.

He dials the number. Pearls of sweat prick his neck while he waits for someone to pick up the phone on the other end.

"This is Superintendent Gren," he says when an assistant answers. "I need you to verify a detail in a report." He gives the man the case number for the murders in Norra Ängby.

"I have the file open here," the assistant says. "Go ahead."

"The report says that nine shells from Lena Franke's gun were retrieved from the underground facility you examined."

"That's correct."

"But you also wrote that no bullets were accounted for."

"Also correct. I was there in person." The lab assistant's tone is short, as if he cannot wait for the conversation to be over.

"Any chance you could've missed them?" Gren asks.

"The room had tiled walls. All of them were intact. We even searched the wall outside the door when we didn't find the bullets, but came up empty."

"Did you–"

"And before you ask, we were as baffled as you are, so we swept the area five times. The bullets aren't there."

"I see." Gren fidgets at the flaking leather on the armrest of his chair. "What do you make of that?" he asks.

"It's not my job to draw conclusions. That's your department."

"Humour me."

The assistant is silent for a few seconds.

"I'd say someone's trying to wind me up," he says. "I mean, what else can you say?"

Gren thanks the assistant and hangs up.

His throat is parched, and his shirt clings to his back. Some water would do him good, but he can't muster the energy to go to the pantry. The phone call has drained him of strength. He is nervous, too, as if the ten-second trek to the fridge will take him through a no-man's-land where anything can go wrong.

The office beyond his room is as familiar as his own kitchen. Perhaps even more so, given how much time he has spent here. Tonight, however, the halls look too narrow and the doors seem strangely small. The stuffy office feels like a slowly shrinking cage of obligations. As soon as he has rallied himself, he will go for a walk outside. The streets will let him think more clearly.

When the phone rings again, he is so startled he bangs his knee against his desk. He snatches up the phone.

"What?" Gren demands.

"I'm sorry." The male voice is hesitant and vaguely familiar. "Is this Superintendent Krister Gren?"

"Speaking."

"I'm a nurse at Lindhaga Hospital. It's a governmental speciality ward, for the treatment of certain criminals."

"I know what that place is," Gren snaps. "Is this concerning John Andersson?"

"How did you know?"

"Lucky guess. Don't tell me he has escaped?"

"No, sir. John is definitely in his room. I spoke with him just a moment ago."

"What is it, then?"

"He wants to talk to Lena Franke," the nurse says. "He says that she's in trouble."

*

The End

Thank you

...for reading this novel – I hope you enjoyed it!

If you liked this story, you can find more on my website at www.wanderingmind.net

You can also subscribe to a newsletter to find out about new releases. I never send spam, affiliate marketing or other nonsense.

If you have the time and would like to support this aspiring writer, please don't hesitate to visit the Kindle Store and write a few words. Your contribution would mean a lot.

Cheers,

Afterword

Norra Ängby is in fact a rather nice place, and as far as I know, its quirks and secrets are neither more numerous nor stranger than those of other suburbs.

That said, it offers a special blend of identical houses, oversized apples, and rune stones. Perhaps it's something in the water.

Most locations in this novel exist. That includes Beckomberga Hospital, and there is indeed a great network of tunnels beneath its wards-turned-rental flats.

There are also a number of outlying facilities which were closed down in the 1980s. Abandoned, boarded up and unguarded, they were ripe for exploration for bored but bold teenagers.

I'd like to write about what we found inside them, but no one would believe me.

Acknowledgements

Tove
The blaze amongst embers

My daughters
For keeping me on my toes

Class of '11
*For continued support, frequent gossip,
and sporadic drinks.*

Everyone who has reviewed or commented on my stories
Your thoughts mean the world. I keep listening.

Dedicated to

Johan Nyberg

I wish we had known.

More by Erik Boman

Printed in Poland
by Amazon Fulfillment
Poland Sp. z o.o., Wrocław